BLOOD WINTER

ALSO BY WILLIAM PATRICK

Spirals

WILLIAM PATRICK

BLOOD WINTER

VIKING

VIKING
Published by the Penguin Group
Viking Penguin, a division of Penguin Books USA Inc.,
40 West 23rd Street, New York, New York 10010, U.S.A.
Penguin Books Ltd, 27 Wrights Lane,
London W8 5TZ, England
Penguin Books Australia Ltd, Ringwood,
Victoria, Australia
Penguin Books Canada Ltd, 2801 John Street,
Markham, Ontario, Canada L3R 1B4
Penguin Books (N.Z.) Ltd, 182–190 Wairau Road,
Auckland 10, New Zealand

Penguin Books Ltd, Registered Offices:
Harmondsworth, Middlesex, England

First published in 1990 by Viking Penguin,
a division of Penguin Books USA Inc.

1 3 5 7 9 10 8 6 4 2

LIBRARY OF CONGRESS CATALOGING IN PUBLICATION DATA
Patrick, William, 1948–
Blood winter / William Patrick.
p. cm.
ISBN 0–670–82789–4
I. Title.
PS356.A788B5 1990
813'.54—dc20 89–40644

Printed in the United States of America
Set in Sabon

this book is for Ian Thomas Patrick

Acknowledgments

My re-creation of Berlin and the war owe much to Robert
Graves and Paul Fussell, to Otto Friedrich, Gerhard Masur,
Peter Gay, Laurence Lafore, Gordon Craig, William Man-
chester, Modris Eksteins, George Bailey, Stephen Kern, Robert Wohl, Robert Harris, Jeremy Paxman, Gwyn Macfarlane,
and, above all, Karl Baedeker. There's also a debt here and
there to Somerset Maugham and to Christopher Isherwood.

Many friends I'll thank privately, but three for whom that
simply won't do are Christine Pevitt, my "case worker," con-
fidante, and champion at Viking; Chuck Verrill, who gave
me more good advice during one lunch than I've received in
the rest of life altogether; and Jonathan Matson, who stuck
it out when others would have gone over the wall years ago.

For anyone who is tired of life, the thrilling life of a spy should be the very finest recuperation. When one recognises also that it may have valuable results for one's country in time of war, one feels that even though it is a time spent largely in enjoyment, it is not by any means time thrown idly away; and though the "agent," if caught, may "go under," unhonored and unsung, he knows in his heart of hearts that he has done his "bit" for his country as fully as his comrade who falls in battle.

—GENERAL ROBERT BADEN-POWELL
Founder of the Boy Scouts

Man ist was man isst.

—German proverb

BLOOD WINTER

1

Black crows hung in butcher shop windows all across Germany that winter. The joke in Berlin was that soon there would be no more rat to eat, only rat substitute.

It was the third year of the war, the third year of the British blockade, and in the city cooks experimented with rice lamb chops, nut cutlet, and pale green vegetable steak. They extracted fats from snails and old boots and hair. Resourceful bakers had learned to make a bread out of potato peel, ground turnips, and sawdust, but then the summer rains came and rotted the potato crop, leaving only the turnips and the sawdust. The government had ordered the slaughter of dairy cows for meat, only now there was no milk. At the front, officers commandeered rations and sent them home to their families. At home, thieves smashed grocers' windows so routinely that a law was passed requiring empty boxes put on display to be labeled EMPTY BOX. The sugar was kept with the war bonds, pepper was stretched with ashes, and only two subjects were talked about in the city streets—food, and the terrifying new weapons that would end the war.

Late one evening in a cinema on the Kurfürstendamm, a hungry young woman sat slumped in her seat with her coat wrapped tightly around her, trying to stay calm. The theater was cold, heavy with the dank smell of wet boots left by the stove, and the images flickering on the screen in front of her were a dreary piece of work about Bulgarian royalty, played, as it turned out, by Czar Ferdinand of Bulgaria, his wife, and two daughters.

The tall young woman looked up for a moment, watched the stilted melodrama and the silly posturing on screen, then closed her eyes. She had no interest in the cinema. She was there because of the little man who had been following her a dozen paces behind as she walked along the Ku-Damm. Military security, the political police, a private detective still working for the Russian Okhrana—there were so many dwarfs from so many agencies wandering about that she could hardly be expected to keep up. At one time in her life she might have been flattered by all the attention. Now, after so many months, the surveillance was wearing on her nerves.

The night before, she had been in a restaurant when two of these detectives came in, showed their cards to the manager, and took the table next to hers. They never removed their coats, they never ordered. They simply sat and stared at her, as if she were going to betray some dangerous radical tendency over her noodle soup. There were times when their ineptness made her want to laugh, but there was certainly nothing comical about their power. It seemed everyone in Germany was a bad actor these days, playing badly scripted parts.

After the second reel she came out of the theater, and the little man was gone. The night was cold and clear, the stars gleaming like distant shards of ice. The winter was tightening its grip, hardening all around her. She raised the worn collar of her loden coat and leaned into the wind.

The Kurfürstendamm was the street that Paris envy had built, Paris envy filtered through a polytechnical/beer imagination. It had been the Kaiser's grand idea to have a boulevard linking the Tiergarten with the Grunewald and rivaling the Champs-Elysées, but all it connected was a railroad station and an ugly church, and even the imperial will could never make it quite measure up to the original. Ornate houses lined the way like huge, antique clocks, but ersatz grandeur was out of fashion now. Against the night sky, workmen climbed on the rooftops, removing copper to be melted down and sent to factories on the Ruhr.

At Kimpinski's they switched off the electric lights, ushering the last stragglers out into the street. The only traffic along the wide boulevard was an elephant led by a small boy. Together they had been conscripted from Hagenbeck's animal show to haul coal wagons from the Anhalfter Bahnhof to the Allgemeine Elektrizitätsgesellschaft. All private vehicles had been confiscated. There was no rubber for tires anyway, no gasoline for fuel.

A lantern hung from a wooden barricade where a crew of women with picks and shovels dug in the street. Margarethe Riesling turned away from the light and headed down Nestorstrasse. A yellow poster plastered on the wall said EAT LESS.

Margarethe had a lean, angular face with a strong, wide mouth. Except for the fair skin and the large expressive eyes, then, her beauty was almost masculine. Her flaxen hair, worn waist length, was tucked up under a gray fedora, and as she walked along in her heavy boots, the loose coat hiding the contours of her body, she might have been taken for a young man. It had happened to her once, in fact. It was during the spy hysteria two years before, when there was talk of cars laden with gold racing to the Russian border, agents on bridges dropping bombs onto trains, and spies dressed as women observing troop movements. It was in August and she was changing trains at Schandau on her way back from vacation when she was surrounded by a mob so sure of themselves that they began tearing at her clothes. With the Hungarian orchestra playing "Deutschland über alles" on the platform, these self-righteous burghers stripped her half naked, then gathered around to individually assess the evidence of her femininity. But even this humiliation gave her some slight pleasure now, in retrospect. She was amused by their assumption that one had to be a man to be a spy.

Margarethe Riesling had been born in Berlin but emigrated with her parents to America before she was three. She grew up in Chicago, a sister city to Berlin in most respects—the same bustling greed, the same urgency to make something of itself. Her father had prospered as a civil engineer, and with prosperity learned to tolerate his daughter's intelligent eccentricity. He allowed her to go off to college, rare enough for a woman at the time, and when her interests led toward science rather than teaching, he indulged even this. She took her medical degree at the University of Michigan, then interned at the Women's Hospital in Detroit. She worked with prostitutes and with opium addicts; she became skilled in managing the chronic diseases of poverty. But for Margarethe, attending the dying and helping the malnourished bring more children into the slums was not an adequate response. She wanted to dig out the root causes of their misery, both medical and economic. In 1910, she was accepted for further study at the Institute for Infectious Diseases in Berlin.

She walked the streets alone now, hearing the slow, steady clomping of horseshoes against paving stones, then the creaks and groans of wooden wheels. She glanced over her shoulder and saw a black van pulled by a single white horse. She brought her collar tighter around her neck and focused once again on the dark pavement ahead of her. There was no reason to be concerned about a wagon.

A newspaper blown by the wind caught against her leg and startled her. She had not realized until then how uneasy she felt. She glanced around for any signs of life, but the street was empty. The men who watched her had never been so creative. Still, almost involuntarily, she quickened her pace. She heard the crack of leather and the stepped-up measure of the hooves. The wagon stayed with her, just fifty feet behind.

She had two blocks to cover before she reached the pension. At this hour there was no reason to assume there could be safety in numbers. The electricity had been shut off at ten o'clock. Above, in cramped apartment buildings, hungry families lay sleepless in the dark.

The leather reins snapped again and the hoofbeats came faster. The horse was nearing her, almost in a trot. She would stay calm. There was no reason for them to arrest her now. But the darkness ahead of her was not promising. The moon bobbed tranquilly above the rooftops, and the stars looked down with serene detachment.

To her left she saw a Bierstube with an oil lamp in the window. She rushed to the door and in an instant closed it behind her, then watched through the glass as the wagon rumbled past. At the last moment the driver turned his head toward her and smiled through a black forest of a beard. Then he was gone.

Margarethe leaned against the door, catching her breath. Then she looked up and saw at least half a dozen old men turned around at the bar, staring at her through an alcoholic haze. They wore their coats and hats. They sat drinking with their gloves on.

"A tall blonde," one of them called out, and all the men laughed.

The bartender complied, setting down a tall glass of Berlin white beer with a dash of raspberry syrup. He looked up at Margarethe contemptuously, and then the men went back to their conversation.

Margarethe stood for a full minute as she watched the empty street. This would be the last time, she told herself, but she had told herself that many times before. A moment later she stepped out and, walking very quickly, made her way to the Pension Hölldobler.

She went up the steps and through the doorway and closed it behind her. For a moment she stood in the marble entry, trying to collect her thoughts. A door opened behind her, but she kept her face turned away. She knew it was only Stumpf, the porter, sticking out his head to see who was passing through his hall. She muttered, "Good evening," then heard the door close behind her.

She climbed the stairs hurriedly, breathing in the smell of boiled turnips and ersatz tobacco. She had made it now, and she could relax, but the knot just below her heart would not go away. At the second landing she turned and walked down the narrow hall.

At room number six she stopped, threw open the door, and slipped inside.

Across the darkened room, silhouetted against the window, Colonel Kraft von Stade sat waiting for her. She saw the orange glow of his cigarette rise to his lips, then flare brightly as he inhaled.

Margarethe Riesling closed the door, then lit the gasolier. "Sorry I'm late," she muttered.

The colonel sat motionless and silent, the cigarette burning between his fingers.

"There were no trams," she said. She turned to face him now, placing her bag carefully on the bedside table, but she knew something was wrong. His moods were like structural shifts in metal or stone, but she had learned to detect them. "I'm late," she said, "but there it is. I told you. I'm sorry."

He remained seated, his cap, gloves, and saber on the smoking table beside his chair. A moment later he leaned over and crushed out his cigarette in the ashtray.

She was surprised to find her mouth so dry, her palms so moist. She had imagined this confrontation for months, she had thought it through time and time again, and she knew that her own fear was the only thing that could give her away.

"Shall I take off my clothes or shall I leave?" she asked him calmly.

At last he rose to his feet and walked slowly toward her. His face was pale and utterly lifeless, his features revealing nothing more than the incredible stupidity she had counted on all along.

"Are we going to make love?" she asked, taking off her coat, her hat, then dropping them in the chair by the door. "That's what I came for, you know. For you to make love to me."

He stood squarely in front of her and looked into her eyes. Von Stade was inert, a machine brought to her to be serviced—clogged lines to be pumped. That, of course, was his only virtue. It was those rare moments in which he tried to be romantic that made her skin crawl.

She looked up and saw a movement at his lips, some subtle change in his eye. He reached out, but she realized too late that it was not to take her into his arms. His open hand caught her at the base of her jaw and for a moment her mind went white. She fell back against the chair, tumbled over with it, and lay sprawled on the floor.

The concussion of his fingers against her face had deafened her. She reached up and felt the blood trickling from the cut beneath her left ear. She touched her jaw and felt it numb and beginning to swell.

From across the room he stared back at her, his eyes blurred by alcohol, trying to refocus.

"I know," he said. He spoke emphatically. Deliberately. He seemed to be waiting for her to lie so he could hit her again.

She looked down at her torn skirt, felt the bruise along her spine. There was nothing she could say, no twisted skein of explanations she could unwind. She merely rose to her feet. Unsteadily then, without looking up, she tugged the ends of her blouse out from under her belt.

Von Stade came forward screaming, kicking the lamp table into her. "I *know*, I told you! You and your crippled Jew!"

She worked hard to concentrate, shutting him out as she unbuttoned her blouse.

"You slut," he growled and slapped her again, this time drawing blood from her nose and mouth. "I know what you are. I know all of it!"

She threw back her head to stanch the flow and looked him in the eye. Her chin was scarlet, the blood running in a single, tiny rivulet down the hollow of her neck.

"You don't know anything," she said, daubing at the blood. Then she tossed away the blouse and pulled her camisole up over her breasts.

▪ ▪ ▪

OUTSIDE the curtained windows of the Pension Hölldobler, Berlin dozed under a blanket of fog. If there had been milk in the city, or horses, there would have been milk wagons creaking through the streets at this hour. This was the time for rolling over and grabbing your wife's warm buttocks. It was not a time for looking at corpses. It was not a time yet for smoking cigars, especially cigars made of cabbage leaves, but together . . .

Criminal Detective Andreas Schiller waved his cheroot before him like a censer and followed the old man into room number six.

The gasolier glowed warmly as Schiller listened to Stumpf describe the circumstances of his discovery, tottering back and forth beside the bed as he displayed the incontrovertible evidence. Schiller glanced past the gray form on the bed, sprawled nude and impertinent, to look at the oleographs on the wall. They were familiar scenes of Lake Constance in summer—a pleasant enough thought for winter in Berlin.

Over his nightshirt the old porter wore a frock coat with medals dangling from the dusty lapel. He had been in the last great war against France, in '66 and '70.

"I was a general's valet," he said. "I know how to look after the needs of officers."

Schiller nodded. "Evidently."

According to "Corporal" Stumpf, Colonel Kraft von Stade was an early riser. He was also very particular about having limitless quantities of hot water, so whenever the officer stayed the night, the old man was up before dawn, stoking the boiler and building steam until the tap was turned on and the pressure dropped. But this morning it had continued to build, so much so that the danger of an explosion had become very real.

"I trust you have let off the steam," Schiller said.

The porter tucked his chin into his neck and scowled. "I still have my wits, God punish England."

Schiller nodded. "May He punish it."

They say the true Berliner comes from Breslau. Andreas Schiller was from Graslitz. He had a soft Saxon accent and spoke near a whisper, and despite the fact that he was half the porter's age, he had the same shuffling gait. In Schiller's case the cause was Parkinson's disease, progressive and degenerative, which in peacetime would have forced his retirement, but with the war meant not only that he stayed on the force but that he was promoted—a war profiteer.

He stood beside the bed now and looked down at the bloodless face. The muscle tone was gone from the once handsome features. The lines of cheekbone and jaw had become indistinct, like clay in a warm room. The lips and surrounding flesh from nose to chin were a deep, cyanotic blue.

Schiller held the green cigar clenched between his teeth, jutting straight out like an instrument he did not have hands enough to carry.

"Died in the best of health," he mumbled, his head bobbing slightly as he formed the words.

The victim's rib cage hovered motionless above the sunken belly. The erection, or what remained of it, thrust up like a stalagmite, sealed in the juices of lovemaking. Schiller held the cigar away, leaned over, and sniffed. Dead fish. The ocean floor.

"You had seen the woman before?" Schiller asked.

"What is to see? A hat, a coat."

"Describe her to me."

"Skin and bones. She looked like a boy," the old man said.

Schiller sat on the edge of the bed, which jostled the corpse and made a deep eructation issue from the mouth. The whores of Berlin were still well padded, he had observed, even on half rations. They were built for an idea of comfort that was maternal, not erotic. They were stuffed like feather mattresses.

He turned to the side and gripped von Stade's chin. Then leaning over, he looked carefully into each ear and along the scalp. As he worked, his hands shook with the palsied rhythm of his disease.

"Help me," he said, motioning to the porter. Together they rolled the body on its side and Schiller ran his hand lightly down the victim's back. There were no wounds lying hidden, only the purplish bruises where blood had pooled beneath the skin.

Schiller let the body fall back into place. Then he looked at the pillow, where a filament of hair glistened and caught his eye. There were three strands, actually. Golden, with highlights the color of burnished copper, and all nearly a meter long.

For a moment Schiller tried to imagine the colonel's nocturnal visitor. He had never seen one of the Ku-Damm's matrons of the evening with hair like this. The new morality of the war made a bona fide mistress the norm for senior officers—their wives were too busy cavorting with younger men. And an officer with von Stade's responsibilities would have to be selective. He would need a room like this, and, if he was smart, a circumspect, reliable lover. Schiller wound the strands of hair around his index finger and, with a sigh, dropped the coil into his pocket.

Colonel Kraft von Stade, head of the Chemical Section of the K.R.A., had until this unlikely event commanded five thousand workers in the suburb of Moabit, manufacturing poisons for the chemical warfare corps. These workers were an essential cog in the war machine, their goodwill, good health, and productivity the underpinning of a victorious German army. So black market procurement at the level and scale of von Stade's was something the civilian police were supposed to ignore. It made no difference if the rest of the nation starved—the armaments workers had to be well fed and contented or the slaughter could not continue.

A key broker in raw materials—chemicals, equipment, even food—the colonel was also a key source of vital war information. Schiller sank his teeth deeper into his cheroot and exhaled a cloud of smoke as he looked down at what was left of the man. Von Stade had stood at the juncture between German might and German hunger. Surely hundreds of people had perfectly good reasons to kill him. A nation starving. A nation looking to its laboratories to compensate for the muscle that had been worn down by three years of war. There were secrets brewing now, plots and intrigues, talk of miracle weapons. And yet, for all that, Schiller knew his investigation was simply over. However indelicate the circumstances, this was nothing more than a heart attack, and a trail of corruption come to an end. The army would take charge and the body would be "discovered" again, in its proper place at home. His prick would be washed, his socks removed, and all talk of scandal laid to rest.

Schiller looked out the window to the apartments across the watery courtyard, and he wondered how many corpses were being rearranged in Berlin this morning, dead men stuffed into closets not because their wives were ghouls, but because they were hungry. It was simple bureaucratic truth that if you report the death you lose the ration card. And these were the people his section of the Berlin Police Presidency—Criminal Detectives B-1—would arrest. Not the goulash millionaires or the officials protected by layers of Prussian bureaucracy, diverting Dutch cheese and Danish meat into fortunes for themselves. It was the von Stades of this world, dragging out the war while the nation starved, lining their own pockets from scarcity, that Schiller wanted to nail. But of course resources were limited, and the department had quotas to meet. The widows were an easy catch anyway. In time, they were always betrayed by the smell.

Schiller stood up and removed his cigar from his mouth. "My friend, your powers of perception are undiminished. The man is dead. Now I must ask for the use of your telephone so that I may contact the appropriate military authorities. The death of a senior officer is not a matter for the police."

The old porter stood aside as Schiller walked hesitantly toward the sink to wash his hands. "A corpse is a sea of contagion," he said.

And as he leaned over, awkwardly gripping the soap, his partner, Axel Kadereit, entered the room.

"Blind, deaf, and dumb," Kadereit said, glancing at the naked corpse. "No one in the building saw a thing."

Schiller nodded, a look of resignation on his face. The death of von Stade would not be the opening he had hoped for, the chink that would expose the dry rot at the heart of Berlin. He did not want to accept it, but without more to go on he had to face facts.

The younger man slowly pushed up his hat brim. "So. Andreas. As representative of the January Murder Commission, what is your finding?"

Schiller looked up. "The colonel fucked himself," he said. "And us too."

Then he turned on the tap with his left hand and placed his right underneath. The water was quite warm.

2

At Base Hospital #12 near the Belgian border, the officers' mess was warm despite the drizzle outside. Two stoves made out of oil drums were built into brick flues inside the Nissen hut. The sullage water evaporated, the steam went up the flue, and the grease left behind was saved for glycerine to make explosives.

"Nothing like the morning air in Flanders. That invigorating medicinal stench."

Eli Gordon turned around in line and saw Glendenning holding a tray of steak and eggs and smiling under his service cap.

"That direct hit at zero four hundred was the apothecary tent, or did you know?"

"Must have missed it," Gordon said.

"Shell the latrine next and splatter us all with shit," Glendenning went on as they made their way to a table and sat down. "Bloody germ warfare! That's how they'll do us in. One minute in my funk hole last night decided me I'd sooner go in a blinding flash than work toward pneumonia in such bloody discomfort. How *do* the Frogs endure this weather!"

Glendenning paused to pick up his fork, idly spearing a rissoléed potato as Gordon sipped his coffee, warming his hands around the cup. He usually slept through the shelling now, just as he usually worked through dinner. At this point in the war he could sleep through the Rapture and Second Coming if he had to. The only sensation Gordon could not screen out was nausea at the sight of meat after sixteen hours of surgery.

The Englishman looked into Gordon's dark eyes, then turned away. Defensively, he popped another small, crisped potato into his mouth and launched into a story about the Turcos at Mont des Cats, brought up during the night and billeted in the cloisters just as the white-robed and hooded monks got up for their devotions.

"Wholesale mutiny, I tell you!" Glendenning stopped and slapped the table, carried away with his own sterling wit. "Chants and candles. Bells and smells. Those dinges were off on foot all the way back to Calais. Eyes as white as these plates."

Gordon smiled and lit a Caporal but said nothing, wondering why he always felt as if he were listening to music now, the notes reverberating, piling one on top of the other. His mind had become like a piano with the sustain pedal down.

In time Glendenning drifted off to have a word with Colonel Evans-Moore, the District Medical Officer, a balding, doughy man, who had given up a lucrative Harley Street practice to join the R.A.M.C. in August 1914.

Gordon finished his coffee and smoked his cigarette, then reached into his pocket and pulled out an envelope. Distracted, he turned it over in his hands. The paper was fragile and white, with the porous texture of thinly sliced bread.

The guns rumbled low in the distance as Gordon stared at the peacock blue ink, the perfectly crafted script used to form his name. The letter had been postmarked in Boston six weeks before and had been clipped to his shaving mirror for days. He had thought of having his batman read it just to be sure there was nothing pressing, but that hardly seemed fair to Lavinia. Lavinia Gibson of Beverly Farms and Back Bay. Lavinia Gibson of the perfect skin and teeth and hair. He imagined for a moment the hours it had taken to arrive at such absurdly perfect penmanship. Then he ripped open the envelope with the tine of his fork.

My dearest husband,
I read the news from France today and think of you there . . .

He hated the letters. He hated the artifice and the formality. He hated the Ladies Auxiliary tone about bravery and honor and sacrifice. But most of all he hated them for what was missing. Four thousand miles from home, he could still make believe his daughter, Abby, would wake up this morning in the big house on Marlborough Street.

Eli Gordon, M.D., Professor of Surgery at the Harvard Medical School, first came to France in the spring of 1915, when the war was only six months old and families with picnics still drove out to the Marne to gather the wildflowers that covered the shallow graves. For Parisians the impulse was a kind of religious pilgrimage to see the spot where Gallieni's troops had come in taxicabs to stop the German advance. The farmers were afraid to go back out into the fields for fear of unexploded shells, but the gamines were there in force, gathering souvenirs to sell along the boulevards.

French troops still wore bright red trousers in those days, and it was still the height of chic to die in white gloves. But that was before the gassing at Ypres, the slaughter at Verdun and on the Somme—names given to battles to imbue the war with structure and meaning.

Gordon had traveled with the Harvard Unit for the Ambulance Américaine in Neuilly, setting up a hospital in a girls' school on the Boulevard d'Inkermann. He delivered his students and his surgical residents and two new Ford motor ambulances, and then for reasons not entirely clear to anyone, including himself, stayed on.

All Gordon knew for certain was that he could no longer share that big house on Marlborough Street with Lavinia Gibson, and that he could no longer stalk the cobbled paths of Boston like a man without a brain. If Lavinia had been able to express her grief, if they had been able to grieve *together* for their daughter, then it might have been different. Maybe sorrow could have brought them closer, maybe opened up some well of feeling between them that had never really existed before. But the best Lavinia could manage was a stiff upper lip, and her typically cheerful optimism buoyed by good works. Blue-blooded families like Lavinia's did not do well with feeling, and they did not discuss divorce.

Two years later now, Gordon sat waiting for spring to come to the trenches again, and then another summer, fall, winter . . . the war that was always going to be over by Christmas. He thought about the smells that would come with the spring and he tried to find something in it to look forward to. The blackthorn hedges white with blossoms, the Boulogne Forest floor purple with wild-flowers. In the spring Nancy Astor would come in her riding cap and taunt the patients to cheer them up, and in the spring the hops would ripen outside the red-tiled cottages. The Tommies would fish in the canal at Rousbrugge. The surgeons would golf at Wim-ereux, and the coolies would bury the dead and mark the tennis courts for the Camier tournament for officers and nursing sisters. The war never really changed, it seemed, merely the souls of the men who fought it.

They were examining brains that night in the postmortem tent when the Chinaman appeared with the note for Evans-Moore.

"Captain Bessy say hully-lah." The coolie stood soaked to the skin, the rain coming down in sheets behind him as he waved his flashlight and malacca cane.

Taking his own sweet time, the colonel stepped back and pulled off his gloves and unfolded the soggy message.

He read the note, then looked up wearily at Gordon as he reached for his cap and his waterproof. "Come along, my boy," the colonel said. "We'll expand your medical horizons."

A motor ambulance—"Gift from Tongoo District, Burma"—

splashed up in the mud alongside, glistening in the light of the electric RED CROSS. Gordon followed the D.M.O. and the Chinaman, keeping to the duckboards that led off into the dark.

The labor battalions were in an old cement works to the north, beyond the camps for the dark-skinned brigades. The three men walked past turbaned cooks squatting over their "chuputty" and Chasseurs d'Afrique hiding from the rain in long cloaks and burnouses. The Hindus refused amputations, and the Zoaves were useless in the trenches because they insisted on looking over the top.

Beyond the pavé the duckboards came to an end, and mud sucked at Gordon's boots as he followed the p'aitou's light past the cemetery wall and the ruined windmill. To his left, the wreck of a Nieuport Bébé stood alongside the divisional whorehouse— blue light for officers, red for other ranks—where a dozen men stood waiting in the rain.

Evans-Moore remained silent about what was waiting for them, but Gordon had harbored an odd, indulgent delusion ever since the coolies first arrived from the coast. He remembered seeing the boxcars filled with grinning Chinese as a kind of premonition, but until now it had remained something fleeting and unfocused, something he could not pin down.

Just past the narrow-gauge railroad that carried ammunition up to the front, they entered a cinder courtyard, then stepped through a doorway out of the rain where the smell of burnt ginger and human sweat hit Gordon in the stomach like the sickening sweetness of a latrine.

Shivering in the damp and cold, a hundred coolies lay spread out across the floor, the orange tips of their cigarettes burning in the dark like joss sticks in a temple. The p'aitou swung his cane to clear a path, and the two surgeons followed him across the main room, dripping rainwater as they stepped over arms and legs. Then they turned down a corridor off to the left where they saw a glimmer of light.

The commander of the Coolie Labor Corps, a Russian named Vessy, stood in the glow of an oil lamp, holding a handkerchief over his nose and mouth. At his feet, a Chinese practitioner ministered to three sweat-soaked men.

Breathing in the spices steaming from the kettle of medicinal herbs, Gordon looked at the blood-splattered tunics, the gray-green faces, then glanced at Evans-Moore.

The colonel raised his brows but kept his hands discreetly in his pockets.

Gordon knelt down and said, "Get rid of him."

The p'aitou cracked the old medicine man with his cane and spat out, "Shun, shun."

Two of the coolies lay utterly still; the other had the shakes under his blanket. Gordon reached for the light and peered into the third man's dilated eyes, then put his hand at the carotid and felt a fluttering pulse. He pushed back the waterproof and the tunic to expose the shoulder and saw black patches rising like blisters against the yellowish skin.

Gordon shifted his position, then tugged at the Chinaman's drawstring trousers and pushed them down. On one side of the groin was a knot-hard swelling. On the other, the ganglia had suppurated, then split open like an overripe fruit.

Gordon glanced up at the Russian. "The others?"

The man struck a match that made his face reflect utterly white. "The same," he said.

The shivering coolie jerked forward and vomited a pinkish bile that splattered on the ground and sent a fine spray drifting across Gordon's face.

Gordon stood up slowly, wiping his skin with his handkerchief. "Bring me a knife and a small basin," he told the p'aitou. "Also creosol."

Evans-Moore turned toward the moon-faced Russian, who picked tobacco off his tongue with trembling, brown-stained fingers.

"Kaiser Bill told us to 'beware the Yellow Peril,' " Evans-Moore said with grim intonation. Then he glanced knowingly at Gordon. "Perhaps this is what he meant all along."

TWO days later, on the coast forty miles west, Major Anthony Rice and Sir Almroth Wright sat in the makeshift laboratory at the casino in Boulogne-sur-Mer, on the second floor, which had once been the fencing academy, just above the "baccarat ward," where the gaming tables had been replaced by rows of wounded soldiers staring up at lacquered ceilings and chandeliers with the mud of the trenches still on their boots.

On the green baize of the billiard table that served as Sir Almroth's desk, two manila folders lay open and overlapping. The first contained the preliminary descriptions of a rather dramatic outbreak of bubonic plague among the coolies at Base Hospital #12 in Hazebrouck. The second held two single pages torn from different numbers of a German scientific journal, *Annalen der Chirurgie.*

Sir Almroth read the Hazebrouck reports without comment. They had been filed by the District Medical Officer, a Colonel Cyril Evans-Moore.

Then he picked up the pages of German, turning them counterclockwise as he followed the wavering lines of script that had been added in the margin.

In Barbarei mit Gefangenen verwickelt. Können Sie sofort nach Berlin kommen?

Wir müssen sofort bakteriologische Entwicklungen besprechen. Bitte kommen Sie sofort nach Berlin? Teilen Sie nicht den Englandern mit.

When he had gone full circle Sir Almroth looked up. "Now that's a depressing prospect," he said.

The old man settled back into his Morris chair with a sheet of paper in each massive, freckled hand. " 'Bacteriological developments,' " he went on. " 'Come to Berlin' to talk 'bacteriological developments.' I see the connection you're trying to make."

The gold watch chain across his waistcoat rose and fell with his paunch as he slumped and ruminated. For the moment he seemed content to breathe in and out, which was effort enough considering his chronic emphysema. Then all at once he shifted emphatically to the side and said, "But I don't believe it for a moment. 'Tangled up in barbarism.' This has been cooked for our benefit."

The young major, who wore the spectral Mons Star ribbon and a look of weariness far beyond his years, sucked in his cheeks and pointed to the second folder. "The outbreak of plague at Hazebrouck, sir, is a fact."

"But there is no real link between Hazebrouck and this message from Berlin!"

Rice sighed. "There's substantially more connective tissue than you may realize," he said. "A fabric of rumors going back months and months. Germ weapons for the Alberich offensive. Experiments on human subjects. His Majesty's subjects. I'm afraid we have no choice but to assume the worst."

Sir "Almost" Wright, the Paddington Plato, glared over the rims of his spectacles into this young man's deep-set eyes.

"But now this bit of news . . ." Rice nudged the tear sheets from the journal with a pale index finger. "This fellow is the lynchpin. It was he who tipped the German hand on chlorine research two months before Ypres. Likewise T-Stoff, K-Stoff. He's obviously in the thick of it. If he says the Boche have 'bacteriological developments' worth discussing, there is every reason to believe him."

Sir Almroth stared intently at the handwritten message. "This was written in bacterial broth, you say?"

"Invisible until our man in Amsterdam incubates it."

"*Bacillus prodigiosus* red?"

"Or so the laboratory would have me believe."

Ever so slowly, Sir Almroth Wright got up and walked across

the polished wooden floor to the windows facing the sea. Rice watched him, listening to the aged lungs wheezing with exertion.

" 'Do not pass to the British.' That's what it says. The last line of this last note from Berlin."

The major nodded.

"So this Dutch intermediary, then. Why *did* he pass the messages?"

"It would appear he never read them," Rice explained. "Or any of the others."

Wright gave a loud harumph. "What I don't know won't hurt me. Is that the idea?"

"Precisely the idea," Rice said. "Strictly a courier, a middleman. And a bit shaken when our chap showed up to inquire about his sources. He had assumed he was quite anonymous."

The old scientist looked out toward the Atlantic. It was a gray morning and the surf cast up a cold wet spray, but still there were men and women strolling the beach in their military greatcoats. He could see the poilus fishing quietly off the Channel guns. He could see the old pier supports built by Napoleon a century before when it was the French who were planning the invasion of England.

He did not want to think of it, really. The Germans were clever, and they were ruthless, but surely they had not gone mad. The critical fact was that any form of research along these lines first and foremost required an antiserum. Berlin would need massive, foolproof immunization—or at the very least an unheard-of level of antisepsis—before even thinking of deploying a biological weapon. The implications of such a staggering advance were simply too much for British science to accept. And without such an advance . . .

"No," he said, turning back from the window. "I categorically refuse to endorse action based on nothing more than rumors and speculation. An outbreak of disease in Flanders. The Chinks were just off the boat! Plague is rampant in Asia. Millions die of it every year. Common as a sneeze."

"My dear Sir Almroth!" Major Rice paused to take another deep, clear breath. "Our first response to the gassing at Ypres was to tell Tommy to piss in his handkerchief and hold it over his face. That was the best British science could do for our fighting man in 1915. Now, for once, we're trying to use a modicum of foresight. To expect the unexpected."

Sir Almroth avoided his eyes and looked back down at the memo.

"The coolies could have brought the plague from Shanghai, yes. But this much we do know. Days before the outbreak at Hazebrouck those same Chinamen policed a captured German trench. The corpses they buried wore diving helmets and rubberized suits. The dead men were Gas Pioneers, Sir Almroth. The German chemical warfare corps."

Almroth Wright's driver, with his dazzlingly white teeth and thin mustache, had been Sarah Bernhardt's leading man on her last triumphant tour of North America. He careened through the streets of Boulogne, handling the Siddley-Deasey as if it were his own sports roadster, narrowly missing a dog cart of "lait hygiénique" and imperiling the lives of assorted pedestrians.

In the leather-cushioned rear seat, Major Rice sat in silence while Sir Almroth leafed through yet another dossier, a curriculum vitae and security check on the American surgeon mentioned in Evans-Moore's report.

"I heard him give a paper at the Conférence Chirurgicale Interalliée," Sir Almroth said, not looking up. They had left the coast now and were passing through farming country. "Rather *Call of the Wild*," he muttered.

"Ummm." Major Rice struck a match and lit his pipe, filling the car with a heavy, blue smoke. "He comes by it honestly enough."

"And how is that?" Sir Almroth inquired.

"What the Americans call a 'self-made man.' Frontier stock,

really. Cowboys and Indians from the Wild West of Kansas City."

Sir Almroth turned to his companion, gazing over his eyeglasses with a distracted look. "How heroic."

"You should note he's spent the past eighteen months at base hospitals and advanced dressing stations," Rice said, pointing with his pipe stem.

"You're saying that he doesn't mind sticking his neck out."

"Seems positively keen on it. There's really no reason for him to be here, is there, except for the grand horror of it all."

Sir Almroth riffled through the pages as the countryside flew by outside the windows. "He's a good technician. Germans respect that. Studied at Heidelberg. Fluent in the language. Interesting idea of his, I must say, hiring circus workers to manage tents for the mobile surgical units. On the face of it he seems a reasonable choice. But I'm concerned to see that he was in such bad odor toward the end at Harvard."

"Yes . . . well, personal problems, you know. Death in the family, bit of an overreaction. But I suspect he would not be available otherwise."

Sir Almroth nodded uncertainly. "Perhaps. That's one way of looking at it. But what's to make him accept this intrigue of yours?"

The major paused again, sucking contentedly on his good English briar. "I believe our lads have found the string."

"And what is that?"

Rice turned to focus on the road ahead. "For all his skillfully constructed veneer, you see, Dr. Eli Gordon still has the silt of the wide Missouri beneath his nails. That sort of tension between what one *is* and what one aspires to often leads to dissolution. No prizes there. But when a man falls apart you have a rare opportunity— to rearrange the pieces to suit your own design."

The dark clouds and the aches in his bones told Sir Almroth that soon it would be raining again. He looked out at the heavily manured fields, the peasants trimming pollard willows, the women carrying bundled faggots along the side of the road.

This threat of germ warfare seemed so improbable, so completely mad, but yet bacteria from this very soil had already killed more British soldiers than German bullets. Gas gangrene—a simple infection—and Britain's finest minds were powerless to stop it. If the Germans were willing and able to spread a disease this deadly along the Western front, then no doubt they would drive the British Expeditionary Force into the sea.

They passed through Saint-Omer, the dullest garrison town in France, and skirted the market in the Place Victor-Hugo. Sir Almroth found himself thinking about the great wall in Provence built to keep out the plague wind. He thought about the carnival of the masked doctors, the copulations in the cemeteries, and the war that seemed to be recapitulating Europe's grisly past. As they cleared the town, he saw the peasants planting winter wheat and, on the opposite side of the road, beetroot. In the distance, a line of British tanks advanced like armor-plated dinosaurs.

The neurosurgical unit at Hazebrouck was housed in the refectory of a Catholic school just outside the village, a solid stone building with a slate roof and a covering of gnarled espalier fruit trees. From the roof you could see the line of fire all the way to Messines Ridge, and the observation balloons hovering over the trenches like so many uprooted turnips.

The six operating tables were equally spaced under the low ceiling, partitioned by white cloth screens. Eli Gordon faced a routine amputation—sixteen strokes—to be administered under light chloroform. As he reached for the orthopedic saw he heard the children in the room above beginning their evening prayers. He watched them each day as they followed their priest through the camp, wearing the blue hooded capes that made them look like tiny trolls.

The next case was a Welsh fusilier suffering sympathetic paralysis from a gunshot wound through the open mouth, but the boy died on the table before Gordon could make an incision. Then there was an eyeball to enucleate—sniper, shot through his field glasses—and a Frenchman with an undeformed Lebel cartridge lodged in his frontal lobe. It seemed both sides were filling their grenades with all sorts of battlefield junk—nails, razor blades, belt buckles—then tossing it back and forth across the lines. The cartridge was hell to find without X rays, but after fifteen minutes of probing, Gordon was able to place the souvenir inside the young man's pocket.

"Excellent wounded," Glendenning called out. He seemed ecstatic. "Look here. Two-inch strip of steel, half an inch wide, peeled off his helmet and curled in through the temporal bone just over the ear. Right through the brain. You can see the tip emerging there . . . behind the external angular process . . . dividing his meningeal artery. Now how often would you see something like that in London, eh? Fascinating case. Fascinating."

Gordon had seen enough fascinating cases. Exotic gutter wounds of the head, blindness from bullets striking sandbags along the parapets and blowing the stuff right through the lids. Generals talked about normal wastage. Surgeons talked about excellent wounded.

Colonel Evans-Moore stood just inside the door of the refectory now, taking off his cap and giving it a shake. Behind the D.M.O. two equally wet visitors stepped in, a tanned and slightly haggard-looking young officer and a rumpled and wheezing gray-haired civilian. Gordon went on with his work, removing the depressed bone fragments of a fractured skull with Montenovesi forceps. A moment later, the colonel was at the foot of the table holding a mask over his nose and mouth. He said, "Two gentlemen here to see you, my boy."

Gordon kept his eyes focused on the wound in his patient's skull. "Either of them bleeding?"

"Not yet."

"Then what say they count off by twos and wait."

Evans-Moore nodded and smiled uncertainly, then went back to his waiting guests.

After catheterizing the tract of the missile, Gordon washed it clean of blood and disorganized brain tissue with a Carrel syringe. It was a simple procedure he'd done a hundred times, and for the moment he tried to find the pleasure that comes from the mastery of technique. In his mind he reduced what he did to "working with his hands," tinkering with bodies the way other men tinker with machines. At least in this one activity he knew exactly what was required of him, and it was utterly safe.

An orderly lowered an electromagnet, and probing carefully now, Gordon inserted the steel tip. He extended the device its full six inches, then gave a nod. The orderly switched on the current and Gordon withdrew the tip. He pulled it out all the way, but there was nothing attached. He tried a second time, and then a third, with the same result.

"Forget it," he said.

He attached a length of stomach tubing to the suction pump and slowly inserted it into the wound. He activated the vacuum and he felt something dislodge deep inside the brain. He reached in and pulled out a bone fragment, but it was not part of the soldier's skull. It was the tip of a human rib, presumably not the victim's own.

The three men sat on a stretcher by the door as Gordon came over, removing his gloves. The colonel stood and made introductions. "Sir Almroth, I believe you've met Dr. Gordon. Dr. Gordon, this is Major Rice." The men shook hands all around. Then Evans-Moore added, "Major Rice is with military intelligence."

Gordon nodded and ran his hand through his straight, black hair. Then he reached into his pocket and pulled out his pack of ten-centime Caporals. "What can I do for you?" he asked.

The major offered him a light. "There's a bit of a problem in Berlin," he said.

■ ■ ■

A company of Scots Guards next door kept an officers' club in a dugout lined with bully-beef tins. Gordon led the way as the four men tramped along the duckboards in the pelting rain. He had known someone would come about the coolies. It was simply more music in his head, more notes added to the din. But what did Berlin have to do with it? And what did any of it have to do with him?

They reached an embankment marked by a wooden sign—NO WE DON'T KNOW WHERE YOUR UNIT IS, BUT THE MAYOR DOES—and Gordon lifted the plywood door and unstopped a trapezoid of light and the squeal of bagpipes.

They descended the ladder into the dank, underground pub, then stamped their feet as Wright coughed and tried to catch his breath. A captain from the air corps was tending bar, a cat napping tranquilly on his shoulder. He brought a bottle of single malt whiskey to their table and set out four glasses.

"The Jocks have real milk for their tea," Gordon said, taking his seat. The kilted pipe major blasted away at the Skye boat song from the opposite corner. "Three cows travel with them in a box-car. They've got it marked 'Horses, Officers, Three.' "

The colonel poured the whiskey. The major packed his pipe, and Sir Almroth, still breathing heavily, made an elaborate business of drying his spectacles with his handkerchief.

Gordon touched off another Caporal with his trench lighter and looked once more at his visitors, their noses dripping, their teeth set against the cold.

"So," he said, blowing a steady stream of smoke toward the ceiling. "Berlin."

The major stoked his pipe, sending up a great swirling cloud. He shook down the flame from his match and then dropped the burnt-out stub on the table. "Yes," he said, glancing over at Sir Almroth. The old man was at last composed. "We were hoping you'd do us a favor and pop over for a few weeks."

The door opened again, letting in a blast of cold air and a spray of rain. A chorus of "Fermez la porte" went up from the otherwise paralytic officers lounging about.

Gordon leaned back in his chair and smiled. "Pop over?" he said.

"Yes."

"To Berlin?"

"Yes."

"With guns blazing?"

"Not exactly," Sir Almroth corrected.

The four men traded glances. Then Major Rice shifted in his seat and picked up the thread. "Actually, we were hoping you would lend a hand at the American Embassy. Ambassador Gerard is looking out after British affairs . . . the affairs of a number of other combatant nations. We think he is in need of some additional medical expertise."

Gordon turned to face him. "And how is that?"

"Our prisoners of war, our civilian detainees. Hundreds of Englishmen of military age, for instance, detained at a makeshift camp at the Ruhleben Racecourse outside Berlin. But now they're being taken off to work in industry. Some of our men are working the morgue, the municipal crematorium, the Berlin sewerage farms. Obvious problems of hygiene."

"And nutrition," Sir Almroth added soberly.

"Yes. Quite."

Rice paused and stared into the bowl of his pipe, hoping to restore the upbeat momentum of his presentation.

"What with the blockade, Germany is suffering near starvation in some quarters. That's just not good enough for His Majesty's subjects. We're sending food from Blighty, but we're not at all sure the packages are getting through. Much to be done. Much to be done."

Gordon smiled and glanced over at Evans-Moore. "So far it sounds like a job for the Y.M.C.A."

The major lit another match and puffed feverishly, giving his tobacco an even, red glow. He looked back at Sir Almroth and waved the match until it went out. "There's one other thing," he added. Then he took the two reports from Wright and handed them across the table. "We're afraid these men are being used in experiments to develop biological weapons."

Gordon studied the three faces turned toward him ever so attentively. The music inside his head had suddenly stopped. He waited and listened for a moment, then opened the folders and skimmed the reports.

"You know, of course, about the outbreak among the coolies," Rice said.

"I was there," Gordon told him, turning his attention to the handwritten messages in the margins of *Annalen der Chirurgie*. He read them each several times over, then said, "This sounds like something from a dime novel."

Then he flipped the pages to Evans-Moore. "Have you seen these things?"

The colonel swirled the whiskey in his glass. "Indeed I have."

Gordon turned back toward Rice and stared evenly into the major's sunburned face. The fine bones were set firm and resolute. The squint lines around his eyes were as white as mother's milk.

"Let me see if I've got this straight," Gordon said. "You've got some coolies with plague, and you've got a cryptic message from somebody in Berlin about . . . 'bacteriological developments.' That leaves you making something of a stretch, doesn't it? Trying to build a pretty shaky bridge across some fairly sizable, shall we say, *lacunae*."

"Other reports have prisoners from the Ruhleben Racecourse being taken to the Institute for Infectious Diseases," Rice said. "It's our duty as we see it to explore all possible links."

At which point Sir Almroth leaned forward and folded his massive hands, which, like his head, were much too large for his body.

"You're an American," he croaked in a deep, throaty voice. Then he paused and wheezed. "You're a neutral. You've studied in Germany and you know the language. You're also a physician of some distinction. We feel you could be most effective in finding out what the Hun are up to."

"You're talking about a bacteriological weapon," Gordon said. "I'm not a bacteriologist."

Sir Almroth coughed into his fist and cleared his lungs. "No one said you were our first choice."

The pipe major dropped his mouthpiece and let the last captive air squeal out of his bag. A cheer went up—"Ripping!" "Top hole!"—and Gordon looked over at the Scot's brown, ragged smile. The knees below the kilt sat like boulders on tree stumps.

"This note in the journal says 'Do not pass to the British.' "

"It was addressed to an intermediary in Holland," Rice explained. "We're dealing with a sensitive issue here, and, very likely, a troubled individual, caught in the middle."

"And it's the troubled individual in Berlin you want me to contact. The one who's sending these notes."

"Not necessarily," Rice responded. "We might ask you to work independently. Dig up what you can on your own."

"That doesn't make a hell of a lot of sense, does it?"

Rice shifted in his seat, then glanced down and leaned sharply forward. "My dear Dr. Gordon. You must understand that we've been receiving messages from this individual for well over a year. Each one has had a prophetic accuracy, giving us invaluable time to respond to Germany's chemical advance. There is not the slightest reason to doubt the validity of this intelligence now that the focus has shifted to bacteria."

"You're telling me you don't know who it is," Gordon said.

The major smiled uncomfortably and leaned back. "You're quite right. We have no idea."

3

"The first attempt was Madrid," said Major Rice, holding his butter knife as he would a pencil, drawing evanescent rectangles in the white linen tablecloth.

It was the following evening and he and Gordon were at Wright's villa in Boulogne on the Boulevard Daunou, talking over brandy and cigars.

"We don't know whether the ambassador, Prince Ratibor, was involved or not," Rice went on. "But Krohn, the attaché, cabled Berlin with a plan for closing the Spanish-Portuguese border by dumping cholera bacilli into the rivers. Fortunately, the German high command at that point had the good sense to veto."

Gordon glanced over at Wright, then leaned back for a moment and watched the old servant and her pretty daughter as they carried off the last of the dishes.

"The Norwegian venture came next," the Englishman continued. "The Germans were going to wipe out the reindeer sledging arms to Russia, infecting them with glanders shipped by diplomatic pouch to Christiana. Intelligence tipped off the Norwegians, of course, and the pouch was intercepted."

"You read the German diplomatic pouch?"

Rice took a long drink from his water glass, glanced once at Gordon, then went on as if the question had never been asked.

"Now, there was one more incident with glanders. In Bucharest.

We don't know exactly what they'd planned to do with it, but when Romania declared war the attaché buried the stuff in the legation's garden. Observed, to our good fortune, by the Romanian undergardener. He told the American chargé as soon as he arrived on the scene, and the ampules were destroyed."

There was silence as Rice picked up his briar and his ivory-handled penknife, then became totally absorbed in carving out the tobacco caked in the bowl with fingers that were long and white.

When he finished he tapped the pipe on the side of the ashtray and put the knife back in his pocket.

"Until now, the only successful venture has been in Argentina. Sugar cubes of anthrax shipped to Herr Arnold in Buenos Aires, transported, we believe, by Krohn's French mistress. They infected thousands and thousands of sheep, beef cattle, and mules. Food and pack animals meant for our troops in Mesopotamia, slaughtered and dumped at sea."

Gordon looked at Wright again, but the old scientist simply stared back, tapping a quarter inch of ash off the end of his cigar.

"So the incident at Hazebrouck," Gordon said. "These messages in the journal. This means something's changed. You think they've lost their inhibitions."

Rice placed his pipe between his teeth. "Unfortunately, yes. We think it has to do with the push they're calling 'Operation Alberich.' From the wicked dwarf of the Nibelungenlied. Siegfried and the cloak of invisibility. Impervious to blows."

Gordon nodded slowly and then looked away. Ostensibly he had come to Boulogne to inspect the wards at the casino and to pick up some guinea pigs from their lab for Wassermann tests. He could still leave it at that.

Sir Almroth adjusted his position in his chair, placed his elbows on the table, and folded his enormous hands in front of him. Gordon glanced over to see the candlelight reflecting in the old man's rimless spectacles.

"We don't think they're impervious yet," Sir Almroth explained.

"But you're well aware that the Germans have a tremendous lead in this sort of thing. The Institute for Infectious Diseases. Koch and tuberculosis. Cholera and all that. They've been working on plague since ninety-four, when Kitasato brought the bacillus back from Hong Kong."

Sir Almroth paused for a moment, looking pensively at the American. "But the unpleasant truth is that they are much too sophisticated to launch such a campaign without prophylaxis for themselves. Some new antiserum. Some 'magic bullet' that would kill the microbes and leave the handlers immune. Otherwise, using biologicals is Russian roulette. You have no control, so you're putting the same loaded gun to your own head as well."

Gordon took a bit of string from his pocket and began tying knots in it with his thumb and first three fingers. He noticed Rice watching his hand, which was a dark, reddish brown, the backs of the knuckles nicked and scarred. It was Rice who had the surgeon's delicate hands, Gordon who was the surgeon.

"So that's what you want, essentially," Gordon said. "This 'magic bullet' brought back to England."

"We want to know what the Germans are up to with our civilian detainees," Rice said. "We want to know what they're preparing to send our way in terms of germ weapons. And yes, in the event that our worst suspicions are correct, bringing a sample of their protective antiserum back to England would be most desirable."

Gordon untied his knot and started over again. "Then why worry about the prisoners at this racecourse? Why not go to the Institute directly? The research seems to be the key. Not whether or not they're performing it on Englishmen."

Rice removed the pipe from his mouth and held it by the bowl, a tiny trail of vapor rising from the stem that pointed toward Gordon.

"We have other agents in place, you see, old man. Agents whose identities *are* known to us. We can't push harder at the Institute without the risk of exposing them. What we need is a new offensive, not more footprints on the same path. That's why we want you to pursue the prisoner angle. Trace this experimentation rumor, if that's what it is, back to its source, to Ruhleben, then see where it leads. Build it back up from first principles and all that. It's little more than a mosaic at this point. Speculation. But where there is sufficient smoke . . ."

Gordon wrapped the string around his fingertip, jostled his brandy glass, and peered into the amber liquid, not drinking.

"What about these other agents in Berlin, the ones you don't want exposed? They keep you up to date on rumors and war stories?"

"Now and then. But you might benefit. They'll be like little fairies watching over you," Rice said. "If you should need them, they'll appear. Otherwise, they'll stay behind their toadstools."

"This courier in Amsterdam . . . the one who passed the journal messages to you . . ."

"His name is Hendrik Troelstra. He's a surgeon."

"I'll want to see him."

"If it makes you feel better."

Gordon nodded and put the string in his pocket, a problem to be unraveled later, in his own good time.

"And the embassy staff?"

"We've been going through a bit of a rough patch with your Berlin station lately. We thought it best not to implicate them."

"I assume you've talked this over with someone in the U.S. State Department?"

"I can assure you they approve."

Gordon smiled as he looked into the brandy, then drank it down. "Somehow that doesn't give me the warm glow I'm looking for."

"You'll be traveling via Britain anyway," Rice said. "I'll arrange for you to speak with your people in London."

There was a silence, broken finally by Wright asking, "Does this mean you'll do it?"

Gordon leaned back and rose from his chair. "I want to think about it, to tell you the truth. I might be interested and then I might not."

"I'm going back tonight. I'm afraid I simply must know now," Rice said.

Gordon looked down and smiled. "Well, old chap, I'm staying on. I'm afraid I'll simply have to let you know in the morning."

Gordon carried an oil lamp up the creaking stairs to his room and placed it beside the iron bed. Then he took off his jacket and reached for the Gladstone bag he'd brought with him from Haze-brouck. From it he withdrew a bottle of Haut-Brion liberated from a bombed-out château in the Forêt de Compiègne. Gordon blew out the lamp, then fell back slowly onto the pillow.

The room was warm and calm now, and he planned to get drunk in a lazy, comfortable way. He listened in the darkness, and for the first time in many weeks he could not hear a thing, not even the distant rumbling of guns.

He reached for the fresh pack of cigarettes on his bedside table and tapped it against the palm of his hand.

"In Flanders fields the poppies blow. . . ." he muttered to himself. Surgery was more intense than morphine, but morphine was more numbing. Neither of those being available . . .

He couldn't judge the merits of what they were asking him to do, or even the assumptions they were making. All he could see was an open window letting air into a room where he had been suffocating. He was sick of doing surgery like a Ford assembly line. You patched them up and sent them out for one more try at getting killed, knowing all the while that the war would win, that the war had already won. And he was very sick of war this season, sick of the smell of gangrene, the sight of horses in gas masks. He was sick of watching men turn blue from the gas and die with subpleural emphysema solidifying their lungs. He was sick of the cries in the night from no-man's-land, the bones sticking out of the rubble, the body parts hanging in the trees. Just as he was sick of his own guilt. Rationally, he knew he could not have saved his daughter no matter what he had done. But still he was a doctor—he was supposed to save lives. And he knew from the look of hatred in Lavinia's face, in that one moment before she closed off completely, that she would never forgive him, and that he would never be able to forgive himself.

Gordon broke open the cigarette wrapper, pulled out a Caporal, and reached for the ashtray, which suddenly flew onto the floor. The night sky exploded red and silver outside his room and the whole house reeled with the shock wave. A moment later he stumbled toward the window and threw it open to see a pocket of flame shooting skyward from the streets near the casino. Dust and debris flew through the air, and a vague, dark shape rode over the town like a thundercloud. Then he saw the Very lights flare up from the Channel guns and shine red against the surface of the Zeppelin.

"Du der über Cherubinen . . . ," he whispered, looking out. It was a rhyme he'd learned from a P.O.W., a German boy he'd kept up the language with. He'd sent him out to bury amputations one night just before Christmas and a sentry shot him dead.

". . . Seraphinen, Zeppelinen. In der höchsten Höhe tronest . . ."

Then airplane engines buzzed overhead. At least a pair of Gothas flew as outriders alongside the airship. The searchlights caught one of them in its beam and the pilot pitched into a roll, falling away from the light.

There *was* a kind of grotesque beauty to it all, Gordon realized. But now they were asking him to take sides, whereas like a priest or a small child he had always been absolved. His whole life had been hidden behind that priestly role of doctor. He was a surgeon first and somewhere far down the line he was a man with beliefs and the freedom to act on them. "So what do I believe in?" he asked himself. "Survival?"

"I believe in myself," he answered. Then, "Oh no." The most fundamental lie.

Looking down, he saw Wright and his assistant, Fleming, just beneath his window. Apparently they had been there quite some time. They had a makeshift putting green laid out on the bluff below the house. A candle glowed inside the hole, and while Wright fumed in mock outrage, his assistant lay on his belly, his putter extended before him like a cue stick, poking at the ball.

And what if they were right, Gordon thought. What if the issue was not something so essentially trivial as his own personal salvation but was something that could win or lose the war? For all the staff wallah absurdity of their plan, what if these Englishmen were not overreacting and Germany actually had designs to unleash some vast plague across Europe?

He considered the proposition, then before he could answer, the whole sky ignited as the Zeppelin burst into flame.

4

The last time Gordon was at the Savoy Hotel it had been packed with colonial officers and the criminal elite of Brussels and Paris. Now the lobby was crowded with young couples for the "thé dansant," the men in khaki, the women with short hair and short skirts, wearing lip rouge and smoking cigarettes. There were even women waiters in the restaurant now, and an Amazonian hall porter wearing a braided jacket above her dark wool skirt.

Gordon had spent the day on the crossing from Boulogne—a ferry to Dover and the boat train to Victoria Station. He was tired and he was hungry now, but still he doubted he could keep anything down. It was the special perversity of this war that an Englishman could eat breakfast in the trenches and dinner the same night at his club.

He left the hotel at ten o'clock and set out along the Strand toward Charing Cross, where the "beauty sleep" regulations were closing the pubs. He saw soldiers spilling into the blacked-out streets and mingling with newly arrived casualties emerging from the train station. Across the way, a banner hung from the windows of Charing Cross Hospital—QUIET FOR THE WOUNDED.

At Craven Street he stopped to buy a hot potato from a vendor on the curb, then turned left. He could hear the footsteps of the two men falling in behind him.

"We're missing the swordplay," one of them said.

Gordon stopped at the Embankment and turned around. He thought he recognized Rice, standing beside an older, heavier man.

"How's that?"

"The benefit at the Savoy. For widows and orphans of the Fusiliers Marins. They say a sergeant cut a sheep in half with a single blow."

The other man struck a match and leaned toward the flame with his cigar.

"This is Ned Bell," Rice said. "Second Secretary, U.S. Embassy."

Gordon nodded and took a bite of his potato, then they turned toward the river and walked south.

"We're pleased you're doing this," Rice said.

Gordon walked on without responding, then stopped to lean over the railing.

Rice looked over at him uncertainly. "Are you all right, old man?"

"Just a cold," Gordon told him. But in fact he had been sweating since mid-afternoon.

Rice handed him a large envelope clasped with string. "Presents," he said.

Gordon tucked the package under his arm. He could feel the river moving in the darkness below him, swollen like the membranes in his head.

"Diplomatic visa, a letter of introduction to Ambassador Gerard, and a thousand marks in bank notes. There's also a Baedeker, till you know your way around."

"Good. I can see the sights."

"There will be another package waiting for you at the embassy. Sent through the pouch. It contains . . . additional things you may need."

Gordon pressed his arms against his sides to quell the chill, and Bell looked at him for the first time.

"Why are you doing this?" he asked. "Berlin's not one of the more fashionable resorts this time of year."

"Boredom, maybe," Gordon said. "Something different." He

leaned forward on his elbows and dropped the potato into the water. "Despite what your friends here think, though, my death wish isn't all that fully developed. I want to know my status on this."

Bell looked down into the Thames. "You have diplomatic immunity up to a point. It's a gray area with a medical consultant like this. But neither Ambassador Gerard nor anyone else at the Berlin embassy knows the real reason for your being in Germany. Keep in mind that this venture is one hundred eighty degrees against the grain of Washington policy. The President does not ant an incident that trips us into this war. Which means, ultimately, that you should not confide in or expect any assistance from the embassy staff."

"Very reassuring," Gordon said, tracing the line of rooftops toward the Houses of Parliament. The clock tower was dark. It occurred to him now that Big Ben had not rung on the hour. It was another wartime change, like the absence of derelicts sleeping by the river.

"And what about London?"

"Ambassador Page has made the diplomatic pouch available for conveying your reports. Postcards, actually. Addressed to your wife, conveying varying degrees of anxiety about 'the children.' It's all spelled out in that packet. You should memorize it and destroy the memo before you leave London."

"And if there's trouble . . ."

Bell tossed his cigar in a long glowing arc down into the river. "The ambassador will not be available. And I, for one, never heard of you."

Rice tapped the railing with his fist, then rose on the balls of his feet. "The boat train leaves Liverpool Station in one hour," he said. "You should be getting back."

The Holland ferry left Parkeston Quay well after midnight, riding low in the water with two destroyer escorts. Gordon stood on deck and lit a cigarette, letting the match fly out of his fingers and over the side.

His skin felt clammy, "cold turkey," and even though he was shivering in the breeze, he didn't want to be inside. He felt as if he might get sick, and this was the place to do it. More than anything else he needed the open air.

Bell had put his finger on the only real question, the one Rice had found it unnecessary to ask. The truest answer Gordon could offer was that everything in life has its tolerance. You stay with something long enough and the impact wears off. Work, despair, the war. Any of it can leave you numb for a while, blown out like a bang of morphine, but then you dig deeper and find a new level and then sooner or later even that won't hold you. So now he was trying something new.

A wooden packing crate drifted past in the dark water below, and he thought about his first welcome to the war zone two years ago. Luggage and deck chairs and lounge furnishings, wreckage strewn for twenty miles as they sailed toward the coast of Ireland. Corpses in fashionable dresses, corpses in knee pants. It was all that remained of the *Lusitania* that fine spring morning, probed by a trawler collecting bodies at a guinea each.

At dawn the ferry reached the Hook of Holland. Gordon boarded the train for Beurs Station in Rotterdam, then took the two-hour express through Schiedam and the Hague.

At Central Station, he had left instructions for forwarding his trunk, which had been following him from Hazebrouck, and confirmed his reservations for a sleeping car to Berlin. Then he threw his smaller bags into a horse cab and told the driver, "Hotel Amstel."

The cab followed the canal, Gordon looking out from under the brim of his hat at the Dutch rattling past on their bicycles. Amsterdam glistened in a fresh coat of ice, and the morning sun was painful, the horse's hooves clattering loudly against the stones. He shaded his eyes and tried not to think.

▪ ▪ ▪

Four hours later, Gordon woke up perplexed. Covered with sweat, his heart pounding with tachycardia, he looked through the rails of a brass bed, saw plush gold curtains and Biedermeier chairs standing around him like bored attendants. He could not for the life of him remember where he was. Then he lifted his head and it all came back to him with the full weight of ever-evolving reality. He had the most expensive room in Amsterdam. He had a private bath and a view of the Buiten-Amstel.

On the wall beneath the curtains he saw a suggestion of sunlight. It was mid-afternoon and he heard the sounds of water traffic, not shelling. The smells were of dry heat, musty furniture, and perfumed disinfectants. He rearranged his body slowly, almost ceremoniously, and put his feet on the floor. Encouraged, then, he stood and made his first tentative step toward the bathroom.

He felt safe and reasonably calm as he stepped in front of the mirror. The glass was absolutely still. He turned on the hot water, breathed in the steam, and inhaled the fragrance of soap. Maybe spring will come early this year, he thought. The poppies will bloom again.

He stood in the bathroom and shaved, his surgeon's hands skillful with the razor, and he studied his face—the whites of his eyes, the heavy creases beneath his eyes. His skin was dark and oily and in reasonably good shape, all things considered.

When his jawline felt smooth he washed off what was left of the lather, dried his hands, and took a moment to palpate his abdomen. There was no enlargement. His efforts at self-destruction had been no more successful than his efforts at moving on.

For the next half hour Gordon soaked in a tub of ornate porcelain, steaming like a lobster. In France he had bathed in a canvas tub for which some sahib in some dusty part of the empire had decreed three inches of water a day. Now the Brits were covering expenses and he felt obliged to bolster their confidence in him. Despite all evidence to the contrary, he knew how a gentleman ought to live.

He dressed and packed again, then ate lunch overlooking the canal in the Amstel dining room, where an enthusiastic waiter netted a trout for him from a glass tank, then afterward brought over a strawberry plant in a silver pot for him to pick his own dessert. The Brits would have been impressed.

He lingered over the coffee, watching the boats on the canal and the Dutch on their bikes, but the lights were already coming on across the water. He had been hiding since Abbey's death— in a bottle, behind a surgical mask—and three years was long enough. It was time to come out now and see what, if anything, was left.

At four in the afternoon Gordon's cab stopped at the corner of the Heren Gracht and Rozen Gracht Straat, outside a shop with multicolored bottles in the window. Over the door was a black-turbaned figure carved in wood, the sign of the Turk's head. Gordon got out and walked across the bridge as the wind blew in thick, dark clouds off the sea.

A wagon was parked at the edge of the canal, and beside it, a metal drum with orange flames licking up from inside. Workmen walked in and out of a charred ruin, carrying loose boards and debris, dumping what was salvageable, burning whatever was of no use. Gordon read the plaque by the door of the empty town house.

227

DR. HENDRIK TROELSTRA
Surgeon.

He stood by the drum as the blindered draft horse stared dumbly into his eyes, its head shrouded in clouds of steam. His first thought was that there had been some mistake, but the sign had the name as well as the address. Then he realized that the error could not have been anything so simple.

He saw a wheelbarrow and a thick-necked laborer coming out with a load of debris. The boy pulled up beside the drum without

taking any notice of Gordon and began tossing books and papers
into the fire. After a moment he stopped to flip through a heavy,
green volume, an anatomy text, examining each drawing and pho-
tographic plate with a critical eye. At last he came to a schema of
the female reproductive system and smiled, his teeth like brown
pegs as he turned the book toward Gordon. He muttered something in Dutch, made a pumping motion with his fist near his
crotch, then tossed the book into the fire.

"What happened?" Gordon asked in German.

The boy grumbled something and nodded back toward the
apothecary's shop.

"Who did this?"

"Nay, nay," the boy said, still nodding toward the shop.

Gordon's stomach fluttered. He rose to take a breath, and then
he saw the car parked across the canal, a fat man with a square
head staring at him with binoculars from behind the wheel.

If the British had known about this, why hadn't they told him?
If they hadn't known . . .

Gordon pulled his hands out of his pockets and warmed them
over the fire. The wind blew down his neck and suddenly he felt
very cold.

The boy tossed in a stack of books, sending up a swirl of cinders.
They were unbound copies of a journal printed on sand-colored
paper. *Annalen der Chirurgie.* Gordon glanced again at the man
in the car, then reached in and pulled one of the volumes from
the flames. It was addressed to Dr. Hendrik Troelstra, Heren
Gracht 227. Above the label was stamped:

> With our compliments.
>
> Isidor Katz
> Maker of Surgical Instruments.
> Friedrichstrasse 134
> Berlin.

■ ■ ■

THE train slowed at Spandau, then came to a halt at Charlottenburg. From the elevated tracks Gordon could see the lights of munitions factories, the smoke rising above the skyline of chimneys. He gathered his coat around him and shoved his bags with his feet, then waited as the brakes took hold and the doors opened, letting in a burst of bracing night air.

Off to the left a crowd of German women stood under the arc light of a tram stop. Their faces were white, their clothes black. They looked like factory workers without enough to eat, and they did not appear to have much energy tonight for spreading "Kultur" throughout the world.

On the other siding, a westbound train rumbled past with soldiers packed into cars marked with patriotic slogans. OUR POSTERITY WILL BENEFIT. YOUNG LIONS—DO NOT ROUSE. Above the groaning of the wheels, Gordon could hear them singing the "Hymn of Hate," but the faces in the windows looked too young to be convincing.

> French and Russians they matter not
> A blow for a blow and a shot for a shot
> We love them not, we hate them not
> We hold the Vistula and the Vosges-gate
> We have but one and only hate
> We love as one, we hate as one
> We have one foe and one alone,
> ENGLAND! . . .

A moment later his own car edged forward, and the train began crawling the last five miles into central Berlin and the Bahnhof Friedrichstrasse.

The trip from Amsterdam had taken six hours, but the incident outside Troelstra's house was still very much on Gordon's mind as he stood in the cold wind that swirled around Friedrichstrasse and tried to gain his bearings. It was as if he had been led to

Amsterdam to be deliberately exposed. Which did not strike him as a terribly good beginning.

There were no motorcabs and only one creaking wagon, both horse and driver nodding forward as if half asleep. Gordon stepped over and hoisted his grip into the seat of the droshky and asked for the Hotel Adlon.

"Marke," the old man said. He shook his head but did not look up.

Gordon was tired and still half sick, and he stared at the inert driver with a growing, inordinate rage. Then he heard footsteps and turned to see a young man in an Alpine hat and white silk scarf, holding up a numbered brass disc.

"This is what he wants," the young man said. The cold had painted red circles on his cheeks. He took the cigarette out of his mouth and said, "You have to get a token from the gendarme at the door."

"There's no line," Gordon said. "There's only one cab."

"Welcome to Prussia, Dr. Gordon." Then the young man handed the disc to the driver and climbed aboard. "But here . . . you can ride with me. I'm Jay Adams, from the embassy. Come on. You must be tired. Let's get you to your hotel."

Gordon looked up at the darkened theater across the way. He was too tired to question now, too tired to insist on things making sense. He climbed aboard and the driver nudged the old horse into motion.

They turned south toward the Linden and the wind blew in their faces. Gordon felt as if the sound of the hooves and the rhythm of the carriage could easily lull him to sleep. Sleep would be good, he realized. Sleep and a bottle.

"I didn't know anyone would be meeting me," he said after a while.

"My own improvisation, really. I thought you deserved fair warning. A fighting chance, perhaps."

Adams lit another cigarette with the butt of his first, his fingers sheathed in gray kid gloves. In the dim light of the streetlamps he held out a small case covered with mother-of-pearl. "Care for a smoke?"

Gordon took one, then struck up his trench lighter.

"Is it so bad in Berlin?" he said.

"How bad do you need it to be?"

Just then an army staff car came up out of the darkness and rumbled past them on iron wheels.

"No rubber," Adams said. "None for tires. None for gloves— you're a surgeon, aren't you? Harvard Med?"

"Was."

"Oh really?" Adams paused, testing the silence for implications. "Class of Fourteen myself. How about you?"

Gordon let the question pass, looking instead at the long line of women on Dorotheen Strasse, standing outside the Staff College, waiting to read the casualty lists.

"You were going to tell me how it is in Berlin," he said.

"Tense," Adams replied. "I think it is fair to describe the situation in Berlin as tense." He took a long drag on his cigarette and settled back into his seat.

"Von Tirpitz is spreading rumors that the Kaiser's lost his mind, spends all his time learning Hebrew. But no one really knows. 'Lehman' they call him—it's illegal to criticize the Kaiser by name—rarely comes to the city for fear of someone taking a potshot at him. Supposedly there's a scheme afoot to sacrifice one of his sons as a sop to public opinion."

Adams glanced over with an air of confidentiality. "But don't take too much comfort from any of that. Hostility toward America is the national pastime. We're arming the Allies. We're supplying them with food. And the embassy's right in the middle, with 'God Punish England' postmarking every letter we send out."

Adams let the smoke linger for a moment at the tip of his tongue, then inhaled deeply. He seemed to derive some voluptuous pleasure from it, as if he had just taken it up.

"I'm the ambassador's aide," he said. "He and my father were partners in New York. Now, you know this new Foreign Secretary Zimmermann is a stitch. He's convinced a million German-Americans will rise up if we come in with the Allies. He was at the embassy for dinner the other night and blurts out over his strudel— 'Don't you ever send reports!' He'd gotten bored reading Gerard's mail! Desperate for something salacious."

Gordon tried to manage a smile, but he was not quite up to it. Then they turned onto the Linden, Adams grinning at him from behind his tortoiseshell spectacles, still smoking like a cherub testing sin.

The driver pulled off toward the front of the hotel and Gordon tossed his cigarette into the gutter.

"Well, here we are," Adams said.

The droshky came to a stop and Gordon stepped down. "Thanks for the lift."

Adams handed him his bag, then paused. "Doctor . . . One thing I should say, just between you and me. The German legal system is not terribly progressive. There's no such thing as innocent until proven guilty. In fact, it's quite the other way around."

"Good point to remember," Gordon acknowledged.

"As I said . . . just between you and me. They still have a headsman, Doctor. And they still shoot spies."

Jay Adams tagged along like a younger brother as Gordon checked into the hotel. There was the ordinary registration form to be filled out, plus the identity and address forms for the police, in triplicate, plus a new set of triplicate forms for ration cards.

"Let me buy you a drink," Adams said when they were done.

Gordon gave a lame smile. "Thanks, old man, but I'm a little under the weather."

"Another time, then." Adams grinned with no sign of disappointment, tapping his newspaper against his leg. "Ambassador Gerard would like you to have luncheon with him tomorrow. If you ask for me when you arrive, I can help you settle in."

They shook hands and parted, then Gordon followed the bell-man up to his room.

At his window looking down on the Linden, Gordon could follow the line of barren trees along the wide boulevard to the palace and the university. He looked to his left, beyond the Pariser Platz, where the Brandenburg Gate rose up toward the night sky. Its horses and chariot seemed to be moving against the background of drifting clouds. Beyond the gate, out in the Tiergarten, a giant bonfire roared, giving the Victory Column in the Königs Platz an orange glow, lighting up the crowd surrounding it. The Germans and their forests, Gordon thought. Getting mystical at the first sign of dense vegetation.

This business with Adams troubled him, almost as much as the business in Amsterdam. The middleman Troelstra was dead, he had been spotted by the German in the car, and his real purpose in coming to Berlin seemed perfectly obvious to everyone. He wanted to talk to Rice, he decided, and not just through a coded postcard. The British had a rather peculiar tradition when it came to underlings. He had seen them send their troops in waves toward German machine guns—walking slowly in broad daylight—because officers thought the other ranks too stupid to handle tactics any more sophisticated. It was not terribly reassuring for Gordon, but then he had not come to be reassured. He had come for whatever happened next.

The American Bar downstairs was dark and smoke filled, and looked like any hotel bar in London except for the cut of the uniforms. Prussian field gray, the black-and-white tunic ribbon of the Iron Cross. Gordon took a seat at one end of the long expanse of mahogany and pulled his lighter and cigarettes out of his pocket and placed them just so in front of him.

He ordered American whiskey and the barman set down an empty glass and proceeded to fill it as Gordon looked around. In the corners of the room were fat Turks in fezzes, awkward Japanese dwarfed by their Western clothing. In the center, a single table of officers and, with them, three women.

Gordon poured down the first drink and watched the brunette who laughed so energetically at whatever her shaved-headed Prussian was saying. He watched her eyes against the cadaverous mask of face powder and lip rouge. The girls at the front could retire well fixed after three weeks, or so he was told, provided they could last for three weeks. But this was a different matter entirely. It had been a while since he had seen a beautiful woman in the right clothes, in the right light, tarted up. Lavinia had been beautiful in the right clothes, but that too was a different matter.

A small man wearing a sprig of parsley in his buttonhole and a bad toupee stepped into Gordon's line of vision. His head looked as if he'd been upended and dipped in ink.

"Ah, sorry," he said, moving closer to the bar. Then he glanced back at the women. "Actresses. A remarkable bargain these days."

Gordon shook his head, letting his eyes linger on the bare white throat of the pretty brunette. "Contradiction in terms," he said. Then he lifted his finger to the bartender and ordered another drink.

EARLY the next morning, Eli Gordon sat in a café on the Oranienburger Strasse and cleared a small circle on the steam-covered window beside him. Across the small Platz, where three streets converged, the shades were still drawn at the shop of the instrument maker Isidor Katz.

The name had come from a journal being burned in a trash barrel, but still it was more solid than anything else he had to go on. He lit a cigarette, pulled his Baedeker out of his pocket, and unfolded the general plan of Berlin onto the table.

The city depicted before him was a gray field lying under the tangled red lines of tramways. The heavy black of the Stadtbahn and the thick gray of the Spree intertwined from east to west across the center. The Ruhleben Racecourse would be far off to the left, almost to Spandau. Gordon ran his finger along the line of the Ringbahn to its point of intersection with the Berlin-Spandau Ship Canal. And on the northern bank, just over the line in Wedding, the Institute for Infectious Diseases.

The waiter came back from the bar and handed Gordon his coffee. He was an old man, his leathery face drawn and desiccated, his oversized shirt hanging around his neck like a horse collar. "Twenty-five pfennigs," he said.

Gordon reached into his pocket for the money. Then the waiter went back to the bar and Gordon raised the cup to take a sip. It was a liquid, fair enough, brown and hot, but it wasn't coffee.

Gordon set the cup on the table next to his and looked back at the extended map. The Institute for Infectious Diseases. The Ruhleben Racecourse. This instrument maker was near the Charité and the medical school, nowhere near the Institute. But that didn't rule out a connection. How many instrument shops could there be in one city, even in Berlin?

Gordon reached into his pocket and pulled out a blank postcard and his fountain pen.

My dearest wife,
   I am safely at my new post and missing you more than you can know. I have heard nothing about you or the children in many days now. I trust I'll hear from you soon.
   With deepest affection,

                                        Your loving husband,
                                        Eli Gordon, M.D.

He glanced up. The shades in Katz's windows were being raised. He folded the map back into his Baedeker and pocketed the card and pen. Then he put on his hat and coat and went back out into the mist.

■   ■   ■

The instrument maker might have been five feet tall standing erect, but the point was academic. Scoliosis had turned his spine into a question mark, and it left him with a posture fit for little more than work or prayer.

Overhead, a glass shade did little to soften the glare of a single incandescent bulb. Isidor Katz stepped forward behind the display case on a pair of canes, his twisted legs popping like springs, his arms on the canes as rigid as metal struts.

"You've come a long way for instruments," he said, sliding Gordon's card off the glass top. He wore a gabardine coat, black homburg, and gloves. Around his neck, a silver magnifying glass hung from a piece of ribbon.

Inside the case, forceps, rib spreaders, and orthopedic saws lay side by side. Here and there the blue felt had a darker tint in the outline of instruments sold but not restocked.

"Dr. Troelstra sang your praises," Gordon said.

"Troelstra?"

"In Amsterdam."

Katz looked down at the brown slush dripping off Gordon's boots onto the floor. "And what were you doing in Amsterdam?"

"Coming to Berlin," Gordon said.

Katz rubbed his chin with the back of his hand, his sallow skin visible through a black beard with the quality of pubic hair. He did not look frightened or unsettled by Gordon's appearance on his doorstep. He merely looked displeased.

"I'm not sure I know anyone in Amsterdam. Not anyone named . . . Troelstra, was it?"

"I take it he's on your mailing list. Copies of *Annalen der Chirurgie*."

"I have hundreds of people on my mailing list."

"The issue dealt with 'bacteriological developments.' That's where I got your name. 'Compliments of Isidor Katz.' "

Katz tapped Gordon's card against the glass, then slipped it into his pocket. "Where is Troelstra?"

"He had complications. I came instead."

Katz reached up to his beard once again, uncoiling a single tuft of hair and stretching it out from his chin. This whole tack could be completely wrong, Gordon realized.

Then the instrument maker tucked the magnifying glass into his pocket and said, "Come with me."

Outside the winter light was soft against the monotonous brown of the apartment buildings. The cold, moist air was brittle, almost frozen.

"So you represent what? The British?" Katz asked, stopping to lock the door behind them.

"Not exactly," Gordon said. He watched Katz pocket the keys, then followed him off the icy curb and into Friedrichstrasse.

The instrument maker had a four-footed gait that used the two canes in rhythm with his legs. Gordon followed him across the trolley tracks and the Platz toward the café where he had waited. The circle he had cleared in the window was clouded over again now with steam.

"So what kind of complications did Troelstra have?" Katz said as he labored along the sidewalk.

Gordon glanced over. "They were sifting through his ashes when I arrived."

Katz continued on without speaking for a moment, his steps punctuated by the squeak of hinges. After a while he asked, "You came alone?"

"Not entirely."

"What does that mean?"

"Why don't you tell me who I am going to see?"

"You want to talk bacteria, yes? For the British, yes?"

"That's right."

Katz said nothing more for a while, twisting from side to side like a swimmer.

They passed the Oranienburg Gate and continued east up Linienstrasse, the narrow street making a graceful arc between the two rows of apartment buildings stretching into infinity. The sun still had not made its way beyond the terra-cotta rooftops.

"It's a delicate situation, you realize," Katz said over his shoulder. "Attention from anyone can be dangerous. Especially attention from the British. You can understand that."

"I thought it was worth the risk."

"That's good," Katz said. Then he turned into the passageway between two buildings.

Gordon followed through a wide wooden door with trash bins lining either side and a tattered cat bathing herself with her paw. Katz stepped through the opening to a second passageway and Gordon walked quickly to keep up—a right turn, then farther ahead a low archway. Gordon stepped through into a second gravel courtyard, hidden from the light.

He did not see Katz spin on his heel, or see him swing his right arm. He did not see the cane making a wide arc through the air until the instant before it hit him just below the hairline. He did not feel the second blow at all, or the third. The weighted canes smashed into his head and neck in rapid succession as his body crumpled forward.

There was an infantile comfort in the gesture, like being readied for bed. As he lay prone in the frozen gravel, Gordon was vaguely aware of hands rolling him over and going through his pockets. He felt helpless and foolish too, marginally conscious but unable to move on his own. He heard a tapping on a windowpane. He opened his eyes and felt blood on his face. He looked up and saw a narrow swath of gray sky. Then he heard a woman scream. He raised his head and saw Katz standing over him, pulling apart one of his canes. Katz hobbled forward, off bal_nce, then thrust toward Gordon's face with an eight~en-inch blade.

Gordon rolled to the side and grabbed Katz's arm. The cripple toppled over, embedding his sword-cane in the dirt beneath the gravel. Gordon swung his right fist but hit only air as Katz moved back.

Dazed, unfocused, still reeling from the blows, Gordon gripped the sword handle and used it as a lever to pull himself up. He was sick at his stomach. His head was swollen and bleeding. The cartilage in his left ear burned and with his best efforts he could not move beyond a crawl, but Katz was already up and hobbling through the archway.

Gordon came over to one knee, assimilating the event in stages. He had been out only for a moment. But now he concentrated on the astounding distribution of pain across his upper body.

He forced himself to his feet, picked up his hat, and lumbered dizzily through the passageway.

A faint snow drifted down as he reached the street again. He squinted in both directions and thought he saw Katz limping around the corner to his right. Light-headed, he ran after as the instrument maker hobbled across Friedrichstrasse and back toward the shop, but then Katz stopped and turned and Gordon darted behind the stone monument. A streetcar pulled up and blocked Gordon's view. Then in a moment he saw Katz in the vehicle beside the driver, making his way toward a seat.

The tram jerked forward and headed south and Gordon felt like an imbecile as he ran after it, bleeding from the head, his hat in his hand, propelled by nothing more than an impotent rage.

After a block he was far behind and winded, but then the tram came to a stop and he narrowed the distance. He was going to be sick and he suspected he might black out. He stopped and walked a few steps, struggling with his equilibrium, tottering but refusing to go down. The tram took on two passengers, then pulled away, and Gordon began to run again, trying to make some sense of it. Katz had mailed the journal containing messages for the British. If Katz worked for the British, why would he try to kill him?

The car outdistanced him once more, and once more the chase

seemed pointless. He slowed to a walk, then just beyond the river the tram stopped and he came close again. He had to suppress the urge to vomit, suppress the urge to lie down and close his eyes. Then the car pulled away, quickly regaining speed, and Gordon fell behind.

He kept going, but by the time he was on the bridge he felt too dizzy and he knew he would not make it. He had made a mistake, breaking away from the script, but now he wanted to know exactly what that mistake was and what it meant.

He saw the tram stop at the Bahnhof Friedrichstrasse and a small twisted form hobble off and into the station. He ran on, focusing on the tracks. If no trains pulled in or left in the next sixty seconds he would be okay. The moments passed as he ran, no trains came, and he reached the station and bolted through the doors.

At the ticket window he fumbled for money, out of breath and bleeding. "End of the line," he said.

The ticket seller, refusing to be hurried, stared back at him through the metal grate. "The line does not end," she said philosophically. She had a round face that looked unamused, squatting on a thick neck. "Where do you wish to go?"

Gordon could hear the rumble of a train coming from the east. He thrust a ten-mark note under the bars and said, "A ticket."

The woman began, "Any five stations fifteen pfennigs second class, ten pfennigs third. Beyond that distance thirty pfennigs second class, twenty, third. Monthly tickets . . ."

"Monthly," Gordon said.

"Local or distance?"

"Distance."

"Class?"

"First."

"There is only second or third."

"Second then."

She shook her head and ripped out the ticket. Gordon put his hat on his head and raced up the stairs.

Katz stood under the second-class marker as Gordon reached the platform and came to rest behind an Imbiss stand. He stayed hidden there, leaning against it for support as the train pulled into the station and stopped. Katz edged into the first car, seemingly unaware. Then Gordon gulped in a breath and dashed for the second as the closer blew her whistle.

He hung from the strap and caught his wind as the train lurched forward. They rolled across the milky surface of the river with Gordon standing feebly just inside the door. They skirted the Charité off to the right, then crossed the river again, already slowing for the Lehter Bahnhof.

Gordon adjusted his position to look into the other car as the train came to a stop. Then he pushed the door open and watched the platform. Two older women got off and walked methodically toward the stairs, hand in hand. Then the closer blew her whistle, the doors slid shut, and the car jumped forward with Katz still on board.

With the snow a faint stippling against the dark cityscape, they rattled across another bend in the Spree. Gordon daubed at the blood still trickling down his face, then looked at it on his fingertips, an extravagantly bright red.

They crossed a brickworks on the left, and Gordon hung by the door. Then they slowed for the Bahnhof Bellevue. The train stopped and Gordon slid back the doors again as an old man with a brass-tipped cane teetered on board.

There was a moment of uncertainty, then the doors closed again and Gordon sat down to light a cigarette. He was tired of the game now and he wanted to regroup. He looked at his bloody hand trembling slightly as he fumbled with the lighter. He watched it with a perverse fascination. Nothing made his hands shake.

He stayed seated at the Tiergarten, watching the platform. The cigarette made him sick and he put it out. The train continued south with Katz securely on board.

Passing through the Hansa quarter and the southwest corner of the park, Gordon could see the fresh dusting of snow through the bare trees and, in the far distance, the small pavilion at the edge of the Neue See, where a few isolated skaters glided across the ice.

They crossed the canal, smoke rising from cooking stoves on the small barges moored there. Gordon glanced up at the map above the door to see that the Bahnhof Zoologischer Garten was next, but then he kept his seat. He could see the platform well enough now. He had been stupid to blunder in without knowing more about Katz. He would not be stupid again.

The doors slid back and a man in loden knickers stepped down with a burly woman tagging after him, her arms filled with packages.

Gordon watched through an exhausted haze as the door closer blew her whistle. Then he saw Katz at the top of the stairs.

The train rolled forward and Gordon shot up and grabbed the door handle but it would not budge. They were gaining speed, the car ahead already bursting into the light beyond the barrel dome of the station. Then Gordon pulled the red handle above his head and the brakes screamed and everything stopped. He ran to the rear and threw back the door, teetering over the end of the platform as he leapt out, then ran back to the stairway with the stationmaster shouting red-faced from his window.

Gordon raced down to the tunnel and, forced to choose, turned right. When he came out on the street he saw the instrument maker already across the Platz, black homburg and twisted body, making his way toward the Berlin zoo.

Gordon crossed the empty traffic lanes to the other side of the street, then ran along the fence that led to the gate.

The zoo was mostly silence now, having shed its summer foliage of children and balloons. The only life was a solitary duck waddling across a frozen brook. The snow was building, falling with commitment, but Gordon could not see so much as a footprint on the smooth expanse of white. It seemed impossible. Gordon was sure he had seen Katz go through that gate. He turned to his left and walked past a still fountain, a snow-covered barn. He heard the crow of a single, persistent rooster, then wild dogs barking from across the way. He followed the gravel path until he came to a crossroads and saw the viewing tower, rising up into the swirling white of the sky.

Gordon unhooked the icy chain across the stairway, then slowly began to climb, revolving higher and higher until he stood at the top, looking out over the rooftops and fences toward the Kaiser Wilhelm church. The frozen ponds, the snow-covered gardens, and the undisturbed white paths lay below. He could hear the wind and the howling of the dogs now even louder. It seemed the instrument maker was a magician as well. He had disappeared.

5

The Exhibition Hall at the Berlin Zoological Garden had been turned into a free tearoom for students, artists, and intellectuals—a warm place, in theory, where they could read and work. Margarethe Riesling, her long blond hair piled on top of her head, went there each morning when there was no heat in her flat and still no heat in the lab. It did not matter to her that the space had become crowded with pretenders—typists passing as writers, artists' models as artists. The press of bodies was more reliable than the coal.

The bearded man to her right slept as the young woman across the table cried quietly into her handkerchief. Margarethe leaned closer to her work and tried to narrow her concentration. Everyone in Berlin had problems. She could involve herself only in so many.

Wearing her loden coat and her gray fedora, holding a blue examination booklet atop a copy of *Berliner klinische Wochenschrift*, she leaned forward and dug at the lined paper with the stub of a broken pencil, jotting down nouns and verbs as guideposts to what she was reading.

After a time she sat up and raised her fingers to her lips, fingers stained a dark blue-black with bichloride of mercury.

"Saliva. Tears. Three to ten percent. *Staphylococcus pyogenes.* Lysis—certainly."

She bit into the soft wood of the pencil. The act of writing was like a Greek rattling his worry beads. The notes were gibberish. They meant nothing the moment the pencil left the page, even to her.

Now and then she glanced up at the center table, where the tea was served. She was famished, but she had not been able to eat, and she was sleeping less than eating, spending each night curled in the fetal position, her mind racing like the cogs in a wheel until she woke up at dawn more exhausted than when she had lain down. And each morning the same vision was there to greet her—the face of Kraft von Stade, taking on that strangely bluish tint. She had known how his mind would work once he learned what she was all about. She knew he would have come up with something operatic to avoid disgrace, something out of *Tristan and Isolde*. She had simply been quicker.

She closed the examination booklet and folded it into the journal, then placed them, along with her gnarled pencil, back into her bag. The Exhibition Hall was stuffy, the noise of people coughing and of chairs going back and forth rising louder and louder.

Staring past the crying woman, she thought of the station this morning where the men were brought down from the train. She was impressed by the way the women actually maintained their dignity, maybe even their hope, right up to the moment they saw their sons and husbands. Dismembered bodies hanging on crutches, corpselike figures on stretchers. But there were so many hysterical women in Berlin. She had turned away to the boy lying untended on the stretcher. Bright blue eyes and mud ringing his mouth like chocolate licked from a baking pan. There was a T marked on his forehead with aniline pencil, diagrams of his broken bones on the plaster casts. He was deathly pale and beginning to convulse, with the officer standing over him yelling, "The German wounded will lie at attention!" That was when she had begun to scream, hitting the officer with her fists. That was when the orderlies carried her away to save her life.

Margarethe looked up and saw a small man limping on a cane

come in the far entrance and join the line waiting for tea. She picked up her things and walked slowly across the room, past the tea table, and out the door.

The aviary was steaming, a few square meters of rain forest set down in the center of Berlin. She could hear cockatoos and parrots against the muffled roar of an artificial waterfall as she unbuttoned her coat and removed her hat.

The small man at her side wiped his eyeglasses with his handkerchief as Margarethe leaned over the rail and stared into the banana leaves. Hanging above her was a band of orchids strung like Christmas tinsel.

"We had a visitor," Katz said.

She glanced up, holding her hat by the brim. "Not Ostriker."

"No, not Ostriker."

"Troelstra?"

Katz shook his head. "An American." He put his glasses on his nose, then immediately took them off again and pulled out his handkerchief. "He says Troelstra had complications. He says that's why he came instead."

She looked back into the undergrowth of dark green ferns and said nothing.

In time she heard a gurgling, flutelike call and looked up where a green-breasted bird was hanging upside down on a lichen-covered branch. He spread his wings, made them vibrate, then pointed the rectrices toward the ceiling. Swaying from side to side, he opened his flank plumes until they formed a brilliant white halo around his body. The Emperor of Germany bird of paradise.

"Oh God," she said, and then she sighed.

Katz waited, still polishing the lenses. "I tried to get rid of him," he said, "but I have my limitations." He continued his task for a while, then, distracted and impatient, he stuffed his glasses into his pocket and looked into her face. "Why don't you just get out!"

"Out where? Where I can work? That's what Troelstra was supposed to fix."

Katz sighed, his hands trembling. "You might as well place a notice in the newspapers now, Gretta. Troelstra isn't going to be able to get you anywhere. You gave the British too much encouragement. They've come to look for themselves."

He drew himself in, then reached up to smooth his beard.

"You're going to be exposed by this, you know. The letters. Gunther. The whole thing."

"Exposed?"

"He's a doctor. His name's Gordon. He doesn't know it yet but he's looking for you."

She stared into the trees where smaller birds flitted about the blade-thin buttresses.

"So tell me what happened to Troelstra," she said.

"I don't know. I think he's dead."

She thought for a moment, then acknowledged the obvious— that, of course, they were all going to die. She looked at Katz and said, "An unlikely trio of helpers, huh?"

She unbuttoned her coat farther, and after a while she reached over slowly and took his hand. It felt cold, even surrounded by this tropical warmth. "Von Stade, Troelstra, Gunther . . . There's really no one left to help me now, is there."

She squeezed, and Katz pulled his hand away and put it in his pocket. "You make a strong case, Gretta. Dead men and exiles. Excellent company to be in."

She looked up toward the glass canopy, the latticework of steel. "I'm under a lot of pressure, Isidor. I've taken help where I could get it. I act like a whore but I'm sorry, I can't work in thimbles."

The instrument maker leaned against the railing in silence for a while. "You need a brewery, Margarethe. You need corn steep liquor? You want vats? I'm not von Stade. I can't get that for you. Take it to Switzerland. Find a way to do your oh so sensitive research in nice, neutral Switzerland. Sell it to the highest bidder, if that's what it takes, but I can't help you anymore."

Margarethe smiled to quiet him and gently touched his arm. She did not want to think about those options. And he knew she would not leave. There was never going to be such an easy out for her.

After a while he reached over and took her hand. "I can't say no to you," he said. "You know I'll do what I can."

She tried to relax for a moment, listening to the water and the birds. She used to walk in the country, she remembered. Even in Berlin there used to be moments of peace. Before Gunther left. Before she started taking risks.

She looked back at her companion and said, "So what does this new man really mean? Did the Germans kill Troelstra?"

He brushed the handkerchief against the tip of his nose. "Or the British. All it would take is getting too close. Calling attention to him."

"I wouldn't give the extract to the British any more than I would give it to Hindenburg."

"I know that."

"*I* will develop it, and *I* will control it, because *I* discovered it. And I won't have this American getting anywhere near me. Do you understand?"

Katz sighed. There were times he could read her and times he could not.

"You took care of von Stade easily enough," he reminded her, pulling out his glasses and putting them on again, ignoring their fogged edges.

Margarethe looked away, staring at the preening bird of paradise. "I had one great advantage," she said. "Von Stade thought he was in love with me."

THE American ambassador, Lawrence Gerard, was a tall man with narrow shoulders and pale blue eyes that gleamed like surgical steel. The German officer rising from the cretonne sofa beside him was much more massive, his bald head a great egg, the features pinched forward into one small portion well below the crown.

"I've been telling Major Baron von den Benken about your important hygienic mission," the ambassador explained as he handed Gordon a glass of sherry. "The baron heads the Inspection of Prisoners for Brandenburg, by the way."

Von den Benken raised his glass in a gesture of greeting. "Chinese Gordon," he said. "The martyr of Khartoum."

"No relation," Gordon told him.

The baron took his drink in one gulp and poured himself another. "Pity," he said. "An engaging man. Though still better to be Lord Kitchener."

The embassy stood on the Wilhelm Platz just opposite the Chancellor's Palace and the foreign office in a three-story granite mansion, originally built for the Princes Hatzfeld. It had passed briefly into the von Schwaback banking family before Ambassador Gerard purchased it in the fall of 1914. His private office was on the third floor, an oasis of potted palms and Oriental carpets looking out toward the Kaiserhof Hotel.

Gordon had gone back to the Adlon to change his shirt and to wash the blood out of his hair, but he had not had time, really, to think through what had happened or what he was going to do next. He had no choice but to show up an hour late, looking as if he'd come in second in a bare-knuckle fifteen-rounder.

"But now you are interested in sewage," von den Benken continued. He downed his second drink, then placed the empty glass beside a brightly painted hootchy-kootchy dancer standing motionless on the lacquered coffee table. "You're quite fortunate, you know. We have the most advanced drainage system in the world. Eight farms on twenty-two thousand acres. All of it you should consider . . . at your disposal."

The baron touched the back of his hand to his lip, catching Gerard's glance as well as the one errant drop of sherry. Gerard smiled vacantly, flashing his ball-bearing eyes from man to man. Then he gathered up the humidor of cigars from his desk, and tucked it under his arm. "Gentlemen," he said, "let's have lunch."

In the dining room, immediately adjacent, Jay Adams was already supervising the butler, who was supervising the placement of serving trays by a stout German woman in white lab coat and white paper hat. When the men came in and took their seats, the baron was to the ambassador's right, Gordon to his left, and Adams, like a good child, well below the salt, where he could be seen and not heard.

Von den Benken's medals rattled across his chest like a tray of loose coins as he bent and sucked aggressively at his soup. He held his spoon with short, thick fingers to scoop up the bits of eel, chatting all the while about "chronic Bosnias" with rail lines in the East, a new investment syndicate building a Rhine-Danube ship canal, the death of Rasputin. The German dominated the table by his size and by his endless stream of talk.

Gordon was surprised by Gerard's passivity, as well as his deference to the baron. But then it made sense. American neutrality, giving offense to no one, sitting on the sidelines making speeches about "peace without victory." When Gerard did enter the conversation it was with a searing remark about drinking restrictions in Britain. It seemed he and the baron were perfectly capable of talking about most anything—the war, the prospects for peace, the prospects for the next American baseball season—anything and everything except the raw and bloody abrasions on the side of Gordon's head, who might have put them there and why.

After lunch they drove in silence through the Tiergarten—Gordon, Major Baron von den Benken, and Adams. The ambassador had excused himself for a series of meetings in anticipation of a trip to Munich.

They passed through Charlottenburg with the snow still falling gently, then picked up Doberitzer Heerstrasse for the ride through the Grunewald, across the Havel, and beyond the citadel to the city of Doberitz.

The road narrowed through a forest that eventually thinned out,

leaving a snow-covered field. Gordon could see the compound—
a fifteen-foot wooden fence stretching off into the distance.

There was a guard house about three hundred yards from the
gate. A sentry stepped out, saluted, and waved them on. The massive doors swung open to accommodate the car. Then there were
two more fences, both made of wire, twenty feet apart.

The car stopped at the administration building and von den
Benken got out to talk with the commandant. Beyond them was
a clearing—the whiteness lacerated by tracks of mud—surrounded
by low wooden barracks.

The baron's driver leaned against the car to catch a smoke as
the two Americans sat inside. Gordon looked out the window and
read the notice listing the enemies of the German empire.

Montenegrins	Gunds	Rajputs
Russians	Senegalese	Sikhs
Servians	Belgians	Australians
Turcomans	Fijis	Kyberi
Annamites	Welshmen	Tartars
English	Zulus	Usbegs
French	Canadians	Kalmucks
Scots	Irish	Kerghis
Japanese	Portuguese	Baluchis
Cossacks	Italians	Burmese
Romanians	Basutos	Yakuts

Gordon looked at Adams, who was smiling above his red bow
tie. He asked, "Why this camp?"

The young man pulled out his mother-of-pearl cigarette case.
"Something of a model," he said, "provided you avoid the Russians."

He offered Gordon a smoke, then took one for himself. "The
baron wants to impress you, I think." Adams lit a match and held
it out. "I think he likes you."

Gordon ventured a smile and looked off into the distance.

"He sold insurance before the war," Adams went on. "Not the knightly poverty sort of aristocrat. Thought himself quite the entrepreneur, till he got burned in Florida citrus."

"Was he in the States?"

"No, no. He has some kind of investment partner. An American. Here in Berlin, I think."

They smoked in silence. Then Adams said, "Yes, indeed. I think you're quite a lucky fellow."

The camp at Doberitz held twelve thousand men, including the work commandos spread around Greater Berlin. The English were actually a small percentage of the total. There were Frenchmen, Serbs, Turcos, Muhammadans, and Russians—mostly Russians—in six battalions of two thousand men each.

Gordon was led through the kitchen, the jail, the food stores; he inspected the concrete cistern latrines and urinals and found that, in true German fashion, they were emptied daily and kept spotlessly clean.

Germans would keep their secrets equally well tended, he was sure. The question was would they use prisoners as guinea pigs to test a biological weapon.

Behind the kitchen there was a central bathhouse where he watched peasants strip and leave their clothes with tags for sterilization. It was run like an assembly line—when they got out of the showers their clothes were ready. Some of the Russians had never had a shower before and they refused to leave. The guards had to drag them away.

There was a hospital tour and then a military formation outside the barracks, two hundred surprisingly well-fed men lined up in the cold. Gordon was supposed to ask for complaints from them, en masse, but under the circumstances, their major grievance was the rate of exchange—20.33 marks to the English pound.

After the formation Gordon followed the men back into the whitewashed barracks with wood stoves burning in the center of the room and bunks lined up along either side. The mattresses were straw, the pillows were paper or seaweed, but there was nothing in sight to make any man's mother fret or complain. And tucked up into the rafters like insulation, piled against the walls, were hundreds and hundreds of packages from England, mountains of brown paper containing tea and coffee, cheese and hams, tinned meat, and English white bread with butter and jam and honey.

Outside, the winter light was failing fast and it was time to ride back into town. In the distance, a crew of British prisoners emptied handcarts onto the rubbish heap where the British and Russian compounds met. On the other side of the fence, a crowd of ragged men had gathered. Many had long beards like "startsi" holy men. Others had not yet begun to shave. The ones in front leaned through the wire to grab what they could as an old man wrapped in a blanket licked the inside of a can. A younger man on the edge of the group held something through the wire. He saw Gordon and grinned excitedly. He waved his hand and Gordon, walking toward the fence, could see now that the object being offered was a small wooden carving.

Von den Benken was at his heels. "Time to go," he said.

"Just a minute," Gordon told him and reached into his pocket.

"No money," von den Benken said. "It leads to more trouble than you can ever know."

Gordon pulled out his last two packs of French cigarettes and gave them to the Russian. The Russian smiled excitedly and mouthed words of praise as he backed away from the fence and melted into the group.

Gordon glanced at the wooden figure, then slipped it into his pocket, a memento of his daring secret mission.

That evening in the Adlon dining room, Gordon watched their waiter pour the wine, then step away and take his place in the cluster of white ties and long white aprons standing between the grand piano and the pillar that looked like ivory.

Gordon turned the carving over in his hands—a warrior draped in skins, holding a scimitar above his head—then let it rest in the center of his plate on the small table he shared with Jay Adams.

"They call them the 'godmothers,' " Adams said, in a tone that was purely informational. "One prisoner gets the name and address of an old lady and sells it to another. Then they both send their wish lists. Something on the order of eighty thousand packages a month for twelve thousand men. Much of it ready for resale."

Gordon twisted the carving around in his plate, then glanced up at Adams. "So the Germans administer all this," he said. "They distribute the packages, I mean."

"Very efficiently."

Gordon glanced up at the ornate mirrors reflecting ornate mirrors into infinity, then stared into the chiseled face of the carved warrior. It was not much to show for his day, but at least it was tangible, a very real piece of wood.

After a while he said, "The guards looked as hungry as the Russians. If this were New York or Chicago you wouldn't expect to see all that food stuffed up in the rafters."

"Self-discipline," Adams came back. "The German virtue."

Gordon reached for his wine, tasted it, then drained the glass. "You said Baron von den Benken had an American business partner."

"That's what one assumes."

Gordon wondered. He *assumed* that Adams was one of his "fairy" guardians, but it was always dangerous to make assumptions. Adams had seemed annoyed when Gordon showed up bruised and too late this morning for their briefing about the camps, but they hadn't discussed what happened.

"The other inspections," Gordon said, letting his gaze drift slowly around the room. "Are they all as rigorous and productive as ours was today?"

Adams smiled, leaning back in his chair with his legs crossed, one arm wedged stiffly between shoulder and table. He tilted up his chin, inhaled deeply on his cigarette, and let the smoke rise majestically from his mouth. "The first thing we learn in the State Department is to take everything at face value. We're under strict orders to believe everything we're told."

Gordon poured himself another glass of wine as Adams leaned forward now and let his elbows rest on the table. Gordon twisted the stem of his glass for a moment, creating a uniform vibration across the surface of the wine. Then he took the first sip.

He heard the rattle of china and crystal, a sharp cry, and finally, the loud slap of skin against skin.

He turned and saw a young girl with cascades of auburn hair grabbing up her gold chatelaine bag and shawl. Across from her, an older man sat staring aghast. Gordon glanced back at Adams, then they both watched as the young woman spun on her heel, caught the tablecloth with her skirts, and brought the wine down with her as she stepped away.

The waiter rushed over, ripping off his apron to soak up the spill. Then, coming toward Gordon with her face buried in a handkerchief, the girl stumbled into their table. Her green eyes darted back and forth as the two Americans rose to their feet. She wore a gown of champagne-colored silk, a delicate brocade across her breasts. Her face was round, her eyes almond shaped. She focused briefly on Gordon with something akin to recognition, holding him a moment too long in her gaze. Then she grabbed at the tablecloth to make it right, muttered "Sorry," buried her face again, and started for the lobby exit.

Gordon watched as she crossed the room. He could still smell the faint scent of rose water lingering after, and it gave him a discomforting déjà vu. It was his wife's face he remembered and, by extension, his daughter's.

"Gentlemen . . ."

Gordon turned back around and saw the man from the other table weaving their way, pulling his napkin down from around his neck. With the Burgundy splattered across his waistcoat he looked as if he'd been shot. His napkin fell to the floor and he walked across it, carrying it half a pace forward on the toe of his shoe.

"Terribly sorry for the disturbance," he said. "Apologize profusely for my companion." He hovered for a moment, sweating alcohol, then dropped into the nearest chair. "May I join you? Table over there's a mess."

This man's accent was American, his face handsome in a way but aging fast. He had a large head with a great chiseled flint of a nose, and he wore his hair swept straight back, long enough to curl in wings behind his ears.

"Dr. Gordon," Adams said, "a fellow countryman ... Dr. Fisk."

Fisk looked up with his red-rimmed eyes and said, "Oh yes. So sorry." He tried to get to his feet, then settled for extending his hand. "Knew you were from the States. Quality of your teeth."

Gordon nodded as he watched the young woman disappear from view.

"But now she's British, of course," Fisk said. "That's the problem." He looked at Gordon now as if he were noticing him for the first time. "You're new, aren't you." He stared at the abrasion across Gordon's head. "Princess Bucher, you see. English girl, married to a German prince. Father raised kangaroos. Damned tight spot she's in. Beside herself with grief because her lady's maid ran off." The dentist sniffed twice, smiled, then rubbed his nose. "I tried to offer a little advice but the dear girl took offense. That's why the damned British got into this damned war, you know. No damned sense of humor."

Gordon pulled out a cigarette and tapped it against his lighter.

"Dr. Fisk is the doyen of the American dental community," Adams said. "He is, in fact, the Kaiser's dentist."

"European dentists are butchers," Fisk said with fire in his eyes. "Barbers!" Then he leaned back and reached for the bottle in the ice bucket. "You mind?"

Gordon shook his head.

Pouring himself some wine, the dentist noticed the carving from Doberitz sitting in Gordon's plate. "For a child?' he asked pleasantly.

"Just something I picked up," Gordon said.

"Ah." Fisk nodded, his eyes still on the wooden toy. "That's good. None too pleasant for a child."

He sipped the wine, then set it down. "You know, I have a boy. Fine boy . . . but sickly. Anemia. In Switzerland now, you see. Needs milk. Needs red meat. Can't get that here, but then we might be going back. Business entanglements. Son of a bitch back in Cleveland trying to cheat me out of my porcelain tooth. My own goddamn invention!"

He stared at Gordon for a moment, then said, "If we go, I'll be giving up the perfect location for a professional man—Bendler Strasse at the Tiergarten. Overlooks the park. Don't suppose you're planning to set up shop?"

Gordon shook his head, then set cigarette and lighter on the table, perfectly even, perfectly parallel.

Fisk seemed tired suddenly, the crazed energy in his eyes fading to a glimmer.

Gordon spun the carving around in his plate again, turning it slowly from the base. He thought about the pretty girl at their table, the spilled wine, the slightly theatrical arrangement of the whole encounter.

He looked up at Fisk and said, "Why isn't this good for a child? A while back when I told you this wasn't a toy you said 'good.' What'd you mean by that?"

Fisk smiled indulgently at Adams. "Doesn't know his history," he said.

Adams shrugged and Fisk turned back to Gordon. "The siege of Kaffa? The Crimea?"

Gordon gave no response, and the dentist reached over and picked up the carving to examine the whittled face. "This little fellow is something of a legend in parts of Mother Russia. But a bit grisly for children."

He looked up, smiled first at Adams, then at Gordon. "Timur the Tartar," he explained. "Enterprising man. Broke the longest siege since Troy by catapulting the corpses of plague victims over the city walls."

6

Criminal Detective Andreas Schiller stood against the low hedgerow looking at the metal plate attached to the widely spaced bars.

SIBERIAN TIGER
Panthera tigris altaica
Distribution: S.E. Siberia, N.E. China.
May attain lengths of 4 meters and weights
in excess of 300 kilos.
A nocturnal predator.

"How did he get over the fence?" Kadereit asked.

Schiller's gaze lifted beyond the ice-covered moat where the reddened snow had first attracted the zookeeper's attention. "It could be climbed," he said. "With the proper incentive."

A man's high-top shoe thrust out of a pile of blood-soaked rags. It was fastened onto the end of an exposed shin bone. Otherwise, the corpse did not look particularly human.

Kadereit reached out and brushed the metal plate with his finger, dislodging a membranous sheath of ice. "I can't see why anyone would work so hard to turn himself into wurst."

The keeper dangled a slab of horseflesh through the small passageway at the rear of the cage. At first the immense beast paid no attention. Then the keeper whistled and banged his foot against the metal door. He yelled, "Nicky!" and the tiger opened his jaws. A great cloud of vapor rose up and a roar so loud that Schiller felt his own lungs begin to resonate. "It's a Russian tiger," he said. "The German fighting spirit knows no bounds."

At last the animal got up and pranced through the snow toward the doorway and the cage beyond, and the two detectives walked side by side back to the keeper's entrance to the pit.

The sky was bright blue now after the snow. Some of it floated off a rooftop and swirled over their heads. There was a freshness in the air, a dry cold, the moisture lying frozen on the ground. But nothing seemed likely to lift Andreas Schiller's spirits today. He had been in a pronounced funk since the discovery of Colonel von Stade's body in the Pension Hölldobler. Without progress in unraveling the black market, his work now seemed increasingly pointless, even morbid.

Inside the cage, where the tiger had been resting, there was a pile of half-eaten entrails. One leg had been chewed off and dragged a few feet from the rest of the corpse; the buttocks and meaty part of the upper thigh were completely gone, leaving only a gnawed and bloody femur above the knee. Below, the severed limb was still partially covered. The victim's trouser leg was gathered around the still tightly laced boot.

Kadereit bent over and cracked open the victim's coat, brittle with snow and frozen blood. Then he stooped down and went through the pockets, looking for identification. With the snow covering disturbed, Schiller could see that the abdomen had been raked away. The spinal column was exposed, the ribs curved and rising like the gunwale of a canoe.

Kadereit stood up, leafing through the leather wallet. He stopped to read a green card, then handed the papers to Schiller. "The Romans fed Christians to the lions," he said. "The German empire feeds Jews."

He looked up. "No offense, Andreas."

Schiller read the name. "Isidor Katz. Friedrichstrasse 134. Maker of Surgical Instruments." Then he knelt down and looked into the man's face.

Gazing up toward the clear sky, the half-lidded eyes were vacant, flat, and clouded. There was no terror, no longer anything to be afraid of. Isidor Katz knew all the secrets now, only he would never tell.

The blood caked in the man's beard was probably from the initial gush when his throat had been slit. Schiller examined the wound. It was not the ragged sort an animal's claw would make, but clean, almost surgical, extending from ear to ear.

He went through the instrument maker's other pockets and found in one a handkerchief, "God Punish England" embroidered on the cloth. In another, a smoking pipe. In another, tobacco and matches, with "God Punish England" on the box. He found a monthly pass for the Stadtbahn, sixty-five pfennigs in coins, and a crumpled business card engraved in English. "Eli Gordon, M.D., F.A.C.S. Professor of Surgery, Harvard Medical School." Written hastily across it in pencil was "U.S. Embassy, Wilhelm Platz."

"I want Hoffman to chew on this," Schiller said, brightening ever so slightly. "See if he can find any gold."

Then he rose stiffly to his feet and added, "Get the man there to bring his shovel."

"For the body?"

Schiller looked back at his partner with one lowered brow. "For snow," he answered.

The zookeeper followed like an amiable child as Kadereit dragged the shovel through the snow outside the fence. Officially, of course, Kadereit was not involved in this case. It was Schiller who had been tapped for the monthly murder commission, but it was incumbent on every policeman to gain experience in life's more sordid details. Kadereit was Schiller's partner in Section B-1, Thefts from Restaurants and Show Cases, and there was only so much of that a man could take.

The professional horizons of Detectives Schiller and Kadereit had already been expanded with the wartime consolidations. Whereas previously separate squads had investigated thefts from delivery wagons versus thefts in saloons, burglaries in jewelry stores versus larceny in flats, the decreased manpower had meant a breakdown of such intense specialization. Murder always remained the most interesting diversion, but by the "turnip winter" of 1917, the black market had become the chief concern for everyone in the Criminal Detective Branch of the Berlin Police Presidency.

"Here," Kadereit said, uncovering a streak of red.

Schiller watched as the younger man drew the shovel lightly back and forth, pushing aside thin layers of bright red ice. There must have been liters of it, saturating an area of one square meter.

"So," Kadereit said. "This time you have your murder, Andreas. They slit his throat. They slit his throat out here and then he climbed over the fence to fulfill his lifelong wish to ride a tiger. How the hell else does he get over there? The fence is twice his height."

Schiller did not answer. Instead he looked down to the glob of meat he found adhering to the shovel blade.

"Oh shit."

The two detectives squatted on their haunches to look at it more closely. Blackened. Frozen.

"What no man should ever be without," Kadereit said.

Schiller found a piece of newspaper, wrapped up the severed organ, and put it in his pocket.

"This is garbage, not a corpse. What do you expect me to do with this?"

The question was rhetorical. The irritation and impatience were a persistent worldview. The pathologist stood with his hands on his hips, looking at the gnawed remains on the necropsy table. His shoulders were stooped, his bald head suspended on arching vertebrae.

"I should take this home and feed it to the cat," he said.

Schiller unbuttoned his coat but left it on. "Good idea."

Now Hoffman had registered the impossibility of the task he was ready to begin, making his ultimate success all the more impressive. He turned to the sink to wash his hands as his assistant, a pale, tubercular-looking young man, weighed and measured the corpse.

Schiller pinched his nose against the smell of formaldehyde and read the inscription above the door: "Hic locus est ubi mors gaudet succurrere vitae." If anyone could rejoice in this place, he thought, it would be the dead.

Hoffman began dictating with his back still to the table. "Isidor Katz . . . thirty-seven-year-old male Semite. Profound scoliosis. Possible infantile paralysis."

The consumptive assistant took notes, standing by with a clipboard and pencil as Hoffman turned, picked up the knife, and made the first incision. For Schiller's benefit he muttered, "If you weren't half dead already . . ."

Hoffman began with the scalpel at the left shoulder, coming down just below the nipples like a zipper, then continuing to the right shoulder to form a large U. Schiller tried to be patient. He knew there was no way of directing Hoffman to the questions he wanted answered. The autopsy protocol had been established by Virchow a half century before, and Hoffman followed it to the letter no matter what was staring him in the face.

Hoffman began the vertical incision that would ordinarily extend through the navel to the pudenda, turning the U into a Y. In this case, a lengthy incision was not indicated.

"You're wearing gloves," Schiller remarked.

Hoffman gave him a condescending glance, and Schiller shrugged it off—an admission of poor form, but old preoccupations die hard.

"It's not an official inquiry," Schiller added in his own defense. Then he watched for a moment, the knife opening flesh like a plow turning over soil.

It was like an image from Karl May, Schiller realized—knives and plows, breaking the plains—and for the moment it offered him a pleasant distraction. Schiller was a great fan of May's adventure stories—*Old Shatterhand* and *Winneatu*, the Wild West of America. The images of open space and limitless freedom had gotten him through many a grim moment in the dreary Berlin winter, but this was his home, his reality. As he fingered the crumpled business card in his pocket now, he thought first about the American in Berlin, the American surgeon at the embassy on Wilhelmstrasse.

Then he turned away from the table and looked once more at the blackened organ now residing inside an autopsy jar and sighed, wondering who disliked Isidor Katz quite that much.

He turned back to the pathologist.

"So how did you get them?" Schiller said. "Not even army surgeons can get rubber gloves, you know. I'm honestly impressed."

Hoffman methodically snipped the last rib, then lifted off the sternum like a lid. "A U-boat delivers them to me up the Spree."

He gave Schiller another withering look, then peered into the open chest cavity. "Paper bandages. Autopsies with bare hands. I have no desire to be buried at sea, victim of the British navy and their fucking blockade!"

Schiller watched as Hoffman carefully lifted the heart out into an enamel bowl. Blood ran down his white rubber apron as he made a preliminary examination, then lifted the organ out again and placed it in a stoppered bottle.

At long last the pathologist turned to the head and neck. He made an incision across the scalp, then massaged the loose skin until it slipped down around the eyes and ears. With the necropsy saw he cut along the crown of the head, then removed the top of the skull like the lid of a pumpkin.

He stood for a moment picking and probing at Katz's brain, shining his light into the cranium. In time he took two slices of tissue, then set down his instruments, straightened his back, and turned to the detective.

"Aside from the marked absence of intestine, genitals, kidneys, liver, and spleen, there are no gross abnormalities of the internal organs. There is, however, massive swelling of the brain, which I would say is the result of the proverbial 'blunt instrument.' "

Hoffman reached up and touched his forehead with the crook of his arm. "I would also consider this blow to be the most likely cause of death. The gash of the throat, which you correctly noted as not of animal origin, was a coup de grace. Probably redundant."

Schiller pulled a fresh cabbage-leaf cigar out of his breast pocket and rolled it between his fingers. It was gratifying to have one's own observations confirmed, but somehow he had hoped for more.

"I'm afraid there are no immediately apparent residues or other evidence that may lead to the killer," Hoffman summarized. And with that he slowly began removing his precious surgical gloves, staring at Katz's infinitely relaxed face.

"It's a great pity," Hoffman added. And for a moment he seemed almost wistful. Schiller wondered—had the man at last seen so much death that the sad truth of mortality was once again able to move him?

Then Hoffman held up the limp rubber. "I'd like to know where the hell I'm going to be getting these from now on."

Schiller looked at the gloves. "What do you mean by that?"

The pathologist sighed and, with a sheepish admission, let his thumb tilt down toward the eviscerated remains.

Schiller put the cheroot between his teeth and bit down hard. "Katz? It was Katz sold you blackmarket gloves?"

Hoffman shrugged, and the linkage fired in Schiller's brain, working backward through a syllogism of criminal deduction. Isidor Katz and Colonel von Stade were both dead. Two men dead, both black marketeers. Two dead black marketeers—two murders.

7

The white light of morning seeped through the curtained windows of the Esplanade Hotel as Princess Bucher, née Lady Evelyn Wattlesby-Ross of Rainhill Hall, burrowed deeper and deeper into the feather mattress and pulled the quilt up over her head. Her room was cold and bleak and she simply could not face it. Not yet. Always before, with Lucy here, the curtains would be thrown back and there would be rolls and coffee and a warm dressing gown waiting for her. With Lucy about she could lie in bed all day. Now she was forced to stay under the covers and starve or get out of bed and freeze.

Her husband was on a hospital train in the East, her maid had mysteriously vanished, and now, as if merely to compound her miseries, the hotel employees were out on strike. The manager had appropriated their ration cards for the guests, and they said they could not work if they could not eat and so took to their beds. Then just last night the manager himself was arrested for selling butter meant for the wounded, and nothing was clear now except that the guests were left without services of any kind, not the least of which was heat.

Princess Bucher wanted her coffee—even ersatz—and worse, she had to pee. Even if she were arrested and shot, she surmised, at least she wouldn't be so cold.

She scooted herself up along the headboard, clutched the heavy

Federdecke to her chin, and looked fretfully around the room. She took a deep breath and readied herself to throw back the cover. Then she heard a key in the lock and froze in place.

A man leaned his head through the doorway, a man wearing theatrical base and eyeliner, a lurid grin, a thin mustache, and a conspicuously bad toupee. He also had a sprig of very wilted parsley stuck in his lapel.

The princess fell back with a sigh and said, "And what are we today, my darling, roast duck?"

Count Billy de Beauford stood just inside the door, coolly removing his gray kid gloves, giving the activity his temporary but complete attention. "I am desolate to have been away from you so long," he assured her. "But one does have to earn one's living."

He dropped the gloves into his black Borsolino and placed them on the bedside table. "And voyeurs abound. But now all our little hotel spies are on strike, are they not?"

She moved her legs slowly back and forth beneath the covers and said, "I've missed you, Billy."

"How dear of you to miss me." He sat on the edge of the bed, bent down, and gently kissed her.

"How was Düsseldorf?"

"Düsseldorf was Düsseldorf. And you, my love?"

"I'm making progress," she said. "The American's here. I saw him last night."

"Oh really?" Billy sat up.

"I literally just saw him, that's all. I was at the Adlon. With Fisk. I was getting nowhere, so I concocted a scene to bring us all together."

"Well, that's daring. Surely a medal for that one."

"Here . . ." She pulled him down and kissed him. "Let me show you where I'll wear it."

Billy smiled. "I don't mean to steal your applause, but being the intrepid journalist that I am . . . I must confess I ran into him too. At the bar. All of an hour after he arrived off the train."

She looked at him skeptically.

"We talked about women, you see, but to no great effect. That's what men talk about in bars, of course. Man to man. A chance encounter."

"What do *you* know about women?" she said. Then she grabbed up the extra quilt, wrapped it around her as tight as she could, and dragged it with her into the bathroom.

De Beauford smiled and whistled quietly. He stood and removed his topcoat, his jacket, his extravagant cravat, and at last his shoes. Then he sat barefoot and cross-legged on the bed, unbuttoning his shirt as he listened to the sound of water hissing into the toilet. He loved the sound of a woman peeing. For him it meant only good things to come.

In time the stream of water stopped. Then the young lady in question bounded through the doorway, pressing her arms against her breasts and making them rise in great mounds up to her collarbones. She leapt back into bed and wriggled under the sheets. "Now warm me up! Warm me up!"

"I say!" Billy found it remarkably easy to adapt to her moods whenever she was naked. "Was that Princess Bucher who just ran by, her ass for all to see, her bosoms bobbling?"

"They weren't bobbling," she said, exhilarated by her own vulgarity. "They were demurely constrained. Now warm your hands."

De Beauford slipped off his trousers and rolled onto her, his erection already protruding through the gap in his underpants. He was a jaded man in many respects, but she was so young, so ripe. And he fully understood and appreciated her need for distraction now. It was his duty. The war demanded constant stewardship, and service to those in need.

He leaned over first and gave her an enormously wet kiss. She received it with a vengeance, pulling at his tongue with hers.

"Wait!" he said. "I do believe . . . why yes, I swear I saw a public notice. Let me check." He threw the covers over his head and began nibbling down her body as she laughed. He loved her laugh—the ring of fine crystal. He began kissing her belly just below the navel, then, ultimately, nuzzled his face between her thighs. Licking her lightly, just once, he raised his head and gently traced his fingertip above her maiden hair. "Verboten," he said. "I knew it. Just above your lovely little cunt."

"No exceptions," she announced.

"Wait." He rolled her over, gripping her buttocks in a firm massage. "Just as I thought. Here too."

"Oh God."

"And what about the titties?" He rolled her back over and buried his face in her breasts. "Yes. Same story. Both of them." He licked each in turn, then took the left nipple between his teeth while she caressed his head.

"What glorious breasts you have," he said, gathering them together in his firm grasp. "Your big mistake, of course, is that I'm not German. You write 'verboten' and that's all there is to it for your lovely Kraut—no further precautions required or taken."

"So?"

"So I, quite naturally, a foreigner lacking such internal controls, see 'verboten' and I translate: 'Opportunity!' "

"And what will you make of your opportunity?" she murmured.

"Your lovely English ass."

"I still can't believe this," she whispered after their first fit of passion. She knelt forward against the bedpost, her face turned to the mirror.

"Accept it, darling," he said, upright on his knees behind her, leaning out just slightly so as not to obscure the view. Admiring herself, she rose up and arched her back, aroused again by the thrusts that took her breath away. She watched amazed, her body glistening, as his stiffened member continued sliding in and out of her. It was as if this lurid scene she was witnessing had nothing to do with her, a proper English lady married to a German prince.

"My God, it's huge," she said. "And for such a tiny little man."

He clenched his teeth, closed his eyes, and muttered, "God is just."

Nearly spent, still tenuously connected, they lay under the heavy quilt with his arms draped around her and her bottom nestled into his belly. Her hair, despite the cold, was pressed against her temples with a salty coating of sweat.

"I don't trust him," she said, gazing into the distance.

Billy lifted his head from the back of her neck where he'd been nuzzling her with his teeth. "Is it Dr. Gordon that we mean, or merely Dr. Fisk?"

She did not respond. Instead, her eyes lost their focus as she singled out a curling strand of auburn hair and began twisting it again and again around her finger.

"Fisk was drunk and vulgar."

"Does that surprise you? Why on earth did you see him?"

"I think he knows something about Lucy. And Lucy is the key to everything."

"That's what Gordon's here for."

"I still have to do what I can whether he's here or not. We don't know how far he'll get, do we, or how long he'll last."

Billy cupped her breast in his hand, squeezing the nipple. "Are you saying he doesn't share our 'intense idealistic commitment'?"

She shuddered and he felt the muscles deep within her contract. "I'm so frightened, Billy. Don't be cynical."

He drew her closer to him, sliding his hand gently down between her legs. "I heard of a Turcoman once," he said, stroking the warm fur. "He was in one of the camps, you see, and he didn't know what to make of the bed. At first he wouldn't get into it. Then in the morning he wouldn't get out. 'Paradiso!' was all he could say. 'Paradiso!'"

"Oh God, Billy. You have corrupted me."

"I've awakened you."

"And when my husband comes back?"

"He'll be the beneficiary."

"Hardly." She glanced back over her shoulder to look at him. "I feel so guilty. Enjoying you. And him freezing in some hospital train."

"It's none too warm here, love."

"Don't joke, Billy."

"Look, my darling. Rice wants you to fade into the background for a while, does he not? To watch and wait."

"It could take Gordon weeks to get anywhere near Ruhleben, much less the Institute. And no matter what London says I know we don't have that much time. Whatever happened to Lucy could just as easily happen to us."

He thrust once more as his hand pressed against her pubic bone. "*This* happened to Lucy. She ran off with her lover—the charming and eloquent Ricky. End of story."

"He says she didn't, Billy. She stumbled onto something she shouldn't have that last trip to Ruhleben."

"Your Ricky's lying to protect her. And for all the rest you have very slight evidence, my love."

"It's my fault. I sent her in once too often."

"Now look. You're projecting guilt everywhere you look because you've been unfaithful. But unless you're Anne Boleyn that's hardly cause for a charge of treason."

"We have to give Gordon some guidance. We have to move it along to at least get him inside the camp."

"And when he comes up empty-handed, will that put your mind to rest?"

"No. I'm still going to talk to Fisk again, when he's sober."

"No, no. Shhh. Let the American run with it for now."

She began to speak again but he silenced her with a kiss. "Stay out of it for now, my darling. That's why they've given us our stalking horse. Let Gordon take the risks. That's what he's come for, isn't it, to take the risks?"

8

In a basement room at Königergratzerstrasse 70, a small man with rust-colored hair struck a wooden match against the box, letting the smoke flare up toward his dilated nostrils. He loved the smell of phosphorus. For him it was like Proust's madeleines—a reminder of a pleasant time long ago, a time that was, like any true paradise, paradise lost.

He held out the match now, but the boy's lips trembled so much that it took several tries to bring flame and cigarette together.

"Relax," Major Ostriker said reassuringly. "You don't have to do a thing."

The room would have been cramped even without the sandbags along one wall, damp without the water pooling into the central depression of the floor. The stones bled moisture like the walls of a cave while, beneath the blindfold, the boy heaved in rapid breaths.

Major Ostriker adjusted his steel-rimmed spectacles and admired the way the arms tied behind the back improved the posture, thrusting the chest forward. The major watched for a moment, fascinated. They stood at life's most significant border, he and this boy. In one instant they could talk and touch; in the next, they would be infinitely remote.

"Ready!" the lieutenant barked.

It was time for Ostriker to move away. God only knew what could happen with these reserve troops.

"Take aim."

The boy began to pant. His lungs pumped in such shallow breaths that if he were held in suspense much longer he would pass out from hyperventilation. The cigarette burned idly, held in place merely by adhesion to his lip.

Ostriker stood to the side and watched the handsome young body pulsing with life. What were this boy's thoughts as he waited? How exactly would the stream of consciousness end?

"Fire!"

The concussion shot back and forth across the room and filled it with the smell of nitrate. Ostriker inhaled the chemical odor, shut his eyes, and thought back to his days in the lab with Dr. Haber, the days when he was totally secure in the knowledge of a commanding sense of purpose. Without Germany's chemists, after all, the guns would have been silenced long ago.

There was no mystery left in this business for him now. For Ostriker, nothing remained here but a corpse, and he had seen more than enough of those. "The will cannot will backward," Nietzsche said, remaining as it does "an angry spectator to the past."

The major adjusted his eyeglasses once again, turned, and walked briskly toward the door as the whack of the coup de grace reverberated behind him.

Major Walther Ostriker, Under-Director of Counterintelligence, Department IIIb of the Great General Staff, did not like spies, particularly, or spying for that matter. The first great passion of his life had been molecules, and it was in chemistry that he had planned to make his mark. The smell of sulfur, the bubbling of flasks, the pulsing of liquids through coils of glass. Through intense effort he had learned to find some of that same elemental fascination in people. A low-interest loan to a British financier could bind him to you for life; sleep deprivation could reduce the most tight-lipped agent to vapor.

The spying trade had opened up for Ostriker purely by happenstance, well before the war in fact, while he was living in France and working as a chemist, cracking the French dye works at Tremblay at the behest of his employer, Bayer I.G. But then came the mobilization and he was called back to Berlin, making certain that the first green cloud of chlorine wafting over the trenches at Ypres took the British by surprise. He was caught up in the excitement, the staff cars pulling up at all hours outside Haber's lab, but then success meant a promotion and a summons to headquarters. Suddenly he was responsible for resurrecting a counterespionage effort decimated by the rapid military expansion. There was no one minding the store for the Berlin district itself, and he set in with a vengeance, cleaning out the counterfeit comtesses at the Blumensale, rounding up bogus businessmen, sending home attachés who did not understand the limits of German hospitality. But even so, the arcana of weapons research remained his special passion. The twentieth century, after all, would belong not to poets or aristocrats, but to technicians like him.

Walther Ostriker had been born in Bitburg in the Rhineland, educated at the Polytechnicum at Karlsruhe. Unlike the more illustrious intelligence officers, who were products of the war college, then, he actually knew something other than banners and parades. But he had never been the heroic type. The son of a provincial physician, small in stature, sickly and weak, he had compensated through rigorous self-discipline and the development of military bearing. It worried him, Ratzel's maxim that all unevolved peoples were also spatially small. He knew all too well that the prejudice applied to individuals as well. But beyond basic stature, the one aspect of the self he could not alter and overcome was his face. The hard-won dueling scars along his jaw merely added to the clutter of eyeglasses and a large and bulbous nose. At thirty-five he still looked like the homely, intense little boy he had been at six or seven.

The woman standing provocatively in his outer office was the little stew responsible for this morning's execution. She smiled brightly, all paint and flattery, as she saw Ostriker come in from the hall.

"Good morning, Major."

He nodded and walked on, followed by Lieutenant von Laudermann, his aide, who quietly closed the door behind them.

"What does she want?" Ostriker asked, stepping quickly behind his desk.

"His watch. She said she gave it to him for Christmas. She says it's worth twelve marks."

Ostriker said, "Give it to her." Then he took his seat and brushed his nose once lightly with his handkerchief.

Behind him on the wall was a series of maps, eighteen centimeters to one kilometer, of Kiel Harbor, Bremerhaven, Wilhelmshaven, and the mouth of the Elbe. In the file cabinets to his right he had dossiers on every man to have graduated from Sandhurst and Saint-Cyr during the past twenty years. He preferred the French as adversaries, given a choice. The Russians were degenerates. The British were fools. But the French . . . At least the French professed rationalism, and they knew how to live.

Ostriker looked first at the latest dispatches from Potsdam and the Marineamt. As he read, he felt the annoying presence of Lieutenant von Laudermann hovering over him. "Something of interest from Montagne de la Coeur," the young man said at last.

Ostriker adjusted his glasses and reached for the new folder. Tall and athletic, well born and well married, von Laudermann was blessed with perfect Germanic features, including the nose curled up as if constantly detecting some foul odor. The major avoided his gaze and spread the papers on the desk in front of him.

The photographs were poorly lit, poorly focused, and grainy. Ostriker was fascinated that they had been taken at all, and at the same time irritated that the quality was not better. He studied the man getting out of the car, the tall American with the lean, dark face. There was a second photo of him, standing beside the driver, the Boulogne casino visible in the background, waiting as the venerable Almroth Wright emerged.

Von Laudermann screwed in his monocle and then, as if explaining the more difficult math said, "The chauffeur. It's Llewellyn. The matinee idol."

Ostriker was not impressed or particularly interested. "Who is the third man?" he asked.

"Anthony Rice. British secret service."

Ostriker nodded. He knew of Rice. Their paths had crossed before. "It all stands to reason," he said, not at all certain what reason he would be referring to. Then he fanned out the pictures across his desk and said, "Tell me about our visitor."

Von Laudermann opened another file, crisp and new, and began to read. "Eli Gordon, Professor of Surgery at the University of Harvard. Has served in British field hospitals since '15. Traveling with diplomatic visa. Supposedly here to inspect prisoners of war."

The major tapped his pencil on the desk and stared up at the ceiling. It was an interesting sequence actually—snooping around Berlin on the heels of a secret meeting with Almroth Wright, Britain's greatest authority on bacterial chemistry. Ostriker had heard rumors of prisoners, experiments, devious plans. With this, perhaps, the rumors began to take on substance. The British could not act on every rumor that reached London. And the British were legendary for their cheese-paring methods. The criminals and crazies, the Jewish knife grinders sent out to inspect fortifications. Amateurs were cheap, and Britain did not budget for pensions or indemnities. This man Eli Gordon matched the description from Amsterdam, the man outside Hendrik Troelstra's office. It appeared, then, that what Ostriker had before him was another amateur trussed up to be killed. But why?

"What do you make of it?" he asked von Laudermann.

"I'm not quite sure, sir."

Ostriker looked at his aide with the placid smile of the Buddha. He had read some of Wright's work before, elaborate notions of "opsonic indexes" as a guide to managing infection. The work made no sense according to German science, but perhaps it was Britain's ignorance that now was more significant.

"Almroth Wright is a bacterial chemist," he said. "Infections. Bacteria. It covers a variety of sins, not true?"

Then Ostriker rose from his chair and looked out across the Wilhelm Platz to the embassy beyond, where flurries drifted diagonally against the black trees. He hated snow. It was like sunlight—the whiteness made him feel exposed, vulnerable. He had felt the danger closing in for months, but now at least it had a face and a name, a direction and a velocity. The British had gotten wind of something and had come to investigate. Of course Ostriker wanted to know what they knew about German research and how they knew it. But more than anything else, he wanted to know why they appeared to know more about it than he did.

The Hindenburg reorganization had wiped out almost the entire Prussian War Ministry in a day. Ostriker had survived, but now the city was swarming with rumors of new waves of radical militarism. Soldiers were being pulled from the front and sent back to their factories. Females were being conscripted for labor and prisoners enslaved as Germany retooled and rearmed for one last desperate push for victory. It was a Götterdämmerung, with all speculation focusing on one great new plan to end the war. It was a plan called Operation Alberich—a plan so secret that no one in power had ever seen fit to discuss it with him.

This was not just an oversight. A bacterial weapon, if that's what it was, not discussed with him? It was absurd. And now his sense of duty placed him in the even more absurd position of protecting secrets he did not know himself.

If he exposed his vulnerability they would pounce on him and tear him apart like dogs. The only course was to investigate discreetly on his own. Then, once he had the facts firmly in hand, he would decide what course of action to take.

Ostriker looked back down at the guileless American face in the photograph before him. Rumors were dangerous paths to follow, and yet there were so many rumors. He was the man who was supposed to *know*. And he would never truly know as long as he could not admit his ignorance. So why not remain silent, he thought. Why not remain silent and let this American be his curiosity.

Ostriker gazed calmly through his steel-rimmed spectacles, focusing on von Laudermann, the pretty boy, true officer material because his name began with "von."

"I want daily reports," Ostriker told him. "And call in Mayr."

Then, as the young man turned to leave, Ostriker picked up his telephone and dialed the American Embassy.

"OUR crisis room," Jay Adams said, making a slow, 360-degree turn as he walked across the embassy parquet. "From time to time, half the Americans in Germany decide they have to leave over-night. But still it's Zeno's paradox. We still can't get them all to go."

Gordon made his way through the file boxes and typewriting tables scattered here and there across the ballroom floor. He watched Adams watch himself in the mirrors on three walls.

"That's for you," Adams said, nodding toward the desk nearest the window where a package had been placed on the blotter. "Came through the pouch."

Gordon glanced at the brown paper and string, then stepped over to the French windows and looked out at the garden. The frozen snow had formed a crust over the flower beds like a sheet of canvas.

"We have some clerical help for you," Adams went on. "But you might want to spend the next couple of hours catching up on the state of play." He picked up the telephone on one of the desks and pressed a button. "Fräulein Kleist . . . Dr. Gordon is here now. Would you please bring in the inspection files for . . . say, July–December."

He put down the receiver, sat on the edge of the desk, and reached for his cigarettes. "Care for a fag?" he said, holding out the pack.

Gordon shook his head.

"There are actually one hundred five camps in Germany," Adams went on, one foot on a chair, the other toe just reaching the floor, "governed within the twenty districts. At last count there were one million, six hundred forty-six thousand, two hundred and twenty-three prisoners . . . mostly Russian. Eight percent in work commandos, like the sewage detail you'll be seeing this afternoon."

Adams stopped to inhale magnificently as Gordon took a seat in a straight-back chair near the windows, his hands in his pockets.

"Permission to visit is obtained from the Prussian Ministry of War, except in the kingdoms of Bavaria, Saxony, and Wurtemburg, which have their own special ministries. Procedure requires that you first call on the general of the army corps involved and leave your card. Then you call on the Inspection of Prisoners of War and present authorization papers. For Berlin that's von den Benken. Ordinarily he would detail an officer to accompany your party."

Adams looked at Gordon and smiled his Cheshire smile. "Fascinating, isn't it? Boxes within boxes?" Then he reached for an ashtray and delicately tapped his cigarette.

"Otherwise, you proceed just as we did at Doberitz. Reports are filed—two copies to the German Foreign Office, two to the British Foreign Office via Ambassador Page, two filed with the State Department, and two . . . with Fräulein Kleist."

As if on cue a robust young woman came through the door wearing a black skirt over sturdy hips and a white blouse straining against a mountainous bosom. She could not have been more than twenty, all red curls and rosy cheeks. A sailor collar seemed designed to certify her youth and, presumably, innocence.

"Good morning, Doctor," she said, very formally. Then she curtsied with downcast eyes. She carried three cardboard binders the way a schoolgirl might, cradled against her left breast.

"Fräulein Kleist is the very distillation of modern German efficiency," Adams said, holding out his hand for the files. "The telephone has an interconnecting line. You press this button . . . here."

He gestured to the apparatus with one hand, then dropped the files on the desktop with the other.

"Is there anything you wish me to do now, Doctor?" asked Fräulein Kleist.

Gordon hestitated for a moment, studying her face. She looked constrained, troubled by something. If pressed he would have to say it was as if she were ever so slightly ashamed.

He reached into his jacket and said, "Yes, actually, there is." He handed her the postcard to Rice he had written at the café before his meeting with Katz, the words "I trust" crossed out and the words "I'm sure" in their place.

"If you'd be kind enough to send this on through the pouch . . ."

She took the card without looking at it, curtsied once more, then turned on her heel and walked out.

"Work to do," Adams said, slipping off the desk and stubbing out his cigarette. "You have a date with von den Benken at one, remember. I'm only down the hall. Just ring the operator and ask for me."

Adams glided out the door, and Gordon stepped over to the desk and sat down. Then he dropped his cigarettes onto the blotter and reached for his lighter and the stack of folders.

He opened the binder and slowly flipped through the files. The repression camp at Langensalza. Minden. The typhus camps at Wittenburg and Gardelegen. The Irish camp at Limburg, where tuberculosis had taken over. And at last the only folder circled with an elastic band, the thickest one of all, marked "Ruhleben."

Gordon scanned the flimsy second sheets that had been typed by Fräulein Kleist's muscular fingers through too many carbons— the faint impressions of letters completely illegible where strike- overs had been made. Ruhleben was a racetrack in the Grunewald filled with civilians, mostly university students and their professors, businessmen and vacationers with the odd luck to be passing through the Reich in the summer of 1914. If the Germans were experimenting on prisoners, aside from the issue of the convenient suburban location, why on earth would they choose this place as a source of subjects? Hypochondriacs from Bad Nauheim and Kissingen, seamen whose ships had been taking on cargo at Bremen or Hamburg. They had black servants from the colonies, cabin boys from the ships, and—the war had begun in August—a large contingent of professional golfers.

Why try to experiment on the best-educated and most articulate group of prisoners in the whole country? Why *not* experiment on Russian peasants, people who would not understand what was happening to them, people who could simply disappear whenever it was convenient? Gordon reached into his pocket and pulled out the carving from Doberitz. He studied the face again, but the wooden features had not changed. They still offered no clues.

Perhaps the complete lack of logic was the beauty of the plan. But what guaranteed there even was a plan? Gordon went back to the reports and read on, smoking cigarettes and turning the pages, and after a while he began to make out a curious pattern. In contrast to the other camps, most of the investigations reported at Ruhleben were not initiated by prisoner complaints or by anyone from the embassy. In the Ruhleben folder, hygiene, disease, the quality of food—these were not the issues. Report after yellowing report detailed the investigation of *German* complaints, struggling to verify that German allegations were unfounded. Sabotage, drug trafficking, forged documents, homosexual prostitution. No rumor, it appeared, was so outrageous that it did not find its way into the official correspondence. At one time or another it had all been laid at the door of the Ruhleben prisoners.

Gordon leaned back in his chair, wondering what he had found. More evidence of British gullibility or the ineffable deviousness of the German mind? He had seen the note in the journal, he had seen the coolies with plague, and all the rest was rumor. But rumor instigated by whom?

Glancing at the package from London sitting on the edge of the desk, he reached for his penknife to begin cutting the string and ripping off the paper. He pulled apart the adhesive along the edges of the pasteboard box, tore back the flaps, and looked in to find it stuffed with crumpled pages from *The Times.* He pulled these out and dropped them haphazardly around the desk, uncovering three smaller boxes. The first contained fifty rounds of ammunition, the second a pair of Colt revolvers, and the third a full carton of Players cigarettes.

The empty plain stretched for a thousand meters in each direction, broken only by the grid of smaller embankments that divided the rectangular sand filters, each as big as a football field. The prisoners worked against the distant line of trees, shrouded in fog, pulling huge canisters on wheels, which spread the sewage collected from some central holding tank. It was remarkably like a no-man's-land, Gordon thought, especially the smell. He looked out across the open space, half expecting to hear German troops singing in the distance.

"We, of course, are the ones at risk," said Dr. Fichte, standing beside him. "God knows what these British swine will attempt to do when we least expect it." Dr. Fichte was in charge of the experimental sewage station, a member of the sanitary police. He had an abrupt mustache, suspended well above his lip, which gave his face a look of continuous surprise.

Gordon nodded, half listening, then raised his collar against the faint drizzle.

"There have been attempts to poison the Mugglesee, you should be aware, but swift countermeasures against spies and saboteurs among the prisoners have kept Berlin's water pure. We can thank Major Baron von den Benken for that."

The major, standing behind, nodded slightly and looked at his watch.

The ritual of inspection had gone on all afternoon. Gordon had watched thousands of gallons of sewage dropped onto dash plates, strained through coke filters, trickled through clinker. He had been regaled with the latest glory of German "Kultur," the Imhoff tank, a device that would revolutionize sewage treatment with an innovative lower compartment for the digestion of sludge.

And there were work commandos like this all over Berlin—on the docks and in the factories—where the good baron could drag him around for months.

"Impressive," Gordon said at last, turning back to share a glance with von den Benken.

The baron brought his handkerchief up to his nose and blew each nostril in turn. Then, seeing that Gordon was still watching him, he added, "German technology is far superior in these matters."

Gordon smiled.

"You think it's because we're full of shit," Baron von den Benken said. "Seven meals a day. But you Americans are full of shit too. You've simply directed your energies into other spheres."

"That's what all those wide open spaces out west are for," Gordon said. "You can shit wherever you please."

"Oh no. Not so simple. Not so innocent. The machine gun? The airplane? The U-boat? Even barbed wire. All products of American ingenuity. This is an American war."

"You don't seem to like Americans much."

"I love Americans," the baron went on. "It simply amuses me to see you now, having armed Europe to the teeth, sitting on the sidelines talking about peace without victory."

Gordon nodded.

"Americans are like ships without a rudder that way," he said. "They lack the moral compass of an aristocracy. The American who tried to buy the Kaiser's villa at Corfu, he couldn't understand why he was refused, as if money were the only issue."

The baron folded his handkerchief and tucked it away in his pocket.

"But baseball I like. And also your black singers. Impressive voices, these people."

Gordon looked off in the distance again as one of the teams wheeled their canister around, ripening the stench. He was being had six ways to Sunday by Rice, by the Germans, but there was not a thing he could do about it. For now, von den Benken played the tune, and all he could do was dance.

9

The sky over London was still bright blue as Major Anthony Rice stepped out of his mother's Kensington town house and made his way toward the bus stop at Palace Gate. It was chilly weather for a stroll, but there were no taxis since the war, no butlers left to summon them. He wondered about the weather in Berlin.

With his hands in the pockets of his overcoat, Rice stopped at the curb and looked at the salmon-tinted clouds streaked across the western sky. The days were getting longer now, minute by minute, and he hoped it would dispel the gloom lingering like chimney smoke from an awfully depressing Christmas. Black beads for mourning had been the most common gift this season. The only holiday glow had come from the lights in Whitehall as the Admiralty and War Office worked on into the night.

It all seemed a long time ago now that they had rushed headlong at each other so hot and heavy in the summer swelter, only to bog down with the autumn rains. So they strung wire from Switzerland to the sea and killed a million men at Verdun, fed the bodies in like logs to a furnace, then a million more on the Somme and still nothing changed. In the East it was the same, only the dead were Russians, machine-gunned on the ice, frozen upright waist deep in the snow, two million dead Russians piled higher and higher from Tannenberg to the Brusilov offensive.

Rice had gone off at the start like all the other young men of his class, ready to die with Horace on his lips, speaking of his officer's role as being that of a shepherd, guiding his flocks in a pastoral. They had been oblivious to the irony there, no sense of themselves, at least not in those early days, as lambs being led to the slaughter. In those days they were sure that death would be an "embrace," or a "kiss," or "crossing the bar." But Rice had seen what German steel did to the human body, and it was nothing like a kiss. So now he worked behind the lines. Now he gave men like Eli Gordon the chance to "do their bit."

The bus came and Rice followed the queue on board, out of the cold, then handed his fare to the woman conductor. He found a seat beside an elderly gentleman knitting a sweater. Of the two dozen people on board, half were busily working knitting needles. This was what Defense of the Realm meant—total mobilization! He watched those flashing spikes of steel, thinking how clear the issues were to those who had never seen a man drown in the trenches. They were part of a vast army, created by *The Times* and *The Daily Mail,* still walking about London kicking dachshunds, still talking about clawing Huns' eyes out with their fingernails.

Rice got off at Piccadilly and walked south to the Automobile Club on Pall Mall. The Horse Guards were in plain khaki now. The lake in Saint James Park had been drained to make way for Nissen huts. Half the population was in mourning for some relative or another; the other half was forcing a kind of gaiety born of desperation, trying to claim a little happiness now before disaster struck. Oxford Street had been completely given over to spiritualists' shops, where the bereaved sought to communicate with the Glorious Dead.

Once inside the club Rice went into the changing room and discarded his civilian clothes. He wrapped himself in a large white towel and entered the Turkish bath, then peered through the billowing steam until he found a balding man with the face of a petulant cherub, a petulant cherub smoking a lengthy cigar.

Rice nodded a silent greeting, then walked through the mist and sat down.

"How the devil can you keep a flame in here?" he said.

"By force of will," Churchill replied, and clamped his bulldog jaws tightly around his seven-inch Romeo y Julieta.

Their rendezvous was in the Turkish bath because of the special privacy it afforded, but also because Winston Churchill, once First Lord of the Admiralty, was now, at forty-three, in such disgrace that he no longer had so much as an office to meet in.

Rice waited several moments in silence, uncertain how to begin.

After a while Churchill turned and growled, "How's Prissy? And, of course, your Hermione?"

Rice looked at the older man, his shoulders hunched, his head jutting forward like the muzzle of a gun.

"Both splendid," Rice said, feigning good cheer, but he knew that the Black Dog of Churchill's depression had settled in for the duration.

"Mother's quite taken up with being a munitionette, you know. Hermione's after me to make an honest woman of her, but we still haven't settled on a date."

Churchill gave a false smile, puffing hard at his steam-soaked cigar.

Though a dozen years separated them in age, Anthony Rice and Winston Churchill had once romped together at Blenheim, and their two distinguished families had been intertwined for generations. Rice's father had been one of Lord Randolph Churchill's most loyal allies in Parliament. At the same time, he had been one of Jenny Churchill's most ardent lovers.

"So," Churchill said. "Sir Almroth went along, then, did he?"

"Yes. Like a lamb."

Churchill chewed his cigar contentedly. "Which means this American fellow should be well settled in Berlin by now."

Rice nodded.

Churchill picked up the rhythm for a moment, then added, "The pace of the war is quickening. As always we have no choice but to be bold. You should realize we may not be able to wait for this fellow's result. Or, for that matter, the German antiserum."

Rice raised his head sharply and beads of perspiration dropped into his eyes. "Why the sudden rush?" he asked.

"News from Chantilly," Churchill told him. "And none of it good."

Rice made a valiant effort to mop his brow but to no effect. The air was like Rawalpindi with a fever.

He looked back at Churchill and said, "How could it be worse than before?"

"Joffre merely wanted to push on with the Somme. . . ." Churchill removed the cigar from his lips, looked at it, then put it back in his mouth. "Nivelle wants to drown the entire French army in it. 'À outrance! À la baïonnette!' He's been casting back to de Grandmaison for his tactics. Next, red trousers. Then the cavalry charge."

Churchill paused again, then reached up with the third finger of each hand to rub the perspiration off his eyelids.

"As for General Nivelle," he went on, "he is simply not at all content to wait and see what the Germans' Alberich holds for us. He talks of one glorious push and—'victoire ou défaite depuis quarante-huit heures.' "

Rice felt his hands as wet as his face now. The Somme too had been a French idea, and it had cost six hundred thousand Englishmen their lives. And Winston himself was hardly above error. It was the monumental failure of his Dardanelles counteroffensive that had made him Britain's own Armenian. Persona non grata in Whitehall, hounded by Northcliffe and the press. For all appearances his meteoric career had died on the cliffs at Gallipoli just like so many young Englishmen. The only way Lloyd George had been able to build his new coalition was, in fact, by expressly promising that there would be no role in the government for young Winston Churchill.

"Haig can't possibly agree to anything so reckless," Rice said.

"Afraid he has. Our forces will provide support and try to move the British front as far as the Amiens–Saint-Quentin Road. Haig's only quibble is French maintenance of the Nord railway."

The last competent French general lay buried in Napoleon's tomb, Rice admitted to himself. The English commanders replayed their dusty victories from the days of unchallenged empire—"Whatever happens, we have got / The Maxim gun and they have not." They had squandered a million lives in futile attacks motivated by nothing more than a passion for straight lines. Now "the supply of heroes" was running short, and the old men were getting desperate.

"So what you're really saying is that the entire army of France could be wiped out in a day," Rice offered. "Even without a German disease weapon, or this Operation Alberich."

"Yes. I'm afraid so. Which puts us on a somewhat tighter schedule than before."

Rice looked up.

"Put on your mac and your Wellies, my boy," Churchill told him. "I want you to run up to Gruinard. See what our Dr. Frankensteins have accomplished with the new apparatus."

"THANK God we've been spared the Chaplin craze," said the petite young woman with fiery hair. She was Fern Andra, the American actress. In the last few years she had become a major star of German Kino, and she knew which side her war bread was buttered on.

To Gordon's left, Princess Daisy von Bulow raged against the war of attrition, not at the front, but among Berlin's opera singers and musicians. "Anna Todoroff," she said. "Claudio Arrau! They came from Bulgaria . . . from Chile . . . to Berlin! Berlin! Now all you hear is New York." She glanced away for a moment, her eyelashes fluttering like an ingenue's fan. "Of course," she said wistfully, "so many of the leading men have already been killed."

The embassy party had been seeded with Berlin's Anglo-American upper crust. Mrs. Gerard paraded Gordon past Princess Munster and Baroness Roeder, both English; Princess Braganza, an American, and the Duchess of Croy, formerly Nancy Leishman, daughter of the late ambassador. Even when he closed his eyes he could still see their teeth.

He had spent another pointless day at a camp for officers at Herzberge. He had talked to "Bombulai the Shine King," the shoe-black from Zanzibar, and the demented Belgian in a bowler hat they called the "French Ambassador." He was carrying the wooden carving in his pocket, waiting for the help that was supposed to come, and trying to keep his frustration in perspective. This was the war of the passive soldier, after all, the soldier who merely waits for the next shelling, the next scream.

Stopping a servant for another glass of champagne, Gordon glanced off toward the piano, where Ernesta Drinker Hughes, the young girl from Philadelphia, kissed Jay Adams on the cheek. They had been plotting all evening to pull down the window shades and start dancing—serious business according to the Law of Siege.

But then from behind them, the clumsy young princess from the Adlon dining room appeared in an emerald gown that shimmered in the candlelight. Gordon had caught her eye several times before and each time she had looked off. She had always managed to be on the opposite side as he and Mrs. Gerard circled the room.

He had gotten used to life without women while at the front. The saintly plainness of the nursing sisters, the mannish look of the ambulance drivers from the Pitchley Hunt. But here in the drawing room it was all breasts and powder and soft pink skin. Especially Princess Bucher's.

"Lost her trunk," Adams said. He sat alone now on the piano bench with his own silver-necked bottle of German champagne.

Gordon had escaped from his hostess, and now he stood watching the sheen come off Adams's forehead. "Who's that?"

"Mrs. Hughes. That's where she got the clothes. Someone took her down to Alfred Marie's but she came out entirely too chic to survive in Berlin. God knows a permanent blot on her character if word ever got back home."

Adams held up the champagne bottle and splashed some into Gordon's glass. "Here," he said. "Help yourself."

"Where's the Baron?"

"Otherwise engaged."

"I thought he was coming."

"A very busy man."

Gordon tipped his glass and the champagne ran over onto the floor. He sipped off a quarter inch, then transferred the drink to his left hand.

"But isn't he one of us? You said he had an American business partner."

"Did I?" Adams looked surprised. "Then I suppose he must. I never lie unintentionally. But that still doesn't mean he wants to be seen with us socially."

Gordon pulled out his handkerchief and dried his fingers. "What about your friend the dentist—this man Fisk? Is he likely to be here?"

"Oh, I think not. Why do you ask?"

"I don't know. I noticed the young lady—Princess . . ."

"Bucher. Don't bother. No fun at all."

"Made me think of Fisk, though," Gordon went on. "He seemed like an interesting sort."

"That is, of course, why he's not here. Far too 'interesting' for this particular gathering."

Gordon glanced down. "And how is that?"

"He gets on well enough with Germans because he gets on well with the 'All Highest.' " Adams opened his eyes. "But the Gerards find him . . . Well, it's hard to pin down, exactly. There are rumors of certain . . . proclivities."

Gordon raised one brow, then let it go. "You'd still think he could be useful."

Adams smiled. "How so? Anesthesia? The power of suggestion?"

"Not so much. Just a little insight now and then. Does he really have that much contact with the Kaiser?"

"I don't know. I suppose it depends on the royal gums and teeth."

"I suppose it also depends on where Fisk lines up. You said the embassy was stuck right in the middle. But private citizens are allowed to take sides, I assume."

"True," Adams said, nodding sagely. "But it's considered very poor form to ask which one."

Across the room Mrs. Hughes tapped the window and pointed to the crowd down on the Leipziger Platz. "Look," she said, "it's a demonstration of some kind."

"Oh no," Mrs. Gerard said, rushing over to dispel the notion. "I'm sure it's just people going home from work."

Gordon could see through the window to the plaza, surrounded by the Marineamt and the Landwahr ministry. The crowd down below was so orderly, confining themselves to the paved walks, that it was hard to tell whether they were demonstrating or not. But he could read the banners—BERLIN BELONGS TO US. GIVE US BREAD.

"Well, we can hardly ask them to eat cake," Fern Andra surmised. "Considering Kranzler's decline in quality."

Gordon glanced back to see Adams looking oddly serious.

"In your effort to seek out evildoing at the camps, Doctor . . . There's a man I recommend you talk to."

"Oh? Who's that?" Gordon set his glass on the piano.

"He's a Russian, actually. A man named Beszenoff."

Gordon waited a beat or two. He wanted to be cautious. He wanted to avoid appearing too eager. But a Russian? A Russian like the man who made the carving?

"And where would I find this . . . Beszenoff?"

"At the Ruhleben Racecourse."

Gordon pursed his lips, still biding his time. This was interesting, almost too interesting. He was not to confide in the embassy. Now the embassy was confiding in him.

"And what makes this particular Russian so appealing?"

"He's at Ruhleben only some of the while. Part time . . . when he's not at the Institute for Infectious Diseases."

Gordon looked back down at the crowd in the plaza.

"Curious, isn't it?" Jay added.

"I don't understand," Gordon said.

"He's a bacteriologist. He worked at the Institute before the war and he still has a bit of pull. His colleagues keep getting him furloughed. The army keeps sending him back."

"To the camp?"

"That's right. The prisoners run what they call their 'Grandstand University' inside the compound. He teaches there. So . . . when you make it to Ruhleben, talk to him. By all means give him my regards."

Adams got to his feet. "Do let me know if he has anything amusing to say."

"Ruhleben," Gordon said. "It may be a while before I get there. Tell me how I can speed up the process."

"Good question. But unfortunately one I can't answer." And then Adams sauntered off, leaving Gordon to himself.

He glanced around the room, trying to clear his head, to assimilate this new development. He felt a little drunk suddenly, alcohol and adrenaline vying for his attention. And then he spotted Princess Bucher again, a few feet behind the throng at the window, looking tentative, a bit lost, like a child amid the grown-ups. Gordon walked over to her and stood beside her for a moment, admiring the fine skin at the nape of her neck, breathing in the scent of rose water.

In time he leaned forward and spoke almost in a whisper. "You know the socialists in Prussia will never be taken seriously until they develop a respectable uniform."

She smiled nervously, her green eyes tensely drawn, and then she looked away, showing him a perfect profile framed by hair the color of mahogany.

"We haven't been introduced. I'm Eli Gordon. I'm with the embassy."

"I know who you are," she said. Her smile was frozen in place, her full red lips as moist as a child's.

"You seem embarrassed. No need to be. I understand what you must have gone through the other evening."

"Excuse me," she said.

She began to step away but Gordon blocked her path.

"Why are you afraid to talk to me?"

"You have to be more cautious," she said. "And patient."

Then she turned and walked away, leaving Gordon face-to-face with a German officer with rust-colored hair, a small, pale man, staring at him intently through a pair of steel-rimmed spectacles.

10

Walking through the winter gloom, Margarethe Riesling saw the thatch-covered roof of the Dahlem station barely visible in the distance. She was hungry and tired and eager to get back to Berlin. She drew her shoulders up against the cold and damp and hurried through the dark.

In her gloved hands she carried a rack of stoppered test tubes from the Imperial Health Office and a canister of gas from the Kaiser Wilhelm Institute. Dahlem was quite excited about this new development, but von Stade's directive still required cross-checking in von Broembsen's lab. Concentrated one in two thousand it was said to be faster than phosgene, a hundred times more potent than chlorine. In Dahlem's studies with dogs, exposure had led to death in a matter of seconds.

She entered the station with the northbound train rumbling overhead and rushed up the stairs in wet, dripping boots. She reached the second-class platform as the cars rolled to a stop, then stepped into a compartment to find a crippled veteran and a teen-aged girl facing each other in awkward silence. Their suspended faces gave away the delicate nature of the transaction she had interrupted, but there was nothing she could do about that now.

Margarethe took her seat, resting her packages in her lap, and waited for the car to roll forward.

In another moment, the train passed through the flat suburban landscape, and Margarethe looked out at the dirty snow beginning to pelt the windows. The bourgeois comforts of Dahlem receded quickly, and the relentless gloom of the city came back to her like a birthright. Reluctantly, she admitted a penchant for atmospheres that tested one's ability to withstand despair. Chicago. Detroit. Her apartment.

After a while the disabled man stopped staring at her and his eyes drifted back to his companion's joyless smile. The shop girls and the factory girls were out of work and they all did what they could to get by.

Some people chose to study art in Paris or Rome. Margarethe wondered sometimes what it said about her soul that she had chosen to study infections in Berlin. She had a practical bent, yes, but it was more a sense of obligation, of service, somehow. And it was that notion, combined with sex, that first got her into trouble.

She let her eyes drift down the man's body. He was not bad-looking. Young. Fit and muscular. The German amputees were issued two prostheses—an ordinary peg, and a flexible one like this with a shoe for special occasions. The wooden joint was visible below his cuff where the ankle might have been.

She looked back up at his young-old face and for the moment at least he reminded her of Gunther. She thought about the last time they had been together, on the library table, below the stained glass as in some religious rite. Even with her legs still wrapped around him, the two of them swaying gently from side to side, his erection still probing, he had begun to drift away from her. He had been hiding at this monastery for weeks, en route to Bremen and ultimately Denmark, but it was Liebknecht and Rosa Luxemburg he wanted to hear about, not her. He had no measurable interest in the anguish of her struggles or in the triumph of her discovery, or even in her feeling for him. He was a revolutionary first and foremost, a man only when some "lesser instinct" overtook him.

So why had she let it trap her, she wondered as she rode along toward Berlin. She was hardly the dependent, wifely type, yet she had surrendered so much of her will to him, made his preoccupations hers, more than compromised where she should have held firm. It was his idea for her to put up with von Stade's advances, to see what could be learned from him. So now she could be shot for her troubles, her work was compromised, and Gunther himself had retreated into exile. She was left stranded and alone, suspecting that the passion for radical thought he had awakened in her was simply passion itself.

She reached up to tug at her collar, and the canister rolled out of her lap and crashed to the floor. Cold condensation trickled down the side. The spigot hissed.

"What's that?" the veteran said.

Margarethe did not waste time responding. She put her handkerchief over her face and reached into her bag, rummaging for a bit of string. Holding her breath, she tied the string around the neck of the metal container as it leaked the deadly poison. Then she pried open the glass and let the sputtering canister dangle out of the window the rest of the way along the Ringbahn to the Bahnhof Putlitzstrasse.

Margarethe was impatient as she walked across the auto bridge over the Berlin-Spandau Ship Canal, the factories of Moabit to her back, the red brick laboratories of the Institute directly ahead. She had knotted her handkerchief tightly around the neck of the cylinder to contain what she could of the gas. But what intrigued her most was that, according to the Dahlem test results, she and the two others in that train compartment should have been dead. The fact that they were not was to her a marvelous curiosity.

Outdated display cabinets lined the corridors on the first floor of the building. Dark wood frames held anatomical specimens in thick glass jars—dissected aneurysms, aborted fetuses, a human face in longitudinal section. She walked upstairs and directly to her lab and through it to the containment chamber, where she placed the canister inside and closed the door. Then she went down the dark corridor once again to the animal facility.

"I need a dog," she told the Turkish woman who was the night attendant. Without acknowledging the request, the old woman turned slowly and made her way between the rows of metal cages. A moment later she had returned with an ugly, malnourished animal, growling stupidly at the end of a rope leash.

Margarethe led the animal back to the lab, then picked up a stop clock, a pencil, and a pad from her desk. Next she took the dog into the containment chamber and closed the door—from inside.

Releasing the dog, she put her fingers to her carotid to take her pulse—a rapid sixty beats a minute. She recorded the number on her pad but tried to ignore its implications. Being fearless was not necessary—what was required was to overcome one's fear.

The dog circled nervously in its slightly demented fashion. He looked up suspiciously at Margarethe, awaiting his fate with no particular bias. There was nothing left for her to do now but untie the handkerchief, start the timer, unscrew the broken stopcock, and breathe in the gas.

Her pulse had shot up even further when she put her finger to her throat again, but more than anything else she took the reading to distract herself, to fill those first few seconds. The dog moved aimlessly about, so Margarethe began to walk back and forth with him to keep their levels of activity similar. She wanted accurate results, a quality experiment. What did it matter that she might be shot when she was willing to take greater chances on her own, entirely by choice. Taking risks was a way of exercising control.

After fifteen seconds she felt perfectly normal. The dog seemed fine too, but then he became unsteady.

Margarethe's fingers were still pressed against her neck as before, but now she forgot to count.

At twenty-six seconds the dog dropped to the floor. His tongue protruded and his breathing sounded more and more distressed.

He lay on his side, then started and raced his legs as Margarethe watched and swallowed hard. She checked her clock. At thirty-eight seconds the dog's movement stopped.

She leaned down and checked the animal's vital signs. Then she rose back up and held the clock in both hands, staring into its face. The dog was dead, but after a full minute of exposure to the gas she still felt perfectly fine.

Margarethe took another turn around the small chamber. Two minutes had passed and all the gas from the cylinder was circulating about the room. She picked up the pad and sat down to record her impressions. Dahlem was right about their new gas— it was immediately lethal to dogs. What they had no way of knowing—at least not yet—was that in these concentrations it was harmless to human beings.

She left the dog in the chamber while she went to her desk and typed out a full report confirming the Dahlem research. She did not mention the leak on the train or her self-experimentation. She simply wrote a forceful paragraph endorsing production and ultimate deployment of the weapon on a massive scale. Then, as always, she signed the name of her employer Professor Rudiger von Broembsen, Head of the Department of Experimental Pathology, Institute for Infectious Diseases.

IT WAS past midnight by the time Gordon had walked back to the Adlon and stopped in at the American Bar. A different group of officers was at the large table, but with what appeared to be the same women. Gordon ordered a double bourbon, then placed / it alongside his wooden carving of Timur the Tartar.

A small man with a bad toupee walked over and hopped up on the next stool, his feet dangling in the air. Gordon remembered him from the first night at the bar. White gloves, monocle, pencil-thin mustache—the miniature dandy.

The little man lit a cigarette, rubbed his nose, took a swipe down his face, then began telling a story to the bartender. "A Jew is recommended for the Iron Cross and Hindenburg himself comes to pin it on."

He spoke rapid-fire German in a Dutch accent and a nasal, White Rabbit's voice. This time he wore a different boutonniere—a bit of tissue paper bunched together to form a carnation. He also wore what must have been a different toupee. It was shorter, as if he had just gotten a haircut.

"Hindenburg's going to make a joke and he asks the Jew which he would rather have, one hundred marks or the Cross. The Jew ponders for a moment and asks, 'What is the intrinsic worth of the medal?' 'Oh, about eight marks,' Hindenburg says. So the Jew answers, 'Well, Excellency, then I'll have the Iron Cross and ninety-two marks.' "

The bartender barked out laughter from behind his few remaining teeth. Gordon had heard the joke before, only it was Joffre and the Croix de Guerre.

The little man took another swipe down his face, then turned to watch Gordon playing with his shot glass, tilting it far to one side with the thumb and forefinger of both hands. Gordon's forearms made a protective circle around his cigarettes, his lighter, and the wooden carving from Doberitz.

"Now where did you get this little horror?"

"Father Christmas," Gordon said. He lifted his drink and knocked it back.

"Russian?"

Gordon nodded, tapping his glass on the bar for a refill.

"Amazing people," the dandy said, giving two darts of his tongue. "Nitchewo. Everything is nitchewo—'It doesn't matter.' Have you seen them working in the city, carrying the trash bins? They don't even require a guard. They're perfectly happy here, these people. Something to eat. Perfectly safe. They were going over the top, you know, many of them, armed with nothing but sticks."

He watched Gordon for a moment, taking note of the abrasions along his hairline. Then he snapped into a bow. "I am Count von Maurik de Beauford," he said. "But you must call me Billy."

De Beauford extended a tiny, well-manicured hand, which Gordon shook without comment.

"Ah, yes, a laconic fellow. That's all right. I'm a Hollander myself. Correspondent for the *Daily Telegraph,* but I spent a good bit of time in the States. Loved it. Coney Island. The Great White Way."

The count rubbed his nose and waited for something from Gordon. After a while he said, "When did you leave the States?"

Gordon picked up the carving and quietly slipped it back into his pocket. "How do you know I'm from the States?" he said.

"Ah. American idealism shines like a beacon to the jaded European. You've been in . . . France?"

Gordon studied the Dutchman's face. He was impeccably shaven. His cheeks were matted with talc, his natural hair and his toupee were both flecked with gray that looked artificial.

"You have a certain look," de Beauford explained.

"And what is that?"

"The look of a man . . . without political opinions."

The bartender returned and Billy was silent for a moment, his eyepiece dangling against the bar. Gordon ordered another whiskey, de Beauford a Molle und Korn.

The Dutchman glanced away, then whistled between his teeth. "You must be important," he said.

"Why do you think that?"

"You have two of Walther Ostriker's less conspicuous detectives watching everything you do."

Gordon glanced into the darkened corner where two men stared intently back at him.

"Don't bother," de Beauford said. "They can't read lips. They'll simply ask me to give a full account of this conversation. Anything particular you'd like me to report?"

"I'll have to think about that."

The bartender came back with Gordon's whiskey, and the stein of beer and the small glass of gin for de Beauford. The Dutchman waited a moment, then as Gordon looked back at the table, he explained.

"The one on the right is von Hessenstein, Moltke's nephew. An American cinema operator wants to become a journalist, you see, so he talks to von Hessenstein. Five days later the papers publish his 'interview' with Moltke, typed out in advance and delivered in an envelope."

De Beauford sipped his gin in a tiny gulp, then took a swipe down his face.

"For one thousand marks, plus commission on the sale of a motor car, which I happen to know he stole from the Railroad Department, von Hessenstein handed over a two-week pass for the Eastern front—with one hundred feet of film of Hindenburg. He has film of everybody. For two thousand marks he said he could film the Kaiser moving the royal bowels. One of the Kaiser's A.D.C. is a personal friend, he says. Though a grain of salt is recommended."

"Is that how you get your stories?" Gordon asked. "Cash up front?"

"Oh, no. Most of them I make up entirely."

De Beauford reached into his coat pocket and pulled out a letter on stationery from the German Embassy in Rome.

"Letter of introduction to Hindenburg. I know his nephew. You produce a letter like this and suddenly it is 'zu Befehl' this and 'zu Befehl' that. There's another one I keep under lock and key in my room upstairs. A safe conduct signed by Ludendorff himself."

Gordon scanned the letter, but he couldn't concentrate. He was still uneasy about the men in the corner. "Tell me about the one on the left," he said.

"Rolf Mayr. No highly placed connections, but probably the best operative in Berlin. He has the ultimate advantage, of course— a perfect criminal mind."

"And their boss?"

"Ostriker? Oh, bags of charm. He worked with Haber on chlorine gas. Very much the technician. But you must have seen him, you know. He was with you at Mrs. Gerard's soiree."

Gordon smiled and shook his head.

"A reporter is paid to know the whereabouts of important people," de Beauford said. "People like yourself."

"Let me guess," Gordon said, pushing his fingers back along his scalp. "Short. Red hair. Steel-rimmed spectacles."

De Beauford nodded and raised his glass, a toast to Gordon's perceptiveness.

Gordon let his gaze drift back to the men. Von Hessenstein had the milk-fed look of every bigshot's nephew. Mayr was more interesting. Gordon thought at first that he was missing an eye. Then he realized it was just that the left brow and eyelashes were both stark white.

"What will you tell them about me?" Gordon asked.

"Subtle disquisitions. Nothing vulgar. They'll ask me to be your friend, ply you with drinks, no doubt. It's a dirty business being seen in bars, talking to foreigners, but someone's got to do it."

Gordon pulled a bank note out of his wallet and placed it under his glass. Then he gathered up his cigarettes and lighter.

"You know the real source of German hostility toward the British is that the war cuts them off from their London tailors," de Beauford said.

Gordon placed his palm flat against the bar. "Entirely too much suffering in this war."

De Beauford placed his hand on top of Gordon's. "And my job is to put it into print, where it all makes such perfectly good sense."

Gordon looked at him with rising concern.

"People think reporting is like looking up facts in a history book. But the world isn't broken into chapters. It doesn't have a convenient index. The world is flux, and you don't even know what the story is yourself until after you dig. Everyone has a story, of course, but most of them are the wrong story. Getting to the *right* story, now that's the target."

"I'll keep that in mind," Gordon said, retrieving his hand.

"You know the American Express office on the Linden?"

"Yes."

"You should stop by there more often. At the end of the day perhaps. You never know what Mum might send from home."

And with that Billy de Beauford hopped down and hurried across the room to sit with the two detectives he'd just pointed out.

Gordon could see the Dutchman hold up his child's white hands for silence, then hear his voice above the rest.

"A Jew is recommended for the Iron Cross . . . ," he began.

11

When Gordon came into the embassy ballroom the next morning a Mrs. Ruthven Webb sat waiting for him, a small figure dressed in black wearing a modest hat and veil, her dark gray coat draped over her shoulders.

Gordon came up quietly and introduced herself. "Mrs. Webb," he said, "I'm Dr. Gordon."

"Oh it's too late for that," she said.

"I'm sorry?"

"For a doctor." Her eyes were magnified by thick, rimless glasses, her head circled by dust motes in the sunlight.

"Ruthven," she added. "He's dead."

Gordon walked around the desk and took his seat behind the stack of papers that had mysteriously appeared since yesterday. He glanced at them quickly to cover his distraction—a Civil War pensioner in Wilmersdorf whose check was late, a businessman stranded in Potsdam with the grippe. Any problem even remotely medical was being shunted onto him. Such as Mrs. Webb.

"Your husband," he resumed, looking up.

She nodded firmly and pinched her nose with her embroidered handkerchief. Gordon sat in the light from the window and listened as patiently as he could.

"He was the Munich sales manager with Quaker Oats," Mrs. Webb went on. "We were setting our affairs in order in Berlin, going home to Cedar Rapids. Then a heart attack took care of everything for us—just like that."

She paused, and after a moment Gordon realized she was expecting something from him.

"I'm sorry," he told her.

"I'll bet you are. I suppose there's so many men dying with this war that one natural death seems entirely insignificant. But not to me, it doesn't. I'm really quite upset."

Gordon looked down at the schedule on his desk. He was supposed to inspect the work commando at a power plant in Oberschönweide in half an hour.

"I was told there's some sort of problem with the . . ."

"Yes, there certainly is." Her thin lips trembled as she said it. "Maybe that German undertaker thought I planned to pack Ruthven in my train case! But no one—and I mean that absolutely— no one authorized anyone to cremate my husband's body."

She leaned over and rummaged through the carpetbag at her feet. "I refused to pay for their services," she said into the bag. "And I refused to pay for that urn they'd put him in. And I find it tragic that they would make a mockery of a man's life quite this way."

She rose back up, her face flushed by her exertions. Then she placed the red-and-blue pasteboard cylinder on the desktop.

"That . . . dust . . . is not Ruthven," she said.

Gordon stared at the portrait on the box—the well-fed Quaker smiling under his hat.

"That is not my husband," she added, resolutely.

Gordon paused for a moment, considering his next statement very carefully. "How can I help?"

"You can't. There's not a blessed thing anyone can do now, is there?"

Gordon nodded. "I'm afraid you're right."

And for the next minute the two of them sat in silence. Gordon glanced down at the dull sheen of the parquet, then Mrs. Webb gathered her coat around her. "I just want you to know that I'm not taking a cereal box full of ashes home to my children."

Gordon looked at her. She was a thin woman, but now even her ears and the septum of her nose had started to loosen and droop.

"Would you like me to take care of the box for you?"

"I don't care what you do with it," she said.

Then Gordon helped her up from her chair and walked with her down the marble stairs.

In the foyer he put one arm around her, trying to offer a comforting hug, after which they said goodbye under the watchful eyes of the embassy's lugubrious butler. Then Gordon returned to his ballroom office and his desk and sat down, staring at the carton of ashes.

He lit a cigarette and exhaled a mouthful of smoke, drifting off for a moment, remembering the battered look on Mrs. Webb's face, then remembering the battered look on his wife's face three years ago. Lavinia, dressed in black, staring at him with crazed eyes across their daughter's casket.

The war had introduced the form letter of condolence now, the appropriate space checked off for dead, wounded, or missing. Efficiency was important these days, considering the efficiency of killing.

He leaned back, drawing again on his cigarette, and he brought his mind once again to the present, to Count Billy de Beauford and Jay Adams, the "fairy" guardians guiding him from behind their toadstools. Something did not add up with what he had been shown so far. The duplication of effort was confusing.

Then he glanced up and found Fräulein Kleist in front of him so serenely motionless as to have materialized on the spot.

"Consular Section sent her," the young woman said, scanning the middle distance just past his head. She glanced back through the door and breathed deeply, and Gordon inadvertently focused on her imposing breasts.

"The consul is on leave," she continued.

"And?"

"This woman simply wanted to hear herself complain. That's all."

Gordon lowered his eyes and put away his lighter, then drew on his cigarette. "You disapprove?"

"She is weak," the young woman said.

Gordon nodded.

"And old."

Gordon watched her for a moment as she stood self-consciously in front of him, clutching her elbows at her sides. He had seen Fräulein Kleist coming in this morning with her ice skates over her shoulder. She was the muscular sort of German girl who spent her evenings at the Ice Palace in Lutherstrasse or lifting weights at her Turnverein.

"And what do you complain about, Fräulein Kleist?"

She cocked her head, temporarily speechless. Then she said, "I try to avoid unpleasantness," and stepped forward to hand him a printed card from the Police Presidency of Berlin.

Gordon read the Gothic script, then looked at her.

"A police detective? What does he want?"

"He wants you to come down."

The blond man downstairs spoke in a soft Bavarian accent scarcely louder than a whisper. "Dr. Gordon," he said. "How do you do?"

Gordon studied his fair, not quite Teutonic face. It seemed open, guileless, square-jawed without being threatening. But still Gordon hesitated, letting the question go unanswered.

After a moment, the detective added, "Could we walk perhaps?"

"Outside, you mean?"

Andreas Schiller inclined his head toward the door. "There is," he said, "more space."

Schiller's feet dragged from step to step as he walked back through the marble entry, his arms straight down at his sides. His hat was tilted forward on his head, the brim almost parallel with the bridge of his nose.

"I have no jurisdiction inside a foreign embassy," he said.

The butler helped Gordon on with his coat, then held the door as they stepped out beneath a sky the color of pewter and into a wind that was cold and raw.

They skirted the boy hawking the *Continental Times,* walked between the two policemen in capes and Pickelhauben standing at the curb, and made their way across to the Wilhelm Platz.

"It creates great insecurity in a policeman to be without authority," Schiller said, bracing himself against the cold. "It's like being without one's badge."

Gordon nodded, squinting against the brightness of the snow. He ran an inventory of everything he'd done and everyone he'd spoken to since arriving in Berlin. He thought of Katz, de Beauford, Ostriker, and the detectives already watching him. He had an entourage now. From time to time he would have to serve refreshments.

"Almost like being without one's clothing," Schiller went on.

Gordon nodded. "I can see that it would be."

They continued into the park, where a shortage of manpower, or even boy power, had left the walks unshoveled. The flower beds were hidden by a smooth blanket of snow, a few vestiges of last summer's plants jutting abruptly through the crust.

"What happened to your head?" Schiller asked.

"Slipped on the ice."

"Too bad." The detective glanced up. "But it could be worse. Much worse. Just yesterday a man named Katz was fed to a Siberian tiger at the Berlin Zoological Garden." He studied Gordon's features for signs of recognition. "We assume he did not volunteer for the assignment."

The wind pelted him with frozen snow as Gordon stared into the cold, blue eyes beneath the hat brim.

A few feet away a husky woman wrapped in furs walked her

dachshund beneath the heroic gaze of the half dozen bronze statues lining the path. Schwerin, Winterfeldt, Seydlitz, Keith, Zieten, Prince Leopold of Anhalt-Dessau—the fallen generals of Frederick the Great. The little dog, true to his methodical heritage, raised his leg at the base of each monument in turn.

"I don't understand," Gordon said at last.

Schiller continued walking. "We found the body . . . or what was left of it . . . inside the cage. That was Wednesday." They sidestepped a yellow stain in the snow. "It seems the carnivores are not fed on Wednesdays."

Schiller walked along rigidly as always, watching Gordon's face from the corner of his eye, letting the American work with the image.

"At first we thought he had climbed the fence. Deranged. Suicidal. But we autopsied the remains and found the cause of death to be a blow to the head, followed by a slash across the throat. This latter, I should add, done with and almost surgical precision."

When they came to the statue of Prince Leopold, the victor of Kesselsdorf, Schiller stopped and waited. The prince sat fixed in bronze, stroking his chin and to all appearances gazing reflectively toward the barbershop of the Kaiserhof Hotel.

"You knew Mr. Katz," Schiller said, his intonation matter-of-fact.

"I visited his shop. On Wednesday."

"What was the nature of your visit?"

"I'd hoped to buy an instrument."

"Did you?"

"He didn't have what I needed."

"So you left your card."

"He said he'd try to find what I was looking for."

Schiller glanced back with a look Gordon attributed to profound skepticism. Both men had their hands hidden in their pockets.

"When did you leave his shop?"

"It was early. Half past eight, maybe."

"And then?"

"I came to the embassy."

Schiller looked up toward the windows of the foreign office, and for a moment there was nothing but the sounds of the city, the sound of wind swooping down through the trees.

"Do you have any idea what would take Mr. Katz to the zoo?"

"No."

"Did you see him at any other time during the day?"

"No."

Schiller smiled, and then resumed his methodical pace around the park.

"All perfectly reasonable," he said. He had removed his hands from his coat and was walking with his arms motionless by his sides. "Of course I knew it would be. I am simply following through on all possible lines of investigation. It's the nature of the work. Police work is extremely tedious, did you know? But then you're a surgeon. You know better than I about attention to detail."

For a while longer they continued in silence, Schiller gazing up placidly at the sky.

"You're with the medical school of Harvard University?"

"That's right."

"Your card was in Mr. Katz's pocket, you remember. That's how I know so much about you. So when did you leave to come here?"

"I've been in France. I haven't been in the States for a couple of years."

"Doing surgery?"

"Yes."

"Very interesting. And are you doing surgery while in Berlin?"

"No."

The detective turned to face him once again. "Then why are you buying instruments?"

"Katz had a reputation," Gordon said. "And German steel

is . . . German steel. I thought I'd take advantage of being here."

"Looking after prisoners?"

"That's right."

Schiller nodded as he walked, letting another moment pass in silence. Then he said, "I hope you don't find it impertinent of me, Doctor, but perhaps you would have better luck shopping in France or England. We have a rather inconvenient war going on, and a rather successful blockade." He looked up. "You would do well to find a brass button in Germany. And as for diverting German steel from Mr. Krupp's cannon factories, I would rate it as highly unlikely."

A squirrel ran across a telephone line, dusting off a shower of snow that stung Gordon's face and neck.

"Hardship leads to temptation, Doctor. But for some, it can lead to extraordinary profits."

Gordon stared at him.

"The black market," Schiller said. "Katz was in it all the way up his twisted little spine."

Gordon glanced back up at the small high-wire performer, sensing now that he was just as precariously suspended.

"You don't look the murderous type to me," Schiller went on. "Whether or not you are the type to trade in back alleys remains to be seen. But if you will permit me a suggestion . . . limit yourself to good works while in Berlin."

Gordon nodded, then looked into the detective's emotionless face. Despite all the other uncertainty, he was reasonably sure this was one contact Anthony Rice had not intended him to make.

GORDON left the embassy that evening and walked over to Unter den Linden, turning east. As the streetlamps came on, the trees along the esplanade were black against the snow.

He crossed Wilhelmstrasse and stopped for a moment outside

the *Berliner Lokal-Anzeiger*. A telegraph machine operated in the window, with pen-and-ink maps fixed to the wall behind it. A copy of the newspaper hung on clothespins from a string. GERMAN FORCES ADVANCE ON DOBRUDJA. BRAILA FALLS. HEROIC RAIDS ON THE SOMME FRONT.

Gordon glanced up quickly and scanned the sidewalk on either side of him. He looked for window-shoppers, dawdlers, anyone without an obvious sense of purpose. Specifically, he scanned for the now familiar faces of Rolf Mayr, von Hessenstein, or Criminal Detective Andreas Schiller.

He walked past the expensive shops, their cigar box lettering gleaming in the windows. He passed the Ministry of Religion, the austere facade of the Hotel Bristol, and the darkened shell of the Russian Embassy. He was bucking a tide of civilian commuters hurrying out of office buildings, making their wartime way to the Brandenburg Gate Tor, their connection for the western suburbs.

American Express was part of the Kaiser-Galerie, just in from Friedrichstrasse. Gordon walked into the office and up to the counter and gave his name.

"Gordon's the last name?" the clerk asked.

"Yes. Eli Gordon."

The young man stepped aside for a moment, then turned back with a large, white envelope.

Gordon took it and walked a few steps toward the door, stopping just inside to tear open the flap and read the note. In an intricate, copybook hand that could have been his wife's, the message gave him his first instructions.

"Admire the shop windows across the way."

Gordon dropped the note into his pocket and walked outside. He passed through the Gothic arcade, wondering how many pairs of eyes were on him at this moment. Why de Beauford *and* Adams? Why a second meeting with this cat-and-mouse routine when de Beauford could have said whatever needed saying?

Outside a store window displaying wooden toys Gordon

stopped to light a cigarette. Inside the framed glass were trains and windmills, airplanes and castles carved somewhere in the Black Forest. Gordon stood staring at the circus animals—a whittled bear holding up a ball, another working a pump—which reminded him of other, unanswered questions. The discouraging truth was that any of these carvings could mean just as much or as little as the one whittled by that Russian prisoner at Doberitz.

The shop door opened and a young woman emerged wearing a sable hat and a sable-collared coat.

Gordon bowed slightly and removed his hat. He was not entirely surprised. "Now what?" he said.

Princess Bucher stood beneath the shopkeeper's bells, her lips parted slightly.

"Smile," she responded, handing him a large package tied up with string. "And carry this for me. Make pleasantries. Laugh a great deal. I assume you've paid court to a lady on a chance encounter."

She stuffed her hands into her sable muff and stepped forward through the arcade, leading the way back into the traffic along the Linden.

Gordon scanned the faces coming toward them as they made their way along the slushy sidewalk, the men following the princess with their eyes. There was a time when he too would have been distracted by her, but he had learned his lesson with aristocrats.

"I've arranged for you to spend twenty-four hours at Ruhleben without an escort," she said.

Gordon nodded. He carried her package under one arm, his body leaning toward her. "I'm aflutter with anticipation," he said, smiling broadly. "But what about getting me out?"

"There's a young man at the Y.M.C.A. foyer who will make the switch. His name is Hazelwood."

"Switch with what?"

"I'll explain later. Are you up to it?"

Gordon glanced across the street to the Gause automotive showroom, where the last remaining vehicle stood on cinder blocks instead of tires. He smiled and tipped his hat.

They walked past the Bristol, heading back toward the Brandenburg Gate.

"All rumors lead to the Ruhleben Racetrack," he said, staring up at the huge structure. "You've got eight thousand men housed there. What exactly am I going to learn in twenty-four hours?"

She took a deep breath, waiting until they had passed the crowd outside the newspaper office.

"I used to have access," she said with a sigh. "As a nursing volunteer. Now, restrictions being what they are, I can't get near the place."

Pulling out one small, plump hand, she reached up to adjust her collar. Her fingers were round and white, the nails translucent.

Gordon watched the crowd carefully as they passed the Adlon. A woman on the sidewalk sold copies of *Berliner Tagblatt* out of a baby carriage. He stopped and bought one and tucked it up against the package under his arm. Then they continued walking across the Pariser Platz.

They walked between the sandstone columns of the huge gate, the stone rising up toward an overcast sky that covered the city like a great vaulted ceiling. Their footsteps echoed as they passed underneath and came out into the park.

"My . . . companion," she went on. "A girl named Lucy Geary. She had an uncle at the camp so she left things for him, even after she couldn't visit any longer. After one particular trip she came back quite agitated. I couldn't get it out of her—it seems I'd played the part of German loyalty all too well with her. But that night when I returned from dinner there was just a note. She asked forgiveness. Said she couldn't take living here anymore. She was overwhelmed by the German cruelty. The last straw—carting the prisoners off to a hospital for hideous experiments. She said I'd understand it all when I read about it in the American papers."

"And . . . ?" Gordon asked her.

"Not a trace of the girl since."

They were in the Tiergarten now, and Princess Bucher turned up Friedensallee, off to the right. They followed the footprints encrusted in the snow.

"That's it?" Gordon asked.

"No, I've inquired back in England. I've checked the hospitals, the police. But all I discovered was that she had an . . . association. A jockey. Also an American."

"So is that why you were talking to Fisk?"

"At the beginning, yes." She glanced at Gordon as the wind raced across the park. "Erskine Fisk. Friend to all."

Out in the park, in the Königs Platz, a large crowd had gathered between the Reichstag and the column. A man in a top hat shouted into a megaphone, while high above the platform and the crowd a huge wooden statue of General von Hindenburg loomed inside a frame of scaffolding.

"National Foundation for the Bereaved of the War," Princess Bucher said. "You give some marks, you get to drive a nail."

Gordon stood quietly for a moment watching the people line up to climb the stairs. Iron spikes protruded from the general's face like stubble. Silver had been driven into the head of the sword, gold into the wedding ring.

"So this whole thing is based on one story from a love-struck girl," he said.

"I assure you it goes much deeper than that. She saw something that disturbed her, which is why she made plans to leave the country. All of a sudden she was going to run off with this 'gentleman' of hers to New York, or so she thought. I traced him. I found out the ship he was on and cabled. He said she never showed up for their rendezvous, so he left without her."

"He could be lying," Gordon said.

"Yes. And she could have been arrested or even killed before she ever got to him."

Gordon looked up at the platform. Katz and Troelstra were

both dead, and murder had a way of lending weight to the unlikeliest of premises.

"You'd be trying to find Charles Geary," she went on. "That is, if you're willing. Lucy's uncle. His billet is Stable Six. They call it the 'Palais de Rothschild,' though he spends most of his time in church. I suspect he may know what Lucy was up to when she left the camp that last time."

Gordon watched an elderly woman lift the hammer, then slam it into a metal spike just above the general's eye.

"Then there's the matter of Nigel Partridge."

Gordon looked back at her. "The jockey?"

"The man you'll be replacing at Ruhleben. He lives near the canal, near Mockernbrücke Station. You're to be at his apartment at ten o'clock tomorrow evening. You'll be taken to the camp the next day."

Gordon adjusted the package and the newspaper under his arm. "Anything else?"

"Be careful what you say to Erskine Fisk."

"And why is that?"

"His clientele is more German than American. He protects his interests."

"Fair enough."

"Lucy had an appointment with him her last day in Berlin. The day she went to Ruhleben."

"You think she might have told him something? You think he might have turned her in?"

"With Erskine Fisk I don't know what to think."

12

It was a fine day for winter, bright and cold, with children out
skating on the Hubertussee, adding little streaks of color to a
world of black and white. Andreas Schiller rode the bus from
Nollendorf-Platz to the Grunewald and got off on Bismarckallee
to walk the rest of the way. He could see Frau von Stade's building
above the trees, and he looked forward to the view. The colonel's
apartment would undoubtedly face the lake.

Schiller's interview with the American doctor had generated
nothing more than a subordinate clause in a single sentence in his
report. But embassy personnel usually meet with murder victims
after the fact, not before. The American had seemed furtive, up
to no good, and Schiller knew that he was hardly the kind of
policeman who struck terror into the hearts of the innocent. It
made him want to know more about this man Gordon, about the
dead merchant Isidor Katz, and about the late head of chemical
armaments, Colonel Kraft von Stade.

This whole district of the Grunewald had been farmland a generation before. The same was true throughout the west and south—
Schoneburg, Wilmersdorf. Some farmers lived here still, only now
in imitation palazzos, bought with shiny new fortunes from real
estate speculation.

Schiller's Berlin was in the north and east, where the workers
from East Elbia had come, been crowded into basements, then

crowded all the more with the war and the recall of colonials. The prevailing winds kept these "proletarian masses" in touch with their work, or at least in touch with the grit from their smokestacks. But "out west" here in the Grunewald, the skies were clear and fresh, wild boars ran free in the parks, and there were diving grebes and wood thrushes overhead. Or at least there had been. Schiller's "proletariats" were hungry since the war, and they were not fools.

The doorman who took Schiller up in the lift stood in uniform and glittering medals, a man of his time. Schiller, on the other hand, wore a six-year-old suit that had not been expensive to begin with. If you refused to wear clothing made of paper, which Schiller did, there was little recourse but to become shabby. Pants worn to a diaphanous sheen, jackets perforated at the elbow, shirts with cuffs and collars eaten away by ersatz detergent. In the left pocket of his overcoat Schiller carried his 7.65-mm Parabellum pistol—the strap to his shoulder holster had worn completely through and could not be replaced for the duration.

At the fifth landing they jerked to a stop and the man pulled back the gate.

"What number?" Schiller asked.

The doorman merely bowed and waved him forward. There were no numbers here. Each apartment occupied a single floor.

A frail housemaid led him through a foyer of black-and-white tile. He heard music pounded out on a piano as he glided next across an expanse of parquet that smelled of wax and furniture oils, then took a seat in the parlor facing a formal portrait draped in black. He had seen the face before, under somewhat different circumstances.

Schiller looked around. A Coromandel screen covered the fireplace. Celadon bowls and a Fabergé box sat on the table amid copies of *Kreuzzeitung*. With trembling hands, he lifted the lid and peered inside the small container. Despite the odor of fine Cuban tobacco, there was, unfortunately, no cigar.

The music was wrestled to the ground and pummeled to its conclusion. What seemed to be the final blow was struck again and again, until at last there was nothing but the sustained reverberation. Schiller took a deep breath and settled back in his chair.

A huge woman swept into the room with a military bearing and enough black crepe de chine for a military cortege. Nearly six feet tall, with a wide jaw, she snapped "God punish England" as Schiller rose to his feet, made a slight bow, and kissed her hand. Then she arranged herself in a chair and the detective sat back down.

"You would speak to me about my husband," Frau von Stade began.

"Yes. I apologize for the intrusion."

"If it is to be done, do it right."

The colonel's widow looked down and adjusted her wide hips, seeking bedrock in the chair as if she were about to shoulder some heavy weight. Then with no small amount of apprehension, Schiller launched his frail craft into these deep and uncharted waters.

"It is a terrible thing for a woman in the prime of her life to be deprived of a husband," he began. "The companionship. The comforts of marriage."

He stopped to swallow—his mouth felt dry. All his life he had dreaded being so much as noticed by such people. Now he was laying it all on the line to play out a single intuition. He licked his lips, and as he did so, a kitten emerged from the other room and bounded toward him, scampering up his leg and into his lap. Its coat was black and white, patterned like a man in evening dress.

"Of course there are the children," Schiller went on, stroking the cat perfunctorily. Its tail rose up with a sensuous arch and the fecund odor of digestive excess.

Frau von Stade stared coldly back at him, heavy and inert. She was like a statue of a woman—in anthracite. The kitten kept insisting, rolling in ecstasy, its stomach pumped up with cream.

"There should be some compensation, I believe. Whatever form it takes, even if it is merely philosophical consolation. Perhaps you would call it merely 'peace of mind,' but often—"

"If you are here to sell life insurance you are too late," Frau von Stade barked. "I was told you were with the criminal police."

"Yes. Forgive me," he said, flushed with embarrassment. Why was he such a fool around these people! He picked up the cat and set it awkwardly on the coffee table in front of him. "But the subject is . . . rather delicate."

"We are Germans. We can face death unafraid."

"Yes. Certainly."

The kitten sat down on the newspaper and licked its shoulder.

"Let me be more direct," Schiller said, but then he paused before he went on.

"Before your husband's death, were you aware of any change in his habits, or perhaps in his associations?"

"What are you suggesting?"

"I have reason to believe that the circumstances of your husband's death might not be as they seemed."

The kitten moved away, leaving behind a tiny, brown rosette.

"My husband died of heart failure while at his command."

"I'm afraid I must tell you those are not the actual facts of the case. I have no conclusive evidence of foul play, which is why I am here. The first step would be exhumation of the body. The army, you see, did not do a proper autopsy. However, if we could take your husband's remains down to the crime lab . . ."

There was a tremor in the room. The cat jumped down and scampered away. Frau von Stade's eyes glowed white hot as her lungs drew air like a furnace.

"It is . . . a difficult thing to say," Schiller continued. "But evidence has been found suggesting that Colonel von Stade was engaged in the unauthorized procurement of massive quantities of

black market goods. It is possible that these illegal activities might
have led—"

In one sudden thrust she was on her feet and clanging the crystal
bell that summoned her maid.

"I will have you boiled in oil!"

Her eyes were huge, her mouth coated with froth. "You step
into my house with condolences and then attack my husband's
name and honor! This is the most outrageous behavior I have ever
experienced. You should be shot for insulting your betters. You
will be shot!"

Schiller reached into his pocket for the strands of golden hair,
then held them out—slowly—like a peace offering toward this
seething woman. She stared at his hand, her eyes bulging.

"Your husband's body was found . . . clad only in a pair of
socks, I regret to say . . . in a cheap pension on Spichernstrasse.
The evidence suggests that he was engaged in sexual intercourse
at the time of death. These strands of hair—feminine in length
and texture—were found on the pillow beside him."

Frau von Stade shuddered for a moment. Her eyes grew even
wider. But then, as with the boiler at the colonel's pension, the
pressure dropped.

Another moment passed and the woman settled slowly into her
chair.

"This . . . woman," Schiller went on. "She was with your husband when he died. Undoubtedly, in some sense, she was . . . responsible for his death. If his death was premeditated, it was she
most certainly who saw it through."

The maid appeared.

"You rang, madam?"

Frau von Stade barked, "Go away!"

Then Schiller leaned forward across the table, a posture for
sharing confidences. "Now this woman . . . If your husband was,
in fact, murdered, it was she who is in all likelihood the murderer.
I don't think she should go unpunished, do you?"

Frau von Stade wiped the spittle from her lips, clasped her hands together, then pressed them into a prayerful pose. "You will tell me more about this woman," she said.

At which point Schiller leaned back in his chair and, for the first time all day, relaxed.

MAJOR Anthony Rice could see the cliffs jutting up over the bow as the boat pitched in the choppy waters of Gruinard Bay. The volcanic outcropping of land was half a mile from shore and heavily eroded, with exposed basalt columns like the pipes of a church organ.

Rice stood inside the tiny cabin of the trawler in his yellow slicker and looked up at the harsh, gray sky, feeling desperately ill. He glanced back toward the Scottish coast where they had put in a quarter of an hour ago. The island and the village seemed equidistant now. The nausea would last only a few minutes more if he could just hold on.

He glanced through the glass at Rollins, the explosives expert, then at Pauley, the bacteriologist, huddling together out of the wind and both looking positively green. But what worried Rice most of all was the sheep. In the event of rampant seasickness, they could hardly be counted on to behave like English gentlemen.

Fifteen sheep were on this boat, harnessed together on deck, and fifteen on the boat that had gone before. George Pauley had been roaming these hills for days, bargaining with the crofters for their animals. The Scots had already gotten used to the Nissen huts at Aultbea, the Royal Artillery checkpoints along the coast. They seemed to take this latest English peculiarity in stride, and they were quite happy with the money.

Rice looked up at the birds soaring over the three-hundred-foot cliffs. The ledges up ahead were coated white with guano from the cormorants and gulls. Rice could see gray seals resting on the rocks below, insulated from the cold by their excess pounds of blubber. Wind and water, birds and fish—elements over which even scientists and generals had no control.

In Scotland now, with the execution of Churchill's plan actually upon him, he found himself beginning to wonder just how well it had all been thought through. The cliffs had probably looked very much the same at Gallipoli when the Aussies landed, only to be torn apart by the Turkish guns, and First Lord of the Admiralty Winston Churchill had been in charge of that one too.

The first boat was already tied up when they pulled into the cove. A rocky beach lay ahead, littered with seaweed, and a weathered pier left behind by the fishermen who had once lived on the island. Gruinard had been uninhabited for years. Though no one knew it at the time, the British army was about to ensure that it would remain so for centuries to come.

Rice stood on the beach with his hands in his pockets while the soldiers unloaded the boat. Low tide meant that each animal had to be lifted up and carried onto the dock. He counted the sheep as they were led away up the path, but he knew the exercise would do nothing to help him sleep.

When all the animals were gone, Rollins and Pauley unloaded their equipment. First up on the dock was a wooden crate containing a five-gallon flask packed in straw. The two men walked side by side, carrying the glass beyond the rocks and safely onto the sand. Then Rollins jumped back into the boat and began tossing out duffel bags. In time, he came up with another wooden crate with rope handles and red lettering on the side that was quite explicit: DANGER HIGH EXPLOSIVES.

"If you'd care to suit up, now, Major." The sergeant from the Royal Artillery held out a canvas bag that Rice took and pulled open. It contained a gas mask, a rubberized suit, and boots—equipment that was becoming all too familiar.

The sergeant held out his hand. "Let me take your topcoat, sir."

Rollins and Pauley, looking like deep-sea divers in their protective gear, knelt beside a metal cylinder eighteen inches long and six inches in diameter. Rollins held it upright in the sand as Pauley lifted the flask, pouring in a thick, brown gruel of concentrated anthrax spores. Then Pauley sealed the empty container, and Timothy Rollins sealed the bomb.

The twisting path up the face of the cliff would have been difficult to climb under the best of circumstances. In Rice's ill-fitting boots it was a slow, painstaking struggle over loose boulders and eroded gulleys. And dry land had done nothing to ease the sickness in his stomach.

Rice was the last one to reach the top, a rocky plain high above the water covered with bracken. He turned and looked back across Gruinard Bay, laced with whitecaps all the way to the coast, and took a deep breath of the damp, salt air. His misgivings were irrelevant now, qualms that had no more place in the B.S.S. than at Mons. He dug into the path and made his way to the ocean side.

Beyond the cliffs he saw the great swells of the open sea dashing against the rocks, sending up a white spray. A few feet ahead, on a point of land, the thirty sheep were being tethered in concentric rings around a mound of earth. Each sheep had a metal plate stapled into its ear. On each plate were the letters "PD" and a number in sequence from one to thirty.

While the sheep bleated and tugged at the scant vegetation, Rollins placed the bomb on the mound of earth and attached an explosive charge. Then, walking backward, he paid out the fuse wire that would be attached to the detonator a safe distance upwind.

Rice stood with Pauley and watched Rollins tighten the screws attaching the wires to the mechanism. The four soldiers turned shepherds stood holding their gas masks under their arms, enjoying a last cigarette.

"Pity they're not German sheep, right, sir?"

Rice nodded. He was already dreading the sound of the blast.

When everything was ready, Rollins looked up. "Any last words, Major?"

Rice shook his head and all the men attached their masks.

"For Harry . . . England . . . and Lloyd George!" Rollins shouted. Then he leaned forward on the plunger.

Nothing happened at first. Then a sharp crack exploded and dirt and debris shot out in a symmetrical pattern, covering the sheep and the edge of the cliff in a cloud of dust.

The reverberation ended before the dust had settled. When it did, Rice could see the innermost circle of animals lying dead, and a job thoroughly botched. He was furious. The point was not to blow the animals to smithereens, but to see if an artillery shell could transmit infection. He looked at Rollins through the glass lenses of his protective helmet. It was no good talking now through gas masks, but they all knew the charge had been too heavy. Far too heavy.

Rollins, Pauley, and the soldiers walked tentatively toward the edge of the cliff to investigate the damage. Rice held back, listening to his own respiration inside the mask. It was his job to see that the test took place. It was their job now to follow it through.

Turning down the path, still wearing his mask, Major Rice made his way, painfully aware of each breath he took. The whole experiment might be pointless now, but it was the idea of exposure that troubled him most. Not just exposure to a deadly microbe, but exposure to world opinion. The technical people had had their fun, inept as they might be, and Winston would get his report. The most important objective now was that this whole improbable affair be safely shelved in some dark, secret hole in Whitehall.

The sergeant waited for him at the bottom of the path in his own rubberized suit and mask. He gestured for Rice to follow him up under the cliffs, where a bonfire blazed alongside a wooden shelter. Near it, a metal drum stood atop a wooden derrick and a makeshift shower stall. Rice removed his boots, suit, and mask, and threw each of them into the fire. Then the sergeant hosed him down with blessedly hot water.

Rice was already dressed and waiting when Pauley made it down the hillside. The bacteriologist held his mask under his arm and wore a despondent look.

"Made a mash of it," he said. "He bloody well knows he did."

"What will it mean to the test?" Rice asked.

"I think we're all right. There's a good twenty sheep left to watch. If it worked, we'll begin to see them die within twenty-four hours."

"Then all's well," Rice said, reaching for his pipe. "It's done and that's the end of it, and I suppose Rollins can come down off his mountaintop."

"Not necessarily, Major."

"What do you mean?"

"There's only nine corpses. The sheep nearest the blast—it seems to have been blown over the cliff."

13

"Well. If it isn't Nigel Partridge," the young man said. He stood grinning in the doorway, naked beneath his bathrobe.

Gordon hesitated on the landing and looked into the apartment where a disheveled young woman came out of the bedroom and glided toward the bath. Gordon's hands were in his pockets, his arms cradled against his sides. "We don't look anything alike," he said. "It won't work."

The real Nigel Partridge shook his head and waved him in. "Nonsense," he said, a little drunk. "Come inside and don't be such a booby."

Gordon lowered his head and stepped into the room as Partridge closed the door.

"Really, old man. Our German bureaucrat is a most literal-minded fellow. You show up claiming to be Nigel Partridge and you *are* Nigel Partridge."

Gordon pursed his lips. He was not convinced.

The Englishman gave a petulant sigh, then took on a more serious tone. "Look here. I was never taken before the magistrate. I could be eight feet tall for all he cares. As for the guard detail—they'll show up here at first light, dragging their arses after a night on the razzle. They'll find a Ruhleben detainee just where they left him and be pleased as punch. Male, vaguely Anglo-Saxon. They've had their night on the town. That's all they care about."

Partridge led him into the kitchen, where an oil lamp burned above the table. Gordon took off his hat and unbuttoned his coat.

"You said something about a magistrate," he said.

"A civil suit. You'll appear for me."

"And then what?"

"Nothing. The plaintiff fails to appear, and off you go merrily to Ruhleben."

"How do you know he fails to appear?"

"He's my brother-in-law. Now *do* sit down."

Gordon pulled out a chair and lowered himself into it.

"The wife's family are good for a bit of litigation every other month or so," Partridge went on. "The brother-in-law asks for a postponement the day of the trial. They hold me over in town for twenty-four hours, I have my evening of bliss, then the brother-in-law fails to show again and the suit is dismissed. It's all very creative, don't you think?"

Gordon glanced up at Partridge's slightly blurred face. He was a bank clerk who'd spent the war playing rounders and singing in amateur theatricals. Gordon wondered if he had any idea of the risks they both were taking.

For the next several minutes Frau Partridge drifted in and out of the kitchen in her dressing gown, making herself a cup of tea and straightening up as the two men sat talking. She was still in her teens, but she moved about with a womanly self-assurance as her boy-husband drew Gordon a small map. The Englishman pointed out the location of his billet.

"There's a man name Geary . . . ," Gordon said.

Partridge put up his hands. "I'm not doing this, mate. You are. I don't even want to know about it."

In all they talked for half an hour, Partridge assuring Gordon that he and Hazelwood, the Y.M.C.A. secretary, would be waiting at the camp chapel the next day. Then Partridge stood, gave a thumbs-up sign, and withdrew to the bedroom and his pretty, young wife.

Unable to sleep, lying on the couch and smoking cigarettes long after midnight, Gordon stared up at the faint traces of light brushed against the ceiling. He reached over and pulled the wooden carving out of his kit and held it up, feeling the whittled surfaces that he could not see. Was it Beszenoff or Geary he was after? And why was it like the sword in the stone—everybody taking a crack at offering him leads.

After a while Frau Partridge's high-pitched wail came through the darkness, a string of vowels that carried their energy through the closed door. It was a hell of a choice, Gordon admitted to himself, spending the night in a prison camp so this fellow could spend a few more hours between his wife's soft thighs.

He thought about Katz and Troelstra, the dead men who had made mistakes. And he thought about icy Princess Bucher, and buxom Fräulein Kleist, and this pink little girl getting fucked raw a few feet away from him. He could hear them both panting now, the bedsprings squeaking, her cries getting louder and louder. He blew out a long stream of smoke, put away the carving, and snuffed out his cigarette. Then he pulled the pillow tightly over his head and tried to sleep.

The air was cold when Gordon heard the clattering of horses in the street, a baby crying somewhere in the building. With a shift of his weight he sat up under the one thin blanket, still fully dressed and wearing his overcoat. The morning sun had thrown a long, golden swath across the floor, illuminating his shoes.

He went to the bathroom and washed his face, shaved with Partridge's razor, then sat back down on the couch. He could not shake the chill as he leaned back and had a cigarette.

He had no idea when the guards would be coming, and for once he could not hear anything from the bedroom. Partridge had said "first light" but obviously that was wrong. Gordon got up and went into the kitchen to see what he could find. There was a tin marked "Tee" but it was empty. There was another marked "Kaffee." Gordon pried off the lid and smelled the aroma of ground acorns.

He filled the kettle with water and had set about trying to light the stove when he heard boots in the hall, then pounding on the door. He should have gotten Partridge out of bed. This did not look convincing—the loving wife sleeping in while the husband waits with his grip.

Gordon started hesitantly for the front of the house, trying to come up with the words he would say. But then the bedroom door fell open and there she was, wriggling into her gown like a kitten stretching its back. He felt her heat as she came forward, the fabric clinging to her body. She was half asleep, rubbing her eyes, as she took his arm and led him to the door.

Two ragtag soldiers stood in the hall with their hands in their pockets. They were on furlough themselves in Berlin and did not carry arms.

Young Frau Partridge wrapped herself around Gordon and began to sob. Her skin was flushed red, her hair damp against her face.

"Oh God, I'll miss you," she said. She kissed him as they watched, the smell of sex still in her mouth, and the force of it all hit him like a hammer. He pulled away after a moment, somehow angry. He gave her an awkward hug, then the guards followed him down the three flights of stairs and through the foyer and out onto the street.

Gordon marched along the snow-covered pavement with the guards on either side in their service caps. The morning was cold as they rounded the corner and came to a halt at the tram stop. The blond guard looked at his prisoner. "I guess we all did it right last night," he said.

In the municipal court building Gordon sat for an hour on a hard bench in the corridor waiting for the case to be called. The blond guard sat with his head thrown back and his mouth open, toying with sleep.

Gordon wanted to get on with the business at hand, with figuring out how he was going to get through this without getting shot. Instead he thought about the young girl, the warmth of that kiss, her body damp against her nightgown.

"I saw some real hell at the beginning," the darker guard said, as if someone had asked. He turned his head at each movement in the hall, scanning with impassive eyes. "In Poland. One step up from the colonies. The bastards breed like rabbits, you know. But let me tell you, once you learn to swear in Polish you're fixed for life."

The guard went on to describe his experiences in detail. He had survived on the basis of willpower, he said. He had learned to channel his thoughts to deflect metal objects.

Gordon looked up as the clerk appeared and called out the name of Nigel Partridge.

The suit had been dismissed, the clerk announced. For reasons as yet undetermined, the plaintiff had not shown up.

The road from Spandau Station followed alongside the tracks. Gordon and his two guards walked the icy ruts with the railway stations on the right, and then the high wooden fence of Ruhleben on the left. The grandstands stood empty, like the restaurant and casino below. Wooden barracks were interspersed now between the red brick horse stables. The banners and balloons were gone. The racetrack had been done over with barbed wire.

A sergeant who, if anything, took even less notice than the escorts logged in Nigel Partridge returning from furlough. The guards had already drifted off, leaving Gordon to his own devices inside the gates.

"Grandstand University" was in the far northwest corner of the compound. As Gordon approached the brick horse barn that had been converted into the main lecture hall, he heard the opening strains of a Haydn symphony. He turned back and looked through a crack in the door to see the Ruhleben camp orchestra in the midst of rehearsal.

Ducking his head under a low, sloping porch, he went up the stairway outside the building. There was attic space under the roof where small cubicles had been framed in, one of which was the biological laboratory. Dozens of small potted plants were set against a garret window above a table covered with glass jars containing frogs, fish, and salamanders. There were scales, reagent jars, microscopes—but no students, and no Russian bacteriologist.

Gordon stepped down the hall and glanced into the next cubicle. A young man with spectacles dangling over his nose leaned over a galvanometer.

Standing in the doorway, Gordon said, "Have you seen Beszenoff?"

The young man did not look up. "Never, to my knowledge."

"He teaches bacteriology."

"I'm physics. Try next door."

"No one home."

"Small wonder, is it? Trying to work to the accompaniment of fifty bloody violins! You should see what it does to my instruments. Come here. Feel this vibration."

Gordon declined the offer. "Who's in charge of the lab next door?"

"Ribton-Turner. Plant diseases."

"Do you know where I could find him?"

"Probably at his club!" Then after a moment he added, "And if you have to ask 'which one,' rest assured they'll never let you in!"

Gordon went back outside and walked toward the center of the camp, to the area they called "Bond Street." There were shops of a sort, a newspaper office, a kosher soup kitchen. It all had the look and feel of a small, ramshackle village, only exclusively male.

He passed Partridge's billet, Stable 22, where he would return after dark. He also noted the location of the Y.M.C.A. church, where he was supposed to rendezvous tomorrow. Then he came across the stable named "Palais de Rothschild," where Lucy Geary's uncle was supposed to have lived.

Gordon went inside the billet and called out, "Hello?" There were eight whitewashed horse boxes with no one home.

To Gordon's left on the rough plank wall was a variety of notices of rules and regulations, penalties and commands. On another sheet was a listing of the eight men who shared the billet. With heavy black ink, the name Charles E. Geary had been scratched through.

"Summer House," Ribton-Turner's club, was a made-over shed near the western perimeter of the compound. It was a single room hardly more than fifteen feet in either direction, with an ornate mantel painted on the far wall and a stag's head painted above that. Gordon sat down in a Morris chair next to the English botanist.

As the white-jacketed servant stepped away, Gordon said, "I'm looking for Beszenoff."

Ribton-Turner folded his copy of *Berliner Tagblatt* across his knee. "And why is that?"

"Does it matter?"

"Yes, it does."

"I'm interested in bacteriology."

"Of what sort?"

"Infectious diseases."

Ribton-Turner glanced down and scanned his paper. Then, as if checking his notes, he said, "Canadian, are you?"

"American."

"Then what the devil are you doing in here?"

"Looking for Beszenoff."

Ribton-Turner let the paper drop gently to the floor, then folded his hands across his belly. "The Russians are starving on German rations, so the empress sends them icons."

He brought his eyes back to Gordon, staring with critical detachment. "All I can say is you can't be a German stooge. If you were, you'd know that Beszenoff is gone."

• • •

Roland Ribton-Turner, D.Sc. (Cantab.), had been consulting for the Bavarian government on agricultural blights when the war broke out. He had continued his botanical studies at Ruhleben, using materials from the pond in the center of the racecourse. Professor von Tubeuf of Munich sent him conifers and ferns, and Seward at Cambridge kept him in algae and mosses. He gave a thriving course for prisoners, attended mostly by amateur gardeners.

He sat with Gordon now in a whitewashed horse box with laundry steaming on the radiator. The box and the laundry belonged to Aubrey Welland, one of "The Supermen" who arranged discussion groups on Ibsen, Shaw, and Nietzsche. Before the Russian's last departure, Welland had shared the box with Beszenoff.

"I took him for a Perfect Gentleman," Welland said. "Always. From the start."

"P. G.," Ribton-Turner explained. "Pro-German. They were asked to declare themselves, expecting consideration, I'm sure. A good many technical Englishmen here, of course. One fellow from Heligoland simply never changed his citizenship when Germany acquired the island. As far as I can tell, though, all they received was room at the 'Tee-Haus' and pressure to enlist."

"Beszenoff's Russian," Gordon said.

"True enough." Ribton-Turner averted his eyes, scraping his teeth with the broken point of a pencil. "He's an officer. One of the few genuine prisoners of war held here."

"So why *was* he held here?"

"We had a good many at the start," Welland chimed in. "French too. But they were transferred to Holzminden. Gerard made the case about Russians and typhus."

"But Beszenoff stayed," Gordon said, watching the Englishman massage his gums.

"Right-o. He and the two little boys they captured at Novo-Georgievsk. Messengers. Ten and eleven." Ribton-Turner stopped to examine his pencil, which had a white morsel of food impaled on the tip. "They said Beszenoff was kept on as some sort of guardian angel—Uncle Constantin—but I doubt it. There's plenty of vice in this camp anyway, considering the number of ship's boys. I think Beszenoff simply had friends in high places."

"Beszenoff worked at the Institute," Gordon said.

"On and off still, or so it would appear. I don't think the Germans could decide what they thought about it. For a while it was weekends only out here. Otherwise he lived a normal life in the city."

"How normal can it be when he's a Russian officer? Why would they trust him?"

"No idea."

Gordon sat for a moment looking at his hands, taking in the stable smells of straw and long-departed horses.

"So now you tell me," Ribton-Turner said. "Why *your* sudden interest in our proud Russian ally?"

"Personal matter."

Ribton-Turner wiped the pencil on his sleeve, then tucked it away in his pocket.

"This is a war filled with theater, my dear fellow," he said. He looked back at Welland once more, confidingly. Then his voice took on a sharper edge. "And a kind of inverse skepticism beginning to operate that's really quite extraordinary. We are now conditioned to believe absolutely anything. Anything and everything no matter how ridiculous. Except, of course, official pronouncements."

His eyes were adamant as he stared at Gordon, pausing for a moment's reflection.

"But I for one truly do not believe that prisoners from Ruhleben are being shot full of microbes in some fiendish program of research at the Institute for Infectious Diseases!"

Gordon's skin flushed, his neck and ears burning as he looked up at the rafters.

"I'd rate it right along with the Angel of Mons," Ribton-Turner added. "The crucified Canadian, and all those wheelbarrows full of bayoneted babies."

Gordon had to laugh. "Become one of the classics, has it?" he said mildly.

"Alternative versions," Ribton-Turner went on, "have the prisoners being ground into wurst to feed the starving Hun. Cannibalism or pestilence. We've been referring to 'Prussianism' as 'pestilence' since the beginning, haven't we. And searching desperately for reasons to carry on this war."

Gordon took a deep breath, then sat in silence, thinking it through. Academic skepticism, or mindless gullibility. There could be dozens more equally pointless leads waiting for him by now, all being spun out of the same thin air.

He cast his eyes around the horse barn, feeling angry and foolish. He had been right enough about staff wallah absurdity. But still, Katz and Troelstra were dead. That much was real, like the scars Isidor Katz had put on his forehead.

"So where did all these stories originate?" Gordon said. "Out of thin air? There must have been something. Something to get the ball rolling."

The Englishman shrugged.

"There's a girl who's disappeared," Gordon went on. "A lady's maid. She visited the camp to see her uncle, then came back with some kind of story about strange goings-on with the prisoners. Something unusual about a particular work commando. About one month ago."

"I know it well," Aubrey Welland said dismissively. "And strictly routine. About a dozen men, taken from the lazaret at the Emigrants' Railway Station just outside the gate."

Gordon looked at him. "So what happened to them?"

"Surprisingly enough, the Germans are remarkably terse about their plans."

"It was just an ordinary work commando, then."

"They checked their health and took them away."

"How unusual is that? A health check. Is that why everyone took note of it? There must have been more to it than that."

The Englishmen glanced at each other with raised brows.

Gordon stared back at each of them in turn.

"Neglected that part, did they?" Aubrey Welland said at last. "Idiots! That's the point of the whole bloody story."

"Neglected what?"

Welland rolled his eyes and gazed back condescendingly. "They were all blacks, of course, the ones they took. That's the whole bloody point! Twelve black men. All black as the ace of spades."

14

ndreas Schiller stood over his desk at the Polizei Präsidium and read Dieter Hoffman's autopsy report for the third-depressing time. He still hoped the repetition might coax some new meaning out of the meager selection of words on the page before him. Death through natural causes. An occluded artery to the brain. "Categorically no reason to harbor any suspicion of foul play in the death of Colonel Kraft von Stade."

Schiller dropped the letter onto a pile of reports and walked to the window, looking out at the snow falling in the Alexanderplatz, instantly turning to grime as it hit the pavement.

"Fucked and sewed up," he said. "Fucked and sewed up."

Hoffman's last sentence read like a reprimand to be passed up the chain of command. If you arrange to exhume a corpse as influential as Kraft von Stade's, you also arrange to find something incriminating.

Schiller went back to his desk and sat down, propped his feet up on the corner, and stared into the two-dimensional yet visionary eyes of the All Highest. It was a full-color poster he was looking at, the Kaiser standing at the helm of a ship superimposed on a map of Germany. "Unsere Zukunft liegt auf dem Wasser," the caption read, only "auf" had been scratched out and replaced with "unter." Our future lies *under* the water.

Riveted by the Kaiser's penetrating stare, the detective let his mind drift for a while, back to the vacant gaze of the instrument maker Isidor Katz. He tried to imagine the man's last moments, wondering about the exact sequence of events that day at the zoo. Did they mutilate him first to let him share in the experience, or did they do it after they slit his throat, a simple statement of revenge?

Then Schiller's anger rose up as he began to visualize the contrasting circumstances surrounding von Stade's stiff prick. The most a man can hope for in life is to die quietly in his bed. This aristocrat dies in bed between a pair of fresh young thighs. Justice was a naive expectation, but still the concept of preferential treatment even in death offended Schiller to the marrow. In fact he refused to accept it. The events surrounding the colonel's death could not have been as simple as they appeared.

"Kadereit, cigars! Kadereit, cigars!"

Detective Gottschalk made the same announcement every time Axel Kadereit entered the building. Schiller stood up and watched his partner stroll across the room, slowly unbuttoning his coat.

"Nothing on the mistress," the young man said, shaking the wet snow off onto the floor. Kadereit was like a child that way. He was like a child in most ways. He pushed back his hat and fell into a wooden chair.

Schiller put his hands in his pockets and shrugged, then turned back toward the clouded window.

It was a marvelous institution, the Berlin police department, a monument to humanity's struggle against the forces of chaos. Their handbook had two hundred pages covering protocol between officers, regulations governing the color of autos, the length of hatpins, the methods of purchasing fish and fowl. The all-pervasive Police Presidency of Berlin had laws against falling asleep in restaurants, laws against delivery boys coasting on handcarts, laws against touching a shad to see if it has roe. The police regulated every aspect of German life. The only thing they could not do was catch criminals.

"You know what you get if you dig down deep enough?" Kadereit said, nodding toward the poster. "Pure white sand. Beach sand. Berlin used to sit on the bottom of the ocean. Not everyone knows that."

"Good," Schiller said, picking up the autopsy report on the colonel and handing it to his partner. "We can wait for the tide to come back in."

Kadereit rubbed the pink indention left along his hairline by the sweatband of his hat, moving his lips almost imperceptibly as he read. "Ah hah. 'Nasal congestion.' A finding like that could blow this wide open, Andreas."

Schiller nodded. "The power of forensic science."

Then he reached into his pockets, rattling the few pfennigs he had to his name. "I stick my neck out to have Hoffman tell me that von Stade died with a cold in his nose."

Kadereit glanced back around at Gottschalk, now going out the door, then fanned the air with the report. "So?" he said. "A miscalculation."

"Of epic proportions, all things considered."

"Let me see." Kadereit dropped the paper onto the desk, then held up his fingers, counting off Schiller's sins in turn. "You have outraged the widow of a member of the General Staff. You have impugned the character of this same, late high official. You have wasted a certain amount of departmental resources, pissed off our chief pathologist . . . Anything else?"

"I think you have it all."

"You're lucky, Andreas. If it were me, I'd be shoveling shit on the Eastern front. Within three weeks."

"What makes you think I'm immune?"

"They can't draft you. You're half dead already, remember?"

Schiller sat on the edge of the desk and leaned against his typewriter. A twenty-year-old Mignon, it was a masterpiece of craftsmanship for which you cranked the ribbon forward manually after hitting each key. This is what he should worry about on the job—losing his perks. Nasal congestion, indeed.

Gazing just beyond Kadereit's head, Schiller voiced the moral proposition that had been plaguing him for days. "Why should an evil man die in the arms of a beautiful woman?"

"How do you know she's beautiful, Andreas?"

"Because otherwise he's just dead and my whole theory is shit."

Kadereit laughed, then ran his fingers through his hair, which was still matted together with sweat. The heavy, wide-brimmed hat was an affectation to make him look older. Instead, it made him look like a boy in a big hat.

"I'll tell you this," he said. "It is amazing what power does to protect one's character, even beyond the grave. Nothing but sealed lips. But it worries me, Andreas. At his level the black market is none of our business. We're supposed to look the other way. Perhaps we should take the hint and leave it alone."

"No." Schiller drew up short and put his hand to his shoulder, letting the arm hang across his chest. "The country starves while the von Stades make themselves rich. I can't leave it at that. We go back to where we were before he was killed. The Café Dalles. The Ka ka Du. And this American, Eli Gordon." He looked at his partner. "Put a man on him around the clock."

Kadereit nodded and placed his hat back on his head. "And what about you, my friend?"

"I'm going to do what we always do when the doctor gives us bad news."

"What's that?"

"I'm going to talk to another doctor."

Andreas Schiller shuffled alongside the Tiergarten, buffeted by the wind. He hid his hands in his pockets, the long strands of flaxen hair coiling through his fingers like beads as he followed the row of fashionable town houses across from the park, cursing all the British sailors in all the northern waters who were keeping him in this threadbare coat. He wished them persistent gales and icy rain. He hoped they froze their English asses off.

The brass plaque beside the door matched the number he was looking for. He dropped his cigar into the frozen sewer grate and began climbing the steps.

It was called "the Jewish science" by its detractors, and Schiller wondered how much his Jewish half had to do with his interest in this new and peculiar discipline. The fact was he needed results, and his frustration was such that he would turn to "the Italian science" or "the Polish science" just as readily.

The receptionist on the second landing was Chinese, a boy of twenty or so wearing an elegant striped suit and wing collar. His heavily lacquered hair was parted in the center, his head bisected by a precise white line from front to back.

"May I help you?"

"I am Criminal Detective Schiller to see Dr. Hirschfield."

The boy raised a ribboned pince-nez to the bridge of his nose but never looked up. "Please be seated," he said. Then, inadequately supported, the pince-nez slid off his face. The boy reached down discreetly and slipped it into his pocket.

Schiller lowered himself onto a leather couch and turned to look at the row of framed prints on the wall behind him. "Die Hauptsache." A pen-and-ink drawing of a peasant woman lifting her skirts above a shaggy pudendum. "Stehaufmannchen." A penis erectus balanced on its testicles before an admiring group of females.

Schiller barely had time to react before he was addressed from the doorway.

"Not shocked, I hope, Detective Schiller."

Schiller turned to look at a short, owl-eyed man in a suit of heavy tweed. "No," he said. "Just like at home."

The man threw back his head and barked like a seal.

"Come in, come in." He stopped to compose himself. "I am Hirschfield."

Schiller entered a dimly lit office, where the doctor took his seat behind a small black desk. He offered the detective a large black chair with clawed feet and arms and carved dragons resting atop the straight back. It was incredibly uncomfortable.

"You are seeking my advice in a professional rather than a personal matter, I take it," the doctor began.

Schiller was distracted, absorbing the impact of the room. A lacquered screen stood at the window, blocking the expensive view of the park below. Beside it was a glass case filled with jade carvings. Here and there were helmets, swords, tapestries, and an assortment of gongs.

"Yes," he said at last. He reached into his pocket and withdrew the coil of hair, placing it on the desk in front of the famed alienist. "I want to find a certain woman. A woman who left this hair on a certain pillow beside a certain . . . conveniently dead man."

Hirschfield smiled. "I am a scientist, you know. Not a sorcerer."

"I understand. But certainly the time has come for your science to play a role in criminal detection."

Hirschfield picked up the hair and held it between his plump, white hands. His eyes sparkled.

"Hair, you know, Detective Schiller, is the most conspicuous of female sexual displays. Softness and warmth, the sensuous touch, the bristling response to stimulation."

The doctor lifted the coil and brushed it against his cheek. "Why do you say 'conveniently' dead?"

"Because I assume the death served her purposes. Other facts would point to this."

"Then the man was murdered, you mean to say."

"The man was dead. There was no immediate evidence of murder."

Hirschfield touched the hair to his lips and rubbed it back and forth, closing his eyes. "But this woman was with him at the . . . climactic moment?"

Schiller nodded, then took a deep breath, as Hirschfield smiled and rose from his chair. The doctor went to a library table against the wall and, a moment later, returned with a sheaf of papers six inches thick, held together with string between two heavy pasteboard binders. Still smiling, he handed the tome to Schiller, then pulled over a chair and sat down.

"Open. Read," he said. His knee pressed against the detective's thigh.

A title page in ornate script announced:

ENCYCLOPEDIA OF SEX
MAGNUS HIRSCHFIELD, M.D., PH.D.
FOUNDING MEMBER
OF THE BERLIN PSYCHOANALYTIC
SOCIETY
Editor, *The Journal for Sexual Knowledge*

Schiller looked over at Hirschfield's languorous expression. Then he turned the first page.

The text was scant, interspersed among numerous illustrations— photographs approximating the quality of the criminal identification pictures they took at the Alexanderplatz. There were whores displaying breasts and buttocks. There were tongues pressed against teeth, and rapists in their cells. A section of clinical photos showed the ravages of venereal disease on genitalia. Castrati showed their scars, hermaphrodites showed their ambiguity.

Schiller continued to browse, but he really did not see the point of this, and he had perhaps four hundred pages more to go.

He glanced up at Hirschfield. "This woman I am looking for . . ."

"Murder, Detective Schiller, is a fundamentally masculine act. It's phallic. The plunge, you see, seeking blood. For a woman to kill requires confusion of sexual identity. She has lost touch with her maternal instinct. She might be barren . . . undoubtedly she is promiscuous because her sexuality is the weapon of choice to entrap her victims."

"Again, Doctor, there was no evidence of murder in the strict sense."

"Ah yes. I see." For a moment Hirschfield stared up at the ceiling.

"This is an area in which our records are incomplete," Schiller said.

"Ah, but in the annals of love . . ." Hirschfield's eyes gleamed even brighter.

"I must ask you if such a method of killing . . . with kindness, you might say . . . is within the capability of a normal woman? Or should I say an ordinary woman."

"How old a man was the victim?"

"Fifty-five."

"It is not uncommon for such a man to die in the act."

"Yes," Schiller said, nodding assuredly. "A random occurrence. But to arrange such a death. To induce it at will. To guarantee it, in effect. Is this possible? Are there techniques? And if so, techniques known to what sort of woman?"

"Yes, yes. A man of this age. A sufficient level of excitement, sustained over a sufficient period of time, a virtual guarantee. A woman practicing fellatio—"

"Spelling please." Schiller had begun to take notes.

"F-e-l-l-a-t-i-o."

"This is the technique of killing?"

Hirschfield smiled. "It is a technique of oral sex."

For the moment Schiller's hands were still. He did not know what to write.

"Taking the erect penis into the mouth," Hirschfield explained. "Stimulation with the lips and tongue."

Schiller stared for a moment, his faced flushed crimson. Then he scribbled busily on his pad. "Such a technique . . ."

"A woman sufficiently aggressive and adept could force his arousal repeatedly. His heart, overstimulated, and without intermittent rest, would betray its normal rhythm. The result—sudden death."

"This is incredible."

"No," Hirschfield assured him. "It is quite real."

Schiller tapped his pencil against the pad. "I am fascinated by the possibility, Dr. Hirschfield, but perhaps something more . . ."

"There are, of course, certain toys. Sensual playthings of one sort and another."

"I am not experienced in these matters."

"Scent. Lotions. Chemical stimulants. Amyl-nitrite, for instance. It can be inhaled to enhance and prolong sexual excitement. Perhaps the stimulation was excessive. Perhaps . . ."

"Perhaps another chemical was substituted."

Hirschfield's face brightened with recognition. "Yes. Well, yes," he said. "That's a possibility."

"What would you recommend to such a killer?"

"Oh, a full menu of chemical agents. Carbon tetrachloride . . . hydrogen sulfide . . . Then there's potassium cyanide. That would do nicely. It's deadly, and, of course, it leaves no trace."

"No trace at all? That's too convenient."

"Well, nothing obvious. Nothing definitive. Nothing more serious than, say, ordinary nasal congestion. Like having a cold."

Schiller closed his notebook, then returned both pad and pencil to his pocket.

15

Fiercely hung over in the late afternoon, Cletus Brown lounged in a blue kimono on a satin sofa, pinching the bridge of his nose. He wore a hairnet over his thick pomade. His delicate fingers spread across his face like the darkened fronds of some tropical plant, shielding his eyes from the last light of day and, possibly, from his decor.

Bed sheets in bright colors hung from an old gasolier in the center of the room, radiating across the ceiling like the arms of a pinwheel. A hammock hung in one corner, a huge wooden parasol fanned out across another as if to shade the clutter of white wicker furniture and potted palms.

"It's sadism to remind me of that whole experience," he said. "I've never been imprisoned before. I am not the criminal type."

Brown reached for his cup of tea and lifted it to his face, breathing in the steam as if it might soothe some inner pain.

Eli Gordon leaned forward in his chair and prodded gently.

"The Englishmen at Ruhleben," he said. "They told me you were taken to the Emigrants' Railway Station with a group of prisoners. They said you were all examined at some sort of lazaret. Was it a Russian who examined you? Do you remember? A man named Beszenoff?"

"Oh please." Suddenly Brown was furious. He put his cup down on the end table, spilling half his tea into the saucer. He took a deep breath to compose himself, then after a moment he looked squarely at Gordon.

"They were Guinea men, the ones they took. From Dahomey. Servants and the like. That's what they wanted."

"For what? What did they want them for?"

Brown paused again, to pick vindictively at a loose thread on his satin lapel, his fingers like delicate instruments. When he spoke again he said, "I *don't* know. They wouldn't take me. I can only suppose she didn't want my blood on her hands."

"She? Who?"

Brown looked away, rolled his eyes, and said, "The woman doing the examinations. It wasn't any *Beat-it-off*, it was a woman. And I knew her, you hear what I'm saying?"

For a moment then Brown concentrated on the movement in the next room, the sound of furniture being moved across the floor. Then he turned back to Gordon.

"The rest of them marched off to Berlin as near as I can tell. She sent me on to Weiler's, a sanatorium in Charlottenburg which I shall not recommend. They use it for the prisoner exchange. Men too old, unfit for service. They actually had the balls to give me another examination—charged me twelve marks for it, the shits— then shipped me off to Amsterdam! But all I did was come right back. This is my home, über alles. War or no war."

Gordon glanced through the doorway and saw Brown's young, blond companion setting up a puppet theater.

After a moment Gordon said, "You're telling me it was a woman?"

"Yeh, you know . . . tits, ass?" He breathed deeply and his nostrils widened. "She's quite beautiful, actually. But all I know is she was running the show. Selecting the prisoners . . . whatever came next. She saw me and she didn't want the complications. I'm not at all sure I *want* to know about any of that."

"You said you knew her. How'd you know her?"

"A jazz place I used to frequent . . . for an occasional taste of the low-life."

"Now wait . . . She's not Russian. She's German?"

"She's American, honey. The girl next door."

Gordon paused, and for a while he looked blankly into Brown's dark face. Once again incredulity was swerving over the edge.

After a few moments Gordon said, "Did anyone else go to Weiler's besides you?"

"One pudgy Englishman, as I recall."

"You remember his name?"

"Get serious, darlin'."

"How about Charles Geary?"

Brown cocked his head. "I am *leary* of Mr. *Geary*. You know, I think you're right."

He tapped his lower lip, then looked at Gordon with huge, watery eyes. "I did finally get my American passport. I'm an American for sweet Jesus' sake. They had me down as Jamaican. My mother was Jamaican, but I was born in New Orleans. The white fuckers just wouldn't believe me."

"Cletus! What do you think?" The young man in the dining room was ready now. You could see his head sticking up from behind the puppet theater, then his naked abdomen when he pulled back the curtains. He wore a tiny blond wig on the head of his penis, and hanging below, a dirndl for a miniature milkmaid. He had tied a string around himself and now he jiggled it as he sang.

Glühwurmchen, Glühwurmchen, flimmere, flimmere
Glühwurmchen, Glühwurmchen, schimmere, schimmere.

Brown shrieked with joy and clapped his hands. "Skiddy you filthy boy I love it! Love it!"

"Tell me her name," Gordon said.

Brown glared back, and then his smile faded to radiant hostility. "We never really got that far. Now anything else you want to know, honeylamb, I suggest you ask her. I'm sure you'd have lots in common."

"How am I supposed to find her? You said a jazz club."

"Onkel Tom's Hütte, if they haven't closed it down. She used to be quite a regular feature."

"She did the examinations. So you're saying she's a doctor?"

"Or damn peculiar."

"How would I recognize her?"

"Why, just follow your heart."

"I need a description!"

Brown sighed dismissively. "Look at her eyes, Doctor. Look at her fingertips. If there's any doubt in your mind, you've got yourself the wrong girl."

The snow reflected the lights from apartment windows as Gordon stepped through the stone archway back into the courtyard. The four walls rose up around him, leaning slightly inward against a wooden girder up above. Beside the outdoor privy, a handcart stood idle and full of snow. A sign posted the hours during which tenants could lawfully beat their rugs.

The Russian seemed like a dead end. And Charles Geary was out of the picture too, but at least Gordon had something modestly specific now. An outline to work from. A commando *had* been taken from Ruhleben. A labor detail that required examination by a doctor, who was a woman, and an American. The Angel of Mons, he wondered, or the bayoneted babies? It all seemed to phase in and out of credibility each step of the way, and each time he ran it through in his mind. Was it enough to believe in cause and effect, or did causality also have to be rational?

The evening was cold and clear as he stepped out onto the street. He noticed two planets hovering above the skyline like small silver moons. Then he lowered his eyes and saw the Mercedes waiting at the curb, the engine running.

A young man opened the door and stepped down. Thin and fair-haired, he had the translucent beauty of a consumptive.

"Get in," the young man said.

Gordon looked through the window and saw Major Baron von den Benken, Head of the Inspection of Prisoners of War, smoking distractedly as he gazed in the opposite direction. The boy pulled back his coat to show the pistol protruding from his belt. "Get in," he repeated.

Gordon appraised the cold smile, the rising note of menace in the voice. He lowered his head and got into the car.

They pulled away from the curb and took Friedrichstrasse, turning south toward the Belle-Alliance-Platz. The angular man who sat beside the driver glanced back once with the metallic grin of army dentures.

The car was stifling, and outside the iron wheels ground into the pavement. Gordon breathed once and said, "Do you mind if I get a cigarette?"

No one acknowledged the remark, so after a moment he reached into his pockets.

They rode south under the elevated tracks and past the Hallesches Gate, then crossed the Landwehr Canal with its chestnut trees and willows stripped bare. The streets were dark, and except for the sound of the wheels there was silence. It was as if von den Benken could not bring himself to look Gordon in the face. He maintained the stern and purposeful distance of a disappointed father.

They passed Blucher Platz and then the cemeteries. Gordon could see the Kreuzberg rising up in front of them as he turned toward von den Benken in the seat and said, "I've been meaning to call you, Major. You should have rung me at the embassy."

Von den Benken leaned forward to mash out his cigar. He was having none of Gordon's feigned nonchalance. "Let me borrow your match, Doctor."

Gordon handed him the trench lighter and von den Benken snapped up an inch of flame. He lit a cigarette, then clenched the lighter in his fist, letting it drop to his knee.

"Chinese Gordon," the baron said.

A few moments passed with nothing but the sound of the wheels. Then the baron said, "I thought we'd agreed you'd be a good boy, Doctor. I thought we'd agreed you'd look where I pointed."

"I guess I lost my way," Gordon said.

"Yes. Rewriting the rules. Now, you know, some of my fellow officers seem to think you're more than a meddlesome inspector of camps. And Ruhleben, for the sake of God. Why Ruhleben? The thorn in my side. Everyone hatching plots, promoting insurrection. Very poor taste, Doctor, to encourage such reckless speculation. Or to appear to be taken in by it. So tell me now . . . what was the particular delusion that drew you there?"

"Just thought I'd see one for myself."

" 'From Missouri.' That's the expression, not true?"

"Yeh. That's it."

" 'From Missouri,' " von den Benken said, nodding. "Chinese Gordon from Missouri." He stopped to inhale on his cigarette, then blew the smoke into the ceiling. "Tell me the truth, Doctor. Why are you mucking around in Berlin?"

"They described my purpose as 'humanitarian' on the visa."

"Ah, yes. Working with the wounded in France. Quite the humanitarian. And now you've come here to take a more active role. So what is it, Doctor? Guilt? They say that happens, sometimes. Sometimes you see all that death and then you become guilty because you're not dead. It must be very difficult. How ever can a man like you justify his own good fortune? You're not even injured. The whole war is going by and not even a scratch."

He paused for another long drag on his cigarette, the orange glow reflecting in his face. Then he nodded toward the iron obelisk atop the hill.

"Have you ever visited the monument, Doctor?"

"No." Gordon felt his mouth now very dry as he spoke.

"A lovely view of the city. It was always better on Sundays, though, when the air was less filled with smoke. This is far enough," he called out.

The car swerved to the side of the road and came to a stop.

They were on the other side of the park now, the vast expanse of the Tempelhofer parade grounds lying under the snow before them.

The blond boy to Gordon's left opened the door and stepped out onto the macadam.

"Get out," the major said.

Gordon felt light-headed as he rose from the car. He had taken it one step at a time, but now it was too late for options. There was nothing he could do.

He stood vulnerable just beyond the arc of the open door, the boy holding it from the other side. The air was cold and Gordon took it in rapid, shallow breaths, waiting. He could see the lights of the city in the distance as he looked up, the night sky diffuse with their reflection. The three other men remained in the car.

"Your lighter," the major said, holding it up.

Gordon reached in through the open door and an instant later his hand no longer felt like a part of his body. The pain bypassed his fingers as it raced through his stomach. A feeling like nausea followed the nerves up the brain stem to fill his skull. He tossed back his head and almost laughed in astonishment. Then his knees went weak, and all the pain came racing back into the narrow space of four fingers.

The boy leaned against the metal, sending a second surge of pain. "There, there," he whispered. "Feel better now?" Then he opened the door to let Gordon retrieve his crushed hand.

The lighter fell to the roadway as Gordon knelt on the pavement. The rear wheels of the Mercedes rolled past and filled his lungs with exhaust. He looked up to see the taillights of the baron's car recede into the distance. Then behind him he heard another vehicle, its headlights darkened, pull slowly away from the curb, turn around in the roadway, and head back toward Berlin.

ANDREAS Schiller's apartment was on the fifth floor of a five-story building near Schlesischer Bahnhof. He climbed the stairs slowly and methodically, taking in the familiar smells, unbuttoning an additional layer of clothing as he reached each level. He was sure the exercise was good for him, and living on the top floor had other advantages. Fuel was scarce, but heat invariably rises.

He had done his job well today with Hirschfield. He had made the connections and found the murder, even if he had yet to find the murderer. But that would come. It was not necessary to be brilliant and daring in police work, merely persistent, and in this matter, at least, Schiller had the patience of Job. He would find the woman and he would find the connection between the deaths of Isidor Katz and Colonel Kraft von Stade. If that connection was Eli Gordon, Kadereit would know it soon.

The detective turned the key in the lock, swung open the apartment door, and saw his son lying spread-eagled on the floor. His two daughters knelt on either side of him, their hands to their heads, shrieking.

"What's happened!" Schiller screamed out.

The children all bolted upright—including the boy. He wore a helmet made of newspaper, a wooden sword in his hand. "Playing fallen warrior, Papa. That's all." The boy was frightened too, struggling to catch his breath.

Schiller closed the door behind himself and removed his hat. "Jesus in heaven, you scared me."

The children glanced at each other sheepishly, fear and surprise giving way to pride in performance.

"Where is your mother?" Schiller asked. He was stalling to regain his composure.

"In the kitchen."

He nodded as he opened the closet door. It had been a stupid question.

Hanging up his heavy coat, then his suit jacket as well, Schiller replaced them with a bulky sweater. The children, stiff as new recruits, were still standing when he turned back around.

"Go on. Play your game."

"I'm tired of it," Rudy said. "Will you read to us?"

"In a minute. Give me time."

The two girls fell to playing with a puzzle on the floor, but the young boy looked up at his father. His face was gaunt. A boy's face changes naturally enough, Schiller thought, losing the baby fat, taking on a more sinewy look. But he worried nonetheless. Children needed food.

"So what did you do today?" Schiller asked his son.

"We shoveled, some. We cleared Köpenickerstrasse. Then we collected. I found a tire and twenty meters of string."

"But did you study! Did you learn anything today?"

"Some, Papa. We studied in the morning."

Schiller looked deeper into the boy's face. Rudy was bright enough for the Gymnasium, but he would need a scholarship. And to earn that he would have to learn more than shoveling snow in the Grundschule. Still, Schiller knew he should not complain. Boys not five years older were being shipped off to the trenches.

A corridor separated the living room from the rest of the apartment, a passage like a tunnel with one window overlooking the snow-filled courtyard. On holidays it became the dining room, filled with candles. On an ordinary day it was so dark the children were afraid to pass through it alone.

Schiller stopped just outside the kitchen door. He could hear his wife crying, see her sobbing as she stood by the stove. He brushed against the Advent calendar still pinned to the wall and knocked it off. The cardboard hit the floor and Magda turned with a fright as Schiller stooped over to pick it up.

"Sorry. I didn't mean to scare you."

"Oh fine, fine," she said. She grabbed a wooden spoon and jammed it into the soup pot. For a moment Schiller stood in place, not knowing what to say.

"So," she offered, without turning around. "How was the pursuit of Herr Raffke and Frau Raffke today?"

"We have them on the run."

Magda continued stirring, each stroke more forceful than the one before. Schiller looked at the strands of hair that had fallen from her braid and brushed against her shoulder, remembering that she too had once worn her hair long like von Stade's mistress. She too had played the role of "woman of mystery," long before her body had become as familiar to him as his own. The years and the children had added to her figure, but now she too was growing thin.

Schiller's eye wandered down to the pamphlet open on the table. "War Cookbook," it said. The shape of things to come.

Beer Soup	Potato and Cabbage Pudding
2 glasses beer, boil	1 hd cabbage boiled 30 min
1 well-beaten egg	6 sliced potatoes
2 tbs sugar	boil all together until soft
flour to thicken	1 tbs lard
boil and serve hot	heat, add flour to thicken

Magda flipped the spoon down into the soup, splashing it across the stovetop. "Damned again, Andreas. Damned again." She fell back from the stove and dropped into a chair.

"Do you want to know how I spent the day? The 'butter polonaise'? I was at Carisch at five this morning. I stood in line at Kaiser Kaffee and at Gerold. I have been going from shop to shop until my feet are frozen and this is what I have to show for it." She reached into her basket on the table. "Turnips! Goddamned turnips!" She grabbed a handful and threw them into the wall. Then she shoved the basket without conviction and let them roll onto the floor.

Schiller reached out and tried to take her hand but she pulled away.

"It's ridiculous! All day you're out trying to break up the black market and I'm out bribing the grocer, making deals with the shoemaker for shoes the children will outgrow before they can ever be delivered. We've got to get away from this, Andreas. We've got to get away!"

His face showed no signs of emotion. The doctors would call it a "Parkinsonian affect," but that was only a convenient label. In fact he had nothing to offer his wife but platitudes, which he refused to utter. They had to stay in Berlin. They had nowhere else to go. He could not know how much longer he would be able to work and they would need the municipal pension.

Schiller pulled his chair closer to his wife and put his arm around her shoulders. Her nose was luminously red, her cheeks wet. She tried to dry her eyes on the back of her hands.

"Did Rudy tell you how he shoveled Köpenickerstrasse?"

"Yes. He was very proud."

"They're taking the disabled now for service, Andreas."

"Magda . . ." He drew his wife close. "It will be all right. It has to end soon."

"Will it, Andreas? Will it?"

He looked at her, then lowered his eyes. "War is the highest summit of human achievement," General von Seeckt had said. "It is the natural, the final stage in the historical development of humanity."

Schiller's gaze came to rest on the two oil lamps on the table. The A.E.G. rotated electricity now among the neighborhoods before shutting off the whole city at ten.

"I should take a lamp to the children," he said. "Just in case."

She pulled away from him, and Schiller felt the twinge of guilt. It was always easier to be a father than a husband in times like these.

He lit the lamp and held it in front of him as he walked back toward the front of the apartment. The children were now sprawled on the floor, each with a volume of Brehm's *Naturbuch*. Ilse, the youngest, whispered as she turned the pages, half singing a song from the playground in her faint, distracted voice. "Now all the dogs and pussycats will never more be seen . . . they've all been ground to sausage meat in the Dunderbach machine."

Rudy looked up. "Papa! Will you read to us now?"

Schiller set the lamp on the table beside his chair. "No. No. We'll eat soon."

"A story?"

Schiller sat down in a massive, overstuffed chair, too distracted to really be with them. He hated that playground song. Children should have pets to cuddle, not to eat. He waited and tried to clear his mind. By the same token, it was no good for children to see their father constantly grim-faced.

At last he forced a smile, leaned back, and said, "Once upon a time . . ."

The children gave a cheer and scurried closer.

". . . there was a peasant family from Schleswig-Holstein, where all the children and even the grown-ups have crooked mouths."

His own children were grinning their gap-toothed grins and he looked at them. Absorbing their warmth, he went on.

"One night it was time to blow out the candle, so the father stood and 'phew'—he puffed and puffed but of course his mouth twisted to the left so he could not blow the candle out. So then the mother tried. 'Phew'—like so, but her mouth twisted to the right and so of course she could not blow the candle out either. Next the little boy tried—his mouth twisted upward. No luck at all. The little girl tried—her mouth twisted downward. No luck again! So! They called in the pretty maid from Copenhagen, who had a perfect mouth, and she put the candle out with her shoe."

He paused, looking into each rapt young face in turn. "Now! Off you go. It's time for dinner."

They left and he felt the pang. He wanted to see them grow up. That was all.

ONKEL Tom's Hütte was just off the Kurfürstendamm, on the ground floor of a creamery that had been transformed by changing tastes. The brick walls were painted with bright murals of Negro mammies and banjo-strumming slaves. The smooth concrete was now a dance floor where listless couples stumbled through a smoky haze, and behind them, a monocled piano player banged out his own Teutonic ragtime, the only man other than Eli Gordon wearing white tie and tails.

Gordon had found a cab to take him back from the hospital to his hotel, then a chambermaid to help him dress. He was supposed to be at the Adlon tonight, at a banquet given by the American Association for Commerce and Trade for their German customers. But von den Benken had stepped up the pace. Von den Benken had brought him closer to the heart of the matter.

Gordon kept his crushed hand elevated on the bar as he waited for the man to bring his beer. Two women danced with their German shepherds, the dogs strutting stiffly on hind legs, their forepaws on their partner's shoulders. Gordon stared blankly for a while and then closed his eyes. The medical student at the Charité had put splints on the three broken fingers but had not been able to do anything for the pain. It was a fully orchestrated throbbing now—a real challenge.

The woman sat in the last booth in the corner, her head barely visible over the wooden partition. Her long blond hair was pulled back and gathered in a loose braid that dangled over one shoulder, her skin smooth and drawn tightly across her cheekbones. Gordon waited, staring until she looked up. Her brown eyes held him in focus for what seemed like a full minute, but for all he could tell she was looking at the wall.

He picked up his glass with his left hand and edged down the bar until at last he could get a better look at her. It was not a face you would easily mistake—Cletus Brown had been right about that. And it was not the hair or the bone structure or the skin. It was the go-to-hell look of the survivor you could see in those eyes.

She sat across from an old man who gripped his drink with both hands as if afraid someone was going to take it from him. The old man stared at the table, taking no notice of the woman or anyone else, and they did not speak to each other. She gazed just beyond her companion's head, occasionally lifting her drink to her lips.

Gordon got up, a little unsteady with the pain, and walked to the booth. Then he stood for a moment watching her, wondering.

"Your friend seems to have fallen asleep," he said.

She glanced up vaguely, taking in one more predictable irritation. Then her gaze narrowed and at last focused on him. In that instant it was as if she knew exactly who he was and exactly why he'd come.

She turned back to her drink. "You could be arrested for speaking English," she told him. "Don't you know that?"

"In this place?"

"Yes."

"They told me just being here was enough."

She shrugged distractedly, then glanced at his bandaged hand. Both statements were true.

He watched for another moment as she pushed back an errant strand of hair. Her skin was golden, her body slender and graceful but not frail. She seemed totally self-contained and self-defined, wearing a man's white shirt that was frayed and yellowed in the front.

Gordon stared into her eyes, then turned away and said, "I'd like to sit down."

"Why?"

"I think we need to talk."

She shook her head. "That's a bad idea."

Gordon waited, glancing at the man seated motionless across the table, then back at her. "He keeps away men like me?"

"Usually."

"Let me buy you a drink."

"I have a drink."

"Then let's say I'm a fellow countryman and I'm far from home."

She shook her head. "I'm German. And you are very American."

"I heard you were from the States."

"Oh? Who told you that?" She took a cigarette from the box on the table and put it between her lips.

"Some fellow at the bar. Women in bars cause talk, you know." Gordon held out his lighter, trying to steady the tremor in his hand. In the glow of the flame he could see the stains on her fingertips now—a dark blue-black.

"You assume women in bars are whores?" she said.

"Yes. Sometimes. But I hear you're a doctor."

"No. You see now? You've mistaken me for somebody else."

Gordon reached down and balanced himself against the tabletop with the extended fingers of his left hand. "So what is it you do, then?"

"I'm a whore."

He watched her for a moment. The strong wide mouth, the arched brows that intensified the eyes. "Whores will do anything for a price," he said. "Even talk to me."

She looked up, assessing him, assessing his determination. After a moment she said, "You look pale. So sit down. Sit down while you can."

"That's whiskey?"

She drained the glass and handed it to him. "With a little water."

Gordon made his way slowly back to the bar, edging toward the center, where the bartender rinsed glasses in a tub of gray suds. He tapped the empties on the zinc surface to get the man's attention, then glanced back toward the corner where her blond hair shone above the wooden booth.

She was on the edge or slightly over, a place he knew well. Maybe she was also "tangled up in barbarism," but at the moment he didn't really care. He had paid the price of admission. He could not quite remember how he had come to this point, but it no longer mattered to him. He would ride it through. Tonight. Right now.

The bartender set the wet glasses upside down on a cloth to drain and Gordon said, "One beer, one whiskey."

The bartender nodded, then went to work with the tap, drawing the beer slowly into a glass.

The rush of anticipation overcame the pain now. Gordon had at last cut loose his moorings and was in the stream. It pushed him toward whatever was hidden in those eyes, and he was going with it, eagerly.

Then he felt someone brush against the bar beside him, and instinctively he drew up his hand to protect it.

"A two-fisted drinker, I see."

Gordon glanced over to find Erskine Fisk standing at his elbow, his lips pulled back to form an unpleasant smile. Then a pulse of anger rushed through Gordon's body, and with it all the pain. He had gone to great lengths to make sure he was not followed here. He had milled around in the Beethoven Room with the other guests. He had doubled back and switched cabs on his way across town. He had done everything he could. But Ostriker's men, Schiller's men—the possibilities were endless. He swallowed his exasperation and reached for his cigarettes and offered one to Fisk.

The dentist waved the smokes away. "What happened to your hand?"

"Accident getting out of a taxi," Gordon said.

"Umm. Pity."

Then the two men stood awkwardly side by side.

Nothing was a coincidence in Berlin. The meeting in the Adlon dining room. Billy de Beauford that very first night at the bar. But why Fisk? Why now?

"Took me years to sink this low," the dentist said. "You've found it right off. Onkel Tom's hasn't been Baedekered, God forbid?"

Gordon shook his head as he lit up with exaggerated calm and exhaled the first puff. "Heard about it someplace," he said. "Ragtime. That's hard to find in Germany."

Fisk looked just past his head, scanning the room behind him.

"Looking for someone?" Gordon asked.

Fisk's gaze drifted back toward the corner. "Yes. Or was. Appears not to have shown up."

Gordon allowed himself to glance over his shoulder, where the old man was now sitting alone with his drink. The blond woman was gone. He had let her slip away.

Gordon pinched his cigarette between his thumb and forefinger, then drew on it hard, making the burning end glow brightly against his face.

After a moment he slid the glass toward the dentist, spilling half of it. "Here," he said. "I don't think I can handle this much excitement in a single evening."

"Thank you. Are you sure it wasn't meant for someone else?"

"No. No such luck," Gordon said.

The dentist smiled, then raised the dripping glass and took a sip, after which he reached up and touched his mouth with the back of his hand.

"A fellow I know has the two most exquisite daughters," Fisk said. "Half woman, half child really. One dances naked while the other sits beside you talking Goethe. Breasts ripening upward. A belly like wheat warmed by the sun. Makes for a very pleasant if slightly bizarre evening."

Gordon began to shake from the pain in his hand. "Another time. I was going to get drunk quickly and head home."

Fisk nodded slowly. "That's wise. Hohenzollern moral standards are all very admirable but . . . perhaps a little higher than men like us can maintain." He smiled up at Gordon. "Ragtime's forbidden, you know. Wouldn't want to lead you astray."

Gordon played with the ash of his cigarette, bumping it off with the tip of his little finger. There was nothing he could do until he found her again, and he would find her again.

"You know, I can get you something for that," Fisk said, nodding toward Gordon's hand. "A bang of morphine costs a pretty penny, but it's always there if you know where to look."

Gordon studied Fisk's discolored eyes for anything especially knowing, especially sardonic. "That's okay," he said. "I can manage."

"Now these girls with their dogs are truly fascinating."

"Ragtime," Gordon said. "That's all."

"Yes," Fisk said, leaning back. "I'm sure you're more the man of action. Not someone who gets his pleasure watching from the sidelines."

In time Fisk's smile turned hard. "Just what are you up to, anyway, Doctor? They say you're looking for evil doings in prison camps."

Gordon turned to face him. "Looking for whatever there is to see."

"Hmm." Fisk sipped his whiskey. "We're guests here of course. Have to play by the rules."

The dentist finished his drink, slammed down the glass, and then raised one finger to his face. "You know, the first time the Kaiser came to me for a dental procedure . . . Amazing presence, of course. Blazing blue eyes. 'Fix my teeth well, Fisk,' he said to me." The dentist lowered his head and glowered at Gordon. " 'So that I can bite!' I thought it was a striking indication of character, don't you?"

Gordon raised his stein and drained the beer. He had trusted too many people. He was getting in too deep too fast and he was going to drag this woman under with him.

Turning up his collar against a cold rain, Gordon scanned the darkened side street. If there were cabs anywhere in Berlin tonight they were not here. He sheltered his hand under his coat and began walking toward Leibnitzstrasse. The door of the club swung open behind him and he could hear a last burst of laughter and piano music before it was muffled once again.

The rain rushing along the pavement had driven the usual crowds off the street. Gordon had the sidewalk and the rain to himself. The only sound other than the hissing of water was the clip-clop of a solitary horse and wagon coming up behind.

He wondered where she was now, which way she had gone. If she was the one who examined the prisoners, then she was also the one who sent the messages. The "barbarism," the "bacteriological developments." Or was he simply falling for it hook, line, and sinker? She had disturbed him in a way he did not fully understand. She had made him gullible the moment she rattled his complacency, upsetting his insular belief that life was as it was, and his own mind the maker of its own misery. Something had changed in the instant he saw her, and it was the first real change he'd felt since his daughter had died.

He looked in both directions but focused on a spot a block away, in the center of the street where an arc lamp marked the tram stop. Gordon walked toward it, watching the brown water washing down in sheets against the electric light. The snow was melting down into the sewer drains. If the temperature dropped now, the whole city would freeze as solid as a glacier. He reached the traffic island, stood against the lamppost, then walked once around it.

The wagon that had followed him was pulled by a single white horse, blowing and blithering across the way. The driver had pulled to a stop along the curb and now the horse was shaking his harnesses from side to side. The driver sat in the shadow of the van's overhanging roof, watching. Gordon could not make out his face, but he could see the huge hands holding the reins, resting on the man's knees. It might have been the peculiar light, but to Gordon the man seemed totally out of proportion to his surroundings.

Two figures ran out of the darkness. Gordon heard the footsteps behind him and jerked around. It was a man and a woman, old and small and huddled together against the rain. Gordon looked down the tram lines and saw the single headlight coming their way. The beam jostled and swung from side to side as the car rolled down the imperfect rails, purple sparks snapping and drifting down from where the trolley tracked the power line.

"Some night, eh?" The elderly man breathed heavily as he spoke, looking up at Gordon from under his fedora. His rimless eyeglasses were beaded over with tiny raindrops.

"It will only get worse," Gordon said as the car pulled to a stop. He smiled, then stepped back to let them board the tram.

Underneath a scarf, the man's wife wore the same glasses with the same beads of water. They both looked like insects behind their beaded eyes.

The driver of the van leaned forward to snap the reins, and Gordon caught a glimpse of his face behind a thick, black beard. The huge man eyed him coldly, his body exuding the size and power of a slowly plodding draft horse.

Lying with her back to him, she was warm as the landscape of a dream. Gently, not wanting to wake her, he stroked the soft declination of her waist, the rise of her slender hips. He kissed her shoulder, then, leaning forward to kiss her face, he found it hidden beneath her hair, a golden stream cascading over her shoulders and running like a river between them on the bed. He reached up to gather it in his hands, to pull it back from her cheek. Then the telephone sliced through Schiller's sleep like a razor.

He knocked the book off his chest, swung his feet to the floor, lifted himself up from the couch. He felt foggy. Disoriented. He should have been in bed long ago.

Rainwater beat against the windows as he staggered across his living room in the faint light and picked up the receiver.

"Andreas . . . This is Kadereit. Sorry to call so late."

"That's all right. What is it?" His head ached and his mouth tasted like the inside of a shoe.

"Gordon just met the woman. At Onkel Tom's."

Schiller rubbed the sleep out of his face, his mind still lagging a few beats behind.

"Waist-length blond hair, Andreas. A regular patron. She used to come in with an older man who dressed like a civilian . . . and acted like a Prussian officer."

"You got a description?"

"Von Stade's. To the letter."

Schiller was fully alert now, wide awake with unexpected good fortune.

"He led us right to her, Andreas. Can you believe it? He led us right to her. But it was like Alexanderplatz at six o'clock."

"What do you mean?"

"He had two of Ostriker's shadowy types. Von Hessenstein, and the one with the albino streak . . ."

"Rolf Mayr," Schiller whispered.

"Exactly. They came out of the shadows the minute our boy left. It was all we could do not to trip over each other. But before that, who should walk in the door and strike up a conversation but the Kaiser's fucking dentist. This Gordon is no tourist, Andreas. And her killing von Stade was no lover's quarrel."

Schiller nodded his head, his eyes staring into the middle distance. Then he lowered the receiver and, without saying anything more, let it drift slowly back to its cradle.

16

The wiper motor on the passenger side crapped out before they reached Gairloch. Major Anthony Rice gazed through the blurred windscreen, listening to the metronomic slapping of the blade in front of the driver, wondering how long it would hold.

"Now the tank is what'll win it," Rollins was saying. He sat in the middle between Rice and the driver from the Royal Artillery. "You know what the German word for tank is, sir?"

Rice shook his head, then glanced out the side window into total darkness.

"Schütz-en-grab-en-verr-ich-ti-gungs-au-to-mo-bile," Rollins intoned. Then he smiled, pleased with himself. "And that's why we're going to win this war."

It had been raining, and Rollins had been talking, ever since they left Aultbea in the early morning hours, heading south in the eight-hundredweight lorry. In the back, two armed enlisted men sat on either side of a well-packed wooden crate. Inside the crate, glass flasks. And inside the flasks, the same brown gruel of concentrated anthrax spores that had been showered over Gruinard Island just two days before.

Rice had not been out to enjoy the scenery, but the blur of water in front of him had added an unwelcome touch of nausea to the claustrophobic feeling inside the cab. They had taken the high road as well as the low road, they had careened along precipices winding and falling like some carnival ride, and it had seemed to him as if they would never reach the bonnie banks of Loch Lomond. Now they were past it, rolling through the Kilpatrick Hills northwest of Glasgow. In another hour he could get this traveling bomb off his back. In another day he could board the train for London while Rollins and the others continued south with their cargo toward the Salisbury Plain research center at Porton Down.

"There we are, sir. Glasgow."

From the crest of the hill they could see the lights of the city stretching off into the distance. Rice felt the lorry gaining speed like a horse in sight of the stables.

He took the unlit pipe out of his mouth and said, "No rush at all, Jenkins. Just keep it on the road if you don't mind."

Despite the surge and the miles of slick pavement still ahead, he felt at least some of the tension ebbing out of his body. They had made it through the worst of it, Jenkins had not killed them, and now he could think about getting some rest.

He stared out at the lights, the wonders of the incandescent bulb, and he remembered a summer night a long time ago. The fireworks at the Crystal Palace. Girandoles and Catherine wheels, candlebombs and whizbangs, then two great set pieces—cornflowers and roses—which turned into the heads of the Kaiser and Kaiserin. They had been the Queen's guests for the evening. Rice had been just a boy, dazzled by the battle of the Nile refought with ships of lights moving across the sky. Then a final cannonade, and *L'Orient* blown to smithereens. Looking back now, he realized how much that summer evening twenty-five years before had formed his notion of what war would be like. Uniforms and parades, puffs of smoke, the streak of rockets crossing the night sky. How did anthrax spores blown into innocent men fit into that grand and glorious constellation?

"What shall we do with the lorry?" Rollins asked.

Reluctantly, Rice came back to the lights of Glasgow. "Take it to the police station," he said. "Let them sit on it for the night."

"And then?"

"A decent hotel with a well-stocked bar."

Rollins looked out at the city, seemingly expanding as they grew closer. "I hope this isn't the night the Huns try a Zepp raid on the Glasgow yards."

Rice sucked his pipe stem and said nothing, but self-interest aside, a disaster in Glasgow worried him far less than did the thought of succeeding at their own mission. Perhaps it was the sheep blown over the cliff. He had worked it through his mind all day and the outlook was thoroughly baffling. Without the possession of something like the German "magic bullet," British use of this anthrax device would be utterly suicidal. So what was the point of taking it into France? Was it a bargaining chip? A doomsday threat? A bluff?

Winston's bold strokes had a problematic record at best. The tank was a brilliant idea, yes, but the army sent it into action too soon, with no idea how to capitalize on it. The Dardanelles campaign could indeed have won the war in '15, but the army and the navy worked at cross purposes, and the Turks used the time to make Gallipoli impregnable. Rice knew very well that a man like Churchill had to be ignored or given complete control—there simply was no way to accommodate genius into the normal chain of command. Intermediaries would always vacillate, committees would always stall, and word, he feared, would always leak out.

Next morning, two hundred miles farther north, off the coast near Lochinvar, a wooden fishing boat bobbed in the choppy swells. The two fishermen on board, brothers-in-law, had been out all night and the hold was full of haddock and cod, plaice and hake, whiting, halibut, and ling. Now, as they pulled together, the net came rolling over the side with even more fish spilling onto the deck. Lemon sole and turbot, flipping about in anoxic frenzy, mixed with seaweed and driftwood like the vegetables in a stew.

Enough driftwood floated in these waters to build a roof over Scotland. The children gathered it on the beaches to burn for fuel, saving the coal and peat for harsher weather.

As he worked, the fisherman named Colum Bella looked back toward shore to the green hills rising so steeply that his sheep cut terraced trails. Even in the fairest weather he was a crofter, not a fisherman, a man whose blood was in "the bens and the glens," and who cursed the Sasunnach and the Clearances daily for driving his people down to this soggy coast. He could put out the creel for lobster and gather winkles in the winter tide pools, he would even work for his brother-in-law in this stinking boat, but he never ate fish himself, and he'd be damned before he'd learn to swim.

Bella looked back not out of longing, but because one of his cows was meandering nearer and nearer the edge of the cliff. Rising high above the water, the face of the rock was concave, with the sod cantilevered out over the open air. Fencing the edges was a practical impossibility. They had brought in goats to take the high ground and keep the sheep and cows off, but every few months one took a dive, crashing down to the rocks and the water below.

Feeling a sharp resistance against the net, Bella turned his mind back to his work. He tugged against the lines and felt the net securely snagged. But far from yielding, the resistance actually increased. It made no sense, but the net was pulling away from him.

The water erupted in turbulence, then a shaft of metal broke the surface, followed by cables branching off left and right. Bella's teeth sank into his pipe as he shared a look of total dismay with his wife's brother. The gray shape continued to rise above the surface, steel and smooth rivets, the metal railing of a conning tower, and salt water rushing off like a fountain. Bella, who could read only the least bit of Gaelic, still was able to derive the essential meaning of the letters marking the side. He and Andrew Keith had added to their catch one half ton of whitefish and one German U-boat.

• • •

Standing beneath his periscope, one foot resting on the hydrostatic gear, Lieutenant Wolf von der Ems chewed his amber cigarette holder and took in the morning smells of coffee, oranges, and lubricating oil. He and the crew of Unterseeboot 86 were nearing the end of a two-week patrol between Heligoland and northern Ireland, returning now through the Hebrides toward the Pentland Firth. He needed to surface anyway to run the diesel engines that recharged the batteries, so why not let it be in sight of one of his childhood haunts, his British grandfather's estate.

Von der Ems was a man who loved the northwest coast of Scotland every bit as much as Colum Bella hated it. Waiting for the hatch to open, he thought about the shaggy highland cattle, the grouse, the hut he built once out of an abandoned dory. It had been a mist-shrouded, mystical place for him through fifteen summers that now seemed to have been experienced in another lifetime. The ruins of the priory, the Celtic crosses on the tombstones, the hinds and hounds and twining ivy—instead of the Kaiser's navy.

Inside the control room now the ventilating fan hummed and Tuzcynski, the depth keeper, whistled a few bars from "Puppchen." Then the metal above clanged loudly and von der Ems saw the sky and felt the fresh infusion of oxygen. He was sick to death of breathing the same stale air, all of it smelling like diesel fuel and his able-bodied crew.

He began climbing toward the hatch and the gray sky above it, and as he did he saw the mate's face reappear in the opening, his camel's hair scarf dangling beside him.

"A problem, Captain."

Von der Ems poked his head up through the opening, felt the number six breeze, and confronted two dumbfounded fishermen bobbing not ten meters away. The submarine and the trawler were moored together by a web of fishing net.

Von der Ems climbed out onto the conning tower and lit a cigarette, his first in twenty-four hours. He grinned broadly as he raised up his Voigtlanders and focused on the hills of the distant shoreline. He could see a cow grazing peacefully on the cliff top. He could see the priory and, beyond it, the slate rooftops of his grandfather's estate.

Absentmindedly, he turned back toward the tower, where two sailors in gray leather jackets trained the deck gun on the now completely immobile Scots.

"Shall we allow the fishermen to gather their possessions, sir?" The mate handed him a megaphone.

Von der Ems took an extra moment to focus on what was being said. "No, no. There is no need for that. Proceed with recharging."

Then he looked down into the small wooden boat, surrounded by a sea of oily green. "These men are harmless enough."

He offered them a wry salute, then said, "Pull the boat alongside."

The mate, who had once been a fisherman himself, along the Vistula, ordered the sailors away from the deck gun and over to the tangled net. Using it like a mooring line, they drew the fishing boat closer.

"Good morning," von der Ems shouted out in English.

The Scots puffed their pipes and said nothing.

Von der Ems turned to his men now and told them to clear the net. Then, again in English, he shouted, "Do you know Sir Ian McGeown?"

The two fishermen looked at each other for a moment, wondering if these Germans had taken it in mind to carry off the laird. If this were the case, Colum Bella thought, it was not an entirely bad idea.

"Aye," he yelled. "We know him."

The German nodded. "You probably live on his land, don't you?"

"Aye. We're crofters."

Von der Ems looked down where his sailors were beginning to cut the nets. "No," he shouted. "Work with it. Loosen the net without cutting it."

The crofters looked at each other again, sharing their distrust. "How is the laird?"

"I have no' seen him since Samhuinn, but he was very well then."

Von der Ems took off his cap and tossed it into the boat. "Take this to Sir Ian. Tell him that his grandson sends his respects. Tell him that his grandson Wolf is very well."

Colum Bella bent down and picked up the cap. On first glance there was no secret message hidden it it, nothing for the English to accuse him of. He would take it to the laird if it meant saving his brother-in-law's nets.

Von der Ems watched silently as the men continued working to disentangle the two boats. The net was draped completely across the U-boat. The sailors first had tried to drag it across the deck before realizing that there were still hundreds of pounds of fish trapped in its tapered end. Now they were lifting up the empty middle portion and walking it, and the wooden trawler, toward their stern.

Von der Ems followed aimlessly behind them on the deck, stretching his legs, smoking, breathing the misty air. He looked down in the water and saw the "fairy eggs," seeds of *Entada scandens* that had drifted with the warm currents all the way from the Caribbean. He could see the net being drawn tighter and the catch brimming inside it, and then the hooved foot protruding through the mesh.

"What is this?" he said.

One of the sailors looked back up at him, squinting in the sunlight. "Looks like a sheep, Captain."

The sailors worked to clear the stern and the carcass rolled into clear view, floating on the surface just under the netting. It was shorn, and against its close-cropped wool von der Ems saw the black marks of recent wounds. Who would shear his sheep in the middle of winter? And where would a sheep get such wounds?

"I want to see this animal," von der Ems said. "Board the trawler. Pull the carcass up on deck."

The sailors leapt into the small boat and began working the net. They pulled and fish began spilling onto their legs until at last one of them was able to reach down and grab the dead sheep and yank it up. The sailors still on board the sub pulled the boat closer again with gaffs, and von der Ems climbed on board.

With his men gathered around, the lieutenant knelt down by the animal and probed the wounds. Had some British gunner taken target practice on a sheep? The wounds looked surprisingly like shrapnel. Then von der Ems noticed the brass marker stapled into the animal's ear, and on it—the engraving "PD 17." PD. Porton Down. British weapons research.

Slowly, von der Ems stood up. "Bring it on board," he said.

The mate looked him in the eye. "What about the trawler?"

"Sink it," von der Ems told him. "These fishermen will go with us."

THE heavy black door of Fisk's office looked out on the Bendler Strasse with a wrought-iron gate protecting the glass. Princess Bucher pressed the bell and waited nervously, staring into the dimly lit stairway, burying her chin in her collar of unborn lamb.

Across the street in the Tiergarten, the barren trees were lost in the mist and fog. It was late afternoon, already dark, and she assumed Fisk would be seeing the last of his patients. She had not called ahead. She had opened the letter from the Inspection of Prisoners and come over on impulse.

It had been four days now since she met with Gordon. She had left messages at American Express, she had waited at the Adlon. Now the letter made it perfectly clear that nothing was going to come of this. Charles Geary had been repatriated. According to the "official response," Lucy's uncle was no longer even at Ruhleben.

Glancing up suddenly, she saw two figures pass briefly in front of a second-story window. Then she saw Erskine Fisk stop to look out, then move back from sight.

She turned around to the door again and waited, her toes growing numb in the slush. She thought of ringing once more, and at the same time dropping it all and hurrying away while she still had the chance. But then another moment passed and Fisk was on the stairs, pulling on his jacket as his slippers brushed over the Oriental runner held down with brass rods.

He reached the foyer and unlocked the door and looked at her coldly. His eyes were redder than they had been at the Adlon. Tonight they looked permanently damaged.

"Princess Bucher," he said, standing back. "What a pleasant surprise."

She glanced down, hestitating at the threshold. "I hope I'm not disturbing you," she said.

"No, no. Not at all."

"Yes . . . Well, I'm afraid we didn't complete our conversation the other evening."

Fisk looked beyond her head to scan the empty sidewalk, the park, the Platz surrounding the Roland Fountain across the way. Then she stepped in and he closed the door behind her.

"You're alone?" he asked. In the narrow space of the entryway their eyes met, and her muscles tensed as if she were being touched.

"Yes. Very, I'm afraid." She felt chilled. "You're sure I'm not interrupting you?"

"No, no. You must come up," he said. He stepped aside and gestured to the stairs.

She climbed just ahead of him, holding her skirts, uncomfortably aware of the man so close behind her. They reached the landing and she waited as Fisk opened the door to his rooms.

They stepped into a carpeted waiting area with a roll-top desk and typewriting machine. The examination room to the left was dark. The door to Fisk's office was closed.

"I thought of turning to you originally because of your . . . range of acquaintance," she said. "I simply wanted to know if my girl Lucy had left the country with her 'mad pash' or if she had gotten into some sort of trouble. Your embassy has been useless, of course, in trying to locate the boy."

Dr. Fisk raised his eyebrows. "Our people in Berlin couldn't find their way home," he said.

"But I did find him," she went on. "Ricky Marsten. A jockey. I traced him to Rotterdam, then cabled his ship. He told me Lucy never made it to their rendezvous."

Fisk glanced up. They both stood rigidly in the center of the room, fixed in place, as an odd shadow passed over his features. Then he reached over to the bookshelf to tap one protruding volume of clinical reports flush with the rest.

"But she also planned to visit your office that day."

"She did," Fisk said. "Complained of a wisdom tooth, as I recall, but nothing came of it. I told her to bear with those things we cannot change. To let nature take its course."

"Was that before or after she went to the camp?"

"Now how the deuce would I know?"

"Lucy was never one to hide her thoughts, Dr. Fisk. So maybe you can tell me if she was agitated at all. Upset in any way. Frightened."

"Everyone's frightened when they visit the dentist, my dear. It's difficult to make the distinction."

"Dr. Fisk, I know that you and Major Baron von den Benken are friends. I understand that. But all I'm asking, really, is the same consideration. If Lucy's been detained for some reason, simply let me know. I'm talking to others, but . . ."

"You think she told me what she was up to and I blew the whistle, is that it?"

"No, no. Not necessarily. I simply mean that . . ."

"Become an informer, have I? Sending silly young girls off to prison?"

"Dr. Fisk . . . I'm sorry if . . ."

"Well, I've been accused of worse," he said. He turned with his hands in his pockets and rocked on his heels, sucking his teeth. "I can see you really don't want to let this thing drop, do you?"

He looked at her sternly and she blushed. Then after a moment his eyes softened and he smiled. "You know, I admire your determination. I really do. I can see you're going to stay with it until you get to 'the very bottom of it.' "

He ran his tongue along his lower lip, nodding his head. "Well, you're doing the right thing. You can't be too careful. It's a damned tough spot you're in, being British and all, in this damned city, with this damned war going on."

He looked down, jangling the coins in his pocket. "The fact is, you see, they watch me too. An American. Close proximity to the Kaiser. In fact . . ."

Fisk reached out and gripped her hand. "Here . . . Come over here."

He led her across the floor into the examining room and turned on the lights.

The princess was rigid. "I didn't come here for my teeth."

"Of course not," he said. "I know that. But they saw you come in. They watch from over there. From the park. We have to be careful. You just bear with me. I'll tell you all about it."

He gestured for her to slip out of her coat.

"Dr. Fisk . . ."

"Don't be nervous. Just make everything look normal, that's what we've got to do."

"I'm cold," she said. "Let me leave my coat on."

"Fine, fine. Leave your coat on for now."

She drew her coat around her. "I don't understand this," she said. But then stepped around the dentist's cumbersome apparatus and sat down.

Fisk pulled a white cloth off a tray of instruments and set about draping it over her bosom.

"I used to treat your husband's gums," he said. "I know all the

Bucher family quite well. He's off in the East, isn't he? The Knights of Malta?"

"Yes. That's right. But now what about Lucy?"

"There's really nothing at all to be afraid of, you know? Really."

"This can't be necessary."

"Oh it is, believe me." He picked up a small, silver probe and looked into her eyes. "Now open," he said.

Confused and exasperated, she parted her lips.

"We might as well make use of the visit, anyway," he said, but he seemed agitated inserting the pick and small mirror into her mouth. "I know it sounds odd, but I always feel more comfortable when I speak with someone if I'm examining their teeth."

She realized now how utterly foolish it was for her to come here. She should have left all this to Gordon. Fisk worked the probe between her gums and teeth and in time she began to cry with exasperation. She felt helpless, violated.

He held his breath, scraping for a moment, then noticed the tears. "Even in a mouth so pretty and so young, you see, the seeds of dissolution can do their wicked work."

She looked up at the tufts of hair shooting out of Fisk's nostrils, the tufts of hair curling out of his ears. He was a rude, crude man, with a rash of gray stubble along one jawbone, and she hated herself for not having the wherewithal to tell him to bugger off. He exhaled in her face as he pressed the silver wire against her gums, and his breath smelled of eggs. Not even the Hotel Esplanade could manage fresh eggs.

"Rinse," he said. Then he waited as she drank from the cup and spat into the basin.

She glanced up, her eyes filled with tears, and wiped her chin on a cloth. "Dr. Fisk, this is ridiculous. I need your help with the baron. If that's a problem for you, then I don't need to trouble you anymore."

"First tell me about the baron and myself being such good friends. Where do you hear such things?"

"I don't know. It's in the air."

"So I've really taken sides, is that it? Gotten in bed with the high command?"

"No, no. I didn't mean to intrude."

Once again he silenced her as his long, thick fingers pressed against her lips. He worked the probe again and again into the crevices between her teeth, winding his way into the deepest corner of her mouth. She moved her hand from the armrest, where his thigh pressed against her. He was leaning over her so closely, breathing over her.

He picked and probed in silence for another moment, calmed by the activity, as she grew more and more frightened, the tears streaming down her cheeks.

At last he smiled and said, "How old are you, my dear?"

"I'm twenty-three."

"I don't like the way these wisdom teeth are coming in."

His tone was grave. He withdrew his instruments, then set them down and wiped his hands on a towel. "There's a skin flap. Much worse than Lucy's. A tiny pocket that could cause real trouble. A great deal of pain." He nodded, seemingly absorbed by the challenge.

"Doctor, I appreciate . . . I really don't have time for this today. I'd like to go now."

"No, no. Quite simple." He turned toward the metal drawers at his elbow. When he came back around to face her he was holding a rubber mask.

"Dr. Fisk, I . . ."

He smiled languidly, almost like a lover, as he brought the mask slowly toward her face. "Now, now, my dear. Simply relax."

The black fixture came toward her.

"I've got to go!" she screamed, bolting up.

"Sit back! What's wrong with you?"

She grabbed the metal tray of instruments and backhanded it into the dentist's face.

"You little bitch!" He reeled with the blow where the metal had creased his forehead. He was blinded for the moment as she leapt out of the chair and the room and made her way toward the stairs. She slipped on the runner midway and slid on her bum, wrenching her back, almost twisting her ankle. But she recovered and kept going.

She stumbled through the foyer and out onto the darkened Bendler Strasse, shaking now with the terror and revulsion she had tried to suppress. She looked back once, up to Fisk's office window, and saw him watching her as she ran.

She had left her bag behind but she couldn't worry about that now. She tried to think clearly as she limped alongside the Tiergarten. She kept going, her head down, until she turned onto Friedrichstrasse and screamed. She was face to face with a ragged man, a one-legged veteran selling pencils. "Compose yourself," she whispered. They had houses for men like him. It was bad for public morale to see them on the streets.

A tram rattled behind her and squealed to a stop, and she turned to look at it, breathing hard, figuring there would be just enough time to race across the street and leap on board. Billy would not be back yet and now she was truly afraid. She would go to Hazelwood's apartment and wait there. The tram was a number 91, but then she realized she didn't have so much as a pfennig. She refused to go running after a public conveyance anyway, acting like some shop girl. And as she stood trying to decide, the door snapped shut and the vehicle jerked forward.

She walked on, trembling, the hubbub of Friedrichstrasse behind her, the tears burning down her cheeks. It was just from the wind in her eyes, she told herself. But she was cold and desperate and very much wishing she had taken the tram.

Staggering through the Spittle-Markt, Private Lech Wroblewski had a hunger that could devour Berlin. He had been hungry since the day the war began, and drunk, too, for all it mattered. Now he was cursing the darkness, cursing his stupidity for listening to Schmidt. There weren't any whores here. Klimper had said Chausseestrasse—that's where you find women. So that took care of everything. Where the hell was Chausseestrasse?

It was early yet, six o'clock. The women didn't come out until later, but Wroblewski knew if he had to wait much longer he was going to pass out before he could get his dick wet. It was dark and it was cold and the snow pelting him in the face made him angry. Then he remembered he had left his coat on the back of the chair in the Bierstube. Screw his coat, he decided. He would rip one off the first German bastard stupid enough to cross his path.

Wroblewski stumbled out of the square and made his way down a wide street with tracks down the center. Leipziger Strasse. This would take him back to Friedrichstrasse and then up to the Linden, and sooner or later he would find some money out for a stroll. He had killed Russians and he had killed Romanians and he knew he could damn well kill Germans too if they got in his way. He was going to survive this war to piss on Germany. Then he laughed to think of it as he stumbled into the bushes. He had to piss on Germany right now. He unbuttoned his Turkish medals, and then the steam rose up as the urine splattered onto the thin cover of snow.

Across the way, Princess Bucher saw a gang of French prisoners leaning on the long wooden lever of a pump, emptying the sewers into a huge metal drum on the back of a tipcart. There was no horse to pull it, but there were plenty of prisoners.

She crossed Markgrafenstrasse, walking faster than before, and she passed the darkened showroom of Michels and Company, silk merchants. For some reason, the sound of her own footsteps seemed to echo very loudly. Every other streetlamp was left dark. Of the three bulbs in each lamp, only one was lit.

Fisk was a madman. She was convinced of that now and deathly afraid that he was following her. The chill she'd felt as he came toward her was still all too real. He'd been aroused as he probed her mouth, breathing on her, pushing himself against her hand. Was it just sex, or was it the arousal of a man intent on murder? Is that what had happened to Lucy? But what could she have stumbled onto that was so devastating to him?

She passed Tietz's, crossed Jerusalemer Strasse, then walked alongside a small, wooded park, the Dönhoffplatz. Why was it so dark? Why was no one on the streets?

Then it was as if one of the trees had stepped out of the darkness to block the path. He was a soldier. Huge, muscular, with blond stubble bristling from a massive head. He was smiling stupidly, and he said something to her in a language she did not understand. She lowered her head and tried to step aside, but he shifted his bulk to block her way again.

"Please," she said, her heart pounding. "I have an appointment."

"Don't talk German to me, German bitch." His mouth hung open slightly as he stared at her with bloodshot eyes. "I'm a Pole who kills Russians for you. Understand?"

She glanced down and saw that his trousers were unbuttoned, the front wet with urine.

"I need a kiss," he told her, staring at her breasts. "A little bite for my birthday." He dangled his thick face down in front of hers, smelling of beer.

She held herself steady, rose on her toes, and kissed his cheek. "There you are," she said weakly. "Happy Birthday." Then, trembling, she stepped aside to pass.

He wrapped his hands around her shoulders. She looked up into his eyes but realized there was nothing left there to reach. She screamed once as he lifted her off the ground, but then he placed his hand across her face.

He dragged her into the bushes and stumbled to the wet ground and lay on top of her, slipping his fingers around her throat. "You scream some more and I'll smash your face, understand?"

The fall had knocked the breath out of her, and with his weight on her chest her lungs could not expand. She lay on her back staring up into the sky, her arms crushed beside her, the cold and brittle skin of her hands bleeding on the ice, her eyes focused on the clouds above Berlin that absorbed the lights like cotton gauze. Her mind grasped at that peaceful, calming image, unable to assimilate what was actually happening to her. Was this Fisk's idea of revenge? She could feel her pulse against his fingers. Her neck seemed to swell as he pushed her head back deeper into the snow. The man was angry, pulling at himself, abusing himself, squeezing harder all the while with his other hand. There was nothing she could do but accept that she was going to die, and then when she accepted it the pain and humiliation became more distant. Deprived of oxygen, she concentrated on the distant clouds and a vision of Jesus came to her . . . Jesus standing over her, welcoming her into heaven. She knew she was blacking out, hallucinating, but her eyes were still open. Then she realized it was a man's face she saw, not a vision. Up above the soldier, a man's face with a beard. The soldier grunted and flogged himself as the man raised a wooden mallet high up into the sky. She saw the mallet pause, then come down. Then she saw it collide with the soldier's burly head.

The weight was off her body and she felt as light as air. She crawled away and staggered to her feet, spitting out the taste of blood. She looked back and saw the two men grappling with each other in the snow, but nothing was going to stop this soldier, not if he could survive that blow.

She slipped on the ice as she ran through the trees. For a moment she thought she was in a forest. The branches scratched her face and snagged her coat. Then in a clearing she saw the stone faces of statues and she remembered the park. She was in the city. All she had to do was get to the other side of the park and she would be safe.

She heard footsteps and she knew it was the soldier crashing through the trees a few steps behind her. She ran along the path, screaming, until she came out onto Jerusalemer Strasse and slipped on the ice. Her hand went down to break her fall, smacking the cold, hard surface. The pain shot up her arm and she lifted her palm, leaving a single dot of blood.

She got to her feet and sensed the hand on her shoulder. Then she turned and screamed but nothing was there. She couldn't think. She stood crying and shaking and walking in a circle as she looked frantically for help. The street was empty. The whole block taken up by the Tietz emporium was dark. She had to keep going, but she could not think clearly enough to know where.

Suddenly, as if summoned by her will, hooves clattered against the pavement to her right, and she saw a wagon coming down from Leipziger Strasse, a furniture van pulled by a single white horse. She raised her arm as a faint gesture to the driver, but the effort left her exhausted. She let her arm drop, and in that moment, for the first time ever, she realized how truly much she wanted to live. The driver nodded and pulled back on the reins, and a wave of relief washed over her that made her break down and sob like a child. She no longer cared about Fisk or Lucy or Ruhleben, or even Billy. She had been wicked and dishonest and she had been unfaithful, and if this was her punishment she accepted it now. She had learned the lesson and she would change. She would go back to the purity she had been taught as a girl.

She laughed and cried as the wagon drew up, and the tears streamed down her face. This man would call the police. This man would keep her safe and take her back to the Esplanade, where she would wait faithfully for her husband to return.

The van pulled to a halt. The driver got down and came toward her as she smiled in gratitude. He was a huge, dark man with a black beard. He wore a frock coat and heavy boots. In one hand he carried a mallet. In the other, a curved knife with a four-inch blade.

He came forward quickly and raised the mallet, then brought

it down hard as her neck snapped to the side and she dropped like a weight to the icy surface, dancing to the rhythm of her disorganized nervous system. The bearded man leaned over with the knife and carefully laid open her throat, releasing a cloud of steam. He reached under her skirts, exposing her thighs, and made a deep gash on either side of her groin. Then he scooped her up in his arms, trailing a ribbon of blood, and tossed her into the back of the van.

The nerves that carried messages to her brain still functioned as she landed inside the vehicle. They conveyed something warm and soft beneath her, and then a limp arm falling across her chest. The last image to reach her fading consciousness was the face of the Polish soldier, who lay, like her, with eyes gaping, throat slit wide.

17

In a second-floor laboratory at the Institute for Infectious Diseases, Margarethe Riesling leaned over an autoclave to remove a set of sterile syringes, pausing for a moment to warm her face and hands. There had been no heat in the lab at all today and her fingers were stiff with the cold.

As the steam rose above her head and dissipated into the room, Margarethe took her glassware and sat down at a large, rolltop desk littered with test tubes stuffed with cotton. Patiently, painstakingly, she assembled the pieces in a white enamel tray—needles, plungers, tubing—all the while trying not to overreact.

She was alone now, but Professor von Broembsen had spent much of the afternoon silently watching her from his swivel chair. His head tilted back, his eyes blinking at the ceiling, wiping his lips on the back of his hand. Margarethe had seen him with two different groups of men earlier in the day, listening to their questions, smoothing the white beard beneath his chin. But he had said nothing to her about Walther Ostriker, or about the man with the rumpled and threadbare look of the Berlin police.

Pushing the tray to one side, she placed a wire cage in the center of the space. Inside it were four plump white mice, sniffing and twitching. She reached to a wooden rack on the shelf by the wall and withdrew a test tube containing 20 cc of a clear, yellowish liquid.

It had taken her two weeks to purify the active substance with acetone and alcohol, then strain it through a Seitz filter on a bicycle pump. The extract left behind was still only five percent pure and highly unstable, and the yield was enough for, at best, one experiment. A wisp on a platinum coil, Sabouraud's medium, a culture on an agar plate. But she knew what she had. Virulent streptococci grew up to a point of 30 mm from the gutter and stopped dead. *Staphylococcus pyogenes* would not grow beyond 23 mm. Pneumococci, meningococci, gonococci, diphtheria bacilli—the effect was the same. The extract worked topically even diluted one in eight hundred with no harmful effects. She had injected it intravenously to rabbits, intraperitoneally to mice, and found it utterly safe. In a moment of wild abandon she had eaten some of it and discovered that it tasted very much like Stilton cheese.

Holding the glass tube now, she steadied herself as she inserted the sterile syringe, submerged the hollow tip, and pulled back on the plunger. Then she lifted the first mouse out of the cage and placed it on the desktop, stroking its fur, making soothing noises as she held it in place. She pulled the loose skin from the back of its neck, then carefully jabbed with the needle. Professor von Broembsen needed her as much as she needed him. If the truth came out about her he would be forced to retire. He would no longer have an office to nap in, or syringes to squirt xylene at flies. He might even be shot along with her.

She held the animal in place a moment longer, stroking it, soothing it. She had given it a fatal dose of anthrax an hour before, and now, with the extract in its blood, only time would tell.

But, of course, that was the great question, wasn't it? How much time did she have?

On the Ringbahn home that night, Margarethe Riesling shared the compartment with a middle-aged couple sitting knee to knee and ignoring each other. The woman stared idly, her arms resting on the packages in her lap. Her husband hid behind the pages of the *Berliner Tagblatt*.

Margarethe was tired, and she did not want to think about the police who were closing in, or the American who was leading them to her. She was still waiting to hear from Katz, to learn what help he could provide. If that failed, she would have to reexamine her options. But for the moment it was enough to be warm and looking forward to the idea of sleep.

She removed her hat and shook off the snow. Then she rummaged through her bag. She paid no attention to the couple, or to the tall, dark man who moved into the car and took the seat exactly opposite.

The "Frau Turschliesserin" tested their door, then signaled ahead. A moment later the train rumbled out of the station into the night.

"You never collected your drink," Gordon said.

Margarethe glanced up, then held him in her gaze for a moment. She tried to adjust to his presence—the man who was going to get her killed.

She did not register any particular emotion. She simply turned back to her search as they rode in silence along the northern perimeter of the city. The fact was she wanted to scream and hit him with her fists but she succeeded in holding it in. They crossed the Verbindungskanal, then the lights of the gasworks flashed up in her face as the train sped past.

"Matches," she said, her hands shaking in frustration. "Do you have a match?"

Gordon pulled his lighter out of his pocket as she leaned forward with the cigarette between her lips. For the first time he could see the delicate tracery at the corners of her eyes, the creases like tiny parentheses at the corners of her mouth.

"You are quite persistent," she said, exhaling a cloud of smoke.

Gordon lit one for himself and then leaned back, shrugging his shoulders.

"I could ignore you, but then I suppose you would simply keep turning up."

"You could call the police," he said.

She laughed once and turned her head toward the window. "I wouldn't have to call very loud, would I."

Then for a moment Gordon watched her reflection against the backdrop of city lights. He had waited for her all afternoon outside the Institute. He did not know her name or anything about her, but it had made sense. He was playing hunches all the more, getting fatalistic.

"How is your hand?"

"Better, thanks. Not much, but some." He reached into his pocket and gave her the carving from Doberitz.

"What is this? What are you doing?"

"A gift from a Russian prisoner," he said.

She shook her head. "This means nothing to me."

"Keep it anyway," Gordon told her. Then he took off his hat and set it beside him, reaching up to run his good hand along his scalp.

"I'm with the U.S. Embassy," he said after a while.

"That's very good. Government work is quite steady."

"I can offer you asylum. If we're careful I can get you out of here."

"And who says I want to leave?"

The Hausfrau sitting next to them had been hanging on their every word with rapt attention. Now her husband lowered his newspaper to stare.

Margarethe glared at them, then turned her eyes back to Gordon. "This is ridiculous. We can't talk like this." They were slowing for the Bahnhof Charlottenburg. "Tell me where you're staying," she said. Then, gesturing with the cigarette—"Write it down."

Awkwardly, using his left hand, Gordon reached into his pocket. He tore out a page from his pocket calendar, jotted down his room number at the Adlon, then handed it to her like a prescription.

"I'll meet you there in one hour," she said, never looking at the paper. "I want to get this over with, do you understand?"

He watched her eyes, her mouth, until he was sure she was lying. Then he nodded without conviction.

He put his hat back on as the train pulled into the station. She mashed out her cigarette, gathered her coat around her, and edged forward on the seat. Then she looked at Gordon. "What does Fisk have to do with you?"

"Fisk?"

"He was with you at Onkel Tom's."

"He doesn't have anything to do with me. You tell me what he was doing there."

The brakes squealed and she looked away, staring out at the lights of the station flashing against the windows.

"I think you could use a friend," Gordon said as the train rolled to a stop.

She simply hurried off alone, rushing through the station for the darkness of Holtzendorfstrasse.

As the train pulled away again he saw her turning south under the tracks for the Kurfürstendamm. He felt odd, watching her go. He had thought it impossible to feel any more alone than he had always felt, but here it was. At the next station he got off and took a droshky back to the Adlon. Then for three hours he sat in his room in the dark, a lead sash weight at his side, immensely curious to see who would come through the door.

IT WAS almost midnight when the Kaiser's landaulet pulled away from the curb, drenching the outrider in the thick, brown slush that washed over the running board. Berliners still out at this hour stopped on the darkened Tiergartenstrasse to salute the man they took to be their emperor.

Riding in the back with von den Benken, Erskine Fisk stared

out through the mist and found the tribute an especially sweet turn of events. It was one year ago today that the army had confiscated his eight-cylinder American Mercer.

"I don't approve of your people," the major said. "Never have, never will. And I'm not at all sure this thing is going to work if we continue to be so blatant about it in the city streets."

"All part of the game," Fisk said, nodding confidently. "And their game long before it was ours."

The dentist wore his shapka tonight, a Russian fur hat that made him look more like a shaman bent on exorcism than a dentist on a house call. He turned toward the baron and jabbed his finger in the air. "What I don't understand is why you and *your* people didn't take care of Gordon the same way when you had the chance."

"You see him with this Margarethe Riesling and you turn outraged Latin," von den Benken shot back. "You want him killed. Always before, you wanted him alive. You had to know every detail. Who sent him? What was he after?"

Fisk brushed a speck of ash off his topcoat and said, "And now we know."

Von den Benken shook his head. "The primordial laceration. The old 'taffy pull.' Can it really mean more to you than money? Ever since von Stade brought this Riesling woman into the picture you've been obsessed with her."

"I have money, Baron."

"But not Margarethe Riesling."

"Not yet."

"It all looks the same in the dark, my friend."

Fisk smiled to hide his irritation. "Sex is a battle, Baron. And the average woman is simply not much of a challenge, is she."

They rode on in silence through the park until they picked up Charlottenburger Chaussee. Von den Benken gazed out at the fog nestled between the trees like protective cotton.

"Cash," the baron responded at last. "Cash keeps you warm at night, Fisk—it buys coal. Now look—Princess Bucher, Gordon . . . They're immaterial. We're fine, so long as we have the All Highest. With the imperial blessing we can do what we please. This is a vital social purpose we're serving, but only if we have his blessing. We can't feed Germany with dogs and cats."

Fisk smiled languidly and reached over to pat the major's knee. "We'll see, Baron. We'll see. One has to be ever so delicate with the imperial sensibilities."

They passed under Bahnhof Tiergarten and continued out Berliner Strasse toward Charlottenburg. The wipers still slapping in rhythm, the rubber tires hissing against the wet pavement.

They were nearing the palace when the dentist took a deep breath and said, "Dr. Gordon talked to the princess, and he talked to the nigger, right?"

"Yes. He's definitely on the trail."

"And he's talked to Margarethe. I think he's talked enough, don't you?" Fisk reached into his waistcoat pocket and checked his watch. "Let's discuss some kind of arrangement for him as soon as we get back to Berlin."

"It's settled, then. As good as done. But what about Margarethe? What if she decides to confide in someone else?"

"I will deal with Margarethe in my own way, my friend. You leave her to me."

Von den Benken settled back in the upholstery and nodded his great round head as the guards at Potsdam waved the car through the gates of the Neue Palais. Two men in green livery came out to help the dentist with his bags, but von den Benken stayed behind. This meeting, presumably, would not take long. William the Sudden. The German prince who lost at skat and approached all subjects with an open mouth.

Fisk followed his guides through the shell room and then through a door to the left, opening onto a wide staircase that led to the Kaiser's Garderobe. There was furniture of French design, white and gold, walls covered with gilt mirrors and sentimental paintings.

And in front of the fire, riveted to the floor, the Kaiser's rowing machine with the special grip for his deformed left hand.

The footman set down Fisk's bags and withdrew, and the dentist was left standing awkwardly alone beside the saddle where the Kaiser sat to do his paperwork, the imperial newspaper lying across the desktop. A single copy edited and manufactured each day for his eyes only, printed in gold.

Fisk had never taken this particular enterprise all that seriously, though it meant the world to the baron, yet here he was in deep shit, just to cover his ass. Return on investment was the key— optimizing the value of his real estate. But von den Benken was every bit as cut off from reality now as their demented emperor. Germany was going down in flames, and these patchwork schemes to keep it up were never going to have any effect. Fisk knew that now. And he knew that opportunity lay beyond the border, with radically new developments.

He turned to the newspaper, scanning the marginal notations— "Nonsense with sauce!" "Stale fish!"—as the All Highest himself, Kaiser Wilhelm II, strode into the room.

Fisk made a deep bow from the waist and the Kaiser scowled impatiently, his ears stuffed with cotton, his eyes red and watery, shivering with pain and lack of sleep.

"Look here, Fisk, you've got to do something for me. I can't fight the whole world, you know, and have a toothache!"

BILLY de Beauford opened his door with the sleepy scowl of a man peering into his chamber pot. He wore a silk smoking jacket and nothing else, stumbling backward on bare feet as Gordon leaned forward and pushed his way into the room.

Champagne bottles and ashtrays littered the floor. A half dozen carts—covered dishes and ice buckets—were lined up along the wall, and a German officer wearing the red trouser stripe of the

Staff College lay sprawled across the couch like a beached walrus.

Gordon nodded to the man and said, "Who's he?"

De Beauford looked blankly at the slackened face. "Major Deutelmoser, I suppose. Imperial News Office. It would seem I was working him over for a story." Then the Dutchman sat down on the arm of a chair and at last focused on Gordon. "You look like hell, you know. You really shouldn't be here."

"Because of the way I look?"

The German snorted loudly and burrowed his face deeper into the upholstered cushion darkened now by a thread of spittle. Billy held up one finger, rose to his feet, and motioned for Gordon to follow him into the bathroom.

Once inside, Billy closed the door behind them and leaned down and turned on the water, letting it splash noisily into the tub. Then he came to rest on the closed lid of the toilet.

"You missed an astounding episode at the dinner the other night. The Kaiser spoke on the vegetarianism of your American red Indians. But you didn't stick around, I understand. I understand you'd done yourself an injury."

"Berlin makes me accident prone," Gordon said. He glanced into the mirror. He did look like hell.

He glanced back at the Dutchman. "So tell me why I was brought here."

Billy dragged his hand slowly down across his face, then looked up placidly. "To confirm the story, I suppose."

"Which story?"

"It's all Bohemian villages to me."

"Look." Gordon leaned down and the little reporter recoiled. "Two men have been killed. I've got a homicide detective and this fellow Ostriker following every move I make. It's time I became better informed, wouldn't you say?"

Billy tugged at his mustache, then smoothed it down. "Fatalities always concern me. But I carry a rather small spear in the chorus myself."

"Behind Princess Bucher?"

"Cherchez la femme."

Gordon sat down on the edge of the tub and adjusted the flow of water himself, letting the sound bounce from one tiled surface to another, echoing. "I tried to find your princess this morning but she wasn't at her hotel. I got the impression she hadn't been there at all last night."

De Beauford rubbed under his left eye.

"I've been out of town," he said. "But yes. That troubles me."

"So tell me what I need to know before I really fuck it up. Let's cut the fun and games."

Billy reached up with the small finger of his right hand and poked at his toupee.

"I despise Germans for the most part," he said after a moment, "but oddly enough I do like Berlin. I'm actually not much for cloaks with real daggers—some stories a reporter simply stays away from. Evelyn, on the other hand, is really rather daring. A sense of immortality seems to come with the entitlement of the British upper classes. She's also highly visible, being married to a German prince, you know. We have a certain vantage point here, but very little room to maneuver."

Billy looked away, then slowly brought his eyes back to Gordon's bandaged hand.

"That looks painful," he said. Then he took a deep breath. "Who is it that's dead? Why are the police trailing you?"

"They killed a courier in Amsterdam. A doctor named Troelstra. Did you know him?"

Billy shook his head.

"Then they killed an instrument maker named Katz. In Berlin, at the zoo. They say he was in the black market."

Billy nodded several times. "These things happen."

"So Ostriker's following me makes sense. They picked me up in Amsterdam. And this policeman makes sense because of the killing. But Erskine Fisk, the Kaiser's dentist. He's turned up twice now."

"That's not good news."

"Why?"

"Evelyn. She had it in her mind to go see him again."

Gordon watched as Billy scraped a kernel of sleep from his eye. Then he looked away and said, "He was at the Adlon with your princess the first time. Then he was at the jazz club where I met the American woman. He'd either followed me, or he was there to meet her."

"You've lost me. I don't know anything about an American woman."

"At Ruhleben. I went looking for the Russian, Beszenoff, and I found her instead. I think she's the one who sent the messages."

Billy looked up toward the ceiling, shaking his head. "Why are you even doing this? They're going to kill you, you know."

"Who's going to kill me?"

"I'm sure they're queuing up. But right now I'm much more concerned about Evelyn."

Gordon waited, feeling the steam rising up behind his back, gathering into a moist, gray cloud above his head. "Tell me what you know about Fisk."

Billy leaned forward on his elbows, his head in his hands. "He's a loose cannon. He has no particular loyalty to anyone . . . except his banker. He knows all manner of Continental low-life. Monied Americans. Demented royalty. He brokers deals. He's a facilitator."

"He's in the black market."

"Anyone in this city who *eats* is in the black market."

Gordon stared at the running water, thinking about the dentist at the bar, the offer of morphine.

"I don't like the sound of any of this," Billy went on. "We're not in a good position. You seem to be tripping over all the wires, attracting lots of attention. Something will come of it, probably something useful for British intelligence, but it won't necessarily be good for you."

"I need to get a handle on Fisk. And I need you to track down this Russian. The men at Ruhleben say he's at Holzminden now."

"I can't get involved like that. I don't know anything about this."

"You can learn. I need your help. Beszenoff supposedly worked at the Institute. I can't rule him out completely and I can't pursue both him and this woman. There's still a chance he could have been the source sending the messages to London. If he was, I need to know it before I try to get any closer to the woman."

"This has gotten too convoluted. Evelyn wanted you to check out Charles Geary. I don't understand how this Beszenoff person got into the picture."

"The embassy."

"*Who* at the embassy?"

"Jay Adams."

Billy stood up and pulled the string on his robe, letting it fall open. "You'll have to excuse me," he said. "I feel as if I could well use a bath just now."

The Dutchman stepped into the tub and placed the stopper in the drain, then looked back at Gordon. He seemed angry, exasperated.

"They should have told you," he said.

"Told me what?"

Billy threw off his robe and squatted down naked in the small pool of water that had begun to collect.

"The Brits have been hanging you out to dry," he said, cupping his hands and splashing the water into his face. "They've kept you 'pure.' They've protected you from the same tired, old information that could make you too predictable, or too cautious."

Gordon watched him for a moment, his shoulders as thin and pale as a little boy's, defenseless and frail.

Billy looked up then, letting the water run over his knees. "Walther Ostriker's queer as a snake," he said. "And Jay Adams is his little fag."

18

The twins sat facing their mother on the cold marble floor of the Criminal Courts Building in Moabit. Swathed in rags, each of them had a breast in its mouth like tiny fakirs smoking a hookah.

Margarethe Riesling, her hair piled on top of her head and wearing a pair of gold-rimmed glasses, spotted their red, weeping eyes and climbed over a dozen haggard refugees to reach them. There was only so much she could do for the others, but conjunctivitis was a problem she could solve. And these were the lucky ones. They had come from East Prussia with malnutrition, consumption, scabies, cholera morbus. But hundreds more had been sidetracked and forgotten, their frozen bodies found weeks later, pried out of cattle cars with picks and chains.

Margarethe bent down to speak with the mother, a young woman with sallow skin and bad teeth and the sagging breasts of a matron twice her age. She said her husband had been killed by the Russians. She seemed to have no idea what to do now, or what would become of her children. She seemed to have given up.

Margarethe muttered what reassurances she could, then reached into her bag for the vial holding her few remaining drops of clear yellow extract. She unscrewed the lid and pulled out a sterile piece of cloth.

It was cold in the building and Margarethe wore her overcoat, a Red Cross arm band on the sleeve. A half dozen other doctors and nurses walked through the crowd, passing out soup and medication.

" 'Purge me with hyssop and I shall be clean,' " a man said behind her. "Is that it, my dear?"

She glanced up, saw the topcoat and the Russian fur hat, then quickly looked back down.

"Or are we merely purging our sins through good works?"

Margarethe breathed deeply and let the liquid soak into the small swab of cloth. "Please go to hell, Fisk."

The dentist touched a gloved finger to the tip of his nose and said, "You mean this isn't it! Good God, what we have to look forward to!"

For a moment then he stood over her, gazing across the room at the ragtag collection of peasants and their shabby belongings. Then he smiled back down at her, his face and neck distorted by the angle.

"I understand one of these 'refugees' set herself up at the Esplanade," he said. "She's charging furs to her room and meals at forty marks a day. Says she was the mistress of an English duke and can't be expected to live on an ordinary Red Cross allowance. Fascinating perspective, isn't it?"

He stared at Margarethe for another moment, then glanced back around the room, sizing up the other workers. "So what is it exactly that we have here—charitable outing for the ladies of the Lyceum Club? Somehow I can't picture it. All the Sisters of Mercy sitting down to tea afterward, and you with a double whiskey."

"You're in my way," Margarethe said.

Fisk stepped back awkwardly as she proceeded to daub the liquid into and around the infants' infected eyes. She squeezed the last drops out of the cloth, trying to ignore Fisk standing over her.

The dentist fingered his watch fob as she finished with her patients. He watched her write down the woman's name in a small notebook, then tie a red cloth to her sleeve the way an ornithologist might band a migratory bird.

"Did you hear the elephant died at the Dresden zoo?" Fisk went on distractedly, patting his pockets for a cigar. "A restaurant bought the meat and the customers lined up for blocks." His face brightened marginally as he found the corona he was looking for. From another pocket he pulled out a box of matches. Then he stopped to watch her, his eyes lingering on her throat.

He removed the wrapper and put each end of the cigar into his mouth in turn, wetting it with his tongue. Then he cut the end, struck a match, and lit up, eyeing her all the while.

"We were close once, Margarethe," he said, blowing a dense cloud toward the ceiling. "It saddens me—I'm a far more sensitive fellow than you give me credit for, you know—saddens me now that you don't like me much."

"I don't like you *at all,* Fisk. I loathe you. I despise you."

The dentist nodded and raised the cigar. "I stand corrected. We've had a falling out, let's say. But be that as it may, I take heart. And do you know why, Margarethe? Because in these last few months I've learned something about you. You were naive once, yes. A gullible young girl—I knew that. But now I see that you are, in fact—and I love this word—corruptible. Margarethe Riesling the altruist, Margarethe Riesling the coldly rational scientist. The idealist, the ice princess . . . this same Margarethe Riesling, fucking Kraft von Stade for a few pieces of lab equipment."

"You make me sick."

"I believe we covered that ground already. But can you *ever,* for one moment, imagine how sick it makes me to know that another man is touching you!"

Fisk held her in his gaze for a moment, red-faced with his intensity.

Then he went on. "I accept what it was all about," he said. "It was like a job for you. But do you understand why I'm still in this godforsaken town? It's *you,* Margarethe. *You!*"

She refused to look at him. He continued looming over her, watching her as if hoping to see some effect wrought by his rhetorical flourish.

In time he glanced away.

"You really had the colonel jumping through those hoops, didn't you, Margarethe. I'll tell you this . . . I for one nearly dropped dead when he brought you in. He was like a lap dog . . . his little hard-on, humping your leg. But he never held out on you, I'll bet. He was in love with you, poor man. Materials, information—whatever it was you were after I'm sure he gave it all to you. But what I'm wondering is, how much were you holding out on him?"

"Is this conversation supposed to be threatening, Fisk?"

"Ah. You cut me to the quick to think that I would stoop so low. Black market, yes. Blackmail, no. I don't really care that you fucked over my carefully thought-out business plan, or how much money it's going to cost me now that he's dead. It doesn't take much in the way of brains to figure out what you're up to. I saw you with Katz. There's only two reasons to associate with Jews, and they are buying and selling.

"Now von Stade should have been able to keep you supplied as well as anyone, so nothing to buy, I suppose. Which leaves something to sell, something you've come up with in your little laboratory. Something intriguing enough to keep you around after your beloved fuck-boy Gunther ran out on you. Something dangerous enough, or valuable enough, for you to kill von Stade to protect it."

She stared at him coldly.

"But now von Stade's gone. You need help of a different kind. From a different sort of protector, don't you. You turned to me, once. But now, misguided girl that you are, you turn to this American."

"I don't need his help," she said. "Or anyone else's. Now I've got to go." She stood up and pulled away. She tried to exit gracefully, but her path was blocked. She stumbled through the throng of refugees, climbing over arms and legs until Fisk reached out and gripped her waist.

"Listen to me!"

He threw the cigar at her feet as he spun her around.

"You just don't get it, do you? I have seen the writing on the wall and it is *not* in German. I've sold all my art and antiques for Swiss francs—you can't believe how the prices are soaring given the uncertainty of everything else. My family is in Zurich, where I have excellent contacts in pharmaceuticals. You know all that. You know I can broker this thing for you, Margarethe, whatever it is. We can go all the way with it, war or no war. You can do your science and I'll show you how to do business. You'll be my protégée."

He stood over her, smiling hopefully into a vacuum. "It'll be like old times, don't you see?"

Then as the moments passed and she did not soften, his enthusiasm faded.

"I think about your body often enough, you know? I wonder if it's still as firm, as lovely as before. Time is cruel, Margarethe, especially to women."

She rolled her eyes and loosened her wrist from his slackened grip. Then she looked him full in the face, her lips pursed as if to spit.

He gazed back at her for a moment, assessing the hatred in her eyes. Then he shook his head.

"You are so lovely. But you are just as crazy as the rest of them. The Kaiser and his handlers have it figured out down to the number of calories in an English breakfast, you know. They still think they can win it. They think Britain is going to be the one to starve . . . which is like you thinking you're going to last another ten days in Berlin."

"I'll get by."

"That may be. But tell me, Margarethe, have you checked in with Mr. Katz since your last little meeting at the zoo?"

"What's happened to him?"

"Oh, well. I guess that answers my question."

"Tell me what happened!"

"I don't know. More rumors, that's all. Some kind of accident. But I don't think he's going to be in any position to help you. Which leaves, I believe, Dr. Gordon and myself. You've got quite a following there, Margarethe, but you don't do well in the limelight. So lovely up on stage, but frozen in place, blinded by all that glare, trying to decide. It's getting to be the last act, my love. It's time for you to make up your mind."

THE Meldewesen was a social history of Berlin, twelve million cards on file at the Police Presidency, as gray and immutable as twelve million paper tombstones. They had ten rooms devoted to the letter *H*, fifteen for *S*.

Eli Gordon walked beneath the yellow tiled ceilings of the basement corridor until he found the separate suite of rooms for the Fremdenliste, the foreigners.

There, behind a podium of dark wood, a young woman stood in the light of a single reading lamp. She jotted down the name he requested, then, without ever looking up, dropped the piece of paper into a canister for the pneumatic tube connecting her with the file clerks in the rear.

Since the system had been initiated, in 1836, everyone who had ever lived in Berlin had been listed, along with addresses, occupations, children, servants, property holdings. Anyone moving from the city was kept on the "active list" for twenty years, but Germans, like Egyptians, built for eternity. No cards were ever destroyed.

Gordon stepped back to wait, reaching into his pocket for cigarettes and lighter.

"No smoking," the young woman said, again without eye contact. Gordon put his tobacco back inside his coat and simply paced.

A moment later a "sock" of air surged through the tube and deposited a canister in the basket beneath it. The young woman opened the small cylinder and glanced at the paper she pulled out of it. "Erskine Fisk?" she said, as if the room were filled with possible takers.

Gordon stepped over to retrieve the message, paid his fifty pfennigs, folded the brief transcript and put it in his pocket, then walked back toward the stairs leading to the ground floor.

The Meldewesen catalogued the barest facts of a man's life, not his motives. Fisk's residence and place of business were listed as Bendler Strasse 18. That much Gordon already knew from embassy records. His place of birth was Pima, Ohio. He had a wife and a son, and he owned three other pieces of property. An apartment building on Pestalozzi Strasse in Charlottenburg, an undeveloped lot on the outskirts of Schmargendorf, and the Bowles Brewery on the Berlin-Spandau Ship Canal in Moabit. Gordon had passed through that area yesterday when he went to find the woman from Onkel Tom's. He found it curious that the Institute for Infectious Diseases stood facing that same canal.

Gordon continued through the gray main corridor filled with bureaucrats and lawyers, wondering about the diminishing role of coincidence in his life. Everything seemed connected by some invisible thread, waiting to be pulled tight like a string bag. The most disturbing part was Jay Adams. It was disturbing, yes, Gordon's gullibility, his vulnerability. But, even so, why the lead about Beszenoff? Why would Ostriker encourage him along the same lines as the British?

Gordon came to the main entry and glanced around quickly, past the newspaper kiosk, past the fruit vendor, hoping for another way out of the building. Just inside the glass door, beside a case holding a papier-mâché replica of the city, Andreas Schiller stood setting a match to the tip of his cigar.

The diffused light from the vestibule gave the detective's eyes a glow of China blue. They were pale northern eyes, eyes meant for gazing across snow fields. Schiller saluted with his cheroot and said, "How about some lunch?"

Gordon slowed his pace and came to an awkward hesitation beside the glass display case as Schiller shook out the match and dropped it into an ashtray.

Gordon looked down at the tiny models of the Reichstag and the university. The real city seemed just about that small. It was too crowded here. They were tripping all over one another.

"No, thanks," he said. "I've got an appointment at the embassy."

Schiller smiled and placed his hand gently on Gordon's shoulder. "No, no," he said. "I insist."

The detective pushed back the door and together the two men stepped out into a brisk winter wind.

The midday sun, never more than thirty degrees above the horizon, produced an uncertain winter light. Schiller winced at the cold and said, "What happened to your hand?"

"Accident getting out of a taxi."

The detective gave him a mildly skeptical glance, then shook his head. "It is astonishing to see one man living under a cloud of such incredibly bad luck."

They walked alongside the immense facade of the Polizei Präsidium, Schiller looking up at the apocalyptic sky, the dark clouds rumbling across. "So what brings you to the Alex?"

"Embassy details. The Meldewesen."

"Ah, tracking lost sheep." Schiller nodded, then pulled the cigar from his mouth and looked at it. "It's a good system, don't you think?"

"Very efficient," Gordon said.

Schiller nodded again, scanning the small shops beneath the stone arches of the elevated tracks across the way.

"Bismarck called this city a 'desert of bricks and newspapers,'" he said after a while. "Carbon paper and file cabinets would have been more exact."

The detective put the cheroot back between his teeth and bowed his head against the wind.

He walked with the same rigid gait, his arms extended at his sides, as if he were carrying a pair of imaginary suitcases.

"Of course you didn't see the criminal files, did you? Tattoo and Deformity Register, Nickname and Alias Register, Register of Bodily Measurement. We're becoming quite scientific. Photography files, dactyloscopy files, modus operandi files. You don't keep such excellent records in America, do you?"

"No. We're not so efficient."

Schiller glanced up with a smile, either the smoke or the cold bringing a film of tears to his eyes. "A basic distinction in political philosophy, of course. In Germany we prefer order. In America you prefer freedom."

At last they rounded the corner of the huge municipal building and the wind shifted to their backs. "Where are you from in the U.S.A., Doctor?"

"I live in Boston."

"I take it you weren't always from Boston."

"No. I was raised in the West."

"No kidding." Schiller grabbed the cigar. "And where was that?"

"Missouri. Oklahoma."

"Ah. Then truly we must talk. I am fascinated by the Wild West. Karl May, you know his books?"

Gordon shook his head.

"Much excitement. Cowboys and Indians. *The Winnateu. Old Shatterhand.* The freedom of the trail, where a man's past is his own."

Then Schiller gazed at him with a look of hard-earned wisdom. "All in all, Dr. Gordon, Germany is not such a terribly good place for secrets."

The restaurant was on Kaiserstrasse, between the synagogue and the Realschule. There was dark wooden paneling punctuated by stained-glass windows above dark wooden booths that looked as if they had been carved with an ax.

Schiller peered over the candles and the Zeppelin-shaped menu. "Knockwurst," he said. "Very interesting."

They placed their ration cards on the table for the waiter, who took their order without much ado and disappeared into the kitchen. The restaurant was cold and they sat in their overcoats as they waited.

"It isn't often you see knockwurst on a menu in Berlin. It's good we're here to try it. What have you been living on, mangel-wurzels for breakfast?"

"I'm not sure. Possibly."

"Umm." Schiller folded his hands over his plate and stared dead ahead.

Gordon wanted to know what this very odd policeman had on his mind. He picked up his fork with his left hand, stood it on end, then began to twist it around and around.

Schiller watched him for a while, studying the impatience, the need for tactile reassurance. "*Old Shatterhand,*" he said after a moment. Then their eyes met and Schiller looked away.

"Will it heal properly?"

"I don't know yet."

"That could be a problem for a surgeon."

"That's crossed my mind."

"A little late to choose another line of work."

"That's true," Gordon said. "A little late."

Schiller nodded and unbuttoned his coat, using only his right hand. His disease made it difficult to coordinate both sides of his body, but when he had finished the process, he said, "I have quite another kind of problem, you see. The fact is, I have two. The more immediate is an investigation that keeps bumping into personages of the Reich. A well-connected military officer. A chief of state security. A close personal associate of the Kaiser himself."

Schiller brought his hands together and once again meshed his fingers.

"My second problem is more philosophical. We Germans, of course, are great for philosophizing. Sometimes with a hammer.

But, if you will permit me—how can it matter anymore that a man kills a man when the bodies are piling up in the trenches?"

Schiller's right arm began to tremble and to quiet it he gripped his left shoulder and let the arm hang across his chest. He looked back at Gordon, and there was a hint of embarrassment in his eyes. "To tell you the sad truth, Doctor, I've begun to think of murder as redundant. Murder during wartime, at least. Maybe you've had a similar feeling . . . with the wounded in France. A doctor who can't save lives. A policeman who can't enforce the law."

Schiller let his arm continue to hang, and in another moment the waiter appeared with their orders—two plates, one small knockwurst on each, surrounded by the ineluctable turnips. Schiller glanced down at his meal without seeing it, oddly distracted now for a man avowing such an interest in food.

Working with his left hand, cautiously applying pressure with the edge of his fork, Gordon cut into the sausage.

Schiller watched pensively as Gordon prepared to take a bite. "You can see then why the motive takes on such importance," the detective said. "The 'Why?' of murder. That's the only way we can discriminate, not true? The only hope of hanging on to any meaning, especially now. Not so much 'How?' or even 'Who?' but 'Why?' "

The detective turned to his lunch, picked up his knife and fork, and struggled to stay in control as he sliced through the dark skin of the sausage.

"We rotate the homicide assignment here in Berlin, did you know? Surprisingly, in this one month I have had two murders to deal with. One victim was a high official in an industrial ministry. The other . . . an obscure maker of surgical instruments. Yet lo and behold, a common thread—both men were involved in the black market."

Schiller looked carefully at his sausage, then without taking a bite reached into his pocket. Slowly, he pulled out the coil of hair he had found at the Pension Hölldobler and placed it on the table.

"This belonged to the first killer."

Gordon looked down at the long, distinctively golden strands catching the light. He had seen hair like this before.

"Her victim was a colonel in a very sensitive position—head of an armaments ministry responsible for chemical weapons. He was also quite a skillful entrepreneur, outmaneuvering the cattle-purchasing federations and the town councils to get meat for his workers. But despite his very public position, his death was a most intimate crime. Unusually subtle. In contrast to the death of Mr. Katz," Schiller added.

The detective picked up his knife and fork with a grimace and speared the wurst. "Even with the wide variance, though, some-thing nags at me, telling me there is a connection beyond the black market. After all, half of Berlin is in the black market, one way or another."

Schiller held up his fork, examining the piece of meat again as if it were evidence.

"Despite his ambitious financial entanglements, Isidor Katz was a socialist. He had been linked by some to a radical leader named Gunther Stinnes, who, in turn, was linked to Liebknecht and Rosa Luxemburg. But so far, there is no proof of all this, only specu-lation."

Schiller shrugged, letting the fork bounce like a drumstick in his fingers. "A merchant socialist. A black marketeer. In this country portraits of Marx and the Kaiser rest side by side on many a mantelpiece."

At last Gordon took a bite, still staring at the strands of golden hair. Then without lifting his eyes he asked, "Who is the chief of state security?"

"A man named Walther Ostriker."

"And the close associate of the Kaiser?"

"His dentist. Erskine Fisk."

Gordon sank his teeth into another bite of sausage, eating to give himself time to think. He'd just received a message but he wasn't sure why. The blond woman at Onkel Tom's was supposedly a murderer. Was this a warning, or was it something else?

He looked up and saw Schiller staring ahead in silence, his hands clasped together over his plate.

"You're not eating," Gordon said.

Schiller shrugged. "There've been some problems with the wurst."

"What do you mean?"

"A question of origin. Dogs. Cats. The hospitals. You know about rumors in wartime."

Gordon put down his fork, amazed by Schiller's complacent stare. He swallowed hard, then reached for his glass of water. As the detective gazed flatly into his eyes, he drank it steadily down.

THE first white flakes of another snowstorm blew into the courtyard outside the embassy. Gordon listened to the wind pressuring the windowpanes, then for sounds from the offices next door.

He waited another moment, then reached down to the lower right drawer of the desk and pulled out the two British revolvers and the box of cartridges. Turning his back to the door, he ejected both cylinders in turn and loaded them, put one of the guns in his pocket, then reached down to put the other behind the vertical files in the lower left drawer.

There behind the folders he found Mrs. Ruthven Webb's oatmeal box, the container for her departed husband, the sales manager from Cedar Rapids.

Gordon pulled it out and removed the top and looked inside. The dull gray powder seemed appropriate enough at first. He shook the container and poured a few ounces into the lid, stirring it with a pencil until he satisfied himself that Mrs. Webb was right. This was not her husband. There were no bone fragments here, and the powder was not ash. What was supposed to be Mr. Webb was plaster. Plaster, Gordon assumed, from the walls of Berlin's Municipal Crematorium.

FISK'S brewery sat like a fortress beside the Berlin-Spandau Ship Canal, enclosed by a high brick wall with a thick, cylindrical battlement resting atop one corner. Above the wall, Gordon could see terra-cotta parapets washed in the orange glow of late afternoon sun. The high iron gate stood chained, with no sign of recent traffic.

Turning his head to look the other way, Gordon found himself staring at the spot where, yesterday, he had waited for the woman to leave work. The brewery and the Institute for Infectious Diseases, facing each other across the canal. The brewery and the Institute, one hundred yards apart.

The wind blew sharp and cold down the waterway as Gordon turned and walked east toward the Fohrer Bridge. Lowering his head, he reached down to feel the heft of the revolver in his pocket.

All around him now were the red brick factories for turbines and machine tools. Siemens, Halske, Schwartzkopff, Borsig, A.E.G.—the muscle of German industry, all with workers who needed to be fed. He had found a connection; simply not the one he was looking for.

He turned away from the canal and walked south on Putlitzstrasse. Then outside a restaurant called the Urania he stopped and made a business of looking in at the customers having an early dinner. The thin man reflected in the glass had trailed him since he left the bridge. A thin man in a worker's coat and a worker's snap-brim cap.

Gordon turned back around toward the Bahnhof Putlitzstrasse and took a quick inventory of his options. It was then that he saw the white horse and the black delivery van, and at the reins the same huge man who had followed him that night outside Onkel Tom's.

The man in the snap-brim cap stayed with him, returning his glance with a metallic grin as Gordon went in the station and up the stairs. They issued dentures like that all along the German front, but the image lodged in his mind was very clear. In von den Benken's car. The man beside the driver.

Gordon stepped into the washroom and lit a cigarette. Across the tiled room lit with bare bulbs a soldier leaned over the sink to wash his face.

An old woman with shoulders hunched under a shawl dragged a mop bucket out of the far corner, trailing with her the heavy smell of disinfectant. When she reached the center of the floor she stopped to stare at Gordon. She seemed annoyed. She stood by her table with the dish set out for coins and she looked at him as if to say, "Let's see it. Pull it out. You can't just stand here."

Gordon turned to the urinal trough and smoked his cigarette. The soldier dried his face, adjusted his cap, and left. Then Gordon waited, smoking, listening to the slap of the mop against the tiles and wooden baseboards.

The gun was in his left overcoat pocket. He had never fired it— he had never fired a gun at all with his left hand—and there was no time now for a run-through. His heart raced as he waited. He wanted to get this over with.

The woman backed toward him, trailing the mop after her, the guardian of hygiene. Then Gordon felt the man's presence beside him. The snap-brim hat, the metallic grin, casually unbuttoning his pants to Gordon's right.

Gordon left the cigarette clinging to his lip and wrapped his hand around the butt of the revolver. The German pulled out his member, tilted back his head, and released a bright yellow stream of urine against the orange-tiled wall.

Gordon glanced down. The man's left hand was on his hip, his right wrapped around his penis, but backward, thumb to abdomen.

Gordon looked up and the man smiled at him. Then the German opened his mouth. In a croaking whisper, half singing, he said: " 'Oh Dunderbach, oh Dunderbach, how could you be so mean. . . .' "

The old woman stood at Gordon's side now, her elbow brushing against him as she worked the mop.

"You learn very slowly, Doctor," the man went on, continuing to urinate. He looked up at Gordon and smiled again.

" 'To ever have invented that sausage meat machine . . .' Oh, wait. Need help with your buttons? You seem to have mashed your fingers."

Gordon stared straight ahead, examining the mortar between the tiles. "I don't know you," he said.

"I'm Dunderbach," the German said, jostling the stream. "And you, my friend. I'm afraid you are meat on a hook."

He gave a little shudder as he emptied his bladder. "Ever hear the one about the Englishman and the German peeing off a bridge? It's night, see, pitch black. The Englishman pulls it out and says, 'Ah. Water's cold.' The German does the same and says, 'Yah. Deep, too.' "

The German shook himself dry, methodically tucked himself back into his pants, then pulled an ice pick out from his belt.

Gordon waited too long to draw the gun. The metal shaft arched through the air as he ran through a final mental checklist. They had killed Katz. They had crushed his hand. And now they were going to kill him.

The sharpened steel ripped at his throat as he squeezed the trigger and blew the German back into the wall.

The charwoman screamed at the sound of the explosion, dropped her mop, then tripped over her bucket as she ran from the room.

"Dunderbach" stared wide-eyed as he leaned against the tiles, calm and intent, one hand gripping the ice pick, the other clasped over his abdomen. He opened his mouth slightly and the metal teeth dislodged. Bright red blood trickled over his widespread fingers.

Gordon stepped back, trying to breathe, still pointing the gun at the German's chest. He wanted to stick the barrel into his face and empty the cylinder, but the inhibitors were already back in place.

The German inhaled deeply. He did not appear to be in pain, merely dazed, as he looked down at his blood-soaked middle. Then he rolled his eyes. Then he groaned and threw himself forward as Gordon fired again.

Both men fell to the wet floor and the ice pick sank into Gordon's shoulder. He fired once more, then fell back amazed as the German's skull exploded across the room.

Gordon lay stunned on the wet tiles, the dead man hemorrhaging on top of him. Then he turned his head to focus on a young boy in a big hat standing in the doorway. He found himself staring into the dark aperture of an automatic pistol, still hot from firing.

Gordon pushed "Dunderbach" away and edged into the corner. Then, as the pain from his shoulder rose up and took control, he saw a cloud of cigar smoke in the doorway and, behind it, Detective Andreas Schiller walk disapprovingly into the room.

19

S tadtvogtei Prison was a chunk of stone and steel holding
down the other end of Dirckenstrasse like a counterweight
for the Polizei Präsidium. It housed "political prisoners"
mostly, if only because all crimes were viewed now as crimes
against the state.

Gordon was kept in a cubicle on the fifth floor, staring at the
slats of the bunk above him, and not feeling particularly well. The
police surgeon had bathed his new wounds in saline and dressed
them with paper bandages, but once again there was nothing for
the pain.

At ten o'clock a guard threw back the door and ordered him to
his feet. The light was in his eyes and his mouth tasted foul. He
slid down off his bunk and, feeling numbed and disoriented, grap-
pled for his shoes. Then the cold and the pain gripped him in
tandem and he began to shake.

The triangular cell blocks were segmented like an orange, radiating around a central opening. The guard led him down the
metal stairs through open gangways of glass embedded in steel
grids to the courtyard below. On the ground level they reentered
the building and went into a small room empty except for a wooden
bench, six feet long.

At one end of the bench, sitting like a kid on a seesaw, was
Andreas Schiller.

The detective wore his hat and coat. In front of him, on the bench between his straddled legs, was a long-necked bottle in a twisted paper bag.

Schiller motioned with his hand, giving Gordon four feet of bench to choose from. Then he waited, his hands still in his pockets.

Gordon sat down sideways on the plank and rested his elbows on his knees. He brushed back his hair but the bandage on his fingers became entangled. He reached up with his good hand and tore away the splints and the paper wrappings.

Schiller shoved the bottle a few inches closer to Gordon and asked, "How's your shoulder?"

"It's all right," Gordon said. Then the two men looked at each other. The room was cold and damp but his shoulder was on fire.

"So who was the man who attacked you?" Schiller asked.

"I have no idea."

"You'd never seen him before?"

"That's right."

The only light in the room was a single bulb in a metal reflector hanging down from the ceiling. Overhead, the wire was stapled to a strip of wood outside the plaster. Shaded by the brim of his hat, Schiller's eyes were scarcely visible.

"So where were you coming from when you were attacked?"

"I was lost. I was trying to get to the Charité. I thought my hand needed another look, but I got off on the wrong stop."

Schiller's nodding continued. After a moment, Gordon realized that it was involuntary.

"So that is why you were strolling around the Westhafen docks," Schiller said. "Looking for the hospital?"

Gordon took the neck of the bottle and pulled it up. It was cheap Polish vodka. "I was lost. Like I told you." He took a drink.

"Ah, yes," Schiller said, nodding. "Lost. Lucky you had that revolver in your pocket."

Gordon remained silent, tilting his neck ever so slightly. Each movement made it hurt in an entirely new way.

"Okay," Schiller went on. "Okay. We don't seem to be getting very far with this. Why don't we leave it for a moment and back up? Let's talk about the tall woman with the long blond hair."

Gordon reached down and picked up a copy of the German New Testament lying on the bench beside him. He thumbed through the book, avoiding Schiller's eyes, scanning the printed list of rules for Stadtvogtei, the wages for making paper bags and umbrella sheaths.

"You seem quite taken with her, my friend. Following her about."

"She reminds me of someone I knew in the States," Gordon said, tossing down the book.

"Ah." Schiller smiled. "Boy meets girl. That's really very nice. But then Margarethe Riesling is hardly the girl next door, is she? More 'Little Mary Kafka,' I would say."

Gordon looked up, and the detective gripped the bottle, slid back the bag, and removed the cork.

"I told you about my two corpses, did I not? Katz and von Stade? I said that both deaths were related to the black market, but that's a bit like saying they were linked to the 'rising tide of violence in society' or to 'declining moral standards.' Incredibly vague. Incredibly general."

The detective paused to take a drink, then wiped his lips. "The more direct connection is you, Dr. Gordon. You knew Katz, you know Margarethe Riesling."

"If that's the blond woman, I didn't even know her name until now. I saw her once."

"You saw her twice that we know of," Schiller said, tapping the cork back in the bottle and setting it aside.

"You seemed shaken when I suggested she'd killed von Stade, that she was a murderer. I don't suppose you ever talked about it? I'd really like to know how she did it. My guess is a chemical poison, sprayed into his face during sex."

Schiller raised his head and Gordon looked into his neutral blue eyes, resisting the urge to ask how he had arrived at that particular conclusion.

"Interesting idea," Gordon said.

"Deductive method. Very scientific. Except that it's based on virtually no evidence. A witness would be much more useful. Unfortunately, people don't usually fuck with witnesses."

Schiller paused, then yawned dramatically. His eyes looked heavy and tired.

"She's a good catch for a man like you," he said after a while. "Beautiful, yes? A little grim, but very intelligent. She works in medical research, and you, of course, are a doctor. Let me see now . . . Katz made medical instruments. But Katz also dealt on the black market. Von Stade bought huge quantities of meat on the black market to feed his workers. So von Stade, Katz, Riesling, and you—the black market. That's one theory."

Schiller put his hands in his pockets as if waiting for confirmation or denial, but Gordon could not give him either one. Instead the American leaned back on the bench and stared blankly ahead.

"On the other hand, von Stade's hungry multitudes were munitions workers. Chemical munitions. Involved in experimental work, highly advanced stuff. And the rest of you—medical people, researchers. Katz a merchant doing business across our borders. Von Stade, Katz, Riesling, and you—espionage."

Schiller's mouth held the shape of his final syllable, his gaze prolonged, flat, and neutral.

"It took quite some time before it occurred to me that the two theories were not mutually exclusive."

Gordon stared off at the stone walls rising up from the concrete floor. He was tired of cat and mouse now. He was tired of the whole damn thing.

"My own interest is limited to the black market, of course," Schiller continued. "I don't like what it says about us, you see. Germany had a war that lasted thirty years once. Imaginative people that we are, we called it the Thirty Years War. But it kept us in the Dark Ages. Starvation led to cannibalism, death brought polygamy to rebuild the population. These things are part of our history.

"But now the Section Fours," he went on. "The political police, they run around with their fingers in the air, testing every wind that blows in from Potsdam and Pless and the Great General Staff. They should be all over you. It makes me rather resentful to do their work for them."

Schiller watched Gordon for another moment, then reached down for the bottle and tapped it on the wood. "I'm curious. When we spoke before you mentioned Missouri, Oklahoma—the Indian territories. Your features are also very dark. By any chance . . ."

"My grandmother," Gordon said. "On my mother's side."

"Ah." Schiller smiled. "The lost tribes of Israel. We're practically brothers, then, you know?"

Gordon said nothing, and eventually Schiller looked away. "Being a blood brother, of course, I might warn you that the army, the foreign office, they're much more skillful than my colleagues from Section Four. Walther Ostriker is pretty good, especially on technical matters. His people of course have been watching you. Watching since our first conversation in the Wilhelm Platz. And Ostriker is not a pleasant man. I suggest you do what you can to avoid him."

Schiller rose slowly to his feet, his right hand trembling.

"We seem to have crossed our lines, haven't we, Doctor? Your first 'accident' suggests to me that you've been reasonably successful in getting into whatever trouble you were sent here to find. But this latest attack is not Ostriker's doing. You've stumbled onto something more complicated than you ever imagined. But perhaps I can be helpful to you. All in all your presence has been helpful to me. But this reciprocation would require, of course, that you tell me what you *did* expect to find in Berlin."

Gordon stared back in silence, wishing he had a clear answer to that question himself. A few moments passed. Then, softly, he said, "Bricks and newspapers."

Schiller nodded, putting his hands in his pockets. "I thought as much," he said. Then he looked up at the ceiling, tracing a long, branching crack in the plaster that had the pattern of a varicose vein.

"You know, Doctor, whoever devised this mission for you was not overly concerned for your well-being." He turned to Gordon with his stoic gaze. "Still, it must be a marvelous thing to be a man of action, to engage the world and change it. I very often feel as if my life is a book I'm reading. I keep turning the pages to uncover the plot, but it really has nothing to do with me. Most times I feel it wouldn't be right to tamper with it. I have to let the story unfold without my intervention, just to see. Once you step in you never know the rest of it, do you? How it will turn out."

Schiller walked the few paces to the wall and paused with his arm draped across his shoulder. "So tell me about Hellmuth Muller."

Gordon shook his head. "I don't know anyone named Hellmuth Muller."

"You know him intimately," Schiller said, pulling the ice pick out of his pocket. He came back to the bench and sat down, then stabbed the metal shaft into the soft wooden surface. "The man with the metal teeth."

Both men sat perfectly still, the ice pick vibrating between them. Gordon shook his head. "I have no idea."

"The man in the van? The big man with the beard?"

"No idea."

Schiller waited for the oscillations to stop, then reached into his pocket and pulled out a cigar.

"People who are motivated to murder are usually fairly persistent," he said, speaking earnestly, without inflection.

He found a match, then took a moment to light his cheroot.

"Two Christmases ago we bought a goose. We bought it to

fatten it up, but my wife and I—as bad as the children—we got attached. When the time came to kill the bird we couldn't bring ourselves to do it. We struggled with the decision, then resolved to use chloroform. A brilliant strategy, which we carried out with great solemnity, letting the bird pass peacefully from this life. We plucked it, then went into the other room to trim the tree. Next thing we know, this plucked goose is up running around the kitchen in a frenzy, knocking things off the wall and off the tables and I had to beat it to death with my cudgel. It was horrible. We would all have been much better off, including the goose, if we'd simply wrung his neck the first time."

Gordon stared back at Schiller, his head shrouded in smoke. Then the detective stood up.

"You should get some sleep here tonight and stay out of trouble. I'm not going to hold you beyond tomorrow. You're not much use to anyone sitting here. Out on the street you have the makings of a veritable death squad. As I was saying, though, failed murders often have messy sequels. We don't know who sent Muller to kill you. But keep in mind—whoever it was, he does know you."

20

The night was clear and cold, the sky off to the north as black as jet behind the glittering points of stars. But in the building harbor at Wilhelmshaven, a thousand arc lamps illuminated giant cranes whirring and groaning as they lifted huge, fifteen-inch guns onto a new Kaiser-class battleship. Overhead, a pair of Zeppelins glided above the fitting-out harbor, turning slowly to make their way across Jade Bay, bound for a dawn raid over Britain.

Commander Dr. Ernst Steegmuller had been dressed and out of his house before he realized that he was still wearing his "Schnurr-bartbinde," the facial bandage he wore each night to give his mustache the "erechtite" look of the All Highest's. Luckily, at four in the morning, there was no one about to see the blunder or his resultant embarrassment, at least not along the narrow lane that led from the officers' compound to the main harbor. He ripped it off his face and stuffed it into the medical bag he carried in his prosthetic right hand.

Despite a certain mental and physical numbness, Steegmuller was delighted to have been summoned out of his bed. "Remember that the day has twenty-four hours," Grand Admiral von Koester had said to the men on the building docks. "And if you find that is not enough, take part of the night as well."

The slightly distracted officer on the telephone had asked Steegmuller to report to Slip 13, just beyond the Kaiser Wilhelm Bridge. A U-boat returning from patrol had sent a wireless message requesting medical assistance—for an unusual illness of some sort, not battle injuries. Steegmuller assumed food poisoning, but there were other possibilities. Arsine gas often escaped from the storage batteries, causing anemia, anoxemia, and jaundice. And then the closed quarters of the U-boats themselves were excellent for the spread of infections.

Steegmuller crossed the railroad tracks and saw the ambulance wagons already waiting at Slip 17. He walked along the dock, admiring the sleek gray skins rising out of the water like so many great metal sharks. He looked out across the blackness of the New Harbor to the glare of the torpedo yard and mine arsenal on the other shore. Then he saw the lights moving under the railway bridge. It was the U-boat, sliding through the water at slow speed. An officer and several men rode atop the conning tower, their hands in the pockets of their leather jackets. Their faces looked unusually grim, not at all the smiles and huzzahs of returning sailors.

The boat edged smoothly through the center of the channel, then turned abruptly toward the assigned mooring. The sailors on deck moved to their docking stations, cleating lines to be thrown to shore. There was a wash from the stern, and the boat slowed even more, sending a rush of water ahead of it to cushion its landing.

The officer on the deck was only a boy, and his smooth face was tense with fear. He saluted and beckoned Steegmuller on board. "Please," he said. "Come this way."

Steegmuller followed uncertainly over the steel grate of the gangway. A burly sailor took his bag and helped him on deck, then up to the conning tower and hatch.

Climbing down the ladder, Steegmuller was hit by the smell of diesel fumes and human sweat. He passed the men's quarters, then the narrower officers' quarters, and finally into the captain's individual compartment. The ceiling dripped condensation like a heavy sweat. The electric light flickered over a man lying naked, his abdomen partially covered by a sheet, his eyes glazed, his arms and legs completely black.

Steegmuller looked at the swollen lymph nodes, the rim of edema surrounding the necrotic areas. He was dismayed and also frightened. He had not seen anything like this since medical school. How could he see such a thing, after all, in the Kaiser's navy? How was it possible for sailors at sea, sailors *under* the sea, to contract such a peculiar disease as anthrax?

MARGARETHE awoke surrounded by men in overcoats. She was drowsy and confused and at first she told herself she was dreaming. One man going through her bureau drawers, another jabbing at her, shouting, "Get up. Get dressed."

The fear of this moment had startled her awake many times before. Now that it was actually happening, the whole scene seemed slightly ludicrous.

The man leaning over her wore black leather and was missing an eye, or so it seemed. "Get up. Put on your clothes." He dragged her out of bed clutching the covers at her throat.

"I'm up. I'm up," she shouted.

Freed from his grip, she sat on the edge of the mattress, looking out at her landlady, Frau Schaaf. The old woman peered in from the hall and worked her keys like a rosary.

The man in leather reached over to the chair and scooped up the clothes Margarethe had taken off the night before. He had both eyes, she realized. It was just that the brow and lashes on one side were completely white.

"Get dressed," he said, tossing the clothes on the bed.

Margarethe pushed back her hair and gathered up the skirt and blouse. She rose unsteadily, then started for the door.

"Where are you going?"

"Where the Kaiser goes alone."

"Just put your clothes on," he said. "Now. Or we'll take you like you are."

The morning was gray, the air heavy and damp. They rode in silence down the Kurfürstendamm toward a large office building off the Tiergarten, then around to a side entrance at Königergratzerstrasse 70, where they hurried her inside and past the guard and into a waiting lift.

The man with the white eyebrow closed the grate and put the lift in gear. They began to rise, and she watched each level go slowly past, the floor cross-sectioned like a specimen in anatomy. The movement added to the nausea that had been with her since she first greeted the light of day. She should have left Berlin when the American showed up. She should have left when she heard about Katz.

On the fifth landing the car jolted to a halt. The man worked the lever to bring them perfectly flush, then opened the grate.

"Get out," he said.

She stepped into a vestibule no larger than the elevator car. Beyond it was a suite of offices with the walls stripped bare, the only furniture a single desk pulled out from the wall. A telephone apparatus sat on the floor along with three empty pasteboard cartons.

Five offices opened off this central reception area, each of them vacant. They pushed her straight ahead into the largest of these, where an officer of the General Staff sat in a wooden chair. The man in leather waited outside, pulling the door closed behind her.

With his back to the window, the officer sat just in front of the radiator, which sputtered and hissed. She knew who this man was. She had been living with his presence in her dreams for months.

The blinds were pulled all the way up to the top and exposed a swath of gray sky. The walls were white, marred and stained.

She could see the nail holes where pictures had hung. Nothing was left in the room but the chair and the paper clips and the scraps of paper lying on the floor.

Gazing at her through steel eyeglasses, Walther Ostriker looked utterly placid. He seemed small and unmilitary, lost inside his uniform.

For a moment he let her catch her breath. Then very quietly he asked, "Do you know what the Australians call their British cousins?"

The question disarmed her. She avoided his lifeless stare and shook her head.

"Bleedin' pommy bastards," Ostriker told her, studying her carefully as he talked. "Pomes. From the metal collars the prisoners wore when they arrived on the new continent. P.O.M.E. Prisoner of Mother England."

Margarethe glanced toward him. The room was incredibly warm and her sinuses burned, yet Ostriker seemed oblivious, sitting with his legs crossed, his hands folded atop a manila envelope in his lap.

"Blinded by arrogance. Trapped by illusions of their own superiority . . ."

He stopped in mid-thought, leaning back to glance away at the blank wall. Then for the next several moments he appeared to listen to the radiators as they hissed and rattled.

In time he pursed his mouth and turned to her once again.

"Tell me, Margarethe Riesling. Are you a prisoner of Mother England?"

She shook her head again, parting her dry lips. In time she managed a hoarsely whispered "No."

Walther Ostriker peeled off his eyeglasses and put the wire earpieces in his mouth, letting them hang on his lower teeth. He seemed to be weighing her response, tapping the glasses between thumb and forefinger, letting them sway back and forth.

A moment later, with one earpiece still in his mouth, he picked up the envelope and pulled out a photograph. He handed it to her and, with the same calm, pleasant tone, asked, "Who is this man in the center?"

Margarethe Riesling studied the picture, then handed it back. "I don't know."

Ostriker took his glasses out of his mouth and held them down by his side. "You were seen talking with him at Onkel Tom's Hütte on the night of January nineteenth. On January twentieth, you rode together on the Ringbahn from the Bahnhof Putlitz-strasse to the Bahnhof Charlottenburg."

"I don't know. I can't be responsible for men who push them-selves on me. Whoever reported this should have noted that neither conversation lasted more than a minute. I got rid of him as fast as I could."

"What is his name?"

"I told you, I don't know."

"What did you talk about?"

"He talked rot. He claimed to be attracted to me. He tried to flatter me. It was that sort of thing."

"He's a suitor?"

"He's a nuisance. I don't know anything about him. I avoided him as best I could."

Margarethe Riesling breathed heavily, staring directly into the major's eyes, trying to manage a look of blameless indignation.

"Of course you don't believe any of that," Ostriker said at last, dropping the envelope on the floor.

He raised his glasses and began spinning them around and around. "You can't really expect me to believe any of that, can you? So tell me why he is here. Is he here to sell you something? Is he here to buy something?"

Margarethe was silent. She folded her arms beneath her breasts and stood facing the wall.

Ostriker put his glasses back on and watched her for a good thirty seconds. Eventually, he raised a pale index finger to scratch the point of his chin.

"I interviewed your Professor von Broembsen at the Institute," he said, tilting back his head. "He told me you grind turnips for him. He says you cry into test tubes. He says you're helping him study certain vegetable and bodily fluids, exploring the ways they 'interact' with bacteria."

She nodded several times and said, "Yes. That's right."

"I'm a chemist, did you know that?"

She shook her head.

"I know all about 'interacting' with microorganisms. You 'interact' by killing them. You burn them off the walls of processing plants, off surgical instruments, off the surfaces of wounds. That's old business. Simple. There's nothing to attract anyone's attention in that anymore."

He uncrossed his legs suddenly and leaned forward in his chair.

"But now deep inside the body—there's the frontier for researchers like you. The chemicals that burn and blister to kill bacteria, they also kill tissue. So when the wound is deep and begins to heal . . . how do you reach inside? And what do you do when the infection is coursing throughout the body?"

He waited, as if the question were not rhetorical.

"What you do is you search for a 'magic bullet,' " he said, leaning back. "A miraculous serum that will kill what you want to kill, but which will leave the host organism alone. Where would you say we are on that search, my dear Margarethe Riesling?"

"Salvarsan," she said. "There's Salvarsan, that's all."

"Ah, yes. Ehrlich's discovery. A chemist too, of course. Dioxydiamino-arsenobenzene. But Salvarsan controls only syphilis. A good place to begin, but limited."

"That's right."

"Salvarsan would do nothing for, say, an infection such as anthrax."

"As far as I know, that's right."

"How interesting."

Ostriker stood and stepped behind his chair, gripped the wooden back, and tilted it slightly forward. "It was the Russians, did you know, who first tried to make a weapon out of chlorine gas?"

She shook her head.

"It formed a hydrate in the cold and sank into the snow, then reformed in the spring to kill whoever happened to be passing by. A rather inefficient device, don't you think? Even for Russians?"

She nodded, trying to smile.

"But Russians are mystics, not technicians. What can you expect? We Germans are much more methodical. When chemical weapons were the frontier we tackled the temperature problem first thing, and head on. I worked with Haber in the early days, you know. The result was 'antifreeze,' xylene, and solvent naphtha. And thousands of blue-faced corpses lying dead on the Western front."

She turned away, as if trying to escape the image he had just conjured up for her.

"But now this city is filled with rumors of terrible new weapons that will turn the tide, disease weapons that transcend anything imaginable with chemicals. Still, there's a problem, just as there was with chlorine. You need a 'magic bullet.' Unless you are an idiot, you need a way to control the plague you inflict on your enemy. To protect yourself against this plague. Otherwise, anything could happen. Your own troops, civilian populations, who knows?"

"We're years away from anything like that," she said, turning back to face him. "I wouldn't even know where to begin."

Ostriker smiled. "Apparently the British have far more faith in you."

She waited a moment. Then she pushed back her hair and said, "I don't understand."

"Curious, isn't it? Of all the people studying bacterials in Germany, not to mention those in England, the British Secret Service approaches you."

Ostriker studied her eyes for a moment, testing her, looking for signs. Then he shook his head. "Several things about you concern me, Margarethe Riesling. For one, you are not a citizen of the Reich. That alone should exclude you from sensitive work in a government laboratory. Yet you've managed to stay on since the war. How do you explain that?"

"I've never thought about it."

"Oh, I have. And I have a theory. Let me try it on you. Professor von Broembsen has published two papers in the past five years. One was on insect vision in relation to swatting flies. Another proposed a new method of paring the nails of the right hand. Let us be kind and say that the man is past his prime. The fact is he's senile, but he can stay on because he covers for you and you do his work for him. Isn't that the way it is?"

"Yes, more or less," she said. "That's the way it is." Then she was silent.

"You must be good at what you do," he said after a while. "Suspect, but still valuable because you're talented. Talented enough, perhaps, to actually succeed where others might fail. But that's something else that concerns me. What would you do if you did succeed? This 'magic bullet' is troubling, isn't it, Margarethe? A breakthrough that could save lives, or one that could open up a 'higher' form of killing."

He leaned forward on the chair, watching her reactions.

"You work with refugees," he said. "You volunteer to care for the wounded—a very admirable sensibility. Except perhaps, for someone in weapons research. A grim business. I think your research may subject you to excessive stress. Various 'dilemmas' of the soul."

He glanced away for a moment, then turned back to her.

"Did you know that astronomers can predict the existence of objects in space long before they can see them? That's because the pull of gravity distorts the orbits of other objects nearby." His eyes were flat and cold as he looked at her. "You, Margarethe Riesling, have a distorted orbit.

"Now this American—Eli Gordon. He works for the British

Secret Service. You will not avoid him in the future. You will agree to meet with him, to hear him out. You will sleep with him if that's what he wants. You will do whatever is required to win his trust, to make him reveal himself to you."

"Why? For what purpose?" she asked.

Ostriker nodded in a noncommittal way, rocking the chair back and forth in his hands. "Professor Pettenkofer, wasn't it, swallowed Koch's cholera solution to try to disprove the germ theory?" He looked up at her. "That wasn't so very long ago, Margarethe. Bacteriological chemistry is a primitive field, but still more advanced than this curious trade of catching spies, where loyalty is such a perversely complicated issue."

"I really don't know what you're talking about."

"And I really don't trust you. Still, at this point I think I can expect your complete cooperation. Is that right?"

"Yes. Of course."

"You know, there are so many idiot ideas rattling around Germany today. Reich! Geist! Volk! Kultur! Apocalyptic visions fed on medievalism, Taoism, Zen. Theosophy. Anthroposophy. Stefan George and Zarathustra. It's all flags and sabers, and death as the ultimate experience. They're willing to wipe clean the slate, these people, more than eager to accept annihilation. And what could be more perfect for the mind of a Wandervogel than a disease weapon! The ultimate irrational concept—both deadly and uncontrollable. I deplore it too, Margarethe. But if it is to become part of this war, it must be in German hands, not British."

He paused to look at her. "Sometimes trust doesn't really matter," he went on after a moment. "Sometimes we let our secrets go like spores in the wind. Sometimes it's even useful for the other side to know what we know."

He held up his hand.

"Let me give you the perfect example. Just this morning I was telephoned by the naval commander at a certain U-boat installation that shall remain nameless. I haven't told this to another soul,

Margarethe. But I will tell you because that's how closely I'm going to watch you, as if we were living under the same beautiful skin. And I'll share it with you too because I think it may help you clear your mind, sort out your confusion, find an anchor for your potentially drifting loyalties. It's a very curious business, what this commander told me. It seems a U-boat crew returned last night infected with virulent pneumatic anthrax. It would appear they contracted the disease during an encounter with a mutilated sheep carcass, somewhere off the coast of Scotland. The animal had suffered wounds from an explosive shell. It also had a numbered tag stapled in its ear, with the designation PD seventeen."

Ostriker planted the chair squarely on all four legs and leaned forward on it. "Does 'PD' have any significance for you?"

"Porton Down. British weapons research."

"Precisely."

He noted the flush of genuine surprise that came across her face. A moment later he said, "It appears the British have built an anthrax bomb, Margarethe. And Eli Gordon has come for your 'magic bullet.' "

21

Berlin was a city of animal lovers, Andreas Schiller thought as he stood in the cold, watching the elephant methodically twisting back and forth, scratching her hindquarters against the huge pilings lashed together to form the boundary of her yard.

On the way to the zoo he had noticed a dog's pelt nailed to the fence, brown and white spots with head, tail, and paws, and "Died for the Fatherland" scrawled underneath in chalk. The swans in the Spree before the war had been supported by an endowment from the city's elite. Now the swans had been eaten by the city's workers.

Schiller stared into the elephant's enormous face, searching for the signs of pleasure that would account for all her efforts. The pilings groaned and swayed, yet she remained, at least to this observer's eyes, utterly impassive.

Eli Gordon was not a stupid man, Schiller had decided, just a man beyond his depth, swimming against the current, but for all that entirely capable of dragging others along with him. Schiller was far from certain where that countercurrent led, but he did know that murder was a dangerous business, and that the black market in Berlin was business as usual. And Ostriker? Fisk? Gordon really had no idea how dangerous the currents could be.

In Schiller's estimation, Eli Gordon was fatalistic, perhaps naive, as he blundered along, and sometimes those qualities can pass for courage. But what about the young soldier in the trenches on a freezing night? What about the couple who lose eight sons to the war and get a framed photo of the Kaiser? How can those bathed in experience and still eager for life endure all that they must endure?

Schiller stared ahead at the elephant, her heavy folds of wrinkled skin like the creases under his own eyes. It was a bad joke now. Suddenly life was not all the things that lie ahead but all the things one didn't do. He had never been the author of his own life, never in control—he knew that. He had spent nine years in the army so he could get a job on the police force so his children could go hungry while he solved crimes that had become public policy. And he still lived on 150 marks a week, paying more in taxes than all of the nobility combined.

He looked up at the troubled sky, growing darker gray as it prepared to unload more snow to bury the city once again. Eli Gordon had crossed his path in connection with a pair of black market murders, ever so slightly off the point. And the woman they both seemed to be after? Maybe she was slightly off the point too. Maybe his entire life up to now, Schiller realized, had been spent ever so slightly off the point. He remembered, as a boy, watching the dancing horses at the circus. A pretty girl in tights on a pretty mare, twirling around the ring. And all the while his eye was on the man with the shovel, darting in and out of the spotlight, cleaning up the shit.

An old man in hip boots came out of the shelter now, spreading fresh straw. "That's the girl," he muttered. "Do your dance." He had no teeth, and his stubbled jaws flapped open and shut like a glove puppet's.

"My friend!" Schiller yelled down. "Where do you find enough food for an elephant these days?"

The man looked up, letting his jaw lapse open. Schiller could see now that he was not so old. He'd simply lost his teeth.

"We mix their shit with straw and feed it to them twice," the keeper said, then stabbed the bale with his pitchfork and dragged it farther along. "Same as at the teahouse."

Schiller stared down, not smiling. "Tell me the truth. How do you do it?"

The man stood and leaned on his pitchfork, studying the face above the fence. "She takes herself down on Mondays for a new card like you and me. Elsa the elephant. I nick the corner each time I feed her."

Schiller reached into his pocket and pulled out the leather wallet that contained his badge. He held it down over the rim of the pilings. "I don't know if you can see this," he said. "But it tells you that I am a detective of the criminal police. And I would like the quality of your answers to improve."

The man jabbed his pitchfork into the ground and stepped over to the elephant. "Up! Elsa!" he said, and put his foot on her trunk. In one gliding motion she lifted him high enough so that he could grab the rim of the pilings and lift himself over the top.

Once on the slushy gravel beside the detective, the man put his hands to his hips. "I told you right. There's rations for the animals. That's what we feed them, what the regulations say."

"No more and no less?"

"That's right. Just what the regulations say."

Schiller adjusted the brim of his hat, then looked up with a faint smile of profound skepticism.

"Some of the beasts were killed for mercy," the man said. "Some were shipped to Holland for the duration. My belly's empty, but don't worry, the animals are living well abroad."

"There was a little extra for the tiger not long ago."

"Right. That's where I thought I'd seen you."

"You told Detective Kadereit that you saw nothing suspicious that day. At least nothing other than a man lying gnawed in a tiger cage."

"I learn from the monkeys. See no evil . . ."

"The monkeys are above suspicion. You, however, are not."

"What does that mean? Suspicion of what?"

"Let us say that it is ill-advised to have anything to do with a war profiteer. Including having one die at one's place of business."

"That's bullshit."

"You could be eating it mixed with straw tonight at Stadtvogtei if you do not tell me what you know."

"How am I supposed to know anything? I clean the cages. I don't get paid to know."

"Your responsibilities have just been enlarged. You are now expected to know."

"Know what?"

"After the victim was killed he was thrown over a fence of great height. We can assume, then, that the murderer either carried a catapult, or he was a large and incredibly strong individual."

"I didn't see anything."

Schiller gazed at the man with placid, unbelieving eyes. Then for a moment he looked down, rattling the cartridges in his pocket. "Feeding a dead man to a tiger. It places a fairly unusual signature on a murder."

"So?"

"What was the victim doing here?"

"He came for breakfast—how should I know?"

Schiller was beginning to tremble. He pressed his right arm across his chest once again and let the hand rest on his shoulder. "I think Katz was selling you food under the table."

"I don't buy the food."

"Who does?"

"The boss. Heinemann."

"Who does he buy it from?"

"The butcher . . . the greengrocer . . . I don't know. It comes in a truck."

"And none of it disappears? Finding its way home with the workers?"

"Not with this worker."

"How virtuous. Now I am absolutely certain that you are lying.

I think you will be able to think more clearly at the Alexander-platz."

"He buys from a fellow in a van."

"What do you know about him?"

The keeper explored the gravel with the toe of his boot. "He used to work for Hagenbeck's," he said. "Lions and tigers. An animal trainer."

"Had you seen him that day?"

"Yes."

"Delivering meat?"

"No."

"Tell me his name."

"He's a Turk. That's all I know. A Turk with a black beard."

"And?"

"He's big."

"How big?"

"Big enough."

"Big enough to throw a dead man over the railing on that tiger's cage?"

"Easily."

AT SIX o'clock that evening they let Margarethe go. She left the building in darkness and took the tram home, then climbed the stairs to her apartment, tired beyond tears. As she inhaled the odor of boiled turnips, she felt her predicament like the sudden grip of physical illness.

She swung open the door to her room and stepped inside, sensing immediately that something was wrong. Then Eli Gordon gripped her wrist and wrenched it behind her, smothering her face in the crook of his arm.

She reached up as she tried to scream, but the pressure on her wrist increased.

"I'm not going to hurt you," Gordon whispered.

She pushed her head from side to side, trying to cry out again, but his coat sleeve muffled her voice.

He kicked shut the door, then flipped on the light with his elbow.

"There," he said, leveraging her arm a fraction of an inch higher. "There."

He held the arm up against her shoulder blade until he felt the tension go out of her body. "I don't mean to be so rough but we're going to talk now. I'm going to take this away and if you scream I'll break your arm. You understand?"

She nodded, and he relaxed the arm that was gagging her, letting it come down to her shoulders, holding her in place. His jaw rested against the side of her head, and he could feel the cold still in her hair.

"I'm not screaming," she said. "You're breaking my arm anyway."

Gordon slackened the pressure a little but kept his grip. He pushed her in front of the bureau mirror where he could hold her and still see her face.

"You've abused my honest and trusting nature," he said, breathing heavily. "Twice, in fact. So you'll have to bear with me if I'm being a little excessive. Now, do I have your undivided attention this time?"

"Yes," she whispered. She stared into the glass to see his eyes, but surprise and fatigue had cut through her defenses. Gordon found her smaller and frailer than he had remembered. She seemed genuinely frightened.

He glanced into the mirror at his own reflection. A vein in his right eye had hemorrhaged, and now the iris was rimmed with a splotch of bright red. He would have to take into account how crazed he looked himself.

" 'In Barbarei mit Gefangenen verwickelt,' " he began.

"Please. Just leave me alone."

" 'Wir müssen sofort bakteriologische Entwicklungen besprechen.' "

"Please!"

He pulled her arm up toward her shoulder blade and said, "Who is it trying to kill me?"

"Why shouldn't they kill you? They're killing everyone else." Her voice broke with the pain and then she began to cry.

"You're really not being terribly helpful," Gordon said. "I think you can do better. Let's go back to the prisoners and start from the beginning. The Emigrants' Railway Station outside Ruhleben."

"I checked their health. That's all."

"Who authorized it?"

"Colonel von Stade."

"For what purpose?"

"A work commando."

"Where? What sort of work?"

"I don't know. I had no reason to know."

Gordon studied her face again in the glass, looking for signs to trust or distrust.

In time he lessened the pressure on her wrist and said, "Why you? They have doctors at Ruhleben."

"Von Stade asked a favor and I did it. That's all." She pleaded with him in the mirror. "Please let go of my arm."

Gordon did not respond.

"I don't even know who you are," she said. "Can't you understand that?"

"Why did you kill him?"

"I didn't kill anyone."

"You killed von Stade."

"He was going to kill me!"

"Why?"

"Because he'd been unbelievably stupid."

"Stupid enough to give you information. Information you passed to the British."

She looked at him more tired than angry now. "Yes," she whispered.

"You sent the messages to Troelstra. In the surgical journal."

"Yes, to Troelstra."

"Why was he killed?"

"I don't know. Now please let go of my arm. I'm not going to do anything to you. What can I do?"

Gordon released her, and she steadied herself on the bureau. Then she leaned forward, bringing both hands up to her chin.

For the first time he looked away to notice the postcards slipped under the mirror frame. There was a picture of the Wrigley Building in Chicago and another color-tinted scene, from the Alps. He knew nothing about her life and he didn't trust her for a minute, but he was drawn to her now in a way he'd never anticipated. Directly in front of her was a small, ceramic tree on a piece of lace, with rings on the branches and strands of silver and gold-plated chains.

"What about the others?" he said.

"What others?"

"Isidor Katz. And Princess Bucher very likely."

"What do you know about Katz?" she said, the color draining from her face. He watched the dark shading beneath her eyes turn deeper.

"Why was he killed?" Gordon said.

"Then he is dead. You're sure of it?"

"Somebody slit his throat. Wednesday morning at the zoo."

She shook her head, and after a moment the tears glistened on her cheeks.

Gordon turned away, glancing at the few plants by the window, struggling on their makeshift trellises. He did not necessarily want to expand what he knew about her. It was simpler to keep her the stark figure riding the train or sitting vacantly in the bar. Little Mary Kafka.

"They slit his throat and then they threw him into an animal cage," Gordon went on. "It wasn't as if he'd cut himself shaving, you know."

She sobbed quietly for a moment, and it seemed that the effort left her drained.

"Who would have done that?" Gordon said.

She did not respond.

"Who!" he repeated.

"Fisk! Fisk and his psychopathic friends. Always so concerned that the animals get enough to eat."

"Why would they kill Katz?"

"Because he was trying to help me."

"Katz sent messages to Holland. What did Fisk care?"

"It wasn't the messages."

"What was it then?"

"Katz was helping me . . . in other ways."

"Like what?"

"He was helping me . . . avoid Fisk."

"What did Fisk want?"

"Me! He wanted me!" The tears spilled over and she reached up with the back of her hand and smeared them across her cheek. "Oh hell," she said. "Oh hell."

She turned and bowed her head onto Gordon's shoulder. "Make yourself useful, would you? Hold me. Just hold me for minute." Then she laughed. "Oh God, I have so many protectors. So many gallant men."

The tension in her shoulders did not relax, her body did not soften to his touch. He let his arms close around her, but he had the feeling he was taking stage directions. He had the feeling they were both just reading their lines.

"On the train you said you could help me," she said.

"I said I could get you out of Berlin."

She sighed. Then she laughed, shaking her head slowly from side to side.

"Tell me about Fisk," he went on. "Tell me about the black van with the white horse. The big man with the beard. Dark like a Turk."

"I'm feeling very bad," she whispered. "Really very bad."

"Fisk owns a brewery in Moabit. It's just across the Spree from the Institute. That's where the prisoners were taken, wasn't it? The men from Ruhleben."

"I told you I don't know."

"There aren't any prisoners being experimented on. It's not a research program at all, it's just a little bit of private enterprise, Fisk and von den Benken. That's the 'barbarism' you're 'tangled up in.' That's what he's trying to protect."

Gordon took her shoulder and held her back so he could see her face but she refused to look at him. Gordon gripped her chin. "Talk to me! Tell me what were you going to tell Troelstra that was so damn important."

She raised her eyes. "Why did the British send you?"

She pushed away from him to look into his face, and her eyes seem to penetrate deep into his body.

After a moment he said, "The Alberich push to the Channel. The British think it's going to be an assault with germ weapons."

"They've got it all wrong."

"Then tell me what's right."

"Why? What can you do?"

"They need to prepare a defense," he said. "Whatever it is."

"How could they defend against this?"

"The Prussian army wouldn't launch anything like this without a way of staying in control."

"The rigorously logical Kraut, is that it?"

She closed her eyes. Her hands were resting on his chest, her arms drawn up. "I don't want to talk about it now," she said.

"There's supposed to be a 'magic bullet,' " Gordon told her.

She pressed against him once more, sliding her hands inside his coat. "Sometimes I just need to be reminded I'm still alive, you know? Still alive outside all of this."

Gordon felt the weight of her breasts pressed against him. He touched her hair at the nape of her neck, and for a moment he thought about it spread over the two of them. It was a nice image. But she had killed her last lover, which was not much of a recommendation.

"You wanted me the first time you looked at me," she said. "I could tell."

"It's been a dry season. Don't read too much into it."

She leaned her face up and kissed him. "Usually I try not to notice."

Her eyes darted back and forth, looking into each of his with an intensity that simply didn't ring true. "I just need to get my mind off all this. It's all right, isn't it? There's so little time now."

"The 'magic bullet.' Fisk found out about it, didn't he? That's what he's after."

She kissed him again, trembling.

"So why didn't you come to my hotel that night?" he said.

"I was being followed. I couldn't."

"By who? Fisk? Schiller?"

She squeezed him with finality, gave a kind of shudder, then turned to the bureau, where she picked up a small, drawstring bag made of silk. She walked over and placed it carefully on the nightstand, then sat on the edge of the bed, slipped off her coat, and began unbuttoning her blouse.

Gordon watched as she uncovered the soft skin of her throat, the firm cleft between her breasts above the lace of her camisole. It occurred to him that, given a choice of ways to die, von Stade had done pretty well. But even a lovesick colonel would have known what was going on. She was not that good an actress.

Gordon stepped over to the nightstand and picked up the silk pouch.

"What are you doing?"

She was up off the bed and snatching at the bag. He blocked her with his shoulder, and she followed as he spun away from her.

He reached into the purse and pulled out a crystal aspirator, tightly sealed, filled with a colorless liquid.

"Give me that!" She grabbed again, clawing his hands with her fingernails. He tossed the bottle into the chair across the room and she lunged toward it as his arms locked around her.

"You shit!" She punched with her fists and kicked until he wrestled her back and threw her onto the bed.

He fell on top of her, pressing her shoulders down into the mattress. Then he reached down and grabbed her wrist and rolled her over onto her stomach.

"Let's try it again, now," he said, pushing her arm up against her spine.

"Go to hell!"

"I can't believe a goddamn thing you say. But I am trying to help you out of this."

"Oh yes, Dr. Gordon. Your 'altruism' is so compelling! Tell me about Scotland. Tell me about Porton Down."

He stared down blankly as he leaned over her, her face straining to the side as he pressed her into the pillow.

"What are you talking about?"

"A U-boat crew with anthrax," she said. "From a sheep carcass floating offshore. Shrapnel wounds, Doctor. And a numbered tag from Porton Down."

Gordon loosened his grip and rolled her over on her back, staring into her eyes. For the first time he saw something authentic there, and immediately his mind began sifting through everything that had been said in London, Boulogne, and Hazebrouck. He was searching for the phrase or the offhand look that should have let him see it.

In his preoccupation he let go of her shoulders. Slowly, carefully, she crawled out from under him. He rose to his feet as she leaned against the headboard and drew up her knees.

Looking out from under the veil of her hair, she gathered the edge of her blouse together, sheltering her body with her arms. "But Britain just wants to protect itself, right, Doctor? Is that the story?"

"Where'd you hear this?" he asked her.

"What difference does it make?"

"Tell me!"

"Ostriker! He's obviously been riding you like a monkey since you stepped off the train."

"Why were you talking to Ostriker?"

"Because he saw us together. And now I'm supposed to fuck you and inform on you like a good German."

"So what? It seemed safer just to kill me?"

She looked down, fingering a button on her blouse.

Gordon leaned over on one knee and gripped her face in his hand. "I want to know about this U-boat."

"I just told you all I know."

"Tell me again."

"It came into port. The men were infected."

"Why would Ostriker tell you this? And why would you even begin to think he was telling the truth?"

"Like the way I know you're telling the truth?"

Gordon shook his head. "He's lying. He's feeding you this so he can use you."

"Yes. And it works! Now I know better than to trust *you*. And I happen to think it's true what he says!"

Slowly, Gordon stood back up. He had no reason to believe any of this, except that the betrayal at the very core of it made such perfect sense.

"Start packing," he said. "One bag. Small."

"Why?"

"Because I think we're both in way over our heads."

FRAU Partridge was cautious at first, hesitant behind the closed door of her apartment.

"It's Eli Gordon. Your husband and I traded off a night at

Ruhleben." Gordon glanced back at Margarethe as he heard the bolt being slid in, then the voice through the door.

"Go away. My husband may be shot because of your little stunt."

Gordon rapped his knuckles on the door once again.

"We need a place to stay. It's only for one night."

He listened for her breathing on the other side of the wooden panels. At least he did not hear her stepping away.

"It's fifty marks for you," he said.

They waited another moment in the hallway, their breath making frost in the air. Then the door fell open and the young woman looked out from behind it. She had shadows under her eyes that made her look not quite so young as before.

"Who is she?" Frau Partridge said. "What is this you're getting me into?"

Gordon kicked the last of the snow off his boots and stepped past her into the room. "We'll be gone in the morning," he said. He reached into his pocket and held up a bank note.

Frau Partridge took the money sullenly and stuffed it in her pocket, then tightened her robe around her waist. "I suppose I have an extra quilt," she said.

Watching the snow pile up in the street below, Gordon stood at the window while the two women made a bed on the couch. The night sky was lit up by the reflection off the snow. The city was silent, muffled by the storm.

"There's room for only one on this thing," Frau Partridge said, leaning over to tug at the coverlet.

Gordon turned back around and said, "Fine. I'll sleep on the floor."

Straightening up, Frau Partridge gave Margarethe an appraising look, then shrugged and ambled off. "Suit yourselves," she said over her shoulder. Then she went into her bedroom and closed the door behind her.

From an overstuffed chair near the window, Gordon watched

Margarethe as she sat on the couch, then stood back up and removed her coat, spreading it over the blanket for extra warmth. Avoiding his eyes, she sat down again to take off her boots. Then, still looking at the floor, she reached back and tied her hair in a loose knot at the nape of her neck. After that she turned off the oil lamp and, without a word, rolled under the covers.

Gordon had not persuaded her to trust him, any more than he trusted her. But she could have come up with a hundred unwieldy lies before she got down to the story about the sheep and the British anthrax. The story rang true, he suspected, because it was. Because it was the one obvious, unspoken assumption beneath everything the British were doing, the one element he had simply chosen to block out of his mind. He could not ignore it now. Still, he wanted to believe the British would not go ahead with something like this on a bet. They had to believe what they had told him about German research. But the way he put the pieces together now, there was no German research.

Margarethe's slow, regular breathing was the only sound in the room. He looked toward her in the darkness and wondered about the leap of faith he was making. Why would Ostriker confide in her? Maybe for the same reason that Ostriker had allowed him to move freely around Berlin, even supplied him—through Jay—with the lead on Beszenoff. Ostriker seemed to be running some elaborate experiment, with him and Margarethe Riesling as the rats in the maze.

Gordon knew he was never going to arrive at any clear answers by rolling the questions around in his mind. He was going to have to work through the few facts available to him and narrow down the options one by one, arriving at the truth as whatever was left. The one issue he could get at now was the black market. If he could pin down anything he could label as absolute, he would at least then have a place to begin.

He smoked cigarettes in the dark and watched her for a long, long time. The intimacy of her preparations for bed had intrigued him, the way she had created her own privacy simply by shutting him out. She had brought her own world with her in a Gladstone bag and a cardboard portfolio of drawings. He couldn't believe she was anything other than a victim in this thing, cornered and coerced. The colonel had gotten her into it, and now Fisk wouldn't let her out because he saw money to be made. But how much could he trust that intuition? His judgment had been thoroughly compromised the first moment he saw her.

She had begun by pretending to sleep, but now her rhythms and her stillness seemed genuine. Even so, it was after midnight before he was sure enough to get up and slip quietly out the door.

The roadbed had given in to heavy trucks and uneven settling that made it roll beneath the thickening carpet of snow. As the droshky stopped along the canal, Gordon could see the dark brewery through the white clouds. He stepped down and paid the man. Then the horse and driver padded off into the distance back toward Berlin.

Gordon walked hurriedly, with his shoulders hunched and his injured right hand cradled across his chest. Up to his ankles in snow, he came to the iron gate of the brewery's outer wall. A chain was strung between the bars, but loosely enough so that, turning sideways, he could just slip through the opening.

Once inside the perimeter, his left hand still on the gate, he stopped for a moment, listening to the wind and the sound of the blowing snow. It was piling into drifts along one wall and, above his head, crusting over the inlays around the windows. A watchdog would have smelled him by now. He had to assume it was safe to go ahead.

A carriage house with three wooden doors occupied the far corner of the courtyard. Gordon approached it silently, then lifted the latch and stepped inside, leaving the door open behind him.

He stood still and waited for his eyes to adjust. Then he heard a thump that sent his pulse pounding into his ears. He struck up the flame from his trench lighter and saw two large eyes reflecting the light, then a white horse nodding its head. Gordon kept the flame burning in front of him and walked beyond the stall, where he saw a crowbar leaning against a wooden post. He picked it up and put it under his arm, then turned to his right. In the third section of the stable, backed in with its crosstie pointing up toward the ceiling, was the black delivery van he had first seen that night outside Onkel Tom's.

Gordon stepped back outside and closed the door and walked across the yard to the main building. He walked along the wall, careful of his footing, until he found the shallow well of a basement window. He stopped, leaned down, and struck his lighter. The opening was large enough for him but the window was locked. He reached down with the crowbar and tried to pry it but there was no way to gain purchase on the opening. He looked inside, then over his shoulders, then firmly tapped the pane nearest the latch. He reached through the shattered glass and opened the frame.

Awkwardly, straining with his one good hand, Gordon lowered himself inside and dropped down hard on the concrete floor.

The downdraft from the window was an icy chill, colder than outside. He looked around, waiting again for his eyes to adjust, and he heard movement. He pulled out his lighter and kicked up the flame and saw a half dozen black faces staring at him through a steel grate. Their eyes were wide, their mouths open.

"Who be you, sah?" one of them said.

Gordon looked past the man's head into the cell where the rest were huddled together, wrapped in thin blankets. "The cavalry," he said.

"Who, sah?"

"It's a long story. You're from Ruhleben, right?"

"Yes, sah."

"A woman checked your health? At the lazaret?"

"Yes, sah."

"What about the guards here?"

A half dozen voices suddenly came at him in some African dialect. Gordon pulled over the man who had spoken and asked again, "How many guards?"

"Just one maybe, sah, but plenty big. He stays upstairs."

"A Turk?"

"Yes, sah."

"Can you handle him?"

"All of us? Oh yes, sah. With pleasure."

Gordon looked down at the two padlocked chains that held the grate. He worked the crowbar underneath one chain and pushed his end of it upward. The prisoners grabbed the longer end, extending into the cell, and pushed down. Three of them leaned on it, straining until the chain snapped. Then they repeated the process, and the door fell open.

With much gesturing and whispering and hushing of each other, they led Gordon through the basement corridor, past empty bins and kegs until they came to a concrete ramp. He followed up the incline, and after about thirty feet the ramp turned to the right. They climbed an equal distance farther, and then Gordon felt the space open up around him. It was colder here. The glass roof let in a faint light, outlining the steel girders up above. He knew he was on the main floor, but he could make out nothing beyond the vague outline of long worktables and conveyor belts.

"Stay here, if you please, sah. We be back."

Gordon stood at the top of the ramp as the men made their way onto the floor. There was something ghostly about their movements in the half light. In time Gordon heard the sound of metal as they picked up knives and cleavers.

A draft blew down his neck as they passed by again, nodding, smiling, walking silently, trailing off through a door behind him. He was alone now, uneasy in the darkness. He had wanted to see for himself. He was eager to switch on the lights but he would have to wait. He was hyperventilating, struggling to keep his mind and the world moving at the same pace. Without the lights he could still make out the tracks overhead, and what he took to be sides of beef hanging from hooks. He snapped on his trench lighter and walked toward the center of the room. Then he put out the flame.

There was shouting. The Africans yammered, crying out in high-pitched voices, and then over all came one long, loud wail of pain. The screams and shouts converged, then stopped, followed by laughter and whoops of victory as the men came crashing back onto the work floor. The lights flashed on overhead and Gordon winced and closed his eyes. His mind was addled, the world hallucinatory, as he turned to see them drag in the Turk's body. They had a rope around his neck, and his clothes were soaked in blood. Then one of them sank a meat hook through the underside of his chin and back out his mouth.

Gordon turned his head to take in the room now. The meat racks, the trolleys, the tables with treadle-driven band saws, meat cleavers and knives. The Africans hoisted the Turk into the air as Gordon looked up. The skinned sides and quarters hung down red and raw and streaked with yellow fat. He stared at the split carcasses for a good thirty seconds before acknowledging their outline. Then he turned and stumbled into a wheeled cart, steadying himself with one hand on the rim. Looking over the edge, he saw by-products, appendages, waste. On top of the pile, the half-lidded eyes of Princess Bucher stared back at him.

22

Gordon crushed out his cigarette in the foyer of the apartment building, then climbed the stairs. When he reached Frau Partridge's floor a door opened behind him. He swung around and saw a child looking out, a girl about eight years old. He made an effort to smile reassuringly, but he had nothing to confirm that the expression showed on his face.

He had just followed the war to its logical extreme. That's what the British would say, right? Toning it down with public school reserve. Coating it with euphemisms that wear off all the edges. Proper upper-crust stoicism. Good old British phlegm. And now? What was he supposed to do with this vision from Fisk's slaughterhouse? He was not staidly British. He was not upper crust. He was not even part of their game.

He walked on to the door and pulled out the key.

"She's left," the girl said.

Gordon leaned back slowly against the wall. He had not really slept for two nights and it took continual effort to stay in focus, to not drop over the edge. He looked at the little girl, her round face, her orange hair spinning away from her head. Another hallucination?

He said, "Where did she go?"

"The police took her."

He gazed dumbly ahead, shivering, as the little girl stared into his bloodshot eye.

"She's a traitor. She's married to an Englishman, you know."

He studied the child's face for any hint that she was put up to this. He would recalculate, that's all. He would maintain his vise-like grip on reality.

He coughed and his lungs kicked up smoke from his last cigarette. "How do you know the police took her?" he said.

"I saw."

"All of it?"

"I don't know."

"How many women did they take?"

"What do you mean?"

"Was it just Frau Partridge or was there someone else?"

"I was just up to pee. I didn't see anyone else."

"Then how do you know it was the police?"

"It's not my fault what happened."

"Okay," he said. "I understand."

She stared at his eye, the intruded blood like a fragment inside a kaleidoscope.

"What did they look like?" he asked her. "Did they wear uniforms?"

"They were just men."

He stepped closer, then went down on his haunches to look into her moon-shaped face. "A leader?" he said. "Someone telling them what to do? What did he look like?"

"They wore hats and coats," she murmured, and for the first time she seemed afraid.

"Tell me anything you remember," Gordon said. She stared back at him, sucking on a finger the size of a prawn.

He gripped her shoulders as if he could squeeze the words out of her. "Tell me!"

"He was cold," she said at last.

"How do you mean?"

"He shivered. He shook the whole time."

Outside the Adlon Hotel men in overcoats sat in a parked car as Gordon stayed on the opposite side of the Linden and watched.

The eastern sky was bright orange now. Office workers walked past him, gritting their teeth as they hurried through the cold to reach their buildings.

Maybe the war itself had finally won, Gordon thought. At the moment at least his own private war certainly seemed to have been lost. He had never understood the balance that had let him operate in Berlin. All he knew now was that the balance had been disturbed by some outside force, and he was losing his ability to care.

The sun rose like a balloon on a current of air as he watched three men get out of the car and walk toward the hotel. One of them, his hands buried in the pockets of his black leather overcoat, stopped to talk to the doorman. He did not wear a hat, and even from this distance Gordon could see the shock of white hair above his left brow. As the car pulled away, leaving Rolf Mayr on the curb, Gordon followed it with his eyes and made out the pensive form of Walther Ostriker sitting in the back seat.

He could drop the whole thing now. He could get to the station and out of Berlin as quickly as possible. He would be protected from the errors of misguided action, from the threat of being used, from the unintentional results of having even the most negligible impact on the world. He could reconstruct what was left of his life propping up Britain's "supply of heroes." Or he could get Margarethe Riesling out of wherever they had taken her and try to get on with it.

The hotel, Billy's letter from Ludendorff, was clearly not the way. The only option left was the revolver in the embassy ballroom.

■ ■ ■

The Americans gathered in the Wilhelm Platz had the blank look of people reading their own obituaries. Surrounded by Germans brandishing newspapers and chanting slogans, the crowd reached halfway across the park, pressed together in the cold, breathing steam and stamping their feet. Gordon worked his way through, trying to make out from the headlines what had happened. A policeman on horseback came through, compressing the crowd and throwing Gordon up against a man and a small boy.

Gordon pushed an elbow out of his ribs as the man boosted up the child. The man had bad teeth and no chin but his cheeks were as fair and red as his boy's. He turned to squint at Gordon. "Kaiser Bill's declared open season," he said.

"U-boats?"

"That's the idea."

Gordon looked over the crowd toward the embassy and the barricade in front, lined with men in blue capes. Then he turned back to the man with the child and said, "What's happening here?"

"The embassy's closed. That's all I know." The man reached up to wipe his nose, then retreated into his own thoughts. Gordon nodded and turned into the crowd.

He worked his way toward the entrance, trying to protect his hand. He reached the barrier and showed his embassy papers to a policeman, who waved him forward. Then he broke through with a final surge and ran up the steps and into the building.

The first floor of the mansion was empty. On the stairs Gordon passed two of Gerard's young secretaries, bundled in their coats, running down with pasteboard cartons.

"Where's Gerard?" Gordon asked.

"Already at the station. You're going to have to hurry."

"And Adams?"

"Everybody's gone."

A layer of papers had spilled on the landing up above and lay trampled across the floor like carpet wet with slush. Gordon walked down the hall and into the empty ballroom. He went to his desk and pulled out the lower left drawer. He looked behind the vertical file and found Mrs. Webb's box of Quaker Oats. He pushed it aside and then riffled through the files. Both the gun and the cartridges were missing.

The floorboards creaked and Gordon glanced up. Jay Adams stood just inside the grand double doors, pointing the revolver vaguely in his direction.

His forehead was pink and as smooth as porcelain. His smile was patently false. He came forward slowly and said, "I really hate to do this, old man. But a mutual friend asked me to be sure you didn't leave without saying goodbye."

Adams shrugged and Gordon stood upright, still wearing his hat and coat as if he were rushing off to work.

After a moment, Jay smiled again. "Sentimental Germans, you know."

The young man stopped at a desk in the center of the room and sat down on the corner. Then he brought his feet up into the chair and said, "Sit down if you like. We may be here awhile."

"I don't have time for this, Jay."

"Oh please . . ."

Adams pulled his cigarettes and then his matches out of a side pocket with one hand and set them on the desktop.

Gordon took a seat. He knew now that shooting someone was harder than it looked, but he had to assume that Adams was up to it. He had loaded the gun himself; the firing mechanism was not too tricky.

The young man laughed. "I don't see your margin, really. This condescending crap. I'd begun to think the Brits had sent you in just to balls-up. Hoping you'd precipitate some major crisis in German-American relations, or at least stumble into martyrdom. Too late for the first. You may still achieve the latter, of course."

Adams shook a cigarette up from the pack and put it to his lips. Then he slid open the small wooden box, deftly removed a wooden match, closed the box, then snapped the match against the side, all with one hand.

"So what exactly is the point here, Jay? What do you think you're doing?"

Adams lit the cigarette, then blew out the match. He crossed his legs and leaned back stiffly on one arm, perched like a chanteuse on top of a piano.

"You tell me something," he said. "Whatever happened to 'first do no harm'? I always thought germ warfare might be something of a moral burden for a physician."

"I think you've missed a beat in the translation."

"Oh? Delighted to hear it. You can tell me your side in a moment, but in the meantime, where is Margarethe Riesling?"

Gordon shook his head. "This is going to be sticky for you, isn't it? Diplomatic ties broken. You taking up with the Germans?"

"Are you joking? Which side of this gun do you think you're on, anyway?"

Adams pursed his lips, then leaned over to the telephone and pushed one button. "Fräulein Kleist. Step into the ballroom, won't you please?"

He straightened up, then said to Gordon, "Everything with you is so abstracted. Lopsided. Men like you understand absolutely nothing about human relationships."

They heard footsteps in the hall. It was a rapid clicking sound, almost like tap shoes. Adams seemed surprised that the fräulein could arrive so quickly. He turned, expecting to see his buxom secretary. Instead, he found Billy de Beauford breezing through the doorway and flipping through the pages of his reporter's notebook.

"Oh yes!" the Dutchman said. He had the breathless look of a man trying to raise cash in a hurry. "Excellent luck catching you both here in one place. Hope this isn't a bad time."

Adams leapt to his feet and brandished the weapon. "Stay where you are!"

De Beauford kept coming. "Yes, yes. Promise not to take long. Just a few questions."

He looked up at Gordon with a shaky smile. "Adams here, you know, has a wonderful trick—drinking an entire bottle of champagne without removing it from his lips. Makes him utterly useless for social purposes the rest of the evening, of course."

"I'll shoot you, you oily little squid."

"I don't doubt it for a moment, Jay my boy." The Dutchman glanced at Gordon again. "Usually they say that *after* the interview."

Billy's good cheer seemed layered over a more than usual dose of frantic energy. He pulled a handkerchief from his sleeve and fluttered it about his face.

"Get over by Gordon," Adams said.

"Yes, of course, my mistake. New frontiers of etiquette, I suppose. I really don't mean to be a bother. There's just a couple of points I need to hit with you. About the break in diplomatic relations, of course. Immediate implications for the American community here. Implications for American foreign policy, that sort of thing. Everyone's in a bit of a snit and I do need copy. Warm in here, or is it just me?"

"I think it's warm," Gordon said.

De Beauford brushed his lips with the handkerchief. "The ambassador is leaving for Switzerland, am I right?" He stepped toward Adams with a distracted look as Gordon slowly rose to his feet.

"I said stay where you are!" Adams backed away, pointing the gun toward each of them in turn.

"You know, it is amazing the way misinformation proliferates," Billy went on. "Like General Oblovsky . . . offering a bounty for regimental flags and being flooded with banners from East Prussian choral societies!"

"Stay put! I mean it!"

"Goodness, Jay . . ." Billy inched forward and smiled. "I love seeing you be so forceful. I never knew you had it in you." He laughed nervously and took another step. "I've always liked you well enough as is, but you know, this really becomes you. A whole new Jay." Billy stopped and smiled again, but this time the expression seemed strained, incongruous. "What I really mean to say is, Jay . . . don't take this personally . . ."

He stepped even closer and flicked the cloth near Adams's face. There was a loud flash and more blood than he had ever imagined. He jumped back, gripping the small pistol hidden in his palm, and watched frightened and unsure as Jay swallowed hard, dropped his revolver, and reached up to touch his splattered cheek.

Adams's right eye had disappeared. With the other, remaining one he stared at the Dutchman, totally confused. Then the next heartbeat overwhelmed him, and he toppled over like a mannequin.

Billy de Beauford took another step back and stared down at the jumbled body. Gordon leapt over and picked up the gun, then reached into Jay's pocket and found the box of shells.

"I hope I didn't spoil it all," Billy said, trembling and not lifting his eyes. "I've never done anything like this before, you know. Is he dead?"

Gordon stepped over to the side entrance as Fräulein Kleist came running through the door. He caught her with a blow to the back of the neck and she stumbled to the floor, sliding into Adams.

Billy looked nervously at the small derringer cupped in his palm, then back at Gordon. "I don't have to shoot her, do I?"

"No, Billy. I don't think so."

"Ah . . . a relief." De Beauford was shaking from head to toe now. "She's really quite lovely, you know. Wonderful breasts."

Gordon took her by the arms and pulled her over toward a radiator pipe against the wall, then took the cord from around her waist and began fastening it to her wrist.

De Beauford seemed not to know what to do with himself, or with the gun in his hand. He stood over the body, staring distractedly.

"I saw you on the street outside the hotel," he said. Fräulein

Kleist now lay stretched out on the floor, one arm still by her side, the other reaching over her head like a swimmer in a backstroke.

"Ostriker's henchmen had the place fairly well sealed off. I thought you might need some help so I followed you here."

Gordon finished tying the fräulein's wrists together, then looped the cord around the pipe.

"We're in deep shit, Billy."

"But in good company," Billy said, releasing a heavy breath. "I located your man Beszenoff. He's in Holzminden. A bit removed from the Institute. So I think it's safe to say your mysterious woman ought to be the source for your messages."

"This all works much better if she is," Gordon said. Then he looked up and the two men stared at each other.

"Thanks," Gordon added. "Thanks for coming here."

Gordon rose to his feet. "I've got some bad news, though, Billy. About the princess."

De Beauford sighed, then gave a faint smile. "I thought as much," he said. "She's dead, isn't she."

"Yes," Gordon said.

"And was it Dr. Fisk?"

Gordon nodded. "The business at Ruhleben. It was black market, plain and simple. She got too close."

"It's never plain and simple," Billy said. "I should have stopped her."

Then he looked up. "So where is Fisk?"

"I don't think we have time to deal with Fisk just now. The police are on to him. They'll take care of it."

Billy's eyes had welled up with tears and he used the handkerchief now to dry his face. "How very odd," he said. "All this official evil going on in the world . . . Evelyn succumbs to something so private. So pointless." Billy looked at him. "Fisk has a problem with women, you see. But that's where all the really powerful evil comes from, though, doesn't it? It's personal."

He put his handkerchief away, then took another deep breath, staring down at the buxom young woman on the floor. "The embassy train leaves from Zoo Station in about an hour. I'm supposed to cover the departure, so that's what I'll do. I suggest you join me on board if at all possible."

"I need your letter. The one signed by Ludendorff."

"Are you going to the Eastern front?"

"I'm going to get this woman out of jail."

"Won't do you any good, I'm afraid. Guards aren't quite so impressed by signatures at this point. Some of them can actually read now."

Gordon closed his eyes and tried to relax as his hand and neck throbbed.

"It's really quite impossible, you know," Billy told him. "But I can't blame you for trying. I'm sure a woman would do you a world of good."

De Beauford smiled faintly and handed him the other small pistol. "Here," he said. "That's the best I can do."

On the third floor of the Polizei Präsidium, Andreas Schiller sat at his desk in the far end of the detectives' room, sipping a cup of ersatz. He glanced up as Gordon approached, then raised one brow as he noticed the menacing bulge in the American's left overcoat pocket.

"Where is she?" Gordon said. His eyes looked hollow beneath the brim of his hat.

Schiller set down the cup, and for a moment the two men stared at each other. "I hope you haven't created any more work for me," the detective said, his hand coming to rest on the keyboard of his typewriter. He began playing with the *H,* tapping it again and again until it cut a small hole in the ribbon.

After a while he added, "If you're going to shoot me, really you'll have to go ahead. But it won't serve your purposes, will it. I'll be dead, you'll be dead, my wife and children will collect a sizable annuity, and Margarethe Riesling will still be in custody."

Gordon stood motionless, watching Schiller's implacable face.

"It is a difficult thing to threaten a terminally ill man," the detective went on. "Why don't you have a seat so we can talk?" The *H* stuck against the platen and Schiller flipped it down with one finger. "All the men dressing up in funny clothes to murder each other," he said. "We've seen enough of that, don't you think?"

Gordon had at last run out of options, as well as energy. He had to trust someone and the someone he chose was Andreas Schiller. He sank slowly into a chair and said, "What do you want?"

Schiller looked up. "I want to thank you for some excellent investigative work. You've solved at least one of my crimes for me. You've also saved me a great deal of effort. God knows we're shorthanded."

"How did you find her?" Gordon said.

"She paid a visit to the Institute for Infectious Diseases at three o'clock this morning. I assumed that Ostriker would be through playing with you, about to move in. You know about the diplomatic fiasco of course. If I wanted to stay in the game I had to do something very fast."

"So what happens now?"

"That depends."

"I can offer you a trade."

"Really?"

"Erskine Fisk and Major Baron von den Benken. A black market operation and several counts of murder. I can lay it all out for you."

"That is all very interesting but not much of a trade. The Bowles Brewery . . . the Westhafen docks. I was following you when you were attacked, remember?"

Schiller rose to his feet. "Not to further your disillusionment, but I'm also not so certain the lady in question would wish to be traded. You see, it was outside the home of Erskine Fisk that we arrested her. Now . . . I am told there is an embassy train. I think you should be on it. Get all this unpleasantness behind you."

Gordon stared at Schiller. He had rationalized everything—the man she had killed, the black market, the attempt to kill him. He had worked all the pieces so that she came out on the side of the angels. Slightly tarnished, caught in the middle, but not a ghoul, not a criminal.

"What does that mean?" he said.

The detective stared back, checking each of Gordon's features as if to see that it was in its proper place.

"Why am I feeling so fatherly?" he said at last. "You see, women talk to me. I think they consider me harmless, even as a policeman. We've had only a few hours to talk. About anthrax, and about her work. She is a fascinating woman, as we both agreed. And with, she tells me, quite a remarkable discovery. But I'm afraid she doesn't trust you. As indicated by the fact that she saw Dr. Fisk as the safer bet for getting her work out of the country. True, he is rumored to have quite a fortune hidden away in Swiss accounts, but she seems interested only in guaranteeing the neutrality of her research. She's very concerned about your other commitments. I've tried to convince her that you are probably as naive about the British as you seem, but for that I have only my instinct."

The detective stepped over to an office door and opened it.

Margarethe Riesling looked up from the desk where she was sitting, her hands resting on a small parcel wrapped in brown paper. She wore dark glasses with round, metal frames, through which she stared at Gordon with resolute indifference as he walked into the room.

Schiller watched the two of them for a moment. Then he waved a dismissive hand. "You're not out to help the British destroy us all with anthrax, are you, Dr. Gordon?"

"I hadn't planned to, no."

"See." Schiller turned to Margarethe. "What did I tell you?"

Then he looked back at Gordon. "She actually may be able to

save some lives with what she has in that package. But right now I believe Walther Ostriker feels he has a prior claim. It would not look good on his résumé to have a British spy, not to mention a scientist with an important military secret, leaving the country just now."

Gordon studied Schiller's face. "You're letting her go?"

Schiller lowered his head, brushed one finger against his lips, and said, "Yes. That's about the size of it."

"Why?"

Schiller shook his head. "It's February, that's all. My term on the January murder commission has come to an end."

23

E rskine Fisk pulled back the door and said, "My good friend
the baron, come in. Come in and we'll have a drink."
Major Baron von den Benken brushed past the dentist
into the stairway, and said, "You can drink out of my ass."

Fisk glanced through the door and scanned the empty street.
"What a disgusting thought," he murmured. Then he replaced the
latch as von den Benken climbed the stairs ahead of him.

Squaring his shoulders, the dentist followed with halting and
mechanical steps. When he reached the top he found the baron
standing just inside the entry, pointing to the matched calfskin
luggage arranged by the door.

"What's this?"

Fisk stepped over the doorsill and gave a mendacious smile.
"Just a little trip," he said. "Vacation for my nerves. Nerves are
shot. Truly miserable case of it." He closed the door behind them.

"Muller fucked it," von den Benken said. Then he continued
into the darkened reception area. "Then 'someone' got in and let
our niggers loose. Your friend the Turk is now a more manageable
size, by the way. More manageable pieces."

Fisk stopped by his drinks cart and raised one finger in the air,
deliberating for a moment, then reaching for an open bottle of
Scotch. "Sure you wouldn't like a drink?"

Von den Benken grabbed the bottle and threw it across the room, the liquor pouring out in amber spirals. "You will not get out of it that easily, Fisk. Sotting your brain won't change anything."

The dentist sighed and calmly reached into the credenza to fetch another bottle. "I thought you were managing day-to-day operations," he said.

The baron turned to face the window. "I went out of town for twenty-four hours and this is what I find. Why did I ever let you talk me into this demented scheme?"

"Because you're greedy, Baron. Just like me." Fisk tossed back a tumbler of Scotch.

"It's more than greed for you," von den Benken said. "That's what worries me. You honestly seemed to enjoy it. Relishing the whole ghastly idea in some perverted way.

"But that no longer matters," he went on. "Fortunately it is rather difficult for Africans to blend into the landscape here, so that damage is under control. We're rounding them up. But we have to assume some leaks will occur. We have to plan accordingly."

"This is giving me a headache," Fisk said, and strolled off toward his examining room. He pushed away the overhead lamp and lowered himself into his dental chair. "I'll tell you my plan. As soon as a certain young lady arrives I am going to get on a train and leave these piss-ant concerns behind. I recommend you do the same."

"You're not going anywhere quite yet."

The dentist looked up. "Well, she *is* late, but I persist in being optimistic. I'm not going to let this one slip away, Baron, believe me."

Von den Benken stood over him. "The brewery's fully insured, Fisk, and you're about to collect. I have this little intuition the whole damn place is about to burn to the ground. Now I'll take my share of the settlement up front. In cash."

Fisk closed his eyes and bowed his head. "This is ludicrous, Baron. Very unbecoming."

He shook his head, then reached up to stroke his scalp, starting with his fingertips just above his brow, drawing them like a comb through his long, thinning hair. His eyes were still closed when he finished. He opened them to find von den Benken holding a pistol.

"You're the one who put the skeletons in the closet, Fisk. Trying to run a business with street thugs and murderers. You won't walk off and leave it all hanging around my neck. I don't particularly mind letting you live, but it will cost you. I assume you don't have the cash on the premises, so I will accompany you to your bank."

The dentist raised his chin and stroked his neck. "Too late, Baron. The cash is in Switzerland. And Margarethe is waiting."

The movement was imperceptibly swift. Von den Benken felt the scalpel in his throat without ever seeing it in Fisk's hand. It sliced the artery, then gouged deeper into the trachea. The gun fell to the floor as von den Benken's mouth foamed red. He grabbed feebly at the dentist's wrist, then stumbled back and collapsed with a great gurgling complaint.

"You annoy me," Fisk said, wiping off the blade. Then he got up and closed the door.

THE passenger cars extended into the muted sunlight beyond the barrel dome of the station. It was a raw day, cloudy and cold with a wind that seemed more like March.

Beside the great black engine of the embassy train, the men from the German Foreign Office stood like mourners at a graveside. Ambassador Gerard moved slowly down the line past Montgelas, Roediger, Prittwitz, and Horstman, giving out gold cigarette cases and pumping hands as the soot and steam billowed over their heads.

Ostriker had taken personal charge of security on the platform. Military police checked identity papers against a master list, and two officers had been assigned to accompany the train. If Eli Gordon magically appeared en route, Ostriker had arranged for the engine to develop mechanical difficulties well before the Swiss frontier at Schaffhausen.

He stood calmly in the window of the stationmaster's office, watching Gerard and his entourage pass through the final checkpoint. The funereal tone seemed very apt, especially if the U.S. used this latest provocation as reason to enter the war. The whistle gave an endless shriek that Ostriker thought was going to penetrate his skull. Then the diplomat bade farewell to the caretakers he was leaving behind, Polo de Bernabe from the Spanish Embassy and Baron Gevers from the Dutch, and stepped into his private salon.

Ostriker walked outside and touched his chapped lips with the back of his hand, staring down the platform. He had guards posted at every station in Berlin, but this train worried him. It was quick, a clean break, very like a surgeon in that respect. If Gordon made it through here, he could be beyond German control in the twinkling of an eye.

And control was very much the issue now. Controlling information, controlling disease. Ostriker had thought he could control Margarethe Riesling, but perhaps a little too much hubris had entered into that assumption. Still, the doctor and the crew at Wilhelmshaven had been quarantined. Naval security had held all reports of the anthrax incident. Word of something this destabilizing would not rumble through the Prussian bureaucracy until Ostriker knew all the facts, and all the implications.

One part of him had suspected all along that the anthrax incident was staged, a hoax to trip Germany into some self-destructive overreaction just as the U.S. was poised to come in on the side of the Allies. The British were masters of political theater, of course. The faked medal commemorating the *Lusitania,* the crucified Canadian.

On the other hand, he still had no way of knowing what Operation Alberich held out. German research. A German bacteriological offensive. How could he possibly respond to what was going on in British labs if he could not be sure what was going on in German labs?

Gazing down the line in the gray distance, his eye eventually focused on a small man scurrying toward the train with a very large pormanteau. It was a journalist he was supposed to know, the one Mayr had seen with Gordon. But it took a moment to summon up the name—by which time Billy de Beauford was nodding and smiling beneath his wide Borsolino.

"Ah, Major," Billy gasped, coming up. "Good to see you. Yes. Always following the action." De Beauford was out of breath from struggling with the bag, his powdered cheeks flushed with exertion.

Ostriker stood with his hands in his pockets and suppressed a sudden surge of anxiety. "Leaving us so soon?" he said.

De Beauford laughed with great enthusiasm and presented his press pass and identity papers to a fat Silesian guard.

"Ah. Not that easy to get rid of me, Major. Just covering the story. Today the story is on this train, leaving for Switzerland. I'll be back soon enough."

De Beauford smiled eagerly as Ostriker looked down at the huge suitcase between them. It was expensive leather, almost as tall as the Dutchman himself.

"You're taking a full wardrobe?" the major noted, watching Billy's eyes. He did not like the furtiveness he saw there. "Or are you simply smuggling one of your mistresses out of the country?"

De Beauford smiled but faltered as he drew in his breath. "Yes. Caught me at it, I'm afraid. But you'll be a sport. You won't tell, will you?"

The guard handed back his papers and the Dutchman tucked them into his breast pocket. Then he smiled and reached down for his bag.

Ostriker nodded to the guard. "Hold him."

The soldier clasped Billy's arm in a firm grip and de Beauford tried to laugh. "I don't understand. What's the problem?"

"We'll talk about that later," Ostriker said.

The whistle shrieked again as the guards took de Beauford into the stationmaster's office. Steam burst from the engine, the great steel wheels advanced, and Rolf Mayr appeared quietly at Ostriker's side.

"We found the file," he said.

Ostriker looked at him out of the corner of his eye and felt his stomach turn to water.

"Berlin Section Four had been keeping tabs on her, but von Broembsen had it suppressed."

For the moment Ostriker could not breathe. He saw the man and heard the words but as if through some kind of filter.

"And what had they found?"

"She was fucking Colonel von Stade, head of chemical procurement."

Ostriker brushed his lips again with the back of his hand. "You can't imagine how delighted I am to hear this right now, Rolf."

"Amazing what a war can do for a woman's taste. Before the colonel, she kept company with a small-time revolutionary named Gunther Stinnes."

Ostriker pulled out his handkerchief and watched the train as it disappeared into the distance.

"Covers a lot of ground for one woman, Major," Mayr said. "Very open-minded." Then he paused, squinting under his white brow. "You want to know what I think?"

"What do you think, Rolf?"

"I think she's not on our side."

Von Laudermann and von Hessenstein rode up front with the driver. Ostriker and Rolf Mayr sat in the back, with Billy nervously in between.

"So explain it to me," Ostriker said.

"Ah, yes. Explain it."

"You have the best contacts in Berlin. Tell me all the little things that have been going on right under my nose."

"Happily. But where should I begin?"

"An American named Eli Gordon. He stayed at your hotel. You talked to him at the hotel bar."

Billy looked out the window, reading the street signs to gain his bearings.

"Gordon . . . Gordon . . . ," he said absentmindedly. "You mean the American. Tall, dark fellow . . . with the embassy?"

"Precisely the man I mean."

"Sorry, but he didn't have much to say. I'm afraid he's one I took at face value. Something about the prisoner camps. Inspections, health problems. Is there more to him? Did I miss something good?"

Ostriker gazed ahead through the windscreen and said nothing. He felt sick again now, unable to breathe as the whiteness closed in. With a little effort she would have had access to all Germany's weapons research. And if she was sitting on this "magic bullet," she was now very likely about to pass it into British hands. All of it preventable. And all of it his responsibility.

They passed Königergratzerstrasse 70 but did not turn in. Billy looked out and began to lose his studied composure.

"Seriously now, Major, you don't detain journalists for the pleasure of their company. My conscience is quite clear, but still it makes one a little nervous."

The car rounded the corner onto the Wilhelm Platz, and Billy's heart sank as they bypassed the foreign office. Instead of turning in there they pulled up in front of the barricade outside the American Embassy, where a police guard opened Ostriker's door, stepped back, and saluted.

"I want to pick up an associate," Ostriker said, tightening his stomach. "Then we'll talk, Billy. We'll go someplace uncomfortable and compare notes on the good Dr. Gordon."

Gray-faced and limp, de Beauford hung like a cat, his feet scarcely touching the ground, as von Hessenstein and Mayr led him through the police barricade and up the steps. He was a dead man now, every bit as dead as his pretty princess. The only difference was that he had yet to go through the pain.

Von Laudermann led the way inside the foyer. The floor was wet with snow where he stopped and called out. Then their footsteps echoed as they continued across the lobby and climbed the stairs.

Billy could no longer control his sweating as they held him under the arms. He shouldn't have even tried to escape. He should have used the time to take care of Fisk on his own, the one act of retribution that would matter.

On the second floor they passed the open doors of vacated offices. Von Laudermann called out again with no response. Then they heard a whimpering from inside the ballroom and Ostriker opened the doors to see Fräulein Kleist struggling in the corner. He stepped fully into the room and in the center saw Jay Adams' body lying in a pool of blood.

CRIMINAL detectives Andreas Schiller and Axel Kadereit rode up front with the driver, lumbering toward the Westhafen docks in Department B-1's only remaining Black Maria. It had taken all morning to line up the men in the back and arm them with Hotchkiss guns and grenades liberated from the Tenth Uhlans. Still, they were not exactly what Hindenburg would call "crack troops."

Ice and snow had turned the road into a narrow path. Kadereit leaned over as they skidded through the ruts and struck a wooden match to light Schiller's cigar. "I hope you know what you're doing, Andreas."

Schiller smiled pleasantly as the cab filled with smoke. "What I've done, you mean."

Kadereit had never understood cigars, a habit that made even less sense now. He squinted against the acrid cloud, a smell like burning trash. "I suppose that's right," he said.

"We must live in the present."

"But how long does that give us, Andreas?"

Kadereit lit his own cigarette, holding it between his third and forth fingers while he carefully placed the spent match back inside the box.

The windows were steamed and the driver rolled his down a crack. The opening let in a rush of cold, fresh air.

Kadereit looked over at his friend. It amused him to think of Schiller in a defiant role, like Götz von Berlichingen—surrounded in his castle, outmanned but not defeated, yelling "Kiss my ass" to the Bishop of Nuremburg.

"So now we smash the black market and become heroes. Perhaps the triumph will overshadow anything else you did today."

Schiller looked at him vacantly. "What makes you think we'll be heroes?" he said. And then to himself—or succeed for that matter. Fisk and von den Benken had friends in high places, friends he had always been wary of jostling. He had been timid until now. But today was a day for taking risks.

Kadereit inhaled deeply on his crumpled cigarette. Schiller gazed up at the gray clouds that rolled across the sky like Zeppelins over the Stettinger Bahnhof. The police detail passed the Exerzier Platz and turned west into blowing snow.

"So why did you let her go, Andreas?"

Schiller looked at his cigar. "We'd never be able to prove she killed von Stade."

"And what about her passing information to the British?"

"That's not our problem, is it?"

Kadereit nodded, musing as he smoked. "I want to track down the dentist's money, that's what I want."

Schiller looked out across the bleak cityscape, more white than gray now, and he was grateful that he and Kadereit were old comrades who could trust each other without explanations. But how could he explain a lifetime of frustration, set against one moment of complete autonomy?

"When you were a kid, Axel, did you have an apple barrel in your cellar?"

"Sure. Of course."

Schiller wiped the window with his glove, but he seemed focused on something that was not in the visual field.

"My stepmother," he said after a while, merging once again with the present. "She was vicious about waste, you know. Always. We had to eat the ones that were going bad first. Mushy, bruised, half-rotten apples. The trouble, of course, was that we could never eat them fast enough. We could never catch up to eat the good ones before *they* turned."

He looked over at Kadereit and gestured with the cigar. "One day you reach in, you grab a crisp, red apple, and you take a bite."

"Like Adam."

"Yes," Schiller said, nodding. "In a way."

Kadereit flipped his cigarette out into the breeze. "Andreas," he said, "you have tasted sin."

Against the horizon, a black cloud suddenly shot up into the air, licked by bright orange flames. A millisecond later the sound wave rolled past them with the force of an explosion.

"What are the chances," Schiller said coolly, "that that came from somewhere other than the Westhafen docks?"

Kadereit gazed calmly through the windscreen. "Remote," he said.

They could see the smoke at its source now, a single black plume like a growing tornado. It rose above the crenellations of a red brick building facing the canal. The building on fire was the Bowles Brewery.

By the time they arrived the fire wagons were backed out onto the road outside the gate. The smoke was thicker now, the flames from the rooftop reflecting in the nickel-colored water.

The Black Maria pulled to a stop and Schiller climbed down, feeling unsteady. It could be the excitement, or the sudden blast of heat, or merely his disease.

He turned back to Kadereit. "Get the men out but stay close," he said.

The captain of the fire brigade stood outside the gates talking to one of his soot-smeared lieutenants. Beyond them, men in slickers sprayed thick streams of water into the air, the mist forming rainbows, then icicles on the backs of their helmets.

Schiller approached and the captain looked up, his face blackened by smoke.

"You came to direct traffic?" he said.

Schiller coughed in the dry, cinder-filled air. "Has anyone been inside?"

"Take a look."

He could see the flames licking up from the windows, charring the bricks above. He could feel the heat. He could also smell the stench of charred flesh.

"It was set, yes? Explosives. Gasoline."

"Thank God for the detective branch."

"Help me!" Schiller screamed. His stoic face was straining with the urgency now. "Did you see anyone?"

The fireman shook his head. "I see a fire. Now . . . if you're through . . ."

Schiller seethed with a self-directed anger now, a lifelong frustration focused on one event. He had energy without an object and it burned through his clothes. If he had not been afraid, he could have moved in days ago and nailed them all.

He walked back to the truck, wallowing in disgust and eyeing the men fanned out in front of it like bowling pins in blue uniforms. Cripples, grandfathers, mustaches with potbellies. It was the half dead leading the half dead.

"Too late," he acknowledged.

Kadereit looked up at a huge black cinder swirling overhead. "So now what?"

"Let's talk to Fisk."

■ ■ ■

It must be possible, Schiller realized, to gain power over the script. This was not Karl May he was reading. He was an agent of his own will. He could direct events to a crisis of his own choosing.

The driver ground the gears as they pulled onto See Strasse. They crossed the Königsdamm Bridge over the canal, then picked up Beussel Strasse south through Moabit. As they rumbled over the snow-rutted streets, Schiller reached into his pocket, pulled out his automatic, and checked the clip. It held a full eight rounds. Assuming nothing had corroded, then . . . he was prepared. He had never been better prepared for anything in his life.

Physical decline was overtaking him, yes. His hands shook but his grip today was still strong enough. The weapon still felt solid and good wrapped in his palm.

Just before the Gotzkowski Bridge they turned left onto Levetzowstrasse, which carried them over the Spree. The only automobile on Altonaer Strasse, they wove through the horse-drawn vehicles like a skier on a slope.

Schiller glanced over at his partner. Kadereit could still look forward to many good years, provided he survived the war. Schiller did not want his own disregard for consequences to end his young comrade's career. But maybe the fire was a good sign. Criminals with real power did not have to hide evidence from the police.

The snow blew up like dust behind them as they drove across the Tiergarten. Gusts of wind knocked the white powder from the trees onto their windscreen. They passed Rousseau Island and Grosser Weg, and then the Wagner monument. Brunhild and the dead Siegfried carved in stone, the Rhine Maidens and Alberich the dwarf.

In a moment they were on Tiergartenstrasse, rolling east. They had made it across the park. Then Bendler Strasse, the shadows of buildings protecting the ice and snow, and Fisk's town house on the corner.

The outer door at street level was locked. Schiller swung his cudgel to shatter the glass, then reached inside and opened the door. His men were clustered behind him, and he felt immensely competent, a leader, a good policeman. His movements were co-ordinated, almost effortless. He was graceful as he climbed the stairs, swiftly and assuredly, a vigorous young man again, not a terminal case. He reached the landing and the door made of clouded glass and he could see movement behind it—a dark shape. He reached out with the cudgel again, leaning toward the door, and then the glass exploded from inside.

For the moment Schiller's senses were immensely distorted. The lead pipe dropped from his hand and the world became remote, even comical. He caught a glimpse of Erskine Fisk behind a veil of blue smoke, running toward the open window like a fleeing embezzler. Schiller laughed to picture the dentist scampering across the rooftops with his grip. And then he fell back against the wall, feeling first the perplexing embarrassment of moisture trickling inside his clothes, and then the pain. Blood smeared in a wide swath behind him as he slid down the wall, tumbling into the arms of Detective Kadereit.

24

The house in Bedford Square was listed for sale with the firm of Ludgate and Brook, Gray's Inn Road. Their sun-bleached and fading advertisement was propped in the bowfront window between the rather dusty glass and the tightly drawn shade.

Anthony Rice's key was for the front door. He nodded in greeting as he entered the room but he did not expect much from it. There was a brief but awkward silence, endured with downcast eyes, and then the conversation resumed.

The scientific members of the committee already had entered through the garden, which connected to another vacant house on Adeline Place. Dr. Nigel Post of the Agricultural Research Council, Sir Benjamin Denny-Brown of the bacterial chemistry unit at Middlesex Hospital, and Sir Ian Fitzhugh of the Lister Institute.

This was the first meeting of the Committee on Medical Intelligence at this location. They had last convened in a basement lavatory at Whitehall, each member led down separately by a Boy Guide, but the dampness had inflamed Sir Ian's arthritis, and Dr. Post had complained of unpleasant memories from school.

Rice poured himself a glass of Amontillado, but continued to stand apart. The scientists were talking of Sir Eric Geddes, major general in the army, now appointed vice admiral in the navy. "There's nothing left for him but to become archbishop," Sir Benjamin said. Rice found their donnish small talk annoying. Gardening, the music hall . . . It was as if they refused to speak substance for fear of wasting it on their listeners.

But Rice had not slept well and he found everything annoying. He and Hermione had quarreled, but more than that he had lain awake trying to make some sense of this whole project. A doomsday machine is a reasonable deterrent when you and your enemy are both equally defenseless. But what happens when your enemy can protect himself and you cannot?

"Gentlemen, good day."

Rice turned to see Winston Churchill burst into the room, tossing off his hat and stick and cape with a theatrical flair, drawing Colonel Napier of the Royal Artillery along in his wake.

The men muttered and cleared their throats, then slowly took their places, shuffling chairs against the uncarpeted floor. They coughed into handkerchiefs and tucked them away. Then Churchill took up his position at the head of the table, a rotund and balding hero standing guard over the empire, casting his eyes quickly around as he listened to the ticking of their watches.

"Since we last met," he began, clutching the lapels of his long frock coat, "the diplomatic cord binding the United States and the German empire has been cut. The cause of this great schism is, as you know, the resumption of unrestricted U-boat warfare." He paused to study each face in turn, cocking his head to the right and to the left.

"These are perilous times in which to live," he added. "Exciting times in which to live. You have read the report. I am eager to know your finding."

Churchill reached into his pocket for a cigar, placed it between his teeth unlit, and promptly sat down.

Nigel Post took this opportunity to carefully examine the wood grain, smoothing a small circle in the table with his fingertips. Across from him Sir Ian and Sir Benjamin eyed each other like homely sisters at their first cotillion.

"Gentlemen," Churchill said. "This is the time to speak."

"Well," Sir Ian ventured, "the apparatus was certainly effective at killing sheep."

Churchill shot him an impatient glance. "Via this anthrax bacillus, am I correct in that, sir? Not the explosion itself."

"Right you are."

"Indeed." Churchill chewed his cigar and waited for more.

Sir Ian Fitzhugh's pale, crooked face was so thin that every bone stood in stark relief. He worked his tongue once against his protruding teeth and said, "But, as you see, First Lord. The larger effects. The application of this . . . biological device on a grand scale . . . There are still . . . several rifts in the lute."

Then Sir Benjamin chimed in. "This American fellow. I had thought we would be receiving something from him on the German preparations. At least some initial assessment of this much vaunted 'magic bullet.' "

Churchill glanced at Rice, who fingered the one ridiculous postcard from Gordon he had tucked away in his tunic pocket.

"I'm afraid the pace of political events may have overtaken him," Rice said. "We assume Dr. Gordon is en route from Berlin to Switzerland with the ambassador's party, but we've heard nothing as yet to confirm it."

"Then I think we should wait," Dr. Post said rather forcefully.

Sir Benjamin removed his glasses. "I agree. The persistence of the bacillus is very much on my mind. We have no idea what the long-range effects might be."

"Or what we are walking into in terms of retaliatory measures. If the Germans are working the same patch, yet further along . . . then they would be that much better prepared to deal with the inevitable 'boomerang.' "

"And still we have no proof that they're engaged in this at all! I simply do not understand the rationale for haste. It is entirely possible that the Germans are far more reasonable than we imagine."

Churchill patiently gnawed his cigar as the scientists spoke. And in that moment, watching his bulldog eyes, Rice realized for the first time as clear as life that Winston cared not one whit what Germany was up to. This First Lord of the Admiralty would protect England no matter what the odds, no matter what the risk to others. The Wogs begin at Calais.

"Gentlemen . . ." Churchill gripped his corona and thrust out his chin. "We are an island nation. It is said that so long as the British navy rules the sea, 'we can sleep quiet in our beds.' But the British navy has a new and formidable rival—not on the seas, but under them."

Churchill shot his glance around the room, implicating each and every man within his hearing.

"Do not speak to me of German reasonableness. We have witnessed their 'reasonableness' in the past. We have new evidence of their 'reasonableness' which I am not yet at liberty to share with you. But of one thing you may be sure—the resumption of unrestricted U-boat warfare will bring our American cousins into the fray. Inevitably, their arrival will ensure victory for our cause, but the United States is not a nation ready for war. It will take many months to mobilize the forces of that slumbering giant."

He rose from his seat and began to pace, absorbed in the sound of his own words as if he were dictating.

"In this hour of greatest peril, Germany has made its commitment. If Operation Alberich offers them hope of victory, they must grasp it with a steeled fist. Their U-boats cannot sink all the troopships their recklessness helps to launch. This is their moment. They must grasp it. They must pursue it ruthlessly."

He stopped and glared at his listeners. "We all know the story of Alberich's magic cloak. Siegfried impervious to blows." He paused to put his cigar between his teeth. "We can only hope that our countermeasures are equal to the task."

The room was silent for a moment, but then Nigel Post, glancing all around him at his companions, leaned forward ever so timidly to venture one additional remark.

"First Lord, forgive me, but I still fail to understand the tactical specifics of the anthrax weapon. The use of such a device is, to say the least, a matter of great risk for all concerned."

"I blush for you, sir. Britain must defend her frontiers, whatever the risk. And our frontier is not Dover but Calais. We cannot sit idly counting angels on pins, awaiting additional intelligence from Berlin. We must prepare our defense now, even if it means a new English Channel of contagion to stem the German tide."

Churchill looked around him once more. "With the committee's approval we will engage immediately in transporting our new apparatus to France. Pending further information from Dr. Gordon, Wellington House will be instructed to create an appropriate fiction to justify the steps being taken."

Churchill's eyes gleamed with defiance. "Do I sense your approval?"

The men were stunned. Rice wondered if Churchill himself had expected this outcome, or if the decision hadn't sprung full-blown from his own ineluctable oratory.

"Very well, then. I appreciate your coming to this unlikely meeting place."

Churchill turned briskly toward the chair where he had left his cloak and stick, as the scientists rose slowly to their feet.

Rice stood by Churchill's side, dumbfounded.

The first lord did not look up. Instead he muttered, "I want you in touch with our man in Zurich. From the moment Gordon arrives, he is to sit on him. Then you will rendezvous for a debriefing."

"What can he say at this point that will be of use to us?" Rice insisted.

"Anything he does say, no matter what he's found or hasn't found, must conform to British interests. And you will personally ensure that his every utterance does conform to British interests. At all cost. Is that explicit enough for you, my boy?"

Rice turned away from Churchill's penetrating gaze. "Yes, Winston," he said. "You've made it all quite clear."

25

In the palm court of the Kaiserhof Hotel in Spandau, Margarethe Riesling and Eli Gordon sat waiting at a small table in the corner, leaning over glasses of beer neither of them had bothered to taste and looking out through the frosted window to the train station across the way.

"Did you see the listing?" Gordon asked.

"Three forty-seven," she mumbled, then glanced down at the table.

Their bags were by the door. The folder containing her drawings and now her laboratory notebooks was in her lap. She wore her dark glasses, a man's brown fedora, her green loden coat, and a gray woolen muffler wrapped around her neck. Gordon wore a German army uniform with the rank of colonel, Tenth Uhlans— a gift from Andreas Schiller, who had escorted them from the Polizei Präsidium to the Bahnhof Alexanderplatz and put them on the Stadtbahn out of the city.

This was the first resting point Gordon had come to in three days, and now so many things that he had simply filed away and compartmentalized needed to be dealt with. He was, first of all, astounded by the prospect of escape, by the fact that they had prospects at all. He had resigned himself to fate the way men going over the top resign themselves. But then Schiller the observer had taken sides. And now survival was a renewed responsibility, one he was not sure he was up to.

He had blocked the images—the Turk and the Africans, Princess Bucher and Fisk—but now they were coming back to him, associations all the more unpleasant as he looked across the table at Margarethe Riesling's luminous face.

"So if we do it your way," he said, raising his glass, "who is it we're supposed to meet?"

"Her name is Käthe. She has a shop in Bremen."

Gordon gazed out at the soldiers with bayonets standing by the office of the provost marshal, the plainclothes detectives mingling with the crowd beyond the Military Passport Office. Then he looked back at Margarethe. She had been defined mostly by his imagination until now, but suddenly here she was, in the flesh.

"As in the Bremen Left?" Gordon said.

She nodded and kept her eyes focused on the table.

Gordon had never been political. Political people made him nervous. He didn't see her that way, though. He saw her intensity as being more than political. It seemed religious.

"The Bremen Left and then what?" he asked.

"A ship to Denmark."

Gordon waited while she touched her glass to her lips. "So when was the last time you talked to her? How do you know it's safe?"

She looked up. "Maybe there's still time to catch your embassy train?"

Gordon stroked the moisture on his beer stein. She had plenty of room for her own uncertainty, he supposed, her own imperfect grasp of what was between them and surrounding them, and of what lay ahead. But what troubled him most was her complicity with Erskine Fisk. How much had she known? And why had she made the choices she had made?

"This package you picked up at the Institute," he said after a while. "Tell me about it."

She shrugged and said nothing. He had watched her tuck the glass dish inside her blouse before they left the Alexanderplatz, fastening it against the warmth of her skin.

"Tell me what it can do," he said. "Make me believe in it, since we're risking our necks for it."

She shrugged again, raising her eyes behind her dark lenses to look out at the blowing snow. "I can't make you believe anything," she said.

"Try me."

"It works, that's all. You inject it. It kills strep. It kills staph, pneumococcus, meningococcus, diphtheria, gangrene."

Gordon widened his eyes. "That's all?"

She glared back at him. "Yes, that's *all*. All so far. I might know far more if it weren't for the fact that it also kills anthrax."

Gordon looked down. He wanted to believe in her every bit as much as he wanted to believe in their survival. He wanted to believe some purpose could be served by it all. But this disturbed him.

"That's one hell of a discovery," he said.

She raised her glass to her lips and took a long drink. "I don't care if you believe me. That's why discoveries by women remain secrets. The moment a man believes in it, takes it seriously, he also takes it over."

Gordon watched as she tapped her glass, her discolored fingertips, the nails gnawed to the quick. They were still beautiful, delicate fingers, long and golden the way her neck was long and golden.

He thought about the Englishman at Ruhleben, the talk about inverse skepticism. He had seen a lot in the last twenty-four hours he never would have believed. The boundaries change with experience.

"I seem to recall a few hundred thousand soldiers with war wounds," he said after a while. "I've been watching men die with strep and gangrene for two years. It gets monotonous."

"I know that. I've had to live with that."

"But now you can just give them a little shot of this stuff and they snap out of it. Is that the idea?"

"It's not that easy. I'm not that far along. I've had to recycle it out of patients' urine—it's that unstable. It's also unbelievably difficult to refine, which is why I've stayed put. But then there are other military applications for a 'magic bullet' right now, aren't there? I've had to walk a fine line. Scaling up as fast as I can. Keeping it a secret."

She glanced down. "Of course, it makes little difference, at the moment, doesn't it? Your friends on the other side seem to have taken the initiative without me. They don't demand much in the way of caution."

Gordon looked out toward the station, where a vendor beneath the canopy sold mulled wine. The guards stood about, slapping their arms to their sides, stamping their feet. Now and then the detectives stopped someone at random, asking for papers.

Gordon had no idea whether anything coming out of her mouth was the truth and he was probably too tired to know the difference anyway. He wanted to trust her, the same way he had wanted to trust Schiller and de Beauford. But he had trusted Anthony Rice and Almroth Wright. And he had trusted Jay Adams.

"Your lab," he said. "How can you be sure you're the only one this far along?"

"I'm sure."

"Just like that?"

"I was there at the beginning. A meeting with Ludendorff, von Stade, von Broembsen. The directive was clear. The Institute was to explore the possibilities. But nothing was to be done on developing a weapon until the problem of control was solved."

"Okay. But what if—"

"I've done research in Berlin for seven years. I've been exposed daily to the egos and advances of all my male colleagues. If anyone else had come even close, believe me, I would be the first to know."

Gordon looked out at the snow. She was hard to dismiss. She had either made one of the great discoveries of all time, or she was completely out of her mind. So far, he would rate it as a toss-up.

"So you're saying there's no German weapons program at all. Nothing."

"That's right."

"So what is Operation Alberich?"

"I don't know. I only know it has nothing to with bacteriological weapons."

Gordon took a drink, then set down the glass, spinning it slowly on the table. "We get to London and you try to convince the British of that. You tell them they're overreacting, bringing this whole bacterial thing into the war themselves. What makes you think they'll buy it?"

"I don't think they'll buy it. Trying to stop the British is your idea."

She looked at him with a determination he had not seen in her face before. "But the extract is *mine*," she said. "And *I'm* going to be the one to control how it's used."

The stopping train pulled in from Berlin at three-forty and Margarethe Riesling and Eli Gordon watched the Spandau passengers cluster along the tracks, getting ready to board.

"How long would you say it will take?" he asked her, looking away.

"About thirty seconds," she said.

Gordon nodded and called for the waiter. He paid their check, and then they crossed the room and stood by their bags at the door. The detectives had stepped inside. Only the soldiers and a few stragglers were left on the platform. The last of them said their goodbyes and climbed into compartments. Then the station clock struck three forty-six and Gordon pushed open the door.

They walked quickly across the snow-covered plaza between the hotel and the station. They were fully exposed now, facing a raw wind. There was no way to know what would happen as they approached the line of soldiers standing outside the office. The moments passed and there was no reaction yet, no movement.

Then the train whistle shrieked and the soldiers saw the uniform and leapt to attention.

"Hold the train!" Gordon shouted as he and Margarethe walked grandly past.

The platform was empty now except for the conductors looking down the rails to give the all clear. The nearest one turned and bowed.

"We must have a compartment," Gordon said. "We will buy our tickets on board."

The trainman bowed again, engulfed by a cloud of steam. "I'm sorry, Colonel. But first class is filled."

"Nonsense." Gordon reached up and threw open a compartment door. "These men will stand down."

Gordon waited, his hand resting on the hilt of his sword.

The startled passengers looked out at the uniform, the scars, and the bloodshot eye. They were not about to engage in a test of wills with a Prussian officer. They stood quickly, grabbed up their belongings, then climbed down onto the siding.

Gordon gave Margarethe his hand, helping her into the compartment. Then he climbed in and sat down across from her as the conductor lifted up their bags, closed the door, and blew his whistle for the engineer.

The train lurched into motion and Gordon leaned back, astounded that the bluff had worked. He allowed himself one faint sigh of relief, then looked toward Margarethe, thinking they might share their small victory. But she sat gazing out the window, beautiful and passive, and utterly inaccessible.

WHEN they reached Hanover it was too late to make connections on another stopping train. They could catch a corridor express, but passport controls were that much tighter on the main lines, and one awkward question was enough to bring it all crashing down. They chose instead to spend the night in Hanover and travel to Bremen in the morning.

They found a hotel just off the Theater Platz, wedged in between a cinematograph and a vacant storefront. They walked to the desk and the night manager looked up, a heavy, sluggish man, his eyes focused on them with both fear and disapproval.

"Passports," he said, burying his nose in a yellowed handkerchief.

Gordon slipped a bank note across the registration book, and after a moment's hesitation the hotelkeeper scowled and shook his head, but then rang for the night porter.

They were taken to a narrow room with windows hidden behind dingy lace curtains and heavy brocade drapes. Gordon sat on a leather banquette and looked down on the ice-rutted street below.

He watched Margarethe light a cigarette, then trace the same five steps between the armoire and the green-on-green papered wall.

He had been with her all afternoon, yet they had not really spoken since Spandau. Surrounded by people who ate liverwurst for breakfast, he realized how much he had already come to depend on her company. But why had she been willing to go off with Fisk?

"We should eat something," he said.

She looked at him dismissively and kept pacing. "I don't have any money," she said.

"I think we can work that out," Gordon told her. Then he stood to open the door.

They ate at the Rabe in the Aegidientor Platz, beer and a brown noodle soup and coarse war bread. Gordon carried de Beauford's derringer in his pocket, and Margarethe had the revolver hidden in her bag.

In the candlelight of the restaurant she looked softer, more approachable. But that only made him more cautious.

"The Bremen Left," he said after a while, removing a small piece of frayed wood from the mouthful of bread he was chewing. "How much does that explain?"

"Not much."

"You're not political?"

She shrugged and sipped her beer.

"You have a lover and he's political?"

She said nothing, but he could tell by her glance that he had struck home. She sat slowly tearing her bread into little pieces but not eating it.

"So that's why you stayed in Berlin, is it? The lover?"

She gave the observation a flick of one brow, but never committed herself one way or the other.

"So why are you willing to leave now? What changed?"

"No man wants a woman who has more problems than he does," she said, and pushed the bread crumbs away from her.

Gordon let the remark settle onto the table, its aphoristic reverberations subside. He watched her long, delicate fingers with the dark blue stains as she reached into her bag, lit a cigarette, and blew a long stream of smoke into the air.

"So tell me about this lover of yours. He's still in the city?"

"No."

"Let me guess. Denmark, by any chance? Having made his escape via one Käthe the Red in Bremen."

"I don't know where he is now."

"But the escape. I'm right about that, aren't I? This sounds like a mistake, then. Who else knows about this?"

She held her cigarette like a pencil pointing upward, staring at him through the trail of smoke. "I have no idea," she said. "I can't give you any guarantees. It could be in all the papers by now, you know."

Gordon stared back at her deliberately. "The authorities in Berlin seem to know you pretty well. It's not all that great a leap to assume you'd try the same route that worked for this friend of yours."

"If Ostriker had known about Gunther he wouldn't have let me go the first time. And we don't have much choice, do we? Unless you're offering something better."

Gordon looked away. "Not yet," he said.

"What does that mean?"

"Let's see where your plan takes us for now," he said. Then he turned halfheartedly to his soup.

They made their way back to the hotel after dinner, the sky covered with clouds, the city quiet. Margarethe walked beside him, looking into the darkness, keeping pace with her long stride. Her head was bowed slightly under her fedora, her skin glowing in the crisp air.

Gordon felt his kinship with Schiller now in the desire not to intervene, the desire to see what she would come up with on her own. He knew he had been drawn in deeper than he had ever bargained for, banking everything on her own interpretation of events. He wanted to see where her account would lead. And for once it would be so much simpler if he could, in fact, believe her.

"This extract of yours," he said, turning onto the Theater Platz. "How much does Ostriker know?"

"I think he pretends to know more than he does."

"That's why he released you, why he gave me room to operate. To watch and wait. To get all the answers without showing his hand."

She nodded as they turned onto the Theater Platz, and watching her, Gordon felt himself wanting to trust whatever she would have him believe.

"So this . . . extract," he said after a moment. "How did you discover it?"

She lifted her head and her eyes glowed majestically as they entered the hotel. "Blue-green mold," she told him. "Mold I found growing on an overripe pear."

Two policemen stood at the registration desk with the owner. One of them caught Gordon's eye and nodded as if to a colleague.

Then the two Americans walked past, crossing silently toward the stairs.

Off balance and unsettled, now frightened, Gordon led the way as they climbed up to the landing and walked directly to their room. This was not a time to have doubts, but he could never hold on to any certainty with her. An overripe pear?

Margarethe closed the door behind them and said, "It could be nothing. The cop on the beat." She seemed quite rational now, whatever her delusions. Lucid and very reasonably afraid.

Gordon glanced at her, then went for his Gladstone bag. "They've had time to notify the other districts," he said.

"But we could be heading for Switzerland for all they know."

He pulled out the Colt and checked to see that the cylinder was full. He reached for the box of cartridges and emptied them into his pockets.

"I guess we can't wait to find out, can we?" she admitted. Gordon studied her eyes as they waited.

They heard footsteps in the hall—two men, maybe three. There was silence, followed by a knock on the door.

"What is it?" Gordon said.

"Ah. Colonel. I wish to speak with you."

"Come back in the morning."

A second voice called out from the hall. "This is official police business, Colonel. You will kindly open the door."

Gordon looked out the windows. There was no fire escape, no adjoining roof, just the three-story drop. He and Margarethe pressed against the wall beside the door.

"There is no 'police business' with the army," he said. "Go to bed." But he knew the bluff was pointless now. They should have gone for the big lie, the best suite at a first-class hotel.

There was more silence, then the scuffing of feet. Someone coughed, and then the key rattled in the lock. Gordon felt the same rush he had felt when he was cornered by the man with metal teeth, the same vertiginous sense of moral disengagement, the same knowledge that survival carried a price.

He aimed with his left hand. The door swung open and he saw blue uniforms and drawn pistols. He ignored their faces and fired four times. The two policemen sprawled back against the door, then slid down to the carpet.

The hotelkeeper fell back into the hallway and Gordon leapt after him with the gun. "Lie on your face!"

The man froze, cowering on the rug as Gordon turned and saw Margarethe stooped over the policemen, looking pale and confused, trying to help them.

"Let's go," Gordon shouted.

She held up her hands. They were covered with blood.

"Let's go!" he repeated.

She gathered up their bags and climbed over the bodies and followed after him, leaving a trail of footprints down the stairs.

A door flew open and the hotelkeeper's wife came out screaming, pointing a pistol in Margarethe's face. Gordon gripped the gun barrel firmly as it discharged past his head. He wrenched the gun from the woman's hands, then sat her down—hard—on the steps.

He stood over her, pulsing with anger until Margarethe took his arm. "It's all right," she said. "It's all right." She was more composed now, her color returning. She pulled him out into the night.

They ran down Königstrasse toward the station, not really sure which way they were going or why. In the fourth block they slowed to a walk, breathing in the mist that hung over the buildings. They could see the station off to the left now, the lights of the corridor express lined up and ready to leave, but that was still not an option. They walked toward the tunnel and under the tracks.

Gordon's heart was still pounding, expanded by adrenaline, his skin wet. The blood coursing through his veins acted like a tracer, highlighting the pain in his hand and in his neck. He felt lightheaded and sick, but there was no turning back. He was like Fisk now, or the generals, defending his turf.

A single figure came toward them, a patrolman, silhouetted by a streetlamp. Would they have to kill him, too? Would they have to kill everyone between here and the border just to get out of the country? Gordon kept his hand on the revolver, but then they made out the small dog on a leash. The German was in a yachting cap and black raincoat, out for a stroll.

The two men nodded perfunctorily. Then Margarethe and Gordon came out from under the tunnel and onto a block of shops leading toward the Eilenriede. They passed along sidewalks covered with ice and a ragged surface of frozen snow. They passed two blocks of houses, then they entered the woods.

On either side of them now the blackness was so deep that it was like a texture. It was frightening, this darkness. And it was frightening that they had no plan now except to stay out of sight until morning. They heard the train rumbling off into the night. They could see the lighter sky ahead in the break above the path, just enough light to stumble along, trying to stay warm, trying not to think about what had happened.

They walked for half an hour more, Gordon laboring to focus his mind on their objectives. What had happened was unavoidable, and now he could not overreact. Preventing overreaction was the whole point. If the British were tempted to bring on this biological disaster, then only Margarethe's information could pull them back. Unless of course she was wrong. Or unless, of course, she was lying.

They came to a clearing with some sort of structure to their left. Gordon flipped his lighter and saw a caretaker's shed made of stucco, covered over with snow.

"What do you want to do?" he asked her.

"I think we should get out of the cold."

"That's what I mean. We can't cover any distance tonight. We can't just walk out of here."

"I agree." There was an edge to her voice. "I'm saying let's go inside."

She took the lighter while he used the colonel's saber to pry off the lock. Then he pulled back the door and smelled the tang of damp soil and decaying wood. In the flickering light they saw wheelbarrows, pruning hooks, axes. Gordon took the flame and, in the rear now, saw a stack of water pipes covering one wall.

"It looks dry," he said, still agitated. He closed the door and climbed up on the pipes and slid toward the corner.

Margarethe hesitated by the door. She stood with her hands in her pockets, rigid with the cold, her shoulders trembling.

For a while she seemed lost in her own indecision, her own private panic. She could go back outside into the park or she could stay with him. Then a moment later Gordon felt her beside him in the dark, pressing her body against his.

"For warmth," she said.

He nodded and put his arm around her, drawing her close. Her hair smelled of smoke, but it was soft and warm as he buried his face in it.

He could feel his heart still pounding as he closed his eyes, making a determined effort to imitate sleep. But he could not get his mind off the corpses lying back in the hotel. Two ordinary policemen doing a routine job. Two policemen with families. What the generals would call "normal wastage."

Shafts of sunlight tilted in the small window. The warmth bathed Gordon's face as he opened his eyes and saw Margarethe up and moving away from him, pushing back her hair with one hand and fingering Billy de Beauford's derringer with the other. For a moment he thought she was going to shoot him, but for the life of him he could not fathom why. Then she motioned for him to be still. He held his breath and heard the footsteps of someone walking outside the hut. He lifted his head, then reached for the revolver lying beside him.

He heard twigs snapping as someone moved through the undergrowth. He crawled to the window and looked out where the mist had turned to snow during the night. Then the intruders came into view. Kerchiefs and peasant skirts. Two old women stooped under the weight of wood on their backs, picking up sticks and branches.

Gordon watched as Margarethe came back and knelt beside him.

"Stealing firewood," she said, glancing up. It was a modest, girlish look that took him by surprise.

They listened, waiting until the wood gatherers had moved on. Then Gordon stood down and began unbuttoning the colonel's tunic with his left hand.

Margarethe lit two cigarettes and gave one to him. She stood watching now, his body lean and well muscled, her appraisal matter-of-fact. She seemed tired.

"Do you want to go through with this?" Gordon said, the cigarette hanging between his lips.

"What do you mean? What choice do we have?"

"It could get worse. You could probably hide out for a while instead. You have to get away from Ostriker, but not necessarily like this. We don't have to travel together."

"Have I frightened you away?"

"Not yet."

"Then I see no reason to change our plans."

Gordon had stripped off the uniform now and was putting back on his own shirt and tie.

"Let's be very clear about what we're doing, then. We're going to London and you're going to tell them everything you know about the research at the Institute. Its limitations. Everything you learned about other weapons work from von Stade. The work at other laboratories. The whole background. You'll make it credible, right?"

"Yes," she said irritably, then took another drag on her cigarette.

"You're going to tell them that, according to everything you know, there's no threat to British forces from germ weapons. At least not in the foreseeable future. This 'magic bullet' they think they might be able to use . . . it simply isn't going to be part of the picture for anyone just yet."

"That's what I told you. That's the way it is."

"They don't have to take these outrageous risks. The Germans don't have a weapon. Or even a defense against a weapon."

"Right. Yes. Right!"

Gordon paused to slip into his own trousers, then put back on the heavy military boots. "So what *will* you tell them about the extract?"

"I don't know," she said. "We'll simply have to see what happens."

Fully dressed once more, Gordon stuffed the colonel's uniform down under the pipes. Then he took the sword and extended it through the door opening, just beneath the hinge. He closed the door on it as best he could, wedging it in, and said, "Lean on this, would you?"

Margarethe pressed against the door, then he pushed on the sword again and again until it snapped. He was now holding a foot-long blade with a jagged point that fit nicely into the Gladstone bag.

An hour later Eli Gordon stood on the curb outside an apothecary's shop looking through the newspaper. Milk wagons rolled past in the crisp morning air. Now and then he could hear the clanging of a trolley. He turned the pages, rustling like dry leaves, then held them tight against the wind as he scanned each column. There was nothing about the killings last night at the hotel, but this was the early edition. By now the news wires would have carried the story to Berlin.

He saw the tram rolling toward him with the headlamp still burning. When it stopped he climbed on board and paid the fare. Margarethe Riesling sat in the first seat, staring out the window behind her dark glasses. Her hair hidden under her hat, the muffler around her neck, she looked as abstracted as any numbed commuter. Gordon walked past her coolly and found a place at the opposite end of the car.

At the train station in Hainholz, Margarethe was first off the tram and fell in with several others walking toward the ticket window. Gordon queued up behind her five places back.

The line moved quickly and soon Margarethe was at the window. She spoke with the clerk but after a moment she stepped to one side. She turned around and for the first time since leaving the Eilenriede they made eye contact. Margarethe looked uncertain, vulnerable, waiting beside the window. Something had gone wrong. He stared at her but she shook her head.

Gordon glanced around the immediate area. There were no special guards posted, only the random scattering of soldiers. He studied the pained look on her face, but in another minute he was at the window himself, the last passenger to buy a ticket.

"Second class to Bremen," he said.

The ticket agent glanced up at him without moving his head, his eyes bisected by the half lenses of his reading glasses. "One passage?" the man asked.

"That's right. One."

"You're traveling alone?"

"Yes." Gordon had his hand on the revolver. "That's why I want one ticket."

The agent was unimpressed. He tapped the glass. "Fräulein," he said. Margarethe stepped back to the window, glancing at Gordon.

"You are traveling alone to Bremen?"

"Yes," she said, her voice brittle. "What is the difficulty?"

"I have run out of tickets to Bremen," the man told her, "that's all. I have to write out passes. Writing out one pass for two saves time."

Gordon withdrew his hand from the revolver and took a slow, deep breath. Then he and Margarethe each paid for their tickets in turn and boarded the train together.

· · ·

They sat across from each other in an overheated compartment shared with four flappers rattling school maps, their teacher, and a young naval lieutenant from the imperial Zeppelin service.

The girls were up and down each time the Imbiss cart rolled past, and hanging at the window in the aisle to point out every cow. The schoolmistress watching over them was barely twenty, but even so she was older than the lieutenant. He relished the girls' attention as he went on about his exploits over London, bragging like a schoolboy about the drubbing he'd given the other team.

Margarethe stared out at the flat landscape through the glass pelted by snowflakes. Gordon hid behind his newspaper and studied the gray sky and white fields.

The train dusted its soot across the landscape as it rolled past half-timbered farmhouses covered with thatch, dollops of fresh show clinging to the straw like down left behind in a nest. A German officer in knee boots and dress uniform walked out to feed his geese, a pail in each hand.

The roads on the horizon were lined with closely cropped poplars like pins in a map. Gordon saw red brick churches, and silos clustered in fours, roofed like medieval towers. Then he looked back at Margarethe and thought of the miles of Germany and the heavily guarded frontier they still had to cross. And when they were free, what then?

Margarethe had the extract hidden under her clothes, like a baby at her breast. The key to a new and more thorough way of killing? The key to saving lives? Or the product of an overheated imagination?

26

The bicycle shop was near the river, just beyond the Eisenbahn Brücke in the Altstadt of Bremen. Käthe Habermass lived on the second floor in an industrial space she and her husband had converted into a one-room flat three months before he was drafted for the Eastern front.

She lived alone now, with a cat she called Vorwärts. Except that she was never really alone since the last wave of strikes. She pushed back the curtains and looked out along the center of the quiet street that emptied into Grossenstrasse just below her window. She could see workmen and merchants, the rows of brick warehouses on either side. Two schoolboys walked together, pumping up and down between the curb and the gutter with a yellow dog trailing after them, sniffing everything in its path. And in the café across the street, a man in a leather coat sat at the window table staring back at her.

She turned away and fed the cat a bit of scraps, then stood washing herself as best she could in the drafty, unheated room. She had once thought the war would bring revolution. What it had brought instead was loneliness and hunger and cold.

The ersatz soap made her hands bleed. She put it away, dried off, and started getting dressed. Her hands were like a man's now, with calluses and nicks and cuts from working with wrenches and sharp metal. But the war had forced her to take her husband's place in the shop as well as in the Movement.

Most of the old firebrands were dead or in hiding now. The party money was in Switzerland. It had been a long, slow slide since the days they sang the "Marseillaise" in the streets, protesting what they called Germany's "Nibelungen loyalty to Austria's desperado politics." Käthe still believed that revolution would come, only now it had to wait for the death of the military elite.

Just as she finished dressing—a heavy sweater over a pair of man's coveralls—she heard a pounding on the door below.

She looked out the window and saw the man in the leather coat still at his table. She noticed another man with him, a shabby, rumpled man she had seen there many times before. No one in the Movement would come without knowing it was safe. And nobody else knocked on her door now except the police.

She slid back the metal fire door and walked down the stairs, the cat following a few steps behind. Well practiced, she would present a face of calm indifference.

When she opened the door a gust of cold air blew in and the cat raced out between the legs of a man she did not know. He wore a Russian fur hat and a heavy gabardine coat. His face was faceted like chiseled stone. He had an alcoholic's eyes and a great hook nose.

"Margarethe Riesling sent me," he said, staring past her head into the room. "She told me it would be safe."

Käthe shook her head, trying to close the door. "I don't know what you're talking about. Go away."

He wedged his foot into the frame, then quickly leaned in, slipping through the crack and grabbing her throat, slamming the door behind him. "That won't do," he said.

"You prick! What do you want?" He wrenched her up by her arm and throttled her into silence.

"We're going to have a chat," he said. "We're going to spend a few minutes getting to know each other while we wait. Like I said, I'm a friend of Margarethe's. From Berlin."

"That's shit!" she said, as his fingers pressed into her neck. "You're some kind of cop."

"No," Fisk said. "I'm a dentist, actually. Dear Margarethe slipped away without her checkup."

AT THE Bremen station they could see the guards checking papers, the detectives standing to one side as the passengers entered the platform. Gordon and Margarethe moved with the crowd on their way out, then walked south along Bahnhofstrasse to the moat and the wooded park separating the newer suburbs from the older city within the ramparts.

They followed the cobbled streets all the way to the river, crossing rows of warehouses and customs offices. At the next intersection the street emptied into Grossenstrasse at the foot of a red brick building. Gordon could see only a bicycle shop and a lamppost, but Margarethe stood gazing at them as if they were filled with great significance.

"It's not going to work," she said at last. "Keep walking." She stepped off the curb and they continued across the street, then into an alley that led away from the shop.

Gordon was half a step behind her, confused and irritated.

"There should be a bike chained outside," she said, still walking. "There's something wrong. It's not safe."

They turned right at the next corner, then continued on for several blocks into a cold wind.

Perhaps this was the moment of insight he had been waiting for, Gordon realized. The first signs of self-preservation, the first indication that she was not part of some demented plan to deliver him into German hands.

He stopped beside a mailbox and set down the Gladstone bag. Margarethe stared off into the distance, making a concerted effort to avoid his eyes. He lit a cigarette for her and then one for himself.

"I really don't know what to suggest," she said after a while, taking off her glasses and putting them in her pocket.

"You still think Ostriker doesn't know about your friends in the Bremen Left?"

"That's not the point," she whispered.

"What is the point?"

"He's not the only one."

Gordon looked at her, her mouth open and the smoke drifting out of its own accord.

"What do you mean by that?"

"I mean it isn't necessarily Ostriker."

Gordon calmly exhaled his own swirl of smoke, studying the lines in her face. Her brow was deeply furrowed, her mouth drawn.

"I told Fisk I'd go to Switzerland with him," she said.

Gordon pushed back the brim of his hat and sighed. "Fisk's in jail."

"How do you know that?"

He didn't know anything of the sort, Gordon suddenly realized. He had merely assumed it. Maybe it was a failure of the imagination. Maybe it was his still naive expectation that virtue will necessarily triumph. Either way, such assumptions now seemed wildly out of place, even dangerous.

"I know about you and Fisk," he said after a while. "Schiller told me about you and him. But what difference does it make? Why would he follow us?"

"Because he's evil."

"That's nuts. He'd be busy saving his ass. The man's got money in Switzerland, a family there. He wouldn't risk that to follow us to Denmark."

"Dr. Fisk tolerated frustration very poorly," she said. "And he was never a terribly logical man."

Gordon tossed off his cigarette and looked up at the gray sky. "It still doesn't add up," he said. Then he turned to look squarely at her. "There'd have to be more to it. He wouldn't follow us to Bremen. How would he know about this place?"

She was silent.

"He'd have to know about you and this man Gunther, wouldn't he? So there has to be some kind of history there, a history between you and Fisk."

Gordon stared into her eyes and saw his own reflection in her pupils. He remembered for a moment what it had been like to be detached and unambivalent, filled with certainty. He had become human now. Now he doubted everything.

He looked down and shook his head. "You fucking slept with him, didn't you?"

Margarethe looked away as the wind swept down from between the buildings. Her hair blew into her face, clinging to her features like a gold fabric flecked with red as she turned back toward him.

"Fabulous," Gordon let out. "How about the Kaiser? The postman, maybe? Schiller? You probably fucked the whole German army, regiment by regiment."

She returned his cold assessment, still gazing at him through her hair. After a moment she reached up to brush it back. "Are you through?" she asked.

Gordon put his one good hand in his pocket. "Tell me about it," he went on. "Tell me. I'm all ears."

"It's really none of your business, is it?" Then very quickly she added, "I was young, okay?"

"Fisk!"

"It was a long time ago. Before the war. Before the drinking. And the rest of it."

"He's a psychopath."

"I didn't know that then. I was a stupid little girl and I was lonely. I was very poor. He was what passed for 'a charming older man.' He 'took advantage' of me, okay? Victim instead of slut. How's that?"

"It still doesn't—"

"All I know of Fisk is that he's cruel. He's vengeful and he's greedy. Infants would kill if they had the strength. That's what

Fisk is like when his will is thwarted. Murderously infantile. I was stupid to raise his expectations, that's all. But I couldn't trust you."

Gordon stood in silence for a moment. Then he shook his head and said, "We need a change of plans. We need a map. And food, oilcloths, blankets."

"For what?"

A truck rolled by them on the narrow street. "The border into Holland."

"Oh, really?"

"I knew some men in France. Some P.O.W.'s who crossed over that way. There's a stretch of the Bourtanger Moor they say isn't heavily patrolled in winter."

"I don't believe that."

"It's not patrolled because it's considered impassable."

She looked at the sky, threw back her head, and laughed. "Truly a great plan," she said.

"It's marshland. Peat bogs and mire."

"Terrific."

"This is the coldest winter in fifty years. If the weather holds for another forty-eight hours we can skate to Holland."

She leaned against the lamppost, then pinched a fleck of tobacco off the tip of her tongue, acknowledging the point. "And if the weather doesn't last?" she said.

"Then at least we won't freeze our asses off."

Margarethe Riesling waited at a café on the Domshof as Gordon went into a bookshop across the street.

"My wife's birthday," he told the storekeeper, a frail old woman with a sagging face and bosom. "I promised her a motorcar before the war. The map's to show her I haven't forgotten."

Gordon watched the loosely wrinkled jowls, the watery eyes. In Berlin you needed a permit from the General Staff to buy anything like a map or a compass. He tried to decide what to do if she asked for papers. He could steal the map, but that would not get them out of Bremen. He knew how questionable he looked.

The moments passed and his confidence began to fade. Then, almost imperceptibly, the old woman smiled and slid the folded map up onto the counter.

"Did you get it? Would they sell it to you?"

Gordon sat down and placed the heavy paper, folded accordion style, on Margarethe's table. It was a Ravenstein and Liebenow motoring map of the Duchy of Oldenburg, scale 1 to 300,000. He pulled out his penknife and, with his left hand, carefully slit along the creases, then leafed through, selecting only the western sections. Most of these large squares he pushed to one side, leaving only two pieces, which he then cut down into smaller squares, representing the forty-mile stretch between the village of Cloppenburg and the Dutch border at Sellingen.

They strolled down Obernstrasse after a makeshift meal, discarding map squares in trash barrels. They saw policemen on street corners, but there was nothing they could do now. If Bremen was a trap, they were already inside it. And it didn't matter at the moment who was on their trail—Fisk or Ostriker or the Kaiser himself—the outcome would be very much the same if they were caught.

They found a sporting goods shop on the corner of Kaiserstrasse with a suit of armor and a huge stag's head just inside the door. This time it was Gordon who walked around the block while Margarethe went in. She said she was a dutiful sister, buying extra equipment for her brother at the front. She came out with loden blankets, an aluminum water bottle, a flashlight, a compass, and two large oilskins.

The next half hour they hit provisioners' shops to get what they could of chocolate, nuts, tinned sardines—things they hadn't seen in Berlin for months. Then at one o'clock Gordon hired a droshky outside the Ratskeller.

"Where to?" the driver asked.

"Oldenburg," Gordon told him, and slipped a note for twenty marks into his pocket.

SITTING in the small café across from the bicycle shop, Rolf Mayr had been drinking ersatz since early this morning and he was stiff and bored and needing to take a leak. Ostriker was interested in two people only—Eli Gordon and Margarethe Riesling—but the burly fellow in the Russian hat had been in the building for a long time. Mayr was curious to know why.

Schultz, the Bremen detective from the political squad, coughed and sniffed and wiped his nose on the back of his hand. "So," he said, "you want me to check it out?"

Mayr kept his eyes on the doorway across the street. "I want you to do exactly what you've been doing," he said. "Sit on your ass and stare out the window."

They were here on a hunch, Mayr and this detective, and Ostriker's hunches usually were worth more than most. But Mayr had always doubted the Americans would come this way. And if they were going to come, they would have come already.

On the street outside their window a constable walked past toward the bicycle shop, a gray-haired pensioner, hurrying like a man on a mission. Mayr watched him come to the doorstep of Käthe Habermass' building, then stop and knock with his nightstick. A few moments passed, then the door opened and the constable was let in by a crying woman in an apron and cap.

Mayr threw a few coins on the table. "Stay here," he said.

"I'll come too," Schultz insisted.

"I said stay here."

Gathering his leather coat around him as he went through the door, Mayr left the café and crossed the street, looking up toward the loft window. He entered the building and climbed the stairs, listening for voices.

The building was silent as he reached the flat and stepped through the doorway. He recognized the smell of machine oil, the coldness of metal. Then he heard conversation.

He stared across the expanse of empty floor toward a curtain that hid the far corner.

The constable emerged from behind the cloth saying, "Who are you?"

Mayr pulled out his papers and flashed them past the old man's eyes as he stepped toward the barrier. Beyond it he could see the woman sobbing in a chair. And beyond her, a mattress that had soaked up blood like a sponge.

In the center of the bed lay a human form that he took to be female, but then again he could not be sure. Mostly what he saw was bone, entrails, and blood. Mayr was, for once, quite honestly surprised. It was as if the body had been turned inside out by a very strong and very unhappy man.

27

The sky was battleship gray above the Channel as Major Anthony Rice stood on deck in a heavy mist, trying to see beyond the convoyed destroyers ensuring safe passage from Dover to Calais. Eric Pauley the bacteriologist stood close beside him, green at the gills once again.

Beyond the circle of naval ships a French barque sailed toward the French coast. A Dutch tramp steamer, painted with huge red and white stripes, crept the other way.

Pauley nodded toward the merchantman and gave a nervous smile. "Whistling in the dark, I'd say."

Rice looked at him uncertainly.

"Neutral stripes," Pauley went on. "Just makes a prettier target for the Boche now."

"Yes. Quite right," Rice said, but his mind was elsewhere. Word from Switzerland had reached him just before they embarked. Eli Gordon was not on the ambassador's train when it arrived.

For the moment, Rice concentrated on the sea swelling under him, then the bow pitching into the waves. Now all the contingencies and abstract hypotheticals were coming down to one very real possibility.

He turned his head into the wind and said, "Tell me, Pauley. What would it mean . . . the exact effect, you know . . . if we use this new apparatus?"

Pauley took a deep breath, hoping he could get the roiling in his stomach to subside. Then he smiled again. "It's just a bluff, old man. Pointless to speculate. A trump card to make the Hun back down."

Rice could see the ocean reflected in Pauley's eyes, the green corrugated surface constantly changing. "But if we did use it?" he asked.

"Still pointless to speculate."

"Why?"

Pauley shrugged and leaned forward on the railing. He glanced over at Rice, then rubbed his chin with the back of his hand. After a while he said, "It's a death sentence, really. Inhalation. Skin ulcers. Septicemia."

Rice nodded and Pauley looked back down at the water. "We could infect half the Germans' frontline troops in one day. In time there would be a mountain of corpses, festering with anthrax, needing to be disposed of. It would rival anyone's vision of hell."

Rice put his hands in his pockets and looked back out to sea. "We chose anthrax, I understand, because it was hardy. A germ that was hardy enough to withstand the blast of an artillery shell."

Pauley nodded silently and watched the waves.

"So the spores would be around for some time, wouldn't they?" Rice said.

A gull flew by and Pauley raised his head to track it as it grew smaller and smaller over the waves. "This is nothing more than my personal opinion," he said after a moment, looking back coldly at Rice. "But full-scale implementation of this plan could render a good portion of Western Europe uninhabitable for what remains of this very bloody century."

The docks at Calais were bustling despite the fog as Rice and Pauley watched from on deck. A steady stream of wounded were being helped aboard a rusting hospital ship by the ladies of the Pitchley Hunt. Clean new recruits marched in the opposite direction, boarding railroad cars headed for the front.

Descending the gangway through the mist, Rice spotted Colonel Napier and another officer standing by a light standard out on the dock. Horse-drawn freight wagons were circling around them, queuing up to transfer the ship's cargo. The stranger wore the red hatband that gave staff officers the nickname "geraniums." He also wore the green armband of military intelligence.

Napier nodded as the men came up. "Colonel Waithe, Major Rice."

Rice shook hands with no great show of enthusiasm and introduced Pauley. "I thought we'd be met by the depot commander," he said.

Napier raised the collar of his trench coat up to his chin. "Change of plans," he muttered.

Alongside the ship now an Italian labor corps wrestled a huge crane into position, preparing to lower packing crates onto the dock. Rice's deadly cargo was only a small part of the overall consignment of freight.

He turned to watch the laborers for a moment. "These men will be handling the apparatus?"

"Oh, they're perfectly capable," Napier said, signing an order on a clipboard handed to him.

Rice was not accustomed to being dismissed. He found Napier's tone and manner entirely unacceptable. He looked at Waithe, and then at Pauley. "Where will the apparatus be stored here in Calais?"

"Not for fighting, of course," Napier said with a smile. "They turned tail and ran before the Austrians—that's why they're here. But perfectly good laborers. Excellent in fact. You just rest easy, old man. You've done your bit. Now we'll do ours."

"What exactly is the change in plans, Colonel?"

Rice and Napier stood eye to eye for a moment in silence. Then it was Waithe who explained.

"We're moving the new gas . . ."

"It's not a gas!"

The two senior officers glanced at each other. Rice was startled to have heard his own voice at such a pitch. He waited until he had regained his composure, then said, "It's a disease."

There was a moment of wordless censure, after which Waithe continued. "We'll be moving the apparatus out to the divisional command posts," he said. "At that point it will be held pending further orders."

"Oh. Blessed relief, that."

Rice knew this was not what Churchill or anyone else in London had ordered. The plan had its own momentum how, just like the war itself, ranging far beyond the control of any single force.

Waithe's jaw tightened in disapproval as he said, "There are still no plans to go operational."

Rice watched the Italians leaning against the lines hoisted up on the cranes. A large crate swung out over the side of the ship, dangling in the air. It was not one of his.

"This change originated where?" he asked.

"At G.H.Q.," Waithe said, watching the unloading. "In France it is no longer a policy decision, but a military one."

"And Whitehall?"

"They are aware of all new developments."

"And what exactly has developed?"

Before Rice could get an answer he saw the crate beginning to twist. One of the men holding a guide wire had slipped and the huge wooden container was off balance, teetering at an angle. The N.C.O. in charge came running over, screaming and waving his arms, then the crate slipped and tore loose from its bindings and hurtled through the air. A moment later it cracked open on the edge of the dock, then slipped off into the water and disappeared.

Red double-decker buses came toward them out of the fog as they followed the road from Calais. Their car passed a Foden steam engine from the salvage corps, then a caravan of lorries carrying a Pioneer Battalion. In the tents alongside the road, coolies sat playing fan-tan.

Troops milled about with the aimless energy of men soon to be back in battle. The graves registration units had already gone up to the front, leaving the new recruits with an ominous "See you after."

Prison camps, labor camps, base hospitals with tents and Nissen huts. It was like the tawdry development surrounding some South African boomtown.

"Now this Boche prisoner at G.H.Q.," Waithe was saying. "He claims he came over because he was hungry and tired of corpses. He makes a good story of it. On wire patrol in no-man's-land. Simply crawled across and into the English trench—said if he got killed he got killed but he was ready to die to get out of it. Amazing that he didn't."

"So you accept this man's account as confirming Operation Alberich?" Rice said. "One German deserter is your persuasive new 'development.' "

"Old Fritz named the day. February twenty-fourth. The orders have gone out to the divisions."

"And did Old Fritz say what the Germans would be hitting us with? Plague? Tularemia? Fire from heaven?"

"The rest is speculation," Waithe said. "An evil dwarf, this Alberich. And reticent, too."

Rice adjusted his legs in the cramped car seat. "But how do we know that *any* of it's the truth!"

"We don't," Waithe responded coolly. "But what would you have us do until we find out?"

Rice turned away in silence. He despaired at never knowing, yet still having to act. German rumors, English rumors. He looked out the window at the grim filigree of naked branches, wishing to hell he knew where to find Eli Gordon.

FORTY kilometers west of Bremen, outside the Oldenburg station, a group of British prisoners leaned against a fence and smoked cigarettes in the cold. Their single guard stood a few feet away talking to a red-cheeked farm girl. This was the main north-south line to Wilhelmshaven, but still it was not Prussia. The people seemed softened by the Flemish touch.

Margarethe Riesling and Eli Gordon walked past the prisoners to board the local for Cloppenburg, a train with three cars and an ancient steam engine. They settled into a compartment with their bags at their feet, hoping the clutter would discourage other passengers.

Gordon looked at Margarethe and she gave him a perfunctory smile. She seemed drawn and frightened, yet he wondered if he wasn't simply following the logic of desperation, steaming full ahead like the *Titanic,* racing confidently into disaster. He had no idea what lay before him now. Ostriker? Fisk? Further surprises from Margarethe? Or Anthony Rice waiting at the border with some new variation?

The only certainty was that they had to get out of Germany before they could even try to sort it all out. From this moment on until they crossed the border they were hiding in plain sight, which meant blending into the background completely, with no margin for error.

The man appeared in the doorway—a jolly Bavarian, a commercial traveler.

"Ah! Good company," he said, bustling in, filling the space with an odor of eager sweat. "Or at least an improvement in the scenery," he added, winking at Gordon.

Gordon smiled halfheartedly, then nodded. It was just enough so as not to give offense, not enough to offer encouragement. The train lurched out of the station and the man took his seat.

"Well. God punish England indeed, eh? And the United States of America."

His face had a raw, red flush, and his collar seemed too tight, constricting his throat. His eyes were bloodshot and bulging as he stared at Margarethe's breasts. He looked as if he were bursting at the seams.

"Have you seen the late editions? Anything new?"

"Nothing that I know of," Gordon said.

The man pulled out his handkerchief, blew his nose loudly, then peered for a moment into the cloth. "Those troopships will be target practice," he said. "Our U-boats have gotten slack, sitting in the harbor. Our boys need fresh blood, and now they'll get it. The Americans will see. We'll sink all the tonnage they care to send our way."

He folded the handkerchief and put it back in his pocket, then added, somewhat incongruously, "Name is Grundig. Fine wine and champagne." Then for a moment he sat suspended, watching them, as if he were waiting for the verb.

Gordon did not speak, he simply listened to the music rising once more inside his head, the sustain pedal down again just as it had been at Hazebrouck. He thought back to Billy and what he had said about public versus private evil. He knew there were other forces at work as well, and simple randomness was one, the basic blunder hunt of the universe.

Margarethe looked out the window, and eventually Grundig looked out to to see what she found so captivating in the darkening landscape. He tugged his handkerchief again and wiped the glass, then stopped when he realized the grime was on the outside.

"I used to sell it," he said all at once, regaining his energy. "Now I just talk about it and watch their eyes mist over. Business is bad. But soon there will be corks popping. Soon there will be cause for celebration all over the Fatherland."

He nodded his head as if to reassure himself, and as the train rumbled on through the twilight, the sound of Grundig's voice built in Gordon's head like shelling in the distance, getting louder as it closed in on him, crowding out his own thoughts.

"No. It's still a good territory. Hamburg. Bremen. Wilhelms-haven too. Now if I only had the navy contract—there's a gold mine. Crack a few bottles over the bow."

Grundig looked at Gordon and then at Margarethe, smiling. He let his eyes linger on her face, then trail down her body. Gordon wondered when the man was going to step over and sniff her leg.

"Where are you and the pretty lady from?"

"We're Swiss," Gordon told him.

"Ah well." The man pulled out his watch. "I hope you don't mind, but it's been running a little slow lately." He looked from Gordon to Margarethe, beaming, then let loose a great blustering laugh.

Gordon smiled. As he stared off into the distance, he felt the same nausea he had felt so often back at Hazebrouck, only this time he couldn't tell if it was a premonition or déjà vu.

"Now tell me. What do you do in Switzerland?"

"We fix watches."

"Hah! Good man. Good man. A man after my own heart. But now I worked the Geneva office for a while. Where are you from?"

"Bern."

"Not a bad town. Quiet, though. A quiet town. What do you do there?"

"I'm a clerk," Gordon said. "With the city."

"Hmmh. An honorable profession," Grundig said, smiling. Then he looked more closely at Gordon's hand and at his stubbled face.

They rolled through the darkened farmland and after a while Grundig said, "And what brings you to these parts?"

"Visiting relatives."

"Ah, relatives." Grundig glanced at Margarethe. "What town?"

"Spahn."

"Ach! Talk about quiet!" Grundig threw back his head in amazement. "Now who could live in such a place?" Then he looked quickly at Gordon. "No offense to your . . ."

"My wife's sister."

"Hmmh. Yes." The train lurched to the side and once again Grundig took a moment to admire Margarethe's lithe body, his face slack and stupid in the harsh lighting of the compartment.

"So you're just visiting, are you?"

"Right."

"Any particular occasion?"

"Do we need one?"

"She's having a baby," Margarethe volunteered.

Grundig smiled again, trying once more to elicit eye contact, but then he gave up, and the failure made him angry.

"A tough time to bring children into this world," he said, stiffening his body. "So this sister of yours. She's married to a German boy, is she?"

"Yes."

"Stationed where?"

"I'm sorry?"

"He's in the army of course."

Margarethe glanced at Gordon. "No. He's older."

"Oh? But not too old to father children. He's just too old to fight? Is that it?"

"He has . . . a club foot," Margarethe offered.

Grundig nodded, and then with one brow raised said, "I see."

The salesman seemed distracted now, his mind overtaken by some elaborate calculation that diverted energy from his social impulses.

"Spahn's near the border," he said after a moment.

"I believe so," Margarethe answered. "I've never been there."

"You have your Swiss passports with you?"

"Of course. Why do you ask?"

Grundig looked stern, as if he expected the documents to be tendered immediately.

He waited, but then seeing no movement said, "You'll need papers, that's all. This close to the border people become curious. Inspectors like to see papers, you know. They like to keep everything on the up and up."

Grundig picked up a magazine and buried his face in it. And from then on he was distracted, silent, and withdrawn, glancing up from time to time like a guard keeping watch.

Gordon looked at Margarethe, her face ashen, and for the rest of the trip they rode along in silence.

Gordon knew he had saved a great many lives since the war began, but it was the ones he couldn't save that he remembered, the priests prying open their mouths with knife blades to administer the host. The private guilt he felt for his actions now was overwhelming, no matter how surrounded by public mayhem.

Maybe Schiller was right after all—murder *was* redundant now, but in his gut Gordon did not feel it that way. If they were left alone there would be no more problems, no more killing. Margarethe's extract could stop some from dying. What she knew about German plans could stop Britain from opening up a whole new level of horror.

Gordon still wished he could replay that moment back in the hotel, see it run backward like the movies, the two men popping up and going down the stairs and back home. He wished he could rerun the whole war that way—all the men rising up from the mire and going back to those who loved them.

Despite everything, or maybe now because of it, he had to believe in Margarethe. He had to believe in her miraculous extract, and in their own right to survive.

Gordon could see the lights of the village up ahead as the train slowed for Cloppenburg. He was tired of Grundig's furtive glances, enraged that the man could not leave well enough alone.

The salesman dropped his magazine into his lap and looked out toward the station.

"You're going on, aren't you?" Gordon said.

Grundig shot him a quick, hostile glance. "I thought I'd stretch my legs. Buy some cigars."

Gordon looked at Margarethe and felt his stomach churn. He struggled to hold his thoughts above the pulse swelling in his head.

"Mr. Grundig," she said all at once. She turned to the salesman. "We're terrible liars. We're not Swiss . . . you know that. We're running away from my husband. I didn't ever want to marry the man—my parents forced me. He's a brute. He beats me. Now we're trying to get away from him, start a new life, that's all. We fell in love, was that such a crime? Don't make trouble for us. Please. I beg you."

She leaned toward him with her large brown eyes. They were moist and tender and utterly convincing. She touched his arm imploringly, but Grundig was unmoved.

"We can't take chances so near the border," he said coldly. "The police in Cloppenburg will decide what's best."

"What do you mean—police?" she went on. "We haven't done anything wrong."

Gordon had to defuse the situation. They could bribe him, or threaten him, or come up with a better lie.

But then a conductor walked by, and Gordon saw Grundig follow the man with his eyes.

"Please," Margarethe said. "Please understand."

Gordon reached into the Gladstone bag.

"I must do my duty," the German said. "I must ask you . . ."

Grundig rose from his seat and Gordon nailed him with the broken sword. The thrust was quick and precise, splitting the carotid and ramming the blade on through to the backbone. The man was thrown back by the force of the blow, pinned to the wall as blood spurted in great heavy currents. His body writhed, his legs shot out from under him and kicked spasmodically as Gordon let him slide to the floor, trying to avoid the blood.

It took a full thirty seconds for the movement to stop. Gordon withdrew the blade and wiped it on the salesman's coat. Then he looked up from the corpse and felt another swell of nausea that once more he could not give in to.

"Oh God," Margarethe said, beginning to cry. She slipped down off the seat, her eyes glistening, and tugged at Grundig's feet.

"What are you doing?"

She worked in silence for a moment. Then she whispered, "His galoshes. We're going to need them later."

The train pulled to a stop and together they stuffed the salesman's body under the seat and switched off the light.

A dozen passengers got off the train and walked across the snow-covered platform. Gordon knew from the timetable that a connecting train was leaving from the other side of the village in thirty-five minutes. They fell in with the transferring passengers, then walked off into the night.

Tall trees lined the road, but they followed the crowd more by sound than sight as the new-fallen snow squeaked underfoot.

In the center of the village a road branched to the right. The train passengers kept walking, but Gordon and Margarethe turned off. Gordon pulled out his compass but it was too dark to read it. The houses had lost the alignment of streets and had taken on a more random distribution. There was a lamp up ahead. As they walked under it three girls passed by, arm in arm. Inquisitively, the girls turned their heads but then went on, smiling and laughing. Gordon could see the face of the compass now. The road led west, toward Holland.

A few hundred yards farther up Gordon wanted to check the map. They stepped off the road into a thin belt of trees and flipped on the flashlight. They heard the sound of the railroad off to the south, then a dog barking. There was a farmhouse closer than they had realized. They knelt down to shield the light as they looked at the map.

This road led to the village of Vahren. Then they could turn north to Magdeburg to pick up what looked like a less-traveled communications road. They would have to take the most obscure path and then only at night. They put away the map and the light and then walked on.

THE village was not on the map and neither was the branching road that they did not take. The main road, smooth where the snow had been ground down to form a second paved surface, curved west and then south. They pulled out their oilskins and wrapped their shoulders against the freezing rain that would gradually wash away the salesman's blood.

They passed through flat forestland with fields now and then marked by hedges. Telephone lines followed on the left, sagging under the weight of their own sheath of ice. There was a sign up ahead, crusted with frozen grime, reflecting in the beam of Gordon's flashlight. "Dangerous curve. Motors to slow down."

After a half mile or so they came to another iron signpost, with the sign itself missing. They dug around near the base of the post and found it lying in the snow. "To Molbergen."

They turned off and followed the secondary road. The pelting ice blew in their faces and down their collars. They were both soaked to the skin below the knee. Their coats below the oilcloths grew heavy with moisture.

Gordon wanted something more from her now. He had made a heavy commitment to her account of things, and now he wanted something in return. More reassurance, somehow. More candor. They had spoken very little since Hanover and he wanted to know what she was thinking. The price of this venture kept going up, and how convincing could she be that Germany did not have a disease weapon of its own? And even if the British did believe her—assuming the two of them could make it across and reach the men in authority—who could say whether the government would be discouraged or encouraged by what she had to offer?

He looked over at her struggling on the frozen roadway and realized that he was too tired for such issues now. They were both sickened and numbed by the killing, burdened with it like the weight of the ice forming on the brim of his hat. But at this point they could go on or they could lie down and die. He asked about her feet.

"Perfectly dry," she answered sadly, walking ahead, Grundig's heavy galoshes scuffing against the roadway.

She and Gordon were side by side in the darkness a few moments later when she added, "I had thought they would fit you, you know."

"You don't have to explain," he said.

She looked at him cautiously. "I'm not so sure."

They walked a little longer in silence, their heads bowed to the wind and the rain, and Gordon began to imagine a trail of duck-boards leading across the moor to Holland. They needed the marshes to be frozen, and for that they needed colder weather.

A vaguely defined structure appeared off to the right beyond a grove of oak saplings. Gordon gave a quick snap of his flash-light and saw a loft barn on strong, rough-cut timbers. They walked closer. Half the space below the uprights was closed in with boards. The open half showed a wagon with ladders lying across it.

"It'll be dawn soon," he said.

She nodded.

Gordon flashed the light again and saw that the closed-in area was filled with straw but that it was not very inviting. Up above, in the gable, there was a window showing a black interior. They climbed up and found warm, dry straw.

They took off their boots and left them and the dripping oilskins on the edge. Then they burrowed down, lying on their sides in the straw. They had little choice but to roll together. Gordon wrapped his arm around her, nestling his face in her hair. This was the way it worked, he remembered. This was the way a man and a woman fit together lying side by side.

"What's going through your mind?" he said.

"We've killed three people."

He pulled his arm more tightly around her and her shoulder felt surprisingly strong. "*I've* killed three people," he whispered.

"No. No, this is a joint venture."

"Okay. But we're still not there yet. It could get worse."

"And what happens when we do get 'there'? Wherever 'there' is?"

"We get the British to turn back at Porton Down. Then you go back to work. You refine this thing and you save the whole damn race."

"I can't save anything without a lab."

"That won't be the problem," he said.

"Oh really?"

"I know people in Boston. Maybe that's not an option, but there are plenty of others. I know people in London, too. I'm trying to say that I could help. If you want me to."

"Yes? And what about the British?"

He let his hand drop down between them. "I agreed to do a job. If what you say about Scotland and the anthrax is right, it was a double cross. I can't see that I owe them much of anything. Except to have you tell them what you told me. Try to convince them not to bring this thing into the war."

"And as for the rest?"

"I thought what happened to the extract was up to you."

She rolled onto her back, and after a while Gordon could hear her breathing in the darkness.

"So we're cutting our little swath across Germany so I can go back to the States and be your 'protégée.' Is that it?"

"No. That's not it."

"Fisk was looking for a protégée," she said, glancing back condescendingly. "I've been through this before, remember? The shameless woman."

"It's not like that."

"Let me guess. You have a wife, but there's no love left between you. You're very different people now than when you first met. And while you still need to protect her—"

"Does it really matter?" Gordon said. "It all comes down to a cliché at some point."

She waited, then rose up on one elbow facing him again. "Clichés are clichés because they're true," she said.

Then after a moment he could hear her digging at the straw.

"You have children?"

"We had a little girl."

"Had?"

"She died. Three years ago."

"I see."

There was the sound of more digging. Then she said, "I'm sorry. How did it happen?"

"An infection. Complications."

Another few moments passed in silence. Then Margarethe said, "So you went away to the war?"

"No. Everything went to hell in a basket. *Then* I went away to the war."

"Another cliché, huh?"

"Yeh. I have no imagination."

She looked toward him and he thought he could see her smile. There was a tiny sequin of light reflecting against her pupils. They were immensely dilated, as black as jet.

"It must hurt," she said, "hearing me talk about something that might have kept her alive. It must make you angry."

"Maybe."

"You don't know?"

"It doesn't do much good, does it?"

"You saved my life that first night in Hanover," she said. "That woman at the hotel would have killed me if she'd had the presence of mind."

"I suppose," Gordon said.

He looked at her, but she turned her eyes away.

"It's too late for that," she whispered, shaking her head. She looked back at him and said, "Too late or too early. I don't know anymore." And with that she rolled back over, and after a while it felt warm enough to sleep.

IT WAS daylight when Gordon heard the sound of water dripping all around. He rose up on one elbow and saw the narrow sheets of sunlight coming in through the cracks in the wood, his movement sending dust motes swirling through them. Just beyond the window, icicles hung suspended from the eaves. A steady trickle of water ran down the surfaces, hesitated into droplets at the end, then fell.

He lay back down, letting his body conform to Margarethe's sleeping shape. Her hair was camouflaged against the straw, her breathing calm and her body warm. Without thinking, he reached down as he stretched and gently stroked her hip. How could it be too late, he wondered.

He had no certainty of accomplishing anything with either the British or the Germans. And with Margarethe? Maybe after a certain age we're all so battered and bruised that we can barely tolerate ourselves, much less anyone else. He had thought he'd even lost the desire, but clearly it was not too late for desire.

He looked at the flush across her cheekbones now, the down glistening beneath her hairline, the fine smooth texture of her skin. Then she breathed deeply and began to stir, and instinctively he brought his hand up across her belly and toward her breast.

The impulse was so familiar, so strong, but still he hesitated. He wondered if it was the threat of death that was bringing him to this now. He had blood on his hands, but not as a surgeon. It was more like the blood of birth. He had gotten beneath the surface, gotten down to something primal, and it scared him. It was getting too very German, all this love and death.

But was it such a peculiar notion that another human being can take away the pain? Was all this Sturm und Drang really necessary? Shouldn't it be simpler than that? You let them in. You trust them and they help make it right. Before he had seen only manipulation and abuse, and he had avoided love the way prisoners avoid entanglements. At other times he'd hoarded it, the way refugees hoard food even after there's plenty all around.

Impulsively, disengaging his mind, he slipped his hand around her right breast and he felt it large and firm. He found the nipple and she arched her back and sighed as she turned over to look at him.

Then he rose up. He had heard something—a dog barking. He

looked out and saw a half-timbered farmhouse not a hundred yards away.

"Get up," he said. He was wide awake now, on his feet. "We've got to get up."

She rose on her elbow.

"We slept too late. We've got to move. Someone's coming."

They gathered up their oilskins and put on their boots. They climbed down through the loft to the hay wagon below, then ran into the woods, keeping the loft in a line between them and the house.

They ran through snow until they came into the denser forest. There the tree trunks were black and bare. A mist blew through the lower branches as a receding cloud exposed a few arcs of winter rainbow—yellow, red, violet. They walked on and began to come across firewood cut into three-foot logs and stacked against the trees, still green just under the bark. It marked a trail running east and west, parallel to the main road. They could make up for the time they had slept.

They walked and ate chocolate and biscuits, but Margarethe was all the more silent now, even more remote. Of all the risks he was willing to take, the most dangerous seemed to be trying to reach her.

The sky was bright blue, and Gordon could feel the sun warm on his face through the breaks in the tree cover. Having touched her, he could still feel the comfort as he walked. He fixed his mind on the sensation and it kept him going on.

In mid-afternoon they found a clearing where a storm had blown down a line of trees, hidden from the road but exposed to the sunlight. They spread their oilcloths and for a few moments sat down to rest. Protected from the wind, they could absorb the sunlight and feel almost warm. But it was a warmth that could get them killed.

"You don't believe me, do you?" she said, pausing to adjust the hook on her galoshes.

"Don't believe what?"

"I saw it in your eyes when I told you about the extract. The possibility of such a thing disturbs you, but still you don't think it's real. You think I've gone over the edge, that I'm a mad-woman."

"I don't think I'm qualified to judge," Gordon said earnestly.

She took the last morsel of chocolate out of the foil and put it into her mouth. "Bacteriology?" she asked. "Or women?"

Gordon watched her for a moment as she lifted her face toward the sun. Then he opened the tin of sardines and set it beside the bag of nuts, their lunch alfresco.

Was it female softness that he needed? Was softness going to save him? She was hard too, tough-minded, much tougher than he was.

"I'm more worried about proving what you say about German research," he said. "Proving it to the British."

"I only know what I know."

"And the extract?"

"I've tested it."

"How?"

"In the lab. On myself. With the refugees."

"The most dramatic discovery in the history of medicine."

"Very likely, yes."

"From mold? From a rotten piece of fruit?"

"Yes," she said, looking back at him. "From a rotten piece of fruit."

Gordon stared into her survivor's eyes, and he saw something new in them, some suggestion of the heat he'd felt as she turned toward him this morning.

After a moment he smiled.

The light was failing and the temperature dropping again as they walked on, branches rolling under them in the snow. The sun had been reduced to a red trace in the west, and the forest was giving way to the moor. Their path petered out into a quagmire. They turned back and made their way through the trees until they found the road again. The night stayed reasonably warm, the same mixed blessing. They would be more comfortable now, then sink in the Bourtanger Moor.

Gordon stopped from time to time to check the compass, but the telegraph lines were a more reliable guide wire, dimly visible against the sky.

Trudging on, his own flesh exhausted, Gordon thought about her body, the ripeness, the fullness like some pomegranate engorged with seeds, ready to replenish the earth. He thought of the orphanages at Biscay, the incubators set up to replace a generation of lost Frenchmen. But how many more people would die if Britain went ahead with this weapon? Or would a weapon this dramatic save lives? Would it save American lives at least? Outraging American sensibilities, keeping his own country from diving in?

"The peasants bury their horses out here," Margarethe said as they walked. It was the first piece of idle conversation he'd heard come out of her mouth. She looked over at him. "The moors were sacred. Some sort of fertility thing, you know. Life getting renewed."

Gordon walked beside her in silence, listening.

"Can you imagine it?" she asked. "Life after all this? The war and everything. Do you think about it?"

"Sometimes," Gordon said. And then he turned to watch her moving in the darkness.

They crossed a frozen brook. They could see the lights of a farmhouse in the distance, and between it and them, a covered well. They heard the lowing of a cow, and then the rattle of a chain, but the chain was not attached to the cow. The metallic sound came from a bicycle coming toward them down the center of the road.

Before they could get to one side a light shone in their faces. They heard the bike fall to the ground and a man's voice shout, "Halt! Hold it right there."

They saw a uniform now, a heavy Mauser rifle, and their spirits sank.

"Oh, you scared me," Margarethe said, trembling. She covered her mouth with her hands, improvising. "I thought you were a robber."

"Who are you?"

"We're going to Magdeburg," Gordon said, his uncertainty forgotten. "Off the train. My sister's husband must have had a drop too much and forgot to pick us up. Where are you from?"

"I'll ask the questions," the man said. His voice sounded hoarse. He was older. A member of the Home Guard with an ancient Pickelhaube strapped tightly to his head. "I want papers. From both of you."

Gordon nodded. "We have papers," he said, but he felt himself grow numb as he patted his pockets, watching the man's face. To Gordon it looked demonic, a jack-o'-lantern above the light, the eyes like slits above heavy jowls. He looked at Margarethe, and for a moment wondered why he was doing all this. Was it for her? For himself?

There was the man on the train, the policemen, all the blood. Now it seemed routine, the price of admission. There were no Pankow tickets, no glass bullets, no cloaks of invisibility. And now there were no excuses. Gordon was tired and they had to get across.

"I remember now," he said. "They're in the bag."

"Nothing funny." The guardsman shoved his rifle close to Gordon's face. "I know what I'm doing."

Gordon opened the bag and rummaged around for a moment with his left hand. He had injuries, he reminded himself. He was at a disadvantage.

Taking the sword in hand, he looked up.

"Here we are," he said.

He gripped the rifle barrel and thrust it upward. Then he rammed the blade, which struck hard but did not penetrate, glancing off the belt buckle—"Gott mit uns"—big and brass. The guardsman fired his Mauser, then grabbed Gordon's arm. The two men spun around and the German landed a heavy boot in Gordon's groin.

They fell to the ground, the German on top, and his elbow ripped open the wound in Gordon's neck. The guardsman raised the gun to bring it down like a club, but Margarethe came from behind and grabbed the barrel. The German held on like a monkey with its hand in a trap. His arms were above his head, tugging at the rifle, but indecision left him vulnerable. He watched defenseless, horrified, as Gordon rammed the blade once more through clothing and skin to penetrate the rib cage.

The man rose in the air as if in a seizure. He was rigid, shuddering like a striking fish, then he doubled over, hitting the ground hard with his head. He rolled forward in the snow convulsing, gnawing his tongue, and the blood poured out in a torrent.

Margarethe held the rifle in her hands, trembling as she listened to the German's last labored breaths, watched his final spasm. Gordon was still on his hands and knees, bent over in the snow. Then in time there was only the sound of the wind in the trees and their own breathing in the cold.

Gordon climbed slowly to his feet, staying clear of the blood.

"Are you all right?" she whispered.

Gordon nodded and closed his eyes against the pain at his throat and his hand. There was no point thinking about it anymore. It had become too easy now to just survive.

He grabbed the guardsman by the foot and dragged him toward the well, a simple matter of logistics now—one more victim to dispose of. His hand throbbed and his whole body ached but he thought of other things.

Unceremoniously, Gordon hoisted the German over the side. Then he walked back for the bicycle, carried it to the well, and dropped it into the darkness below.

When he came back to where Margarethe stood, leaning on the rifle in the cold, he was close enough to see her tears in the moonlight. She looked at him, then she lowered her head and kicked at the snow, covering up the trail of blood.

Without the plane of the earth to guide them, struggling to see the road in the darkness, they had the sensation of running up an incline. Gordon carried the rifle over his shoulder, and Margarethe carried the Gladstone bag.

They passed a railroad crossing, the steel bands covered with ice, and beside it the arch of a birch tree weighed down with snow. The temperature had dropped and the wind blowing cold in their faces made it impossible to breathe. They were numbed with exhaustion now, but at least fatigue and the forced, plodding rhythm made it easier not to think.

They walked on until the first signs of morning came from the farmhouse windows, the lamps casting yellow light down in the snow like mirror images. A single planet shone in the sky, which paled behind the trees and left a jagged outline that turned from turquoise to silver. Then a smudge of orange appeared, only to recede behind the clouds.

They saw the yellow glow of a lantern moving slowly toward them in the distance and Gordon took Margarethe's arm. They veered off into the woods past a roadside shrine, then snared themselves in a noose left to catch birds.

Kneeling down, they watched the milk cart roll past them toward the village.

"We've got to stay off the road now."

Everything along the way was clearly visible and well defined, including them. They spotted a windmill off to the left and made for it.

The sails had been taken down. The bare blades were tethered to the ground with heavy ropes. They climbed up inside and shook off the snow, then once again nestled in each other's arms.

Margarethe's eyes were blank as she stared off into the ceiling. After a while Gordon saw the tears well up and slowly flow onto her cheeks.

Gordon lay on his side next to her, silent. Then he watched the sun rise even higher, and for the moment tried to absorb the transient illusion of safety.

28

Walther Ostriker rode back to Berlin through a morning that was clear and cold. He had spent last night at Pankow, at the sanatorium, trying to get something useful out of Billy de Beauford, but the doctors asked to stimulate his memory had, instead, wiped it clean. The Dutchman lay corpselike in his hospital gown, staring at the wall, his bald head in the pillow like a poorly hidden Easter egg.

Ostriker found this whole exercise in futility profoundly depressing. The incompetence, the waste, the frustration in not being able to regain control. Was it the physical law of entropy at work, or just an error in perspective? Satan's fall itself was nothing more than an error in perspective.

But what perspective could he bring to the wire from Bremen, the young woman ripped open in her bed? A young woman linked to Gunther Stinnes and, by extension, then, to Margarethe Riesling. As the colonel had been associated. Colonel von Stade . . . also dead. Thought by at least one meddlesome Berlin police detective to have been murdered. A detective shot trying to apprehend an American named Erskine Fisk—the Kaiser's dentist—now also unaccounted for.

These crimes made no sense, fit into no stream of logic. Irrational forces had entered into these events and surrounded him now like the oppressive whiteness of snow.

The car rolled on toward Berlin and he settled back in the seat and closed his eyes, trying to summon up his most calming image, a memory of Boulonnais horses, their big muzzles and woolly legs running past ancient windmills and châteaux with slate roofs. When he had been a young chemist at Tremblay he had spent his holidays bicycling through bright beech forests beside those windmills and canals. He remembered the old women haggling over geese. He remembered the chalk hills where he found fossilized echinoderms and Roman coins and flaxen-haired boys. Those boys were dead now, very likely. Every one fed into the oven of Verdun.

And now anthrax? That was one reality he could not evade. What was to happen to his dream landscape with anthrax drifting across those same quiet canals? Days had passed since Wilhelmshaven and he had done nothing. Naval security there was waiting for instructions but he was suspended by fear. He seemed to know less now than when the first reports arrived, and the passage of time would make his caution look like incompetence. He was forced to admit that he had no certainty of stopping Gordon and Riesling now. He had overestimated his own ability to manage events, even comprehend them, and the result could be catastrophe. If these two gave the British the means to control their anthrax weapon, no-man's-land would look like a garden party compared to the devastation of northern France that would follow.

Just beyond the Exerzier Platz at the Guter Bahnhof, a motorcyclist raced by Ostriker's car on the other side of the road, shooting up a spray of slush behind him. As the car continued past the Schultheiss brewery and the market hall, Ostriker turned and looked out the rear window to see the young soldier spinning his bike around and coming after them along the Schonhauser Allee.

"Pull over," Ostriker told his driver.

They veered off the shoulder alongside the Jewish cemetery, the monuments jutting through the snow like some sort of wreckage. In a moment the courier pulled up to Ostriker's window and saluted. He was a boy not more than fifteen.

"If you would please follow me, sir. There have been new developments."

"What is it?"

"I don't know, sir, but Lieutenant von Laudermann is waiting for you at the airport."

Ostriker nodded, then distractedly waved the motorcyclist on, and then in a rare moment of vulnerability thought about Jay. It was as if he suddenly felt the cumulative effect of two and a half years of death all across Europe. An entire generation of young men struck down and mutilated. A boy of twelve is cherished and protected—at seventeen he is expendable. The death of a single woman or child prompts outcries and indignation. But by what perverse moral reckoning can the death of five million young men possibly be accepted?

" 'It was' must be changed to 'Thus I willed it,' " Nietzsche said. But the will can achieve only so much. As his driver followed, Ostriker reached into his valise, withdrew paper and pen, and began to write.

The airport at Johannisthal, southeast of Berlin, had been the center of German aviation since its beginnings. It was here that Pegoud first lit up the skies with his stunt flying, and here that Fokker built his Fliegerschule alongside the Albatros Works.

Now the showrooms were quiet. Aviatik, L.V.G., Rumpler. There was only one customer for airplanes now—the military. The young bloods who had learned to fly before the war were already dead. The men taking to the sky now were grim professionals at twenty-one.

As Ostriker's car pulled onto the barren airfield he could see von Laudermann standing beside a Halberstadt CL II outside the hangar. He was wearing his overcoat, talking to a young man in an aviator's scarf and leather jacket.

The car pulled to a stop near the airplane's tail and Ostriker got out. Both men saluted as they came forward.

"This is Captain von Teubern, sir. Mayr is waiting for you at an army airfield near a village called Werfte. Decent weather, sir, and a car at the other end."

"What exactly have we found, Lieutenant?"

The captain turned toward his plane and climbed up the steps to the cockpit.

"A civilian murdered on a train near Cloppenburg, sir. A member of the Home Guard killed with the same sort of weapon, in the same district, only hours apart."

The two men exchanged a glance, and then the pilot signaled to his mechanic to turn the propeller. There was the concussive wock-wock-wock of the blade going around, but the engine did not engage. They went through the procedure once more, the motor caught, and the propeller disappeared into a blur.

Ostriker vacillated for a moment, touching the edge of the folded paper in his tunic pocket. But even time and space were relative now, so where did personal loyalty fit?

This was no time to trust von Laudermann. The young man handed him a fleece-lined helmet, and Ostriker strapped it on and climbed up into the observer's seat.

"It will be cold," von Laudermann yelled over the roar of the engine. "The temperature is dropping."

Ostriker settled in behind the machine gun, focusing on the inscription on the metal—"Si vis pacem, para bellum." "If you want peace, prepare for war."

The small plane taxied immediately onto the runway and into the wind, picking up speed. In a moment they were rising over the roofs and treetops. Von Teubern executed an Immelmann turn, and they headed west, toward Holland.

THEY traveled through the woods most of the day, then in the late afternoon near the edge of the forest they saw a half-timbered barn. Twilight was coming on and they smelled a peat fire. At this moment the shelter seemed worth the risk—they could be shot and killed warm or they could be shot and killed cold.

They left the cover of the trees behind and started across the field, hoping to get out of the weather while they waited for dark.

They traversed a frozen brook, then climbed through a wire fence that bordered the meadow. The wind was from the west and they heard the sound of a train a mile or so ahead moving along the tracks that ran beside the river. They had seen cavalry patrols before, but the river would be the challenge. The river and the border itself.

Gordon climbed a rail fence into a small pen, and they heard the bleating of sheep as they approached the building. He pulled open the door to the barn. The animals were skittish and fell back, stirring up the dust inside.

Margarethe followed and then he closed the door and they climbed the ladder to the loft. The straw was dry and warm and they were up off the ground and for a few moments at least they could rest.

In the failing light they could barely see each other's faces. Gordon pulled out the map fragments and his lighter to study the route before them. Margarethe leaned against his shoulder and stared at the map with him, tense and frightened.

"Maybe we should reconsider," she said, smiling nervously, brushing back her hair. "Maybe we should try Switzerland after all."

Gordon studied the fragments. The route ahead did not look particularly promising. He saw the highway, the railroad, the river. At these temperatures it would probably not be frozen solid. They would have to commandeer a boat or a barge, and even after that they would still face the restricted zone between the river and the border. There would be peat bogs and canals, and by now German soldiers.

He looked up at her and for a moment tried to forget about the men he had killed, to forget the British and the anthrax, to forget about what was to come. He tried to imagine the two of them getting on some boat and floating downstream, floating out into the North Sea toward Denmark.

"And what do we do in Switzerland?" he asked her.

"We find a hotel with a bath."

"And then what?"

"Sleep for a week."

He glanced out through a crack in the boards, trying to gauge the path they would have to take. Then he looked back into her eyes. "And then what?" he said.

She smiled. "You're on your own, buddy. This is *my* fantasy."

At long last it was as if they had reached the dropping-off point on some medieval map. This was an unknown territory, full of hazards, and he expected to confront the whirlpools and sea serpents as he studied her eyes, but they did not appear. There were issues of trust as well as danger, and some of those issues, like Fisk, troubled him, but what he saw now was also the chance that there could be some bond. They were both damaged goods but neither of them seemed to care, or even care if what people called love was all fatuous mysticism. They had already absorbed each other's hurts and losses and guilt, already accepted the limitations imposed. Without saying a word, she had convinced him that all this sorrow and deep regret was part of some other lifetime.

He kissed her, then touched her, and it was a lover's hand he used, not a surgeon's. He willed himself ignorant of the muscle and bone underneath her skin. He blotted out the technical knowledge and gave in to the warm illusion.

She kissed him back and he felt the strength of her arms around his shoulders. He touched her breast again and felt himself swell with wanting her.

There were no petty stratagems, no question of world enough and time—they might have two hours. So what could this mean? A new lifetime in a few minutes?

He catalogued all the things he might never know about her: What would she name her children? Would she keep a cat? But again he had to act without knowing. He had to cut loose from the shore and float downstream. He would have to let go of loneliness, his last support. He would have to let go of all the doubts that had occupied his mind, sustaining him, and accept that all the questions were answered.

They loosened their clothes. Neither of them had bathed in days, but the tang of sweat was like a messenger, one molecule in one hundred thousand wielding its primitive power. Their kisses were wet and strong. She drew on his tongue as if there were something nurturing in it. He kissed her throat, her breasts, then moistened his fingers between her legs. He followed with his tongue, caressing her, sating his hunger but making the hunger grow until she was wet and glistening. Then he touched her again and brought his hand up to her lips. She took his wet fingers into her mouth and he spread the moisture across her face and kissed her again. This was the smell of spring that he wanted, the smell of life.

THE checkpoint was just south of Ter Appel, on an isolated stretch of road that crossed the Bourtanger Moor from Meppen on the Ems. The only other crossing was at Nieuwe Schanz, fifty kilometers to the north.

Walther Ostriker stood at the window of the small cottage, watching Rolf Mayr interrogate peasants under a sky that was as bleak and cold as the faces of these shabby, black-clad farmers. Ostriker warmed himself with coffee, real coffee, brought in from Holland, as his soldiers tossed down the baggage that had been so carefully piled onto creaking wooden carts.

Gordon and Riesling had been on quite a rampage, or so it seemed. The woman in Bremen, the man on the train, the Home Guard. Ostriker knew perfectly well now that Gordon had killed

Jay, just as he knew that Margarethe had killed Colonel von Stade. Two cold-blooded killers who now had found each other. How very touching.

Soon, he knew, they were going to kill everything else he cared about, everything that was good or true, unless he could find them and stop them. The Alberich offensive would proceed as planned, and the British, with Margarethe Riesling's new development, would make their catastrophic response.

Ostriker took another sip of coffee, then set the cup aside. The hot liquid was like acid scorching his troubled stomach. He had not eaten. He was much too sick at heart to eat.

He looked out across the border into Holland with all its calm neutrality. He still believed that the moor was impassable, but he had been wrong before. Time was running out, time for holding in place. He could only guess what Margarethe was carrying to the British. He still did not understand what had happened in Bremen. And even though he fully expected to find their bodies frozen out in the bogs, if any chance remained, however slight, that they could escape with some "magic bullet" that legitimized germ warfare for England, he needed to react.

A roar like an airplane flying low broke the silence of the forest. Ostriker looked out and saw a motorcycle courier coming down the road from Meppen with Lieutenant von Laudermann in the sidecar. The motorcycle spun on the ice and skidded to a stop outside the cottage. Then, stiffly, the young lieutenant climbed out.

Ostriker stepped out into the cold as the driver shut off the irritating roar. Von Laudermann walked toward him through the snow, removing his helmet and goggles, glancing up at Ostriker with a look of remarkable arrogance for a man so red-faced and cold.

"Everything's in place, sir."

Ostriker nodded, exhaling a gray cloud. "Yes," he said. "Perfectly in place."

If he had learned anything in this war it was that optimism was the first sign of a clear and present danger.

"We're radiating out from where the guardsman was found. We've narrowed the search to one area within six miles of the border between Spahn and Borger. It is quite hopeless for them."

"Yes," Ostriker said. "Quite hopeless."

Von Laudermann smiled. "The stretch they've chosen is an artillery practice range, you see."

Ostriker nodded, but he was not impressed. They had already defied probability, and the law of averages was not reassuring. As they approached the end of the game, Ostriker could at last feel his own firm adherence to logic crumbling beside something much more visceral.

The last of the peasants passed on into Holland, pulling their carts. Mayr stood with the soldiers in the cold, lighting a thick, hand-rolled cigarette.

"Rolf!" Ostriker called out. "Come here."

Squinting his colorless brow against the smoke, Mayr ambled forward like a street-corner tough.

"You like Holland, don't you, Rolf?" Ostriker trembled as he spoke the words.

"Yes sir, Major. Holland's fine with me."

"Good. I have some work I want you to do in Amsterdam. Just in case things don't turn out as we would hope."

Ostriker reached into his pocket and handed him the two separate notes. One for Colonel Devereaux, French Deuxième Bureau. And one for Major Anthony Rice, British Secret Service.

29

When Gordon awoke it was dark and he heard a tugboat's horn on the river, then a train rumbling along the tracks that ran north and south between the highway and the Ems. They had slept for several hours, and as he rose up now to gaze out of the loft the sky was black.

He looked down where Margarethe lay sleeping, then slowly nestled into the straw beside her once again. There was an urgency now in the outer world as well as in this loft where they lay side by side. They had to cross the border before daybreak, but the mere act of brushing against her body had aroused him. He could not yet dismiss the warmth and comfort of this moment and face the cold uncertainty of what lay ahead.

This was the primal bond, a man and a woman. Maybe it was as simple as returning to the womb in the face of danger, but he doubted that. This felt adult. Not at all regressive. He wrapped his arm around her and kissed her neck, burying his face in her hair. He held her until she was awake, still warm and soft, massaging her shoulders and then her hips until she smiled and returned his kisses. Slowly, gently, he raised her skirt up over her hips and caressed her thighs, then the warm moisture between them.

He had never before made love with the passion and commitment he had experienced in this same darkness just a few hours before. The questions in his mind *were* answered, but the decisions were far more than cerebral.

He was still tired and he was hungry now, and, as he touched her, he was slow to respond. Then he felt her reach out for him in the darkness, taking him in her hand with her own special urgency. The pressure of her hand was warm and firm, encouraging. Then she kissed him and the urgency increased. She pulled at him now longingly as she slowly moved her hips. She moaned softly. Her grip tightened, rising with her own desire. Then she began to tug, flailing away at him until he was more rigid than he had known possible. The pressure was almost painful, as if he would burst. Then with a little cry she guided him into her, impaling herself with one graceful thrust of her hips.

They shared the pleasure as if their nerves had been interwoven. It was a bond they wanted to last forever, but the intensity was such that they were both quick to come, merging their bodies without any reservations, without precautions. This flow of life was beyond control, the possibility of a child their only protection against strategies and logistics, against the cold reality of logic.

When the crisis had passed they kissed and held each other in the darkness a little longer, and then when their heartbeats calmed it was time to go.

They set out due west over open fields. There was now a freshness to the night air, an excitement that took them well beyond the acknowledgment of danger. They were on a higher plane. They had already surrendered to something larger.

After half an hour they came to the railroad tracks and skirted the red light of a signal bridge. They could see the station and its bored attendant, rocking on his heels under a floodlight two hundred yards to the north.

They kept on in the darkness and crossed a frozen brook, then a wire fence, then started across a meadow. Gordon, leading the way, walked into another fence in the dark and stumbled over it. They slid down a deep ditch and back out again and through a hedge. The frozen surface cracked underfoot. If the temperature rose any more than this, they could be up to their waists in quagmire.

They crossed another fence and then a road that was not on the map, and then they heard the river. It was frozen along the banks but still moving in midstream. They could see the lights of a tug pushing its barge, and then the sheen of the water itself.

Steinbild was to the north but they were not sure how far. They began walking, not along the riverbank but through the edge of the forest on the other side of the road. The sky was bright over the water and they could see clouds moving against the sky.

After about fifteen minutes they heard horses, than saw a cavalry patrol silhouetted against the river. But then, just south of the village, near enough to see the lights from outlying houses, they saw a small barge tied up to an earthen pier.

Gordon stepped out onto the road to get a better look. Crouching low with the Mauser, about to signal for Margarethe to follow, he spotted the solitary German guard resting on a piling.

Gordon crept back into the tree cover and the two of them watched for a while and listened. They seemed to be breathing in unison, thinking the same thoughts.

"I love you," she said.

Gordon took her hand reassuringly. "Yeh, I know. I love you, too."

Margarethe watched nervously for another moment. Then she whispered, "But how does that get us across?"

The guard sneezed, then wiped his nose on his fingers.

"We'll have to get rid of him," she said. "Are there oars or what?"

"I don't know," Gordon said. "I don't think we'll find anything better."

The guard sneezed again, then reached into his pockets. He struck a match and lit a cigarette, and in the light his face was smooth and young. He was a boy of maybe twelve.

Gordon pressed his lower lip between his teeth and did not move.

The young guard began whistling "The Watch on the Rhine." Then he tossed the match into the water and walked upriver.

"What's he doing?" Margarethe whispered.

"I don't know. He might be just stretching his legs."

"Maybe he's patrolling the whole river, not just the barge?"

The boy had gone a good fifty feet now and showed no signs of turning around.

"Let's hope," Gordon said, and stepped slowly out onto the road.

With the Mauser in hand he walked out onto the earthen pier. Its sides sloped down into ice, except at the end where the current flowed swiftly by. The barge was tied against the current with heavy lines front and back, and there was nothing even resembling an oar or a pole.

Margarethe watched upstream for the boy as Gordon untied the forward line. The front of the barge swung out into the current.

"Climb aboard," he said, and Margarethe stepped onto the platform. Then Gordon untied the other line and then with all the shoving power he could muster, leapt on.

The current carried them quickly along, but downriver, not across. They lay flat on the wooden deck, adding their weight to the outward side and pumping, catching the current and angling themselves gradually into midstream.

The river was swollen with winter rains and snow and moving swiftly. It bent slightly to the right up ahead, helping their cause as it continued north, but their lateral progress was still not enough. He wanted to check the map to be sure what they were getting into, but he could not risk the light. They might be floating past Emden at midday, then into the North Sea. But the fact was they had no control over their fate just now anyway. Any hope of control from this point on was purely an illusion.

In time they could make out the shapes of trees and bushes on the other shore. They had no way of telling if these woods were deserted or if there were guards standing in every shadow, watching them.

They continued downstream, the barge slowly edging closer and closer to the ice along shore. Eventually they brushed against it. Gordon reached out and tried to gain hold but the effort was pointless. He scanned the shoreline as they drifted, grappling with the ice. Then a tree trunk appeared, fallen over from the bank. Margarethe reached for it but the barge slipped past. Then Gordon stretched out and gripped a branch and they came to a stop.

"We made it," he whispered, leaning over the edge. He began to pull, maneuvering the barge out of the stream, then pulling hand over hand against the trunk to work the barge closer to shore. Eventually they hit the bank and Margarethe climbed out and held the line while Gordon followed. Then he turned and gave the barge a shove back into the stream.

It was midnight when they struck out across the marsh. A thin layer of new ice had formed over the more solidly frozen surface, and it creaked under their weight and broke through in great shattered footprints.

They crossed over the sluice gates of two wide drainage ditches. Then it was open marshland for more than an hour, frozen solid.

Then a road, and then a sort of dell with small copses on three sides. They squatted down for a moment to rest.

Margarethe tapped him on the arm. "Here," she said.

"What?"

She reached out in the dark and put something in his hand. "Horlick's Malted Milk Balls."

Gordon let the chocolate melt on his tongue, then turned back to face her. "It's going to be okay," he told her. "We're going to make it across."

"Yes," she said. "I think so too."

"You don't look very convincing," he said. "You look tortured."

"Of course I look tortured."

He strained to see her face against the night sky. "Tell me," he said.

"I don't know. Maybe I'm just not so sure I believe in happily ever after."

"Is that specific to me?"

"Not at all. Maybe I've just . . . seen too much."

Gordon watched her for a moment. "Too much of the war?"

"Yes. The war. I'm not sure it stops with the war, though. Maybe I've just seen too many men."

"Men like Fisk."

"Yes. Like Fisk."

"That can change. The world can change."

"I don't know. I hope so."

"We can change one thing. We can make each other happy."

"Maybe. If we get the chance."

"What does that mean?"

"I want the chance. I really do."

She leaned over and kissed him, sharing the taste of chocolate. He held her for a moment, but there was something left unsaid, something she refused to tell him, and that he refused to ask.

In time they got to their feet. They went on, obliquely crossing a field until they came to the second road, and for a while they were able to walk along on reasonably firm sand. Gordon knew they were going to have to make their own chance together. No one could survive the war, not entirely. Some part of you would always die no matter what. But at least he knew he loved her. At least he had that.

Up ahead he could see two shelters in front of them, perhaps three hundred yards apart. He dropped down on one knee and waited. There was no smoke coming from the chimneys, no guards.

After a moment they walked straight ahead, equidistant between the two huts, and eventually they found a path. They continued on the firm sand, but then the surface turned to ice again. After this their movement became as much lateral as westward, constantly shifting to avoid pockets of deep mire.

Gunshots broke out from the woods to the north. They dropped to their bellies, then heard two more shots. They could see the flashes from the muzzle of the rifle.

They waited with their heads down low, the blood pounding, but there was no sound except the wind blowing across the moor. They could not see any other suggestion of movement. Someone else was crossing tonight—these shots were not meant for them. But from then on they corrected only to the south, away from the drier forest and the guards.

They did not talk again. Gordon needed to believe they were going to make it. He did not want to be affected by her pessimism, or by her premonition, if that's what it was. She had brought him back to life and that's where he wanted to stay.

Toward dawn they came to an area of peat cuttings, gravelike slits running east to west. With each step they had to test the ground until they found the narrow bridges of standing peat, which wobbled and swayed as they walked across. Their southerly corrections had kept them away from the patrols but had gotten them deeper into the marshes. They were going in circles trying to guarantee a shallow crossing.

Then the sky lit up like day. It was to the south. A great concussion, then a whistle, then the sound of a freight train rushing past.

They dropped into the mire and a massive explosion rocked the earth, sending mud and water hundreds of feet into the air. There was another flash, the whistle, the roar, and then another explosion fifty yards south.

"What the hell is going on?" Margarethe screamed.

"We're on the artillery range."

"That's miles from here."

"They're testing bigger guns. They must have moved north."

He took her hand and they turned west and ran on deeper into the marsh. They broke through the ice, and the muck was over their boot tops. Then it was up to their waists. The shells fell behind them as the flash from the explosions lit up the surface ahead and cast them in silhouette. Their feet and legs went numb but they had to keep going. The water level became shallower, the surface more solid. They kept running until they hit a barbed wire fence. They snared their clothes on the metal points, then ripped them free. They tumbled down the slope of a ditch but caught themselves before they landed on the ice. They jumped across it, then climbed up the other side on rubbery legs.

They crossed a field without really knowing it, then another ditch, another field. Then they stood on the banks of a canal, stationary and confused. For the first time in hours they were faced with an obstacle that could not be overcome by a simple reflex action.

"Is it Holland?" Margarethe asked. The canal was still under construction but water stood frozen in it.

"I don't know."

"There was a canal on the map."

"That's south of here. Maybe fifty miles. There was supposed to be a river."

"They're turning the river into a canal. The marsh runs all the way to the border. I think it's Holland."

"I don't know," Gordon said. "Keep down. Keep quiet." They ran to a makeshift bridge of ladders and planks and climbed across.

They reached the other side and kept going. A hundred yards farther they came to another canal, but this time they ran straight across it, breaking through the ice into the water up to their waists, drenching themselves in the spray but getting across. But by then it was all they could do to climb the bank.

Maybe they had made it after all, Gordon thought. He had not wanted to fully indulge the luxury of hope, but now it seemed within reason. Her pessimism was wrong. Her fear was out of place.

They walked on and colors began to emerge in the dawn. The ground was gray and level as they ran toward a green background of dense woods.

Then a voice called to them in German.

"Halt!"

The sound came from dead ahead, where a man emerged from behind a tree, a dim outline holding a gun on Margarethe.

"We're in Holland!" she shouted. She was directly in Gordon's line of fire as he came up.

"No. You're on German soil. You're an hour yet from Holland."

The man stepped back and pointed the automatic at Gordon. "Drop the rifle," he said.

He was small, in civilian clothes, but Gordon saw him flip the gun off safety. And he had no way of knowing how many other Germans were around. The man might miss but then the shot would bring the rest. How far were they? The border couldn't be another hour. But Margarethe had the Colt in her bag, didn't she? Or was it in her pocket?

"You're lying," Gordon said, breathing hard, trying to think. He slowly gripped the gun on his shoulder.

"We're in Holland!" Margarethe shouted again. Then everything was out of control. The Colt exploded in an orange flash and Margarethe screamed once more as the guard fell to the ground.

The gun seemed frozen in her hand. She tried to shake it loose as Gordon reached out and took her by the arm.

He dragged her off, running west. The night receded. They could see the spaces between the trees. Gordon pulled Margarethe along a sandy path with ice and the litter of pine needles leading to a road. She was crying uncontrollably.

A farmhouse stood up ahead with flowers painted on the door. A Dutch design.

Gordon shouted and kicked at the door.

He heard a voice from inside shout, "Holland! Holland!"

And then the door opened and a red-faced man in his nightgown greeted them.

"Orlog gefangenen?"

"Yah, yah."

"Roosland?"

"Nay, nay, American."

The farmer's two little girls emerged from their cabin beds in the wall. The wife was up and lighting the kitchener.

Gordon stood in the doorway, holding Margarethe as she cried. They had reached the other side. They had left the war behind. But the war was by no means over.

30

General Headquarters, British Army, had moved from Saint-Omer to Montreuil with the Somme offensive. Set high on its steep, cobbled hill, the city had been fortified centuries before to keep the English at bay. Now the Union Jack fluttered above the citadel, and three thousand French civilians needed a pink "permis" to pass in or out.

G.H.Q. itself was officially located in the Ecole Militaire in a narrow street a few yards from the eastern ramparts. But the commander in chief actually directed his forces from the château of Beaurepaire, four kilometers away. There was an electric bell to warn of Haig's approach so the sentries could honor him with a full present arms. Haig was keen on military tributes. He would never visit the trenches, though, for fear the carnage would cloud his judgment.

Major Anthony Rice walked along the ramparts, huddled in his greatcoat, having just left a conference with the Royal Artillery. The tactical specifics worked out by the staff were now being implemented. The anthrax spores would be fitted into special shells for the 9.2-inch howitzer, guns with a range of 27,000 yards and transportable by rail. Special units from Dunkerque to Saint-Omer to Saint-Pol-sur-Ternoise had been selected to hold the line. If that line was overrun by the Germans' Alberich offensive, the Royal Artillery would fire the anthrax weapon to cover the retreat.

This was a ragtime war, Rice had come to realize, a Cubist war with no center, no focus, completely inside out. It had everything to do with the smell of rum and blood and nothing to do with classical heroics. They could date the corpses by the style of the uniform now. The fight for Derby Day and Grandfather's mustache had turned to carnage, and England's youthful promise had been turned to dead and rotting meat. The Neverendians were right. The war had become the permanent condition of mankind.

Rice stood beneath the blue and white banner of Saint Andrew's Cross that flew over the Church of Scotland hut. The wind was at his back as he looked down at the British encampment and beyond.

Spring would try to give birth once again to the French forests. Lilies of the valley, anemones, beech trees surrounded by golden narcissus. Behind the lines the Christian Brothers would try to plant their crops, life would try to resume its normal progression despite the war, but he wondered. Flanders, Artois, the Pays du Nord . . . They may have seen their last spring for many years to come.

Rice had surrendered to this process long ago. He knew that literature leads to despair, that introspection leads to pain. Individuals have no control over larger events and they can be judged only on how they do their part. "Play up! . . . Play the game!" That's all that can be asked.

He heard footsteps and turned to see Ross from the intelligence unit running toward him up the cobbled street. As he approached, the young officer reached one hand up to his cap to keep it from flying off.

"Major Rice . . ."

"Hello, Ross. What is it?"

The young man's face glowed with beads of perspiration. "Good news and bad, sir." He tilted his head back for a moment and tried to catch his wind.

Rice looked off into the distance and said, "Yes? Go on."

"There's a wire from Holland, sir. Seems an old friend of yours has turned up and wants to see you. Eli Gordon, sir. He's made it through."

Rice clasped his hands behind his back and sharply turned away. It was too late now. He did not want more ambiguous information. Nothing Gordon could offer could change their course now anyway. Even if he had brought something concrete, even this "magic bullet," they would not have time to deploy it. Events had simply overtaken them. The weapon was in place. The Germans would advance and the British would have no choice but to respond and to accept the consequences.

In time Rice turned back again and saw Ross still waiting for him.

"And the good news, Ross?"

"I'm afraid that was it, sir." The young man looked confused. "Colonel Devereaux's just arrived from Paris, you see. Deuxième Bureau. Colonel Ryan's with him in Haig's office at the moment, but he wants to speak with you as well."

Rice nodded vacantly.

"And if I may say so, sir," Ross went on, "this Frenchman's mad as bloody hell."

A SEA rain blew in over Amsterdam, rattling the elm trees along the canals. The cold snap of the last week had departed, leaving in its place a bone-chilling damp.

Inside the British Consulate on the Keizers-Gracht, Anthony Rice and Sir Almroth Wright sat opposite each other before a blazing fire. The small Indonesian table between them held chocolates, coffee, and short fluted glasses of old Dutch gin.

"How do you know he'll come?" Sir Almroth asked, wheezing quietly into his handkerchief.

"Oh, he'll come," Rice said. "The second wire was quite explicit. He obviously feels responsible for the fate of all the world."

The old man's body was a loose amalgam of worn-out parts. He shifted in his seat, responding slowly and irritably, trying to find some comfortable arrangement for his ill-fitting bulk.

"I take it, then, he still accepts this German story of evildoing on our part," he said.

Rice looked up. "Indeed. Berlin seems to have made him even more 'accepting' than before."

The fire sizzled and popped, and Sir Almroth turned to glare at it. The flue was not drawing properly and the smoke tormented his lungs.

"A dirty business," he said with a sigh at last, stopping to daub at his eyes. But his sentiments were far more complex than the resignation he displayed. Britain had already developed a reputation for duplicity, for wanting to fight to the last drop of someone else's blood. He could not completely discount the German claims for what was going on at Porton Down. He simply could not accept that he himself had been duped, left in the dark by his own scientific colleagues.

"He wants you here to discuss bacterial chemistry," Rice went on. "He doesn't consider me quite up to the task for some reason. I can't imagine why."

"I understand my role in this," Wright added gruffly. Then something deep inside his throat dislodged and rattled loudly. Red-faced and eyes bulging, Wright turned his gaze on Rice. "You mentioned something about a woman," he gasped.

"Yes. Some kind of assistant from the Institute. He says she can prove that what's gone on in Berlin is not what we'd feared. That Alberich does not equate with germ weaponry."

The old man coughed and spit into his handkerchief, then blew his nose. "Then I suppose we can only pray she's right. I suppose we must listen to what she has to offer."

Rice pressed this thumbs against each other, digging at the cuticle of one with the nail of the other. Then he dropped his hands into his lap and let his gaze drift back toward the fireplace bordered with Delft ceramics.

Wright's dour assessment was true enough. But the more un-fortunate truth, the one Churchill had wanted to forget, was that the French held three fourths of the line on the Western front. They had not been at all keen on having their countryside rendered uninhabitable to save Britain from invasion. But then Churchill had never imagined having to ask their opinion.

Whatever the Germans had in store for His Majesty's forces now, they would face the assault with conventional weapons, but without the open revolt of their French allies. The anthrax pro-jectiles had been pulled back. This new innovation in mass murder was being returned to Porton Down.

Sir Almroth put away his handkerchief, then peered into the box of chocolates, seeking whatever consolation he could find there.

Rice propped his elbows on the arms of his chair and gazed into the fire, entwining his fingers in front of his face as if about to play "Here is the church and here is the steeple."

It was an odd business really. So many lies. Everything so lu-dicrously hush-hush, so precariously balanced between overreac-tion and negligence. It was like a mountain road with disaster lurking on either side. Germany was driving along that same moun-tain road from the opposite direction, high above that same pre-cipitous gorge. Someone would have to give way.

This fellow Ostriker in Berlin could have played it much dif-ferently, much more publicly, Rice realized. Telling France about Britain's biological offensive had been quite enough to force Haig to pull back. But the German had saved the threat to American opinion as his trump card. With it, he had extracted a very limited price, and Rice could only assume that Major Ostriker had his reasons.

Rice raised his index fingers slightly, more a cupola than a spire, and brushed the tip of his nose.

"It's all a bit hard, isn't it?" Sir Almroth said vacantly, popping a chocolate into his mouth.

"Perhaps," Rice told him. But conscience was not a consideration in these matters. Gordon was at best a loose cannon. He was unreliable, not to be trusted with sensitive military intelligence. And whatever this woman from Berlin may or may not have discovered, it was useless to them now. New developments were beside the point. You surrender as you would to God and you take whatever comes.

Rice picked up his drink, rumming up for the battle to come, and for a moment slumped in his chair, brooding. Then he stood and made his way to the rain-spattered window to watch the street and to wait.

Standing in a doorway sheltered from the rain, Rolf Mayr watched the brightly lit window of the consulate drawing room. Waiting out in the cold, his hands in his pockets, he had memorized every face, curbstone, and tree. He had enemies enough in Holland. He wanted to get this over with quickly and then back to Berlin.

Ostriker had bungled the job, and Mayr knew it was up to him now to put the cat back in the bag. He was happy enough to see the woman again, happy enough to be the one they call on to clean up the mess. And now maybe there was more challenge to it than he ever would have thought. These two had blood on their hands, a surprising pair. Mayr always liked a challenge.

From behind his vantage point, a black Morris rounded the corner and stopped to idle at the curb. Mayr glanced around at it quickly, then back at the consulate window where the Englishman looked out into the street.

Mayr looked at his watch. It was exactly three o'clock, and that's when Eli Gordon and Margarethe Riesling were expected. All his senses were focused on the consulate, the steps, the street in front. Yet some stimulus in some dim reptilian part of his brain was signaling alarm. Something was wrong with that car behind him. That car was not supposed to be there.

A moment later a man and a woman turned onto the Keizers-

Gracht. Walking arm in arm under an umbrella, they came toward the consulate building from the opposite corner.

Mayr stepped out onto the sidewalk to get a better look at their faces. Their eyes were focused straight ahead. They looked calm. They looked intent on reaching their destination. They were not scanning the sidewalk like people prepared for something to happen, like people who might be dangerous, or in danger, or who might have been warned. They walked arm in arm, oblivious, gliding along in their own private world.

Mayr stepped to the curb and signaled to his partner in the gray Citroën half a block away. Zweck would pull the car into position first, directly in front of the building. Passersby would have their heads down with the rain, huddled under hats and umbrellas. Mayr would approach from the other direction, forcing them inside the car and away.

Then Mayr heard the Morris behind him begin to move and suddenly his attention was split. He glanced back again but the driver's face was indistinct, shadowed. Mayr signaled to his partner to step it up as this other car pulled beyond him and edged toward the spot where they needed to be. This was getting fucked up fast and Mayr did not need complications.

The Morris pulled between him and his targets, rolling forward in front of the consulate. Mayr waved to Zweck again now and began to run. He still could not see the driver of the other car, just the back of his head. But by then the troubling image had registered and clarified itself in Mayr's brain. A Russian fur hat. A gabardine coat. The man behind the wheel was the man he'd seen on the steps of the bicycle shop in Bremen.

Mayr looked ahead to his partner coming toward them in the Citroën. Then the Morris seemed to stall, then backfire. When the car pulled away, Mayr at first thought Gordon and Riesling were gone. Then he looked again and saw two bodies on the pavement. Someone was shouting for the police. A crowd had begun to gather.

The rain was cold as Rice stumbled toward the huddle of men leaning down outside the building. Their backs were bent and glistening as they hovered over the wounded couple. Rice saw the woman first, her face pale but still oddly beautiful. Her coat was soaked with blood and there was bright red blood at her mouth, washed by the rain.

He looked up and spotted Mayr in the crowd, standing wet and impassive. Rice glared at him accusingly. This was not part of the deal, not the way it was to be played out. The German simply gazed back at him and shrugged, then turned and walked off through the crowd.

Rice pushed his way inside the circle and, kneeling down, saw Gordon's face, his eyes wide and searching. He leaned over him and sheltered him from the rain. The American was struggling to breathe, struggling to turn his head toward the woman lying beside him.

"We didn't do this," Rice said emphatically. "It is very important for you to know that we did not do this."

Gordon did not appear to hear him, or to care. The rain came down harder now. He licked his lips and tasted the blood.

"But who did do it?" Rice asked. "Can you tell me who shot you? Can you tell me why?"

Gordon did not respond. He had seen the look in Fisk's eye and that was answer enough for him. A random tremor in the universe, a random impulse acted upon. It was this that Margarethe had feared. A personal matter. Gordon had never understood the war's impersonality. But this he understood.

So the war had not won, after all, he realized. He was astonished. Now it was all he could do to move his hand toward the woman's hand and to take it in his grasp.

31

Andreas Schiller woke with a start, then relaxed and gazed dreamily out the windows of the train. He could feel it moving again, but he could not quite gauge where they were. He remembered the Falls of the Rhine, the dark tunnel, the iron bridge over the Thur. They had to be in Switzerland now, heading into its clockwork interior.

He looked out and saw wide-roofed chalets sticking out of the mountainsides like mushrooms. It seemed to be spring—ice melting on the rock cuts, oozing out of the stone like sap—but surely not that much time had passed. In the distance he saw dark valleys, then bright patches where the sun burned against the rocky peaks and cliff faces.

"How do you feel, Andreas?"

Schiller turned his head and saw Kadereit's young face leaning down at an odd angle, with an even odder expression of tenderness and sympathy.

"I feel good," Schiller said. "Where are Magda and the children?"

"I sent them down to the dining car."

Schiller twisted uncomfortably. His abdomen was stiff and painful, what was left of his digestive tract resentful and bruised. He had thought at the time that this doctor Kadereit had found seemed more like a tailor than a surgeon. He had owned a suit once that fit just as badly as these stitches in his side.

"Don't worry, Andreas. There's plenty of money now, remember? And you're in Switzerland, where everyone becomes healthy. My God . . . vegetarian restaurants, temperance restaurants. The most wholesome place I've ever seen."

Schiller smiled. He did not feel particularly healthy, but he hated to disappoint his friend. Kadereit had nursed him, hidden him away, proclaimed him too near death to be troubled by his superiors. Still, Schiller could not understand why the department had been so generous with him.

"Before you know it, we will be in Schatzalp. Two thousand meters up, Andreas. No bacteria in the air. And no war. Good doctors, too. The best money can buy."

Self-consciously, Kadereit brushed his elbow against the pocket holding the envelope. In it were Swiss thousand-franc notes, as crisp and compressed as the leaves of a cabbage.

The train bumped and Kadereit gripped the luggage rack to steady himself.

"So we've passed Zurich," Schiller said.

"Indeed we have. The beautiful Bahnhofstrasse of the numbered accounts."

Schiller nodded his head, but his eyes had the faraway look of some religious painting. It made Kadereit nervous, this beatific glow. He did not wish his friend such perfect peace quite yet. And it added to the discomfort he already felt in having deceived Andreas to exact these reparations. It was a cynical act, he knew, amoral at best, but because of it Schiller would live a little longer, and because of it Schiller's kids would be taken care of.

Kadereit tried to see it as a simple civil suit—himself as judge—awarding significant damages. Erskine Fisk had shot and nearly killed a good man. Now Erskine Fisk, via his Swiss bankers, had made restitution.

As for departmental interest in procedural irregularities, the police surgeons and all the rest, Kadereit had borrowed the phrase from Götz von Berlichingen and kept it always at the ready. "Kiss my ass" did surprisingly well in answer to almost all forms of official inquiry.

He sat down on the cushioned seat and gripped his partner's hand. Schiller's eyes opened, then sparkled with pleasure, but it was not the human touch that made him smile. It was the sound of his children banging back the door, clambering through the passageway.

Epilogue

On February 24, 1917, the German High Command carried out their long-awaited Operation Alberich. It was an unprecedented wave of destruction, one of the great atrocities of the war. But it was a retreat, not an advance, a fallback to the heavily fortified Siegfried Line. From Arras in the north to Soisson in the south, they poisoned wells, destroyed roads, leveled trees and houses, blew up railroads and bridges. It was the German army, then, not the British, that left an uninhabited wasteland through France—a second "English Channel"—thirty miles across.

For their part, the Englishmen at Porton Down destroyed all records of their experimentation with and limited deployment of the anthrax weapon. The reconstituted alliance of Britain, France, and a belated United States won the war but lost the peace, and within a generation the world was once again engaged in wholesale slaughter. Britain and her allies rearmed, and the work at Porton Down resumed.

The research described in Margarethe Riesling's notebooks was never pursued, but the rare species of mold she discovered in Berlin made one more fortuitous appearance in a laboratory in London in 1928. Almroth Wright's young assistant, Alexander Fleming, noted the mold's antibacterial property and set it aside for further work. He also gave it the name by which it is known today—penicillin.